Stuart Stern was born in England. He studied medicine at the University of London. After graduation he spent three years in research in the chemistry of mental illness before serving as Resident in Clinical Psychiatry in a famous London psychiatric unit. A period of travel and research in the United States followed, including a year's practical medicine in a remote town in the Prairie heartland.
Dr. Stern is currently in specialist practice in London.
He has published numerous articles and technical papers and edited a medical journal.

Also by Stuart Stern:

THE MINOTAUR FACTOR

Stuart Stern

The Poison Tree

Futura Publications Limited
A Futura Book

A Futura Book

First published in Great Britain by
Futura Publications Limited in 1978

ISBN 0 7088 1345 3

Typeset by Art Photoset Ltd
Beaconsfield, Bucks

Printed in Great Britain by
Hazell Watson & Viney Ltd
Aylesbury, Bucks

Futura Publications Limited
110 Warner Road
Camberwell, London SE5

When peace is made between great enemies,
Some enmity is bound to remain undispelled.
How can this be considered perfect?
Therefore the sage takes the left hand tally, but exacts no payment from the people.
The man of virtue takes charge of the tally;
The man of no virtue takes charge of execution.
It is the way of heaven to show no favouritism.
It is forever on the side of the good man.

Lao Tzu
Tao Te Ching

THE POISON TREE

SUNDAY 28 AUGUST, 1977
TANG MANG WU – THAILAND

Breadfruit, mulberries, mango chutney and Darjeeling tea; chocolate from Amsterdam, cognac from Paris, smooth brown Havana cigars, an occasional Stilton cheese; from Rangoon an elegant native girl with almond eyes, sensitive breasts and loins like shantung silk; and when he grew tired of the moody Burmese, they flew in Rose Lips, a robust, prattling child from a whorehouse in Hong Kong, to be his body servant. Everything Conrad Vigson wanted was his for the asking, including the foundations of the CYDAC computerised microscope system that would enable him to delve more deeply into the mysteries of bacterial reagents.

The laboratory was built out from the hill on concrete piers, like an Annamese temple stripped of gilt and graven images; a pilgrim shrine for minor Asian warlords and emissaries from Peking's Social Affairs Department; a hermitage of applied research erected and maintained by courtesy of the White Tiger Pharmaceutical Company. The site could not have been more remote. Tucked into a fold of the Chokhan Hills, close to the Laos-Burma borders, the complex was accessible only by a straggling pack train trail that linked the primitive villages along the narrow valley of the Nagotang, or by the beefy ex-USN Bell Kingcobra that ferried supplies over the Tang Mang ridge every Sunday afternoon.

Remnants of a teak plantation furnished bottom for layer upon layer of jungle that undulated down the steep watershed. In Vigson's imagination, the rim of the blue mountains that bordered the distant rice plains protected him from colonialists, imperialists, nationalists, drifting USAF personnel, the CIA, agents of WHO and the International Narcotics Bureau; also from insurance investigators and any legal piranha that might have been given his scent by his wife – widow, come to think of it – Amelia Cranbury Quinn, the arch bitch of Baltimore.

What Amelia would have made of her husband's reincarnation was a matter that afforded the dead man much speculation. A confrontation with the shameless Rose Lips would certainly have caused her to shriek in horror. She would have been equally outraged by his relationship with Miss Kyoto.

Jackie Kyoto, however, was a pupil, not a plaything, and there was nothing physical between them. The excitement they experienced in laboratory and greenhouse was infinitely more stimulating than anything they might have shared in bed. Miss Kyoto's respect and admiration gave him more satisfaction than he had wrung from ten years of marriage. In the shabby history of defection, wives like Amelia Cranbury Quinn had a stronger influence than whole regiments of double-agents and sly recruiters. But Conrad Vigson's sleep was no longer disturbed by memories of his widow and her symbolic pinking shears.

Recurring nightmares focussed round the movie that Sydney Phillips of the State Department had smuggled up from Washington in the mistaken belief that Conrad would be fascinated by alienative rituals and weird offshots of his work. The ultra-restricted USAF footage of indiginous survivors in defoliated areas of Vietnam had been the final insult. And Conrad Vigson had gone clean over the top.

'What's *wrong* with you, Conrad?' Amelia had peevishly demanded. He had been sprawled on the davenport in the lounge of their mansion in Gunstone Park with his head buried under the cushions, racked by uncontrollable spasms of weeping. 'These people are our *enemies*. For God's sake, they're not even *white.*'

Infants mottled like angry iguanas, babies with heads like basketballs, toddlers tottering around on stumpy pumpernickel legs – how could they be enemies? From that day forth Conrad Vigson's political conscience atrophied and he began to seek a means of escape from the cage of responsibility.

When he had laboured too long at the electron microscope, or imbibed a drop too much of French brandy and the terrors of the past threatened to consume his present happiness, Miss Kyoto would sit with him on the verandah in the warm fertile darkness and cajole him out of his depression. In that profound Americanised voice of hers, she would read aloud from Buddhist texts or Taoist classics, while caressing the back of his hand with her fingertips. Always he would be calmed and feel reassured that he had found the way of truth.

Which made him exceedingly grateful to Chen Yu-lan and Sheng Kittegawa, the gentlemen who had engineered his rebirth and built this Shangri-la specifically for his benefit, far from squabbling committees and heartless government leaders.

The price was reasonable: tutorial advice to thirty Chinese students; an occasional conjuring trick to impress important customers, crumbs from the end of the laboratory table, nothing original or adventurous, by-products from his research at Baltimore, his experiments into bacterial regulators and inhibitors. Naturally, he gave nothing away, except to the biochemist from Peking who was too smart to fool. Besides, he had the feeling that Peking was footing part of the bill, though Kittegawa would not come right out and admit it.

He knew what Yu-lan and Kittegawa wanted. Already he had delivered enough to justify their faith and capital outlay. Now fifty-nine years old, he was good for another ten years. He had no intention of short-changing them. Unlike his former employers in Britain and the U.S., the White Tiger Pharmaceutical Company did not seek to deceive him. They put no pressure on him. On the contrary, they encouraged him to breach unexplored territory in any branch of research that might yield worthwhile results. They never quibbled about costs, even when things went askew.

In addition to cooks, housekeepers, gardeners and maintenance staff, the Tang Mang Wu team was composed of graduates from reputable universities in Europe, America and the Far East. Dedicated, efficient young men and women thirsty for knowledge – botanists, agronomists, bacteriologists, geneticists – they were all English-speaking Orientals. He did not concern himself with their private lives or political persuasions. He did not know or care how much they were paid or what would become of them when they passed out of his ambit.

Miss Kyoto was the exception. He cared very much what would become of her. He had marked her as his natural successor and firmly insisted that she be appointed Chief Research Assistant and remain in Tang Mang Wu until the entire project was completed. Thus he assured himself of her support and companionship for at least another eight years. Yu-lan and Kittegawa were only too delighted to grant Miss Kyoto tenure. She spoke five languages in several dialects and was expert at simplifying advanced research procedures for visiting laymen. A tall, strikingly handsome Eurasian of thirty-three, she was reticent without being coy about her childhood and youth. Vigson picked up a hint from one of the domestics that she had once been the wife of a corps commander in the Kumintang. He probed no further. She made no secret of the fact that she had graduated in chemical engineering from Caltech and had spent three years in post-grad research with Professor Franklin at the Newton Institute in Philadelphia. Her knowledge of molecular biology was exhaustive. Vigson had freely adapted several of her theories on auxin transcription in genetic coding and incorporated them into his experiments with considerable success. Greenhouses, light/dark chambers and the new cloning lab were supervised by the lady, a chore that Vigson was only too happy to delegate to his able assistant.

In Kittegawa's opinion, Conrad and Jackie made a perfect pair. Vigson liked to think so – he with his refined European features and crest of silver hair, she with her solemn oval face and dark tranquil eyes. He trusted Jackie Kyoto more than he had ever trusted anyone.

After lunch each Sunday, Miss Kyoto and Conrad Vigson would rest together in the shade of the recreation block, listening to the rhythmic *tok-tok-tok* of ping-pong balls as the young bloods put off their white coats and did battle within, more gay than inscrutable at the tables, crying out and laughing like children.

Between two and three o'clock, the growl of the helicopter's engines would infiltrate the wide, bell-like silences of the valley. Invariably Miss Kyoto heard it first. She would touch Conrad's knee, lean forward, incline her graceful neck and scan the ridge, east to south. Soon the Kingcobra would tilt over the horseshoe and circle the complex, sun glittering on its blades. All the students, all the servants including little Rose Lips, would scamper from the buildings and stream up the steps towards the pad to light the smoke cannisters that would tell the pilot how the valley breezes blew. Miss Kyoto explained that the smoke flags were not really essential but that the students had been trained to be thorough.

As the chopper steadied and sank towards the pad, Vigson and Miss Kyoto would walk along the path through the flower garden and wait on the paving at the top of the steps to see if Yu-lan or Kittegawa had brought a client to be shown the wonders of Tang Mang Wu. If there were no guests, there was still the pleasure of watching the unloading. Crates of expensive equipment slid gently down the ramp. Bundles of the latest scientific journals were collected from the pilot along with personal little treats that the masters sent in, like wine, candy, hamburger steaks or stoneware jars of Belugia caviar.

Sunday 28th August was just like any other. The air was sweet and jonquil-coloured after heavy rain, the view breathtaking. Smoke from the bright red cannisters rose straight to heaven. Miss Kyoto, Vigson was later to remember, wore the *Ao-dai*, a Vietnamese high-collar coat with matching trousers in lilac silk.

Mr. Kittegawa stepped down from the hatch. For the first time that Vigson could recall, Mr. Kittegawa wasn't smiling. He looked older. His shoulders were stooped and he shuffled slightly as he approached. It was nine or ten Sundays since he'd dropped in. Vigson wondered if the master had been ill. Solicitously he enquired after Mr. Kittegawa's health. With a weak, strained smile Mr. Kittegawa assured Dr. Vigson that he was in good physical shape.

They turned and descended the steps. As they did so, Mr. Kittegawa suddenly addressed Miss Kyoto in a language that Vigson did not understand.

It had never happened before. It startled Vigson and made him awkwardly aware of his position as the only European this side of the rice plains. Like a child sensing a withdrawal of affection, he felt his poise become riddled with vague fears and guilt.

Treading anxiously on Kittegawa's heels, he sought to gain attention by plucking at the man's sleeve. 'Wha . . . what's wrong? Wha . . . what is it? What have I done?'

Ignoring the scientist, Sheng Kittegawa chattered on.

Miss Kyoto's eyes clouded. Her smooth brow furrowed. In a dialect so gutteral that it made her mouth ugly, she rapped out a question.

'Please, please tell me what's wrong,' Vigson begged.

Only when they reached the door of the administration block did Mr. Kittegawa and Miss Kyoto stop and spare a glance at Vigson.

Kittegawa spoke in the alien lingo.

Jackie Kyoto answered.

Taking Vigson by the arm, Kittegawa escorted him into the office building and through it, down rubberised corridors, round the ell and then, as Miss Kyoto had advised, cloistered him beyond the airlock in the greenhouse.

Pale plants erect in plastic pots. An ocean of fronds breaking over trays of earth that had been measured to the last grain. Green seas of leaves. Deeper, neat pert rows of stems poking from porous cups; tuber hybrids, healthy as hell. Through glass doors into a sectioned maze of thermostats and lagged pipes. Upright frames punctuated by teakwood tables bristling with pipettes, Petri dishes, flasks and labelled flagons, tiny birdbath trays sealed tight with Sentorite.

Poppies everywhere. Poppies like paper. In bud. In flower. In dormant state. Poppies chilled like orchids in a Fifth Avenue store. Poppies black. Poppies white. Poppies pink as human tissue excised from the flesh.

Pods nodded drowsily as Vigson brushed heedlessly past. Mesmerised by Kittegawa's monologue, he was carelessly unaware of his cherished blooms.

Mr. Kittegawa spoke calmly.

Dr. Vigson, when he found his voice, shouted.

Mr. Kittegawa told him what they had decided he must do.

Dr. Vigson screamed.

Mr. Kittegawa caught him by the shoulder.

Dr. Vigson spun on his heel and with his free left arm swept dishes and pots from the stand. Tearing himself from the Oriental's grasp, he smashed, stamped and ground glass and poppy petals to powder beneath his enraged feet.

Four students were required to hold the doctor down long enough for Miss Kyoto to fill a hypo and inject a small quantity of haloperidol into a vein in Vigson's forearm.

Mr. Kittegawa stood by, sadly shaking his head.

'Conrad, you must understand that there is no other course open to us,' he said, dolefully. 'We *must* send you home.'

'Upton did this. The bastard. The bloody bastard. Upton, I tell you. He's *always* had it in for me. *He* did it. *Upton.*'

The haloperidol flowed through Vigson's bloodstream and reached the rebellious centres in his brain. He snorted, jerked and lay rigidly motionless under the weight of four young Chinese. *'Upton. Fucking bloody Upton.'*

'Who is Upton?' Kittegawa enquired.

But Jackie Kyoto did not know.

And poor Conrad Vigson, poleaxed by paranoid mania, gave no intelligible answer there and then.

THE WATCHDOGS

MONDAY 29 NOVEMBER, 1976
LONDON

Autumn had at last turned a blind eye and allowed winter to slip unobtrusively into the city. The morning's haze thickened as the day progressed and by three o'clock the gloom in Chancery Lane was palpably due to fog. In legal offices clerks and accountants grumbled over tea, complaining that by dusk the streets would be choked with traffic and the highways to surburbia effectively closed. In courts of law, barristers stalked the spoor of justice while learned judges listlessly watched fog rub against the windows like some gigantic cat come to get their tongues. Sucked into the mist that seeped over the Embankment, Crown Office Row and Temple Church passed stealthily from sight. From a window on the attic floor of the Prince Albert Building in Rialto Street, the American peered out at the river, a column inch of watery murk supported by the roof of a wholesale stationers squared by a warehouse's weeping gable.

In the room behind the American, the Englishman creaked in his uncomfortable swivel chair, sipping tea he had brewed on a gas-ring in the corner.

'Did it not occur to you, Henry, that the fellow may be *personally* as mad as a hatter but that his *professional* self will never lose its objective grip of reality?'

After a pause the American said, 'That's what makes him so dangerous.'

'Poor old Vigson's always been confused. Incorrigibly confused. Not that *we* ever did anything to lighten his darkness.'

The American glanced over his shoulder. He had just lost his glimpse of the Thames and had the feeling that perhaps he had become so insubstantial in the wake of his enforced retirement that the fog would quietly consume him too.

He drank Scotch from a chipped glass. 'If it *is* Vigson,' he said.

Both men were pushing sixty. The Englishman remained lively and quick in his movements while the American tended to show his scars, to be cumbersome and stiff, sluggish in speech and gesture.

The office had been bought and paid for out of Sir George Upton's private income. It was unrecorded in the ledgers of Whitehall. Only his close friends, a mere handful, even knew of its existence.

Long ago, the American had ascribed certain aspects of Upton's behaviour to wilful eccentricity. Now he saw sense in the peculiarities, the cultivated will-o'-the-wisp style. For instance, the ten tall metal filing cabinets that flanked the walls of the office were safer here than anywhere else. No stenographers, no mother hens, no ministers, cleaning ladies nor janitors ever had sight of them. The spartan room in the Victorian block in Rialto Street was a haven from pricked ears and prying eyes.

Secrecy, privacy even, had turned out to be an illusion as far as the American was concerned. In the end, the million bucks worth of electronic gadgetry that was supposed to protect his position as Director of the CIA had failed to prevent political inquisitors tearing him down and stomping on him.

'Supposing it is Vigson, what do we do, George? Blow the bugle? Turn it over to official agencies?'

'What would "official" reaction be?'

'Doubt and mistrust.' said the American. 'As far as the records show, Vigson's been dead for four years.'

'Did you really swallow that plane crash story, Henry?'

'I hoped to God it *was* true. Like you, though, I laid a few contingency plans just in case it wasn't.'

'Plans that include my participation?'

'Vigson was your baby, George. We only adopted him.'

'True.' Upton fished the teabag from his cup by its fragile string and plopped it into the wastebasket beneath the desk. 'Evidently Vigson didn't like America any more than he liked England. The very first thing we must do, Henry, is establish beyond doubt that the fellow is Conrad Vigson.'

'Can't help you. I'm out, remember. Broke. Busted.'

Cocking his head, Upton studied the American ruefully. Mauled by Senate and House investigating committees, strafed by the Bream Commission, betrayed by the Forty Committee and casually abandoned by a departing President, Henry Marks, former Director of the U.S. Central Intelligence Agency, had every right to feel sorry for himself. But self-pity had never been a trait in his character, and Upton suspected that the humility was a piece of play-acting designed to draw him out.

'Come now, Henry. You may have resigned your post under a certain amount of pressure. But you weren't sacked. I'm sure you still have the allegiance of friends in high places?'

'Maybe one or two.' Marks moved away from the window and, as Upton switched on the desk lamp, shifted out a straight-backed chair and lowered himself onto it. He crossed his legs at the knee, twisting sideways, and, squinting, put his hand on the slender unmarked file on the desk top. 'I brought what you asked for, didn't I?'

'Is that, by any chance, one of the documents that you refused to yield up to the Bream Commission?'

'The contents of that file,' Marks said, 'are nobody's business but mine. Scraps of data, rumours, that's all. Some without classification. All unverified.'

'But, taken together with the contents of *my* file,' said Upton, 'cumulatively sufficient to indicate that Conrad Vigson is alive and well and brewing up fresh trouble from a bolthole in South-East Asia.'

'You've got more data than I have.'

Upton opened a desk drawer and removed a much thicker file than that which Marks had brought. He folded back the buff-coloured cover, exposing a wad of invoices, some carbon copies, others Xeroxed.

'Lionel Ballard is a reliable chap, Henry. He's been buried in Hong Kong for the best part of twenty years. Blends well with the landscape. He's chief salesman for Ringworth and Tubbs, scientific instrument makers, a venerable English firm with a plant in the Midlands. Built up their Far Eastern connections far back in the 'twenties by supplying glassware to the opium barons.'

'And Lionel Ballard claims that Vigson's still alive, uh?'

'No. Ballard has simply passed on certain curious facts, plus a tale or two that happen to have wafted his way. Study the invoices. Some are Ringworth and Tubbs originals. Others, including a dozen or so from Mikomoni of Japan, Ballard managed to procure by bribery and corruption, through pals in the trade.'

'Yeah, I've studied the copies you delivered to my hotel.'

'How do you interpret them, Henry?'

'Somebody's ordering pretty heavyweight stuff.'

'Far beyond the needs of any pharmaceutical plant or opium processing factory that I've ever heard of. Do you know what somebody's building? A biological laboratory that would be the envy of any institution in England.'

'That's not saying much.'

'From Japan, from Mikomoni, in bits and pieces, there's a CYDAC computer going into the hinterland,' said Upton. 'Now that *is*, as you say, pretty heavyweight stuff. Not by any means run of the mill lab equipment. Apart from the enormous cost, the requisitions for a CYDAC suggest that somebody knows how to use the system and needs it for research and development. That in turn suggests that somebody's into chemical engineering of some sort.'

'Who says that "somebody" is Vigson?'

'You of all people know how the trade and barter system works in the Far East,' said Upton, patiently. If Marks wished to be nursed through it, then he would cooperate. 'Tracing the original purchaser of cargo can be very tricky. However, Lionel is persistent and persuasive. The large purchases are being made by an agent of the First Provincial Bank of Kowloon.'

'The underworld's slush fund.'

'In Ballard's opinion, it's the White Tigers that are up to no good.'

'I've heard nothing.'

'Of course not,' said Upton. 'Our Chinese friends aren't likely to broadcast their doings to anyone on your domestic circuit. Now all this is very interesting. Quite fascinating, in fact. But hardly reason for us to become hot under the collar. However, Ballard has a lady friend. Several, to be frank. One of these "ladies" skimmed up an item that puts a different complexion on the White Tigers' investment in advanced equipment. There's a white man, a European, heading a very large laboratory. A European with a pedigree and a shock of white hair.'

'Yep,' said Marks. 'That's enough pieces for me, George.'

'The lady has a brother, and the brother is a pilot, a helicopter pilot.'

'Who makes deliveries to this lab?'

'Unfortunately not,' said Upton. 'But there is an outside chance that, for a fee, he may be able to find himself a job that will get him in on the run. Apparently, he has worked for the Triads in the past and is "trusted".'

'Can we put a man on board?'

'I doubt it very much,' said Upton. 'For the moment, we must depend on Ballard, let him handle the situation. He knows what we want.'

'We want Vigson.'

'Eventually, yes, we may have to take vigorous steps to redeem Vigson,' said Upton. 'First we must discover what Conrad's up to. Precisely what he is producing that's marketable.'

'And so profitable that it guarantees a return on a million dollar investment.'

Upton said, 'And why a bacteriologist of Vigson's stature is required to head the project.'

'The White Tigers must have been scouting the field for a top guy on the turn,' said Marks. 'Vigson was a natural. I figure they conned him into co-operating, into going along with that plane crash yarn. Hell, George, when I think of it, the Chinks must have taken out that planeload of people just to throw us off the scent.'

'The Chinese have never been reluctant to use extreme measures to get what they wanted,' said Upton. 'I agree, they *planned* on scooping up Conrad Vigson. They did not pick up a casual drifter. It was Vigson they wanted and Vigson they got. Why?'

'Because the guy's a genius.'

'Because they required an inseminator, a *creative* scientist. We must assume that they have furnished him with a working laboratory and assistants capable of learning from him.'

'Is Peking involved?'

'Can't say.'

'George, why did you send for me?'

'I want Vigson back.'

'Hell, we all want Vigson back – if he's alive. But the agencies . . .'

'Henry, are we exchanging information or practising the arts of deceit on each other? You know why I asked you to bring that particular file.'

'You need my connections.'

'Connections that, I suspect, you sacrificed your job and reputation to protect.'

'Sure, I bowed out of the Directorship. You think that's the end of it? I can be slapped with a subpoena any time. I've no protection, no claim to executive privilege. I don't mind too much for myself. But my "connections" would make fine fodder for hungry pressmen, ammo for those Congressmen who, in the name of democracy, want to emasculate the U.S. intelligence services and lay them wide open to our enemies.'

'I guessed as much,' said Upton. 'It's your close personal connections that interest me.'

'No George. Use the regular channels.'

'If we hand over what we have to either of our governments, we'll be obliged to stand back and watch them trample all over the Far East. And if the White Tigers get one whiff of an investigation, they'll shift Vigson. They'll hide him where he *can't* be reached.'

'Like Red China?'

'That's possible.'

'What do you want from me?'

'Your co-operation. We can't afford to wait until Ballard brings home the bacon. We must set up and be prepared to act.'

Finishing the last of the Scotch, Marks dumped the glass on the desk. His bulky shoulders and large head were outlined against the gray glass, a featureless silhouette. Only his hands had colour, a rich walnut tan he'd picked up in a hire boat during a sulky retirement vacation fishing for marlin on the Gulf. In contrast Upton's hands, folded on the files, were pale as lilies.

'Well, Henry?'

'You have your own network, George. I don't.'

'Contrary to what you may have been lead to believe, Henry, I hold no position in British Intelligence. I'm not a professional spymaster. My job is that of Scientific Projects Adviser to Her Majesty's government.'

'A licence for dabbling.'

'Quite true. I've always been an inveterate dabbler. But I control no agents *per se*. I confess, however, that my relations with certain sections of the national defence system, and its funding ministers, do give me a degree of flexibility.'

'And power?'

'I'm chief watchdog. As such, I have charge of the kennel.'

'Now we're coming down it it.'

'First, let me indicate what *I* require of *you*, Henry. I need an active American agent. Not an executive. Somebody we can trust, who can be given sufficient authority to act to some purpose. I thought perhaps we might enlist that young chap, Feldspar.'

'Send him East, you mean?'

'Not at the moment. Station him in a nice quiet corner of one of your Washington research departments. No need to brief him. Simply lock him in a room and feed him a nourishing diet of paper.'

'That much I *can* manage,' said Marks. 'Who cooks up Feldspar's paper diet?'

'We do.'

'What's on your mind, George?'

'If Conrad Vigson *is* mixed up with the White Tigers – and we may assume that he is – then the situation could rapidly become explosive. We know what Vigson can do. He's a fountain of ideas, the most creative research and development scientist *I've* ever come across. You can bet your boots, Henry, that the White Tiger Company have gone into weaponry.'

'Biological arms dealing; hell, that's nasty.'

'If my assumption proves to be the case,' Upton continued, 'we may be obliged to become rather unscrupulous.' He pushed the swivel chair back from the desk and got to his feet. He unlocked and pulled out a drawer in one of the steel cabinets. 'It's always so much easier to be unscrupulous with one's friends, don't you think?'

Two photographs, framed in black ebony, dusty beneath ill-fitting glass, were laid on the desk facing Marks.

Upton stepped behind the American and, with a hand on his shoulder, leaned over. 'Trophies.' He tapped his pinkie on the glass of one of the photographs. 'This one's a treasure. You'll recognise the faces, of course.'

'I'd no idea there was such a photograph,' said Marks, intrigued.

'Taken at the College. Don't know where you'd got to that

afternoon.'

The group portrait showed a rank of young men kneeling on a ragged lawn, backed by another standing rank. Their clothing was baggy, casual summer wear. Open-necked shirts and short haircuts increased the impression of jocular candour. No back-drop apart from the corner of a cricket net marred the flat horizon. The sky was untroubled by cloud, slightly bleached by overexposure.

Upton said, 'Kingsley Roach was behind the camera. I remember thinking at the time that it was a very discreet means of ensuring that his mug was not recorded for posterity.'

'You looked like a schoolboy then, George.'

'Almost thirty. Quite an old man in that company. Others?'

'Leland.'

'Dead.'

'Muirhead.'

'Dead, too.'

'And Clarence! God, I'd forgotten about Clarence.'

'He's still kicking. Runs a market garden down in Cornwall.'

'Is that Ken Rigby?'

'It is.'

'Jesus, will you look at Walter Stein.'

'Even in those days Walter wore an aura of mendacity,' said Upton. 'Will Go Far.'

'He sure did.'

'Stein's been put to use, hasn't he?' said Upton.

'From time to time,' Marks admitted, cagily.

Upton bent his head as if his eyesight were not up to his memory. 'There's the lad himself – young Lionel Ballard.'

'A wily little mother even then. I remember him now.'

Upton placed the Kingsley Roach portrait to one side and edged in the other group photograph. Great elms spread threatening shadows from the corners of the frame. But the faces were distinct, focus and lighting expert. Ten men and a couple of middle-aged women were seated on a steep grass bank below an English country mansion. Upton said, 'Drayton Down Defence Establishment, *circa* nineteen fifty-one. September, I think. Yes, you can make out the fallen leaves on the lawn.'

'Isn't that Poggendorf?' said Marks. 'And there's Vigson, slap in the middle.'

'Significantly. You won't recognise the others.'

'How many are still alive?'

'Poggendorf's dead, as you know; and this one, and this one. But the majority are still above ground.'

'You keep in touch?'

'Naturally.' Upton pointed again with his finger. 'This chap – Meredith – has a first-class mind. Plant sciences, genetics, that kind of thing. He might prove useful.'

'Where's he located?'

'London. Has a lab of his own. Does good if unexciting work there.'

'Who pays him?'

'The government.'

'And,' asked Marks carefully, 'are they all still loyal?'

'Not so much loyal as guilty.'

As if suddenly fatigued by nostalgia, Upton returned to his chair.

The open drawer, tea-cup, glass, the portraits, were enough to bring to the spartan room an air of disarray, of busy-ness.

'Now, Henry, I've shown you my kennel. Sleeping dogs, some of them. But they can be roused, if needed, and made to bite.'

Marks continued to study the photographs. The silence was intensified by the fog that sifted through cracks in the window frame and brought an unpleasant coppery taste to the mouth.

At length, Upton asked, 'Will you work with me, Henry?'

'Old style, George?'

'A contained operation.'

'Yeah, why the hell not!' Marks shrugged.

'Then you must unmask your active connections, Henry. You must tell me, in absolute confidence, what *you* have to work with? Can they be of help?'

'Sure, they can be of help. If we discover how to manipulate them. I'm not proud of my connections, George. But, Jesus, they're handmade for this operation.'

'Part of your "contingency plan"?'

'You've guessed it.'

Marks slid the thin mauve-coloured file from under the photographs and flipped it open, turning it towards Upton. '*My* rogues' gallery.'

'Who are they?'

'Frank Varese.'

'It means nothing.'

'Arnold Sarsby.'

'Henry, you'll have to enlighten me.'

Marks raised his head and stared straight into Upton's face. 'The Mob,' he said. 'My secret allies.'

Upton did not seem unduly surprised.

TUESDAY 15 MARCH, 1977
OSIRIS – MONTANA

Rain hung heavy in the noon air. Masking Rigby's field of vision, occasional sleet dabbed the Rambler's windshield. In towering valleys to the north a warm front massed. Chivved by freaky winds that boomed out of Alberta, it breached the Parallel with no respect at all for the security of national frontiers.

Spring had come perilously early. In the wake of the deepest snowfalls to cloak Montana within living memory, wayward half-cocked chinooks swept dangerous depressions east from the Bitterroot range, creating sudden snap thaws. Already, so the radio announced, flood crests boiling down the Bald Eagle threatened the dam above Fort Coyle and the Indian reservation at Sholton Creek.

Rigby had enough horse-sense to avoid the main centres of pre-flood activity. He had quit the interstate highway at Missoula and threaded a route up through sodden forests into muscle country along the timberland rim. The overnight haul from Seattle had blunted the edge of his fear. He drove listlessly along the final stretch into Osiris. Sleet, blustering winds, lakes, the big bold shapes of mountains all helped calm him. In robust, friendly North America he was safe from pursuit.

The overwhelming dread that had made his flight out of Hong Kong such a nightmare fluttered from him. Sir George had been right: he must push on until he reached Osiris. A stammered transatlantic call to Sir George had revived his determination. Upton had not lost his charisma. In ten or twelve hours, as soon as Upton arrived hot-foot from London, Rigby's part in the assignment would be over. He would be released from all further involvement.

The summer retreat in Osiris was ideal for a rendezvous. Better than his Seattle apartment or his office in the Botanical Research Centre. By its very remoteness, Osiris must be inviolable.

After he had delivered the box to Upton, he would stay on for a week or so, shut himself off until his nerves recovered from the strain of nine agonising days waiting in a stuffy room in an urban renewal block in Hong Kong's Cat Street, above the remnants of Thieves Market. Din had been constant, hammering up from stall-lined alleyways, from work-sites of new building across Ladder Street. The noise and the smell were debilitating. He was too old now to take pleasure in alien environments.

Home soon. For a week, he would do nothing but cook steaks, drink beer, sleep round the clock, soothed by the knowledge that he was no longer a pawn in Upton's latest game, no longer valuable to the faceless enemy. Perhaps he might persuade Upton to grant him a year's sabbatical from his duties at the Seattle centre. He was due a favour. Eight years since last he'd visited England. Three grandchildren he'd never even seen. Her Majesty's Government had had its moneysworth. He was over sixty and no longer adaptable enough to be a satisfactory courier. Besides, the last world war was long over, the Drayton Down Group long since scattered. Poggendorf and Vigson were dead, and he had completely lost touch with Tabor, Meredith and the others.

Come to think of it, he'd never had much affinity with them. Scientists employed to do a government's dirty work. Acrimony had split the group before its best projects could be brought to fruition. Not even Upton's magnetism could hold them together after Conrad Vigson and Poggendorf developed 'political' consciences. Loyalty to the 'old school'? Faded recollections of a mansion buried in Chiltern woodland, trestle work-tables in temporary laboratories, humourless military guards, barbed wire, identity cards, misty rain, inferior food and too much beer after dinner. Sentiment had no hold on him. He no longer cared about Drayton Down, about England. He must resist Upton's persuasive charm. Refuse further covert assignments. Break the link. Leave security to eager men – like Ballard, his Hong Kong contact. Ballard obviously still enjoyed the cut-and-thrust; he hadn't a nerve in his body or an inkling as to the significance of his actions.

Upton himself probably didn't know what it was all about any more. He had no clear picture of Upton's function now that war had become an underground pastime. What *was* Sir George? What position *did* he occupy? Scientist, administrator, political adviser? Spy? It didn't matter. He wanted no share in Upton's plots. The time was ripe to resign. In fairness, the government should allow him to continue his mundane research duties at the Seattle centre until his official retirement in four years. He had no idea of what he would do then. Go home to England for good perhaps.

Osiris came at him at the tail of a blind bend. Outrigger shacks clustered round the base of the hill on which the town was propped. Left of the road, the Century river was swollen with snowmelt and laden with vegetable debris. It surged and raged, a milky brown swathe, through narrow troughs. Rigby had never seen the Century in full flood before. He'd never visited Osiris at this time of year, of course. The vibrant power of the river impressed him. He glanced at it, stimulated, until it fell away behind the houses.

As usual, the community of Osiris struck the Englishman as oddly incomplete. Files of solid timber-frame houses should have been dominated by mining gear or the messy accoutrement of a lumber mill. There were no signs of industry to give the town purpose. The country road bulged to incorporate stores, offices, church, movie theatre and schoolyard, artificially raked, like an elaborate set from the Lincoln Centre Folk opera.

Rigby cruised gently up Main Street. He thought of stopping off at McNair's for supplies, changed his mind and rolled on over the piebald summit. A quarter of a mile north, he swung with infinite relief into Wolfridge Avenue.

The avenue was separated from the town stem and sparsely developed. Five middle-income lots fanned from it. Their isolated facades were defended by burly evergreens. In this season none of the houses were likely to be occupied. His own refuge was perched high on the upper level, last in the row. Birch and alder-brake packed the ground behind the property. Somewhere below, the river rumbled like an endless freight-train. Discoloured snow patched the lawn that aproned from the picture window and the soaring wing of the porch. Cantilever steps climbed from a short asphalt path that dove impetuously between two oval flowerbeds stuck with the sad skeletal remains of last summer's phlox.

Squinting up at the frontage as he prowled towards it, Rigby detected no signs of life. Even so, ingrained instinct could not be denied. Caution, ridiculous degrees of caution, had saved many an agent during the war. The war, the damned long-lost war! Why couldn't he put it from his thoughts tonight? He was still seriously disoriented. He did not steer the Rambler into the steep drive. Instead he eased it into a slot at the butt of the avenue. A stave fence checked the flow of wilderness. Snow had drifted into a cushioning ramp that, back in January, must have been all of ten feet deep. Still staring up at the house, Rigby paused. He switched off the ignition. Apprehension prickled the hair on his scalp. Quite, quite irrational. He did not ignore the sensation. 'You work with your instincts as well as your brain,' Upton had told them, chalking the phrase on a shiny blackboard in the lecture room of the special training wing at Stanmore Camp where they had first met, in the third year of the war.

Rigby cleared his thoughts of nostalgic detritus. Upton would not laugh at him. Upton, of all people, would understand.

Reaching into the rear of the Rambler, he brought out a scuffed pigskin document case. He opened it. Wrapped in two thick handtowels, the plastic box was intact. Rigby held the bundle thoughtfully in both hands.

Outside the wind tossed wildly through the trees. A gout of slush was plucked from the house eaves and hurled noisily into the shrubs. Windows, large and small, remained dormant and disinterested. Vague doubts persisted.

Rigby snapped shut the lid of the plastic box, wrapped it in towels again and returned it to the case. Leaving the rest of his baggage, he turned up the collar of his overcoat, opened the Rambler's nearside door and, stooping, got out.

Fatigue had made his skin uncommonly sensitive. He flinched from the layer of cold above the fretted surface of the snowdrift, a sharp contrast to the warm Fohn-like air that flowed around his face.

Rising, he crabbed down the side of the Rambler, carried the case across the drive and climbed the steps to the timber platform by the kitchen door. He fished for his keys, found the right one and aimed it at the lock.

Before he could complete the action, the door jerked open. He looked into the girl's friendly blue eyes. His instinct had been right. The girl, a total stranger, told him to come on in.

Fear swelled in Rigby like a tumour as he stepped hesitantly over the threshold.

Mr. Wing considered himself an expert in fear. He had learned his subject thoroughly. His first lessons had come from his father and brothers who had risked – and lost – their lives back in 1947 in the 17-months war between Chiang Kai-shek's Nationalists and the Communist insurgents. More positive instruction had been delivered by a consortium of mixed-blood philanthropists who 'rescued' promisingly barbarous orphans from the smouldering ruins of Hangchow. Two of these 'gentlemen', Chen Yu-lan and Sheng Kittegawa, recognising Wing's unique potential, had adopted the boy and brought him up, diligently instilling in him a religious respect for the profit motive. With a long eye to the future, they had patiently Americanised him. Splitting his personality like a bamboo rod, they had bound it up again, as suited their purposes, to make him even stronger than before.

In Singapore, Hong Kong, Canton and Macao, in Tokyo and Osaka, in Paris and Marseilles, in Manila, Havana, Istanbul, London, Los Angeles and New York, Mr. Wing had added practical experience to his UCLA Master's Degree in the Psychology of Fear.

The moment that the girl admitted Kenneth Rigby to the living room of the house on Wolfridge Avenue, Mr. Wing identified the genus – defiant terror. Rigby was elderly, small, sparse, stooped, balding and obviously in the last stages of nervous collapse. Abraded by his experiences in Hong Kong, he was as frail and ragged as a length of rotting twine.

But Rigby was English. In Mr. Wing's considered opinion, Anglo-Saxons, no matter how chewed-up they appeared, must be treated with respectful caution. Behind the botanist's effete hangdog submissiveness was a faint edge of truculence that kept Mr. Wing on his toes. On the other hand, Rigby was out of practice. He had never been a professional agent. He must have been badly shaken by the confrontation on his own doorstep. Besides, the girl would have a disconcerting effect on a Rule Britannia academic. Wing doubted if Rigby had had much contact with young ladies of Dorothy's class.

Dorothy's presence confused even hardened agents. Wing glanced at her fondly. She cradled a plastic coffee cup in one hand. Sipping from it, she ushered Rigby from the kitchen into the long, cold living room.

She was twenty-four, looked younger, rangy rather than petite, ash-blonde, Dutch stock from Kansas. She wore levis, sneakers, a plaid windbreaker. Her short hair made her seem tomboyish. Her fingers were square, her legs long, her breasts, under grape-purple shirting, small and snub. Her wide mouth was an advertising huckster's dream, made for Pepsi and strawberry shortcake. Her smile was as friendly as a florist's.

In her right hand she held the knife. Her grip on it was light, nonchalant. The knife was an old Boone Huntsman with a scotch-taped handle and a stout five-inch blade honed like a barbershop razor. With that same knife, Mr. Wing remembered, she had dexterously castrated a garrulous Irish smuggler named Rafferty down in the resort town of Ajijic on the shores of Lake Chapala in Mexico to end an argument over possession of a mind-popping consignment of Sandoz LSD-25. Mr. Wing had had to finish the young fellow off, to prevent his screams from awakening the mid-American immigrants in their ersatz adobe retirement chalets.

The stone fireplace was empty. The picture window poked into a gunmetal grey sky, though a band of light across the alderbrake made the snow sparkle fleetingly. Soon, when the storm hit, there would be no sparkle left. Mr. Wing would be glad when this job was over. He did not like snow, dampness, and chill rooms.

Courteously, Mr. Wing expressed himself delighted to meet Mr. Rigby. Rigby did not return the greeting.

Politely, Mr. Wing said, 'May I relieve you of your document case, please?'

Rigby's stubborn fingers tightened on the handle.

'How the devil did you trace me?' he asked, in a bold barking voice.

Behind Rigby, the girl leaned on the doorpost. Two other doors fed the ell-shaped living room, one to the porch, the second to a central vestibule that led in turn to attic and basement. Mr.

Wing had personally checked every inch of the house and had pronounced it 'clean'.

'We are *rather* short of time, Mr. Rigby,' Wing said. 'I would be obliged if you would return the cultures.'

'What cultures?'

With a graceful movement, the girl put down the coffee cup.

'The cultures that were stolen from my employers in Hong Kong,' said Mr. Wing.

'I don't know what you're nattering about.'

'The salesman – Ballard – told us a great deal before he died,' Wing said. 'Now, Mr. Rigby, the document case, please.'

Slowly and deliberately Rigby shook his head.

The girl's movement was swift, athletic and highly functional. The knife blade severed median and ulnar nerves. The document case dropped instantly from Rigby's grasp.

Blood spurted. Rigby sobbed loudly, left hand clutching right wrist. He brought it to his face, stuffed it into his mouth, as if the wound had been caused by snakebite, he crouched over, moaning almost inaudibly.

Mr. Wing kicked the document case away from Rigby's feet and lifted it.

Dorothy returned to her lazy position by the door.

Rigby whimpered. Blood spattered his lips, chin, jowls and collar.

Mr. Wing could not see his eyes. From a pocket in his vest, Mr. Wing brought out a small knife and sawed through the leather strap above the catch of the case. He pulled open the jaws of the case, dug inside and brought out the towel-wrapped bundle.

Apparently, Rigby was concerned only with staunching the blood that flowed copiously from his wrist.

Setting the case on the floor, Mr. Wing loosened the towels and exposed the square box of hard black plastic.

Features contorted with pain, Rigby looked up.

'Listen, I . . . I . . . don't *have* the damned cultures. The box is empty.'

Mr. Wing smiled indulgently.

Grimly, Rigby insisted, 'It's empty, I tell you.'

Typically English last-gasp bid to avert inevitable defeat! How pathetic! Mr. Wing sighed and flipped open the box lid with his thumbnail.

Rigby lowered his head and charged.

'No, Dorothy,' Wing shouted. *'Dorothy, no.'*

Rigby managed three steps, nowhere near close enough to do Wing harm. But even after it was over, beyond redemption, Wing went on shouting, 'No. No. No. No. No.'

She was almost as fast as Mr. Wing had been before he had learned to temper speed with guile. Before the Oriental could do anything to prevent it, Dorothy intercepted Rigby, smothered his charge, locked his arms, jerked back his head and ripped the knife across his throat.

Gurgling, Rigby sagged against the girl's breast. She punched the knife into the side of his neck. Shoving him away, she stepped fastidiously aside as he fell. Face down, Rigby lay on the oatmeal rug, the Huntsman jutting from below his right ear.

Wing said nothing now. He watched in silence as Dorothy studied her handiwork and then, treading carefully round the spreading red stain, kneeled to retrieve the weapon. She flopped Rigby onto his back.

Much to his chagrin, Wing detected a faint glint of life lingering in the Englishman's washed-out eyes. No fear now, only smug self-satisfaction, fading, fading, until, without a sound, Rigby died.

Frowning slightly, the girl looked up.

Mr. Wing held out both hands. Towels draped across his fingers, the hard black plastic box was cradled in the middle, lid wide open.

'Jesus,' the girl said.

The box was empty.

Sir George Upton made the hop from Seattle to Faber Falls in a twin-engined eight-seater Chippewa that was the best that Harold Feldspar could lay on at short notice. The Chippewa had seen better days. It was piloted by a crazy contract artist, a French-Canadian who answered to the name of Pierre. Pierre nosed through the foul spring weather with the kind of suicidal élan that Upton had thought buried with the last of the few.

Darkness had fallen before the plane touched down. Isolated landing lights and the dinky tower of the little airstrip emphasised the vast emptiness of the back country. After checking that his passenger wouldn't require his services before midnight, Pierre tweaked up the hood of his fur-lined parka and set off on foot for the town's one and only bar.

Crossing the breadth of the airstrip, guided by a light in the window of a shack dwarfed by a hangar, Upton headed for the clubhouse of the Faber Falls Private Flying Club where CIA Agent Harold Feldspar waited, alone, by a cold pot-bellied stove.

Feldspar was seated on a scarred pine bench, elbows on knees, sipping gin from the silver cup of a hip flask. He wore a tweed raglan-sleeved trench coat over a grey cashmere sweater and fine cord slacks. It was a couple of years since the men had last met, but age, and increased status, had laid no obvious mark on Feldspar. Hunched on the bench, like a sophomore at the Yale-Harvard game, he lacked only a pennant on a stick to make the impersonation complete. The wormcast scar on his left cheek had been made vivid by the cold atmosphere in the shack. He seemed neither relieved nor irritated by Upton's appearance. Giving nothing away, his greeting was cool and unemotional.

Feldspar had been co-opted to the assignment seven months ago, appointed from a dull, if dangerous, on-going surveillance in Barbados to head a so-called research project in one of the agency's less public Washington properties. As yet, Feldspar had received no official briefing. Natural curiosity and a flair for diplomatic interrogation had unearthed the particular chain of command that he'd been welded into – an *ad hoc* group of indeterminate size convened by a permanent inter-agency committee affiliated to the United States Intelligence Board. Somewhere along the line stood Henry Marks; Feldspar was sure of it. Also involved – though Feldspar could not ascertain the exact extent of his authority – was Vice-President Rainer.

Apart from putting subtle questions to minions in Washington restaurants, Feldspar had spent his days processing – that is, assimilating – a weird assortment of classified data. Taken piece by piece the documentation seemed random and meaningless. This past month, however, Feldspar had begun to discern a pattern to the collection as a whole, though he could not deduce what might eventually be expected of him by way of action. Until that afternoon, he had been unaware that Sir George Upton had a hand in the game.

Feldspar got to his feet and offered Sir George the silver cup. Upton took it and tossed off the contents in a single swallow. He returned the cup to Feldspar.

'Did you lay on transport?' Upton asked.

'I rented a Mustang. It's outside.'

Feldspar leading, the men went out into the cold wet night, followed a paved path by the gable of the hangar and found the rented Ford in a lot adjacent to the field's side gate.

'Shall I drive, Sir George?'

'No. I will.'

Feldspar slid into the passenger seat. He made no apologies for the vehicle – Upton would realise that he had done his best – and he asked no questions.

Upton slammed the shift and shot the Mustang out of the gate. Feldspar tried not to blink.

From Faber Falls, Upton navigated north-west. The Mustang's hacked-out transmission and balding rubber tyres gave it the hair-raising instability of a skateboard and, after twenty miles or so, Feldspar felt impelled to remind Sir George that climatic conditions were not favourable to speed.

Upton grunted. He did not ease back on the throttle.

Along the Falls-Branks loop powerlines were down and local crossings endangered by log-jams higher up the Goose river. Upton was flagged to a halt by a couple of State troopers in yellow slickers. What they thought of the driver the troopers kept to themselves. That night they were too busy to speculate on what a four-square English clubman might be doing champing at the wheel of a '72 Mustang on a backroad in northern Montana. Courteously they told him what roads to avoid and advised him to drive cautiously. Upton thanked them and left them shaking their heads in despair as the Mustang vanished into the darkness at approximately the speed of sound.

It was 23.53 local time when Upton brought the Ford into Osiris. So far he had told Feldspar nothing, not even the name of their ultimate destination.

Long splinters of rain swept the township in the wake of the storm that had raked the county throughout the evening and early part of the night. Under swaying lamps the Osiris main stem was deserted. Used to fierce spring gales, the citizens slept peacefully, unconcerned about the flood havoc that threatened the eastern prairie town along the state lines.

Upton had lost all sense of time. He was suspended in a condition of compacted reality cultivated over three decades of abrupt departures and jagged international jet flights. Of middle height and slender, he was anything but physically imposing. His thin sandy hair was meticulously brushed over a pink scalp. But the muscles of his face were taut and his movements decisive. He could play the sombre elder statesman of the British scientific community when he had to. In fact, he had been yanked away from a Royal Society dinner by Rigby's urgent call and still wore full evening dress, crowned by a Harrow school scarf and an old-fashioned black homburg. Feldspar was not fooled. He had seen Upton in action and knew him to have more power than most government leaders, and even fewer scruples.

Navigating to the end of Wolfridge Avenue, Upton swung the Mustang sharply into the driveway and killed the engine and lights.

'Is this it?' Feldspar asked.

'Yes, a safe house – that might not be so safe after all.'

In the right-hand pocket of his bulky tweed trench coat, Feldspar's fingers discovered a Smith & Wesson Police Airweight .38 Special that he just happened to have with him.

'I would be obliged, Feldspar,' Upton said, 'if you'd refrain from shooting a small white-haired gentleman. He is my courier.'

Feldspar smiled faintly.

Climbing out, Upton walked briskly up the cantilever steps to the kitchen door. He had been here last summer and his memory for detail was excellent. Feldspar waited at the bottom of the steps while Upton rapped on the kitchen door, then rattled the handle to confirm that it was locked. He turned and picked his way back down the steps, past Feldspar, to the Mustang. He lifted an overnight bag from the passenger seat and returned once more to the door. By the light of a flashlamp, using a wedge of flexible steel, he opened the lock and let himself into the house, signalling Feldspar to follow.

The house was hollow and empty. Planting Feldspar in the kitchen, Upton moved into the living room and through it, exploring the whole place from attic to basement. Coming back into the living room he instructed Feldspar to pull the drapes across the picture window and switch on the table lamp. By its light Upton conscientiously examined the room.

Keeping half an eye on the door, Feldspar watched.

As he worked, Upton said conversationally, 'The courier's name is Kenneth Rigby. He's bringing me a package from Hong Kong. He called me last night from Seattle. He seemed rather "spooked" – is that the word?'

'Probably,' said Feldspar. 'With reason?'

'I don't know,' Upton said. 'It's possible that, in view of the inclement weather, he's been delayed en route. Somehow, I don't think so.'

'How long since your man was last here?'

'At a guess I'd say not since last summer.'

'Then somebody's breached the house.' Feldspar pointed with his thumb.

The distribution of dust on the bare floorboards showed Upton where the rug should have been. He got down on all fours and, probing with the flashlamp's beam, found a sticky thread of blood wiped into the fissure where hearthstone and planking met. He dug out a sample on the point of a pen, smeared it on his fingertip and held the finger up to show Feldspar.

'Blood?'

'Still moist,' said Upton.

Moving back into the kitchen, Feldspar found a wet mop in a closet behind the washing tub.

If the proving of a legal case had been Upton's objective he would have preserved these few valuable pieces of evidence. No police detective, he was at liberty to use the findings as the basis for intuitive assessment. With Feldspar's assistance, he searched the house again, very carefully this time, then, opening the living room drapes and putting out the lamp, he stood by the edge of the window and stared down to the butt of the avenue. Instinct told him that Rigby's attackers had fled.

Feldspar said, 'You think he reached here, Sir George?'

'Oh yes.'

Feldspar said, 'Perhaps you should tell me what he was carrying.'

Still staring from the window, Upton said, 'A receptacle, about the size of a paperback novel – a box, like as not.'

Feldspar said, 'The question is, did he have time and opportunity to dump it before he was taken?'

Rather wistfully, Feldspar thought, Upton said, 'Rigby was not a young man. On the other hand, he was always a bit of a bulldog. I knew him during the war. We worked together.'

Upton had been the brightest of Colonel Kingsley Roach's back-room boys. In those days a spy depended on his wits and inductive powers, not on a battery of computers and a network of company executives. Roach had had the freedom to handpick his team, to operate them more or less as he liked, even to the extent of ringing his own targets. Upton had been suborned from his post as a lecturer in biology at Cambridge. Rigby, as it happened, had been a Cambridge fellow too. Later, when hostilities were ostensibly over and the colour of the enemy had changed to Red, they had worked together again at Drayton Down Defence Establishment.

Upton said, 'He was very good at his job.'

Feldspar made no comment.

In that lonely house in Osiris, Montana, Upton recalled Rigby's qualities. Taking it step by step he mentally trailed Rigby from his Seattle apartment to the living room in Wolfridge Avenue. Visualising each stage of the journey, Upton discarded anomalous actions, things that Rigby, a scientist, would not be liable to do.

Finally, nodding to himself, Upton went outside and explored the stairs and narrow area of the driveway, sectors invisible from the windows of the house. Feldspar loitered, his back to the steps, uncomfortably aware that Upton was a wide open target as he poked about by the light of the flashlamp. Backtracking past the Mustang, Upton crabbed to the heel of the sidewalk at the driveway's end and then, calculating, glanced from the house to the avenue, to the woods: a problem in geometry as much as psychology. Feldspar leaned against the Mustang, hand in his trench coat pocket. Sufficient light spilled from the avenue's single streetlamp to illuminate the level of the alderbrake and the stave fence.

As he drew closer, Upton made out tyre tracks churned in the wasted snowdrift. The mud was chocolate brown, wetted by falling rain, tread marks stippled into mushy snow. Crouching, Upton studied the signs. Feldspar waited by the Mustang in the driveway.

Upton touched nothing. He got up quickly and returned to the house. As he passed Feldspar he said, 'Start the car,' then went on up the steps again.

Inside the house, he picked up his overnight bag, adjusted the drapes, tapped the kitchen door lock into place and left. He came down to the Mustang, told Feldspar to move over, got into the driver's seat, and reversed into the avenue. He eased the Ford back so that it fitted cleanly into the furrows left by Rigby's vehicle, almost perfectly covering the muddy tracks by the breast of the snowdrift.

Watching curiously, Feldspar suddenly chuckled.

'Yes, *sir,*' he murmured. '*Yes, sir.*'

Upton opened the driver's door, swung himself round in the seat and, reaching out, raked the snow with his fingertips. He soon found what he sought.

One by one he picked the Petri dishes out of the drift. Four of them had been slotted into the soft-packed snow, thumbed into it like large glass coins.

Upton's mind leapt back to another night, darker than this and far colder, in mid-winter of 1944. Kneeling by Ken Rigby's side he had sifted through a snowdrift in search of a single glass slide that had been smuggled out of the experimental medical block at Auchwitz. It allegedly contained a contagious germ that would destroy the reproductive facility of all females of Jewish extraction. Fortunately the germ had turned out to be a dud. But Upton remembered Rigby's amazement at the hiding place, how impressed they had both been by the German courier's ingenuity under pressure. Now the same trick, done with four sealed Petri dishes, had perhaps cost Rigby his life.

Upton had not intended that his watchdog in Seattle should die. Even so, he did not grieve for Kenneth Rigby. He kept all emotion out of his thinking by concentrating on other matters.

By the dash-light he examined the dishes. They were perfectly intact, the nutrient agar streaked. Hopefully, the bacterial cultures would still be pure and healthy. He had no knowledge of who had carried out the preparation. It might even have been Tony Ballard; the task was simple enough.

Unwrapping the Harrovian scarf from around his neck, he embedded the four dishes snugly in its folds, nested the bundle in the overnight bag and placed it under the flow outlet of the heater. He then closed the Mustang's door and drove off.

'I assume,' said Feldspar quietly, 'that that's what you came for?'

'Yes.'

'Am I also right in assuming that all the classified material I've been obliged to absorb relates to what's in those lab dishes?'

'Yes.'

Offering no more information, Upton cleared the town. It was only then that his excitement deteriorated into a spasm of trembling that took Feldspar by surprise. Prudently, Upton eased the Ford to the roadside.

'Let me drive,' Feldspar said.

'No,' replied Upton. 'I think better when I'm occupied.'

'Are you okay?'

'Just a touch of jet-lag,' Upton said. 'Do you have a cigarette?'

Feldspar lit two Philip Morris Internationals and handed one to Upton. The older man's trembling soon subsided. He watched the highway behind him for three or four minutes then drove on again, heading for Faber Falls and crazy Pierre's plane. He would not stop long in Seattle. He certainly had no intention of depositing the cultures at the Botanical Research Centre. Clearly that establishment was blown.

In getting this far Upton had lost two men. He was convinced now that Rigby must be dead, his body dumped in the river or weighted down in one of the thousands of deep cold lakes that sprinkled the region. He would cover up the cause of death, of course, a dreary subterfuge involving false documents and a tangle of official lies. Rigby's Seattle colleagues would be informed that Rigby had died of a stroke while on vacation. Upton would vet the obituaries that would appear in scientific journals. He would personally visit Rigby's daughter in England. Perhaps then he might allow himself to feel guilty. But the acquisition of the cultures was a salve against an excess of conscience, giving substance to the rumour that had come out of Hong Kong, the crumbs of information so incredible that nobody but Henry Marks had taken them seriously.

Upton was thankful now that Marks had come in on the deal. No fat sheaf of analyses, no reports, no computer read-outs were necessary to tell him that the rumour had a strong basis in fact. Ballard was missing in Macao, Rigby in Montana. It was probable that he would never discover just what had happened to them. It was a matter of no consequence. He could not afford to be squeamish. In a game worth fifty billion dollars and, possibly, a hundred million lives, the lives of two Englishmen counted only as a minor exchange.

The assumptions had been proved. It was time to activate his forces, waken the other watchdogs.

The wind brawled and bullied the Mustang. Upton drove faster now, chasing the storm.

'Feldspar,' he said. 'I think it's time I gave you a briefing.'

'Will I be working for you?'

'Indirectly, yes,' Upton answered. 'But you will act – at first – on orders received through your office. I needn't add that the tale I'm about to tell you must be treated in strict confidence. Only you and I will have possession of the facts as they stand. You will tell no one what you're working on, no one at all.'

'I understand.'

'I hope that you do,' said Upton. 'Because I require your help immediately.'

'To do what, Sir George?'

'To find me the man I must put in next.'

'What kind of a man?'

'A botanist. Somebody well-placed, unmarried – and, most important of all, somebody *clean*.'

'Is that why top college staffing files drifted my way?' said Feldspar. 'All those boring dossiers of bacteriologists, geneticists and botanists.'

'Of course. I imagine you must already have someone in mind?'

Feldspar nodded. He was aware, fully aware, that he might be condemning a man to death. He did not hesitate. 'The most suitable candidate might be difficult to recruit.'

'You may leave that side of it to me,' said Upton. 'What's his name?'

'Rand,' Feldspar answered. 'Professor Gordon Rand.'

TUESDAY 16 AUGUST, 1977
TURKEY

In the heat of the Turkish summer, Gordon Rand lay in the

shadow of the largest of the four quonset huts that marked the upper boundary of cultivation. In the past couple of weeks he had spent more time sprawled in the canvas lounger than in performing professional tasks. Boredom was the biggest hazard. Boredom with the arid vistas of the Turkish back country. Boredom with the limitations of advanced field work. Boredom with the pretty segments of the experimental crop unusually arranged in a chequerboard of white and dark purple that separated the distinct varieties of *Papaver Somniferum*, the opium poppy.

Rand did not much care for Turkey. He had never had much enthusiasm for the project to which he had been assigned by a clutch of Washington top brass. The reality had turned out to be even more depressing than the prospect. It seemed he was expected to do the kind of routine benchwork that any laboratory assistant could cope with – and to ask no questions. In spite of the frightening potential of Meredith's breakthrough, Rand found it difficult to take the cloak-and-dagger stuff seriously.

By inclination he had always been physically lazy. Never an outdoorsman, never one of the heavy-booted, khaki-clad, lobster-kneed fanatics who clumped through jungles and across inhospitable deserts in search of rare hybrids and new species of lichen. He had lost his appetite for that sort of botanical adventure during extended postgraduate trips to Bolivia, Kashmir and Dartmoor, England, fifteen years back. Occasional field trips in the intervening years had only served to strengthen his conviction that he was more suited to studying life forms through a Siemens electron microscope than on some goddamned goat-track thousands of miles from the controlled environment of the Vereker Laboratory of Plant Sciences in Stanford, California, U.S.A. Even in the Vereker he stood apart from his fellows. He was not sufficiently 'mission-orientated' to be comfortable in the rat-race of sponsored research and development.

No matter how thorough the Turkish authorities had been in helping set up this outpost – unaware of its real purpose, of course – the constant *churr* of power generators and the naked modernity of the huts seemed strangely alien to the heartland poppy patch in which thousands of misty green seed pods sweated out their rich amber essence in the sun.

At such a fundamental level, opium was an honest crop, endemic to primitive cultures, the mainstay of entire eco-systems in places as remote as Kahutshir. In central Turkey alone a hundred thousand farmers reaped a living from the juice of the poppy plant. It was difficult to connect such specialised agriculture with the flourishing poison tree of the international drug trade, with squalid Marseilles refineries, profit-hungry smugglers, ruthless syndicates, pushers and users, twitching addicts in city streets. Here, in the sun, poppy growing seemed honourable and traditional.

Opium was non-perishable. Every homestead had its nest-egg tucked away to be used in barter, as a daughter's dowry or a son's birthday gift. Turkish opium was reputed to be the finest in the world, with morphine content as high as fifteen percent: a brokers' dream. Rand had familiarised himself with all the facts and figures. Even so, he could not shake off the feeling that he had become a cog in a cumbersome machine designed to interfere with a natural cycle of mythical historicism. He doubted if the vast network of 'connections' that fed addicts in western cities could be broken by tampering with the primary source.

He had tried to discuss his opinions with Meredith during the cool upland evenings. True to the tradition of die-hard colonials, the Englishman came in from the field or laboratory and changed into a rusty dinner jacket for the ceremony of demolishing the local cuisine and downing a couple of bottles of potent *raki*. Though a relaxed and interesting conversationalist, Ashley Meredith refused 'to talk shop' and, on the subject of the ethics of science, deftly avoided revealing his own position. Rand's curiosity also got short shrift from Laura Meredith, Ashley's daughter and personal assistant. She teased the American for over-seriousness.

In fact Laura and Ashley Meredith were all that made the Kahutshir project bearable, apart from succulent kebabs dished up by the unit cook, a grizzled old rogue requisitioned from the kitchens of the Isparta Hotel.

Anyhow, Rand consoled himself, the field stint would soon be over and his real work would begin. Laden with data, he would return to Stanford, book and computer time, and set about compiling detailed analyses of the Meredith experiment. First he would have to spell out the unit's basic findings in a form that the funding body could assimilate. The committee members, and Vice-President Rainer, could not be expected to comprehend botanical terminology.

Rainer's committee would want to know only one thing: 'Does the stuff work?'

Rand would be obliged to answer: 'Yes, like a charm.'

Watching Meredith stroll up and down the plant rows like a gaunt mediaeval friar in a herb garden, Rand's bewilderment increased. How could a world authority on plant virology treat such a startling discovery so casually? Wrapped in an off-hand attitude, Meredith was defensive about the processes involved in reaching his discovery. Rand did not suppose that Meredith hoped to sell him – and the United States government – a false bill of goods. Besides, the facts were laid before him in the poppy field. It still struck him as incredible, however, that a lone botanist, beavering away in a cash-starved, antiquated institute in London, could come up with such an original bacterium.

But the proof was beyond doubt. Meredith *had* developed a bacterial strain that drastically reduced the morphine content of the opium poppy.

Sitting up in the lounger, Rand shaded his eyes and stared across the patch. The delicate heads of the poppies nodded languidly in the faint noon breeze that drifted down from the mountains. There was no visible evidence of change in the plants. Even the most seasoned botanist could detect no external difference between the treated flowers and the control groups that lay under protective canopies. Naturally, the native labourers and Killick, the government observer, were not entirely unaware that something was happening. Only the records told the whole tale, however. And the records were locked in a tall steel safe in the laboratory. Killick was not admitted to the inner sanctum. Though curious as to the unit's objective, the young Turkish assistant was too proud to beg for information. Perhaps Killick was hoping for some tangible evidence of change in the plants. If so, he would be disappointed.

The damage was done to the structure of the plant. The experiment had yielded a mass of data on the effects of Meredith's bacterium on control groups of both varieties and on a small batch of cultivated variants. In all cases, the results were identical, the morphine content of the plant reduced to less than five percent of normal. The crop had been rendered almost worthless.

The days of the poppy-patch farmer were numbered. Only massive spreads would be commercially viable if the Meredith bacterium were put to use. Massive spreads were too obvious to remain immune to international legislature. Ashley Meredith's discovery could mean the end of the illicit drug traffic from Mexico to Manila, all along the Tropic latitudes. Administration and economic upheaval that would be created in areas like Kahutshir were not Rand's problems. Happily, he could leave the welter of practical considerations to the World Health Organisation and the governments of dozens of countries – including the United States. Quite simply he had been invited to test the effectiveness of the new bacterium; even without long-term analyses, he could solemnly declare that it worked.

It was exactly noon. Shadows thrown by the quonsets had shrivelled. The sepia heat was stunning. In a few minutes Meredith would haul up from the field with the morning's samples, and the ritual of testing would begin. Three or four hours of elementary benchwork in the cool air-conditioned interior of the laboratory would be a welcome relief from the tedious heat. But Meredith was moving up the rows empty-handed. Basins, three-pronged grooving knife and alloy spatula had been stuffed back into the sack slung over his shoulder.

Rand got to his feet. Surely, this departure from routine was significant. A flaw in the methodology? An unexpected hitch that would necessitate another six or seven weeks in Kahutshir? God, what a hellish prospect.

Anxiously Rand moved out onto the pad in front of the huts and, glancing to his left, saw that Laura had emerged from her work-place.

Killick, dark, truculent and insolently handsome, had crawled out of the shade way down by the base poles. The Turk's cheese-cloth shirt puffed up with the sighing breeze and his swarthy skin, even at that distance, glistened with sweat.

'What the hell's wrong? What's happened?' Rand called out.

'Nothing's wrong, Gordon,' Laura told him.

She had tanned evenly and quickly, but she did not appear unfeminine. She had a softness that Rand did not associate with English women, a delicacy that was anything but fragile.

Close to him now, she said, 'What will you have? *Mersin,* or do you feel like risking the *Kavaklidere*?'

It was a camp rule that alcohol was not served at noon. In this heat it made them all too sleepy to work well after lunch. The thought of the sweet, heavy orange liqueur, *Mersin*, did not appeal to him, still less the sickly local champagne.

'What is this?' Rand said. 'What's going on?'

Meredith climbed the earth steps from the field ramp, smiling. 'Do have something, Gordon. By way of celebration. Laura, find our friend a Tuborg.'

'Celebration?'

'It's over, young man.'

'Is this an arbitrary decision?' Rand asked.

The Englishman shrugged. 'There's no point to be served by further testing. We may proceed with experiments in environmental chambers and the like, don't you think?'

'Do you want me to take fresh stem, leaf and root cuttings before we leave, Ashley?'

'No need.'

'But . . .?' Rand hesitated. 'Listen, if we're packing up and pulling out, it's time we have a *real* conversation.'

Meredith's seamed face wrinkled as he grinned.

'I wondered how long you'd be able to contain yourself, Gordon. Let's go into the lab.'

They left the pad, entered the vacuum door at the mouth of the largest of the huts, and passed through the inner door into the laboratory. The Turks had gone out of their way to provide equipment, and the lab was well stocked. Two innoculating hoods stood on the bench nearest the door, a Gillett & Sibert Conference microscope, complete with viewing head and camera attachment, in a screened cubicle. The Turks had even furnished an expensive Uvispek Photo-electric spectrophotometer that had helped speed the research considerably.

Rand wasted no time. 'Ashley, I'm sick of secrecy.'

'It's necessary, I'm afraid.'

'There are too many open-ended issues to the experiment to suit me.'

'Because you are a man of integrity?'

'I like to kid myself that I am,' said Rand.

'If you worked in England you'd be obliged to adjust to deceit of one sort or another. It's part of one's protective mechanism against bureaucratic stupidity.'

'I'm not exactly Simon Pure when it comes to wheeling and dealing for the Vereker's requirements,' Rand said. 'But don't sidetrack me into running down the paymasters, Ashley. I want some straight answers.'

'I'll enlighten you if I can.'

'As you know I was dragged into this project. I didn't volunteer. I admit I'm impressed. More than impressed, I'm fascinated. I'm also confused.'

'Why?'

'Your preliminary report is full and thorough in all respects, Ashley, but you ignore the process by which you developed the bacterium. What's wrong? Are you unsure of its long-term effects?'

'No.'

'Then why keep it secret?'

'I've been instructed to do so.'

'That's what I figured,' Rand said. 'All right, so you go along with a government edict. Maybe I would too. But I did some research of my own in the Stanford library before I left for Turkey, and I found precious little in your published papers to suggest that you were aiming at, or even drifting towards, a major bacterial breakthrough in relation to plant inhibitors.'

'Luck played a major part in my discovery,' Meredith said cryptically.

Rand said, 'I'd be the first to acknowledge the part that luck plays in breakthroughs. But somehow I don't think chance had much to do with it in the case of the Meredith bacterium.'

Meredith seemed less affable. 'Why not, Gordon?'

'This was Conrad Vigson's line of country.'

'Vigson?'

'Come on, Ashley, don't snow me. You worked with Vigson way back, in that top secret Drayton Down establishment.'

'In God's name, where did you unearth that piece of information?'

'In a Vigson paper in *Ethos*. Winter issue, 1956.'

'I don't see the significance of digging up that old stuff,' Meredith said. 'After all, there were ten of us on the Drayton Down team at that period. There was also an official embargo on publication of our findings.'

'An embargo that Conrad Vigson decided to ignore.'

'Only after he left Drayton, left England in fact.'

'But that wasn't the last word from him.'

'What are you driving at? Do you suspect me of thieving another man's ideas? Vigson's been dead for years. Before that . . . well, I really didn't keep in touch with either the man or his work.'

'No, I don't think you'd thieve another man's ideas, Ashley.'

'Your trust is comforting,' said Meredith, sourly.

'Still, I feel I'm entitled to be told just how much of the early benchwork derives from Vigson's research?'

'None.'

'I take it that you *have* read his paper on lysosome disintegration?'

'That early paper, yes.'

'Did it stem from research conducted at Drayton Down?'

'I suppose it may have done. Indirectly. The methodology is very primitive, however. It won't have escaped your sharp eye that my team at the Institute has been conscientiously applying itself to lysosomes.'

'Specifically to a study of transfer of resistance factors in relation to inexplicable behaviour patterns in herbicides?' Rand asked.

'Not quite.'

'Close enough?' Rand persisted.

'You have no valid reason to assume that such a programme excludes the possibility of . . .'

Rand cut the Englishman short. 'Let it go, Ashley. I can see that you're reluctant to fill me in.'

'I advise you not to rush into anything, Gordon.'

'Into what, for Chrissakes?'

'I didn't ask for you to be assigned to this project, you know,' Meredith said. 'You were the choice of the U.S. government, of Vice-President Rainer to be exact.'

'Presumably you went to Rainer because you needed American backing.'

'Facilities, more than funding,' said Meredith. 'But now that I've got you, I intend to use you to the full.'

'That's what worries me,' Rand said. 'What am I expected to

do?'

'Design a mathematical model susceptible to computer analysis, for one thing,' Meredith said.

'Epidemic and population dynamics aren't my speciality.'

'Then adapt.'

'There's more to it than that. What do the top guns have in store for me? Am I being set up as some kind of target analyst? To map out where best to spread the bacterium?'

'I doubt it.'

'Since I'm working under direct appointment of the Vice-Presidential Sub-committee on Narcotics, and Jay Rainer is a highly ambitious politician, this begins to smell like a prestige project.'

'I can't pronounce on Rainer's ambitions one way or the other,' Meredith said. 'I don't *know* what the U.S. intend to do.'

'Who made the initial crosslink between you and the Vice-President's narco squad?' Rand asked. 'Will you tell me that much?'

'Sir George Upton.'

'Did he request my appointment?'

'I really couldn't say.'

'Ashley, I've got to know what I'm into.'

'Poppies.'

'That's all?'

'Isn't it enough?'

Though unconvinced, Rand said no more on that subject. He would do what he had been commissioned to do, prepare a summary for the Rainer sub-committee and utilise the data along programme lines drawn up in consultation with Meredith.

'When do you plan on leaving?' asked Rand. 'A day or so should see to the packing of the equipment.'

'We'll leave tonight, just after dark.'

'Sudden, isn't it?'

'A precaution, that's all,' Meredith said. 'As to the equipment, we'll entrust that to Killick. After all, he was presented to us as a trained lab technician. Can you drive a Land Rover? I never thought to ask before?'

'Yes. I take it you want us out fast, with all our documentary evidence on board. Where's the arranged pick-up point?'

'Afyon.'

'Then on to Istanbul?'

'No, to Ankara.'

'Aren't we compelled to check out with Turkish government officers?'

'They can whistle,' said Meredith. 'I'll feel safer when we're home again in our respective laboratories.'

'It's not really the Turkish government we're shy of, right?' Rand said.

'Other folk *might* be interested in what we're up to,' Meredith admitted.

'Commercial investors,' said Rand. 'Who can blame them? If my government decides to use this bacterium . . .'

'No responsible government would *dare* use the bacterium,' said Meredith.

'Because of unpredictable side-effects, you mean?' said Rand. 'I wish I had your faith in politicians. Government agencies think only of short-term benefits, Ashley.'

'I assume that you are aware of the drastic consequences that would be caused by a world opium famine,' said Meredith. 'Good Lord, Gordon, we have evidence of the kind of suffering that even a modest reduction in international output brings. A scarcity, never mind a famine, of medically essential opiate-based drugs constitutes a disaster.'

'Then why the hell are we playing about with such a monstrously dangerous bacterium in the first place?' said Rand.

'Have you considered that we might be expected to produce an antidote?' said Meredith.

Rand snorted. 'Come on, Ashley. You know better than that. Nobody can *order* us to rustle up an antidote.'

'If we were given massive support, however, the right kind of climate for such a discovery could be fostered.'

'Big science style? Yes, that's possible. Even so, no right-minded scientist would guarantee results,' said Rand.

'Gordon, I'm a servant of my government,' Meredith said. 'I have no say in how my discovery will actually be applied. However, I do know that there are many non-political factions who would be extremely interested in such a bacterium. I think their unscrupulousness might match that of *any* defence department, don't you?'

'Growers, dealers, brokers and distributors, you mean?' asked Rand. 'The syndicates?'

'Precisely.'

'Surely they know nothing of the Meredith bacterium.'

'Secrets are not easily kept.'

'Yeah,' said Rand, 'particularly when testing's carried out in such a cockamamie way as this. I take your point, though. If one illicit dope ring got its hands on your bacterium, it could create a world monopoly by infecting a *handful* of major production areas. It could push the price of raw opium through the roof.'

'And if this hypothetical ring had thoughtfully stockpiled opium products . . . ?'

'Its members would make a swift multi-billion dollar killing.'

'That's true, of course,' said Meredith. 'But consider, Gordon, how much more devastating their intervention would be if *they* had an antidote.'

Rand said, 'I'm beginning to get some idea of the scope of your bacterium and its implications, Ashley. Now that you've developed it, you can't just flush it down the toilet, can you?'

'Unfortunately not,' said Meredith. 'We must learn how to control it and inhibit its effects.'

'And put it to use?'

'Controlling it will be difficult enough,' Meredith said.

'How much clout do you have at executive level?'

'Very little, I'm afraid.'

'I probably have even less,' Rand said. 'Seems like we'll have to jump through any hoops they hold up for us, whether we like it or not.'

'I take it,' Meredith said, 'that you do understand the seriousness of the situation?'

'I certainly understand why developing an antidote is important,' Rand said.

'Imperative,' said Laura Meredith, as she entered the laboratory with a tray of drinks. 'I believe that's why you were assigned to work with us, Gordon.'

'Why the hell didn't my government tell me the whole story?' Rand said. 'Don't they trust me?'

'Ah, Gordon,' said Meredith. 'You forget we're merely scientists. We're not supposed to concern ourselves with major policy decisions.'

Meredith lifted the ugly dark brown bottle from the tray. It was fresh from the icebox and beaded with droplets of condensation.

He poured a glass for his daughter and another for himself, and passed Rand the can of Tuborg.

Rand ripped off the ring and held the can up. 'How does that English toast go?' he asked. 'Happy landings?'

'That seems suitable,' said Meredith, sipping the *Kavaklidere*. 'Lord, what poisonous stuff this Turkish bubbly is. I wonder if it's as inflammable as it tastes?'

'I think we'd best use gasoline,' Rand said.

'Leave that to me,' said Meredith. 'I do so love a bonfire.'

The Hotel Pera Palas in the Mesrutiyet Caddesi stood not ten blocks from the narrow street in which Adnan Killick had been born and raised. Never before had the young man entered its majestic foyer. The Pera Palas had hardly changed since the opulent days of Abdul Hamid. It was a monument to luxury that the urchins of Istanbul's old quarter accepted as a symbol of a life-style to which they might aspire if they were favoured by the Prophet and won themselves a graduate degree and a post with an American-owned company. Killick was pleased that his contacts had chosen the Pera Palas as their base in preference to the Hilton or the Sheraton.

The Chinese masters treated him with an avuncular deference that soon put him at his ease. They seemed to realise that he was no mere peasant but had received the benefits of education. They spoke to him in English and put their questions simply and, Killick thought, with due deference.

There were two Chinese, similar in appearance and build, like brothers. They were identically dressed in lightweight business suits with knob-knotted ties that, had Killick been better versed in the sporting life, he might have recognised as emblems of membership of the Imperial Golf Club of Nagoya. He was not told their names. His college friend, Bahm, who had found him the job, left him alone with them in an airy fifth -floor suite.

They encouraged him to talk and seemed very pleased with all he told them about the happenings at Kahutshir, even sharing his scorn of the English professor's mannerisms.

'And then,' said Killick, 'the English come out into field and spray all poppy flowers, all types. I smell the gasoline. But I not have time to do much.'

'When was this, Adnan?' asked one of the Chinese.

'In afternoon, late.'

'What did you do, Adnan?'

Killick was seated on a low divan, knees cocked. He bounced a little on the soft cushions as he justified his inactivity with unusual vehemence. 'I not able to do nothing. Too late.'

'The plants, they would not burn easily?'

'Took long, long time, yeah,' said Killick. 'Lotsa gasoline. Late harvest crop burn slow. I could have tell them that. But they not ask. Not ask me nothing. Not tell me nothing.'

'After the burning?' prompted one of the Chinese.

'Break down remains with sticks. *Smash*. It take longer. They not expect it take so long. Wind not blow. Smoke go up, strong. *Phaffff*. Smell strong.'

'How long did it take for this work?'

'Four hours, five hours.'

'And then, Adnan?'

'They drive off in Land Rover. No word. Not stop to eat dinner even. Leave. It is near dark. Meredith, he give me keys to all the quonsets. Laboratory, too. First time in seven weeks I allowed to enter laboratory. He tell me to pack equipment carefully. Trucks come tomorrow.'

'Did you not ask questions, Adnan?'

'Killick spread his hands. 'No good to do that. They tell me nothing. After they go in Land Rover, I run to laboratory. Everything gone. All papers. All samples.'

'Why did you not use the radio to inform your friend Bahm of the departure?'

'Radio not work. They take part with them, I think.'

'Will you report all this to your government boss?'

Cautiously Killick said, 'I tell him what you want him told, not any more.'

'Tell him just what you have told us.'

'Trucks come morning. Meredith he have sent for them, secretly.'

Seated a yard apart in wooden-armed, heavily quilted chairs, the Chinese glanced at each other, then one rose and, shaking Killick by the hand, said, 'Your friend has a gift for you, Adnan,'

Killick got hastily to his feet. 'I sorry I not have more to tell.'

'Your information has been of much use.'

As he was guided towards the door, Killick asked, 'But what they do, the professors?'

From his chair by the window, the Chinese called out, 'What do you think they were doing?'

'Killing poppies,' said Adnan Killick. 'Yet all plants seem strong, not sick. Juice heavy, as always.'

'Yes,' said the Chinese. 'Yes, tell your government boss just that.'

Killick's friend Bahm was waiting in the outer room of the luxurious suite. After shaking him by the hand once more and thanking him for his co-operation, the Chinese delivered him over to Bahm.

Bahm patted Killick's shoulder and presented him with a heavy envelope. Killick opened it at once. It contained fourteen one-thousand lira notes.

'*Ne kadar*?' Bahm asked.

Killick showed him the notes.

'Thousand dollars,' Bahm said. 'They are pleased with you, Adnan.'

Then he escorted his old college buddy out of the Pera Palas and tucked him back into the streets and government offices of Istanbul until such time as the White Tigers might need his services again.

Chen Yu-lan uncapped a bottle of tonic water and poured it into the tall glass of vodka. Sheng Kittagawa was drinking Scotch.

Chen Yu-lan said, 'It is imperative, Sheng, that we decide on the Turk's reliability.'

'I am of the opinion that he is too stupid to distort the truth.'

'Do you believe that the poppy plants were strong and healthy?'

'Ah, no,' said Kittagawa. 'That is still a matter for conjecture. If we had copies of Meredith's reports, we would know.'

'Unless they are bluffing us.'

'It is impossible to develop an antidote in so short a time,' said Kittagawa. 'We can, however, be certain that both English and American governments do have our bacterium, or one most similar.'

'It is regrettable that Wing failed with Rigby.'

'There is no help for that now,' Kittagawa said. 'We are to blame for not making Tang Mang Wu more secure.'

'If the American authorities have the culture and have begun analysis, they will pour money into research to press for the development of an antidote. We do not have such facilities.'

'We do, however, have Vigson and a start in the foot-race,' said Kittagawa. 'If we cannot stop them, perhaps we can delay them.'

'Long enough for Vigson to finish his work?'

'We must hope so, Chen. I suggest immediate and positive action to that end.'

'Yes, that is wise.'

'The obvious cannot be ignored.'

Chen Yu-lan nodded. 'Call Wing.'

WEDNESDAY 17 AUGUST
LONDON

At the junction of Cromwell Road and Queens Gate the Daimler ran into a snarl of traffic. Laura had forgotten that London would be choked with commuters in the half hour after five. The maze of one-way streets and filters defeated the navigational ingenuity of the chauffeur who had been sent to Heathrow to meet the Paris plane, and for Laura the long harried crawl towards Eaton Square turned into a nightmare. In panic, she slid open the glass partition.

'Driver, can't you take another route?'

'Sorry, Miss Meredith. It's the same all over the city at this hour. How is he?'

'Worse, I think.'

Turning in his seat, the chauffeur studied Ashley Meredith critically, until the impatient bleating of the herd behind the stately limousine forced his attention back to the wheel. He nosed the Daimler up tight to the fender of a Granada, then sought the young woman's eye in the mirror. 'Looks to me like his heart.'

Ashley Meredith had become unwell on the final leg of the journey from Turkey, the short flight from Orly. As they had eaten lunch during the Paris stopover, Laura at first suspected food-poisoning. It was now obvious that the condition was much more serious, involving the respiratory system.

She wished that she had summoned medical aid at the airport. But the limousine had been so convenient and her father so adamant that he be taken home that she had given in. Now Laura felt like a stranger in the hostile city, torn by raucous clamour, confused by swarms of cars and buses, frustrated by darting, suicidal pedestrians.

During the plane trips she had slept hardly at all. She had inherited a considerable degree of tension from her father on the journey out of Kahutshir. For the first time in her life, she had felt like a fugitive. What made things worse was that her father would not give reasons for his extraordinary anxiety.

From Afyon to Ankara and throughout the commercial THY flight to Paris, she had been aware of mounting stress, not only in her father but also in Gordon Rand. She had been almost glad to part from the American after lunch at Orly, though she would have welcomed his strength now in this totally unexpected and critical situation.

Though Meredith had no record of ill-health and certainly none of cardiac trouble, he had been under great strain during the past months, ever since Sir George Upton had fostered this sinister project. Strain, Laura knew, could cause heart disorder. Because she had been used to taking her father's advice throughout her life, she gave in to his wishes now, drifting into obedience in spite of the realisation that she should treat the illness as an emergency. What else could she do? Leap from the Daimler, find a call box and summon an ambulance? That might take longer than the drive home.

She studied her father again. He looked ghastly, his flesh leeched of all colour like a cellar fungus. A piping wheeze came from his throat, terrifyingly loud in the Daimler's hushed interior. It intensified even as she listened and changed into a spongy seething sound.

Simply for the sake of doing something, to offer him some comfort, she ripped a Kleenex from the box in her purse and pressed it into his hand. The hand rose jerkily to his mouth and crushed the tissue to his lips. He slumped crookedly into the seat corner, the wheeze breaking into a racking bout of coughing that shook him like a rag doll. Laura began to weep.

The Daimler crawled through a green arrow, shot forward and made distance, wheeling right into Beauchamp Place and along Pont Street. Brakes. The chauffeur cursed, drawing back his lips, as the limousine ran into more traffic at an intersection.

Outside the window, close to her father's head, Laura saw a young man on a Honda motor scooter weave to a halt. The rider was oblivious to her suffering, incurious, impersonal, insulated by his electric-blue helmet and plastic visor. For one idiotic moment, Laura thought of screaming at the rider, imploring him to find a doctor. Then the lights changed and the scooter was gone. The Daimler surged forward once more.

The Kleenex was still balled in her father's fist, a pastel pink ear jutting from between finger and thumb. She peered at the paper in horror, expecting it to be soaked with bright red blood. Instead, she saw only a tiny freckle of frothy pink mucus, a shade darker than the tissue itself.

The coughing bout had worn itself out, dwindling into seething inhalations and strenuous sighs. His skin was slick with a creamy sweat.

She pulled away, shouting, 'Where's the nearest hospital?'

Meredith struggled. She leaned against him, pinning him into the corner. The Daimler was travelling faster now, rounding into Belgrave Square.

'H . . . H . . . H . . . Home, La . . . Laura.'

'Father, you're so ill. We . . .'

'C . . . C . . . Call Upto . . . o . . . on.'

'Yes, yes, I will. Later. Don't excite yourself. Don't try to speak.'

'Miss Meredith, we're almost in Eaton Square. A coupler minutes'll take us to your address. We can call for an ambulance from there.'

'He needs immediate medical attention.'

'*Home*,' her father snarled, shifting his weight abruptly so that he craned forward.

'But . . . ?' Laura wept again, confused by her own ineptitude.

She had no experience of serious illness. She had been at school when her mother had died, and her father had kept the nature of the illness secret from her. She was used to the plant spiral of life and death, the slower form. Once though, when she had been little more than a child, she had witnessed the withering of a strong tomato plant in her aunt's greenhouse in Malvern. Malicious boys had smashed the panes and there had been frost in the night. Before morning, the tomato plant had died. Nothing her aunt could do would revive it. That had been her first conscious experience of the mortality of living things. She felt as helpless now as she had then.

'Eaton Square.' The chauffeur snatched at the wheel and, sacrificing the dignity of the limousine, bulled the vehicle through a red light into the familiar environs of the Merediths' house. But the city was still against them.

'Shit,' said the driver, without apology.

Peering forward, Laura saw road-signs, bold warning notices, candy-striped crosspoles on battered Water Board sawhorses. A row of eight orange lollipop night markers were already flashing. Beyond the obstruction a Mini and a Vauxhall were locked in an unyielding struggle to be first through the narrow access gap.

Her father was coughing again. He braced his elbow against her shoulder, propping himself upright. He coughed with a certain fastidiousness in short, harsh, moist gasps into the tissue in his fist.

As the Daimler rocked to a halt by the barriers, Laura saw the plate. Relief poured through her at the sight of the ornate iron railings, the bland Victorian frontage, the tall, sober four-panelled front door, and the plate – a traditional brass plaque engraved in steep sloping copperplate script with the names of the partners.

'*Stop, don't reverse. Stop.*'

'Here, miss?'

'Yes, just here. Pull in, please.'

Glancing left, the chauffeur immediately understood.

'Ah, doctors,' he said.

'My father's practitioner: Dr. Craig.'

The chauffeur already had his door open. 'Stay put, Miss Meredith. I'll dig him out.'

He seemed to move so slowly, the little uniformed Cockney, yet she knew that he was running as hard as he could. She watched him skip round the front of the Daimler and cross the pavement, holding his hat as the stiff evening breeze swirled round the square. She watched him race up the steps, punch the button, and then, twisting the brass handle, barge through the door and run on into the sombre hallway that led to the consulting rooms.

Laura prayed that Robert Craig would be on surgery.

Meredith's eyes flared wide. He seemed astonished, as if the pain had reached down into unexpected regions and took unfair advantage, savage and unrelenting. A life-time of robustness and good health had left him unprepared. He bit down on the Kleenex tissue.

Laura could hardly recognise him now. The short ride from the airport had changed him into a stranger. His hair stood up in grotesque tufts above his ears, and in his features was a desperate emptiness as if his face were a mask crudely carved from soft porous balsa wood to hide a visage too ugly to be revealed.

The Daimler's door opened. The healthy reality of Robert Craig enveloped her. He leaned on her, his hand on her arm. The solid, slightly boozy, slightly tobacco-stained presence brought Laura out of her trance.

Craig had a bulbous nose and, though not yet forty, a pleasant sort of decay that went well with his optimistic effervescence. Her father had once remarked that Craig had never quite recovered from undergraduate glee at being privy to the intimate secrets of mortality.

A stethoscope dangled from Craig's hand. His tie was tugged out from the vee of his Norfolk waistcoat.

'When did the attack begin?' Craig asked.

'On our flight home from Ankara.'

'How long have you been in Turkey?'

'Almost two months.'

'No preliminary signs in that period?'

'None.'

'Did he complain of pains, of feeling unwell?'

'No. He . . . he was perfectly well when we left Ankara.'

'So, the attack came on suddenly, in flight?'

'Just after we left Paris, a couple of hours ago.'

'Coughing?'

'Yes, but what . . . ?'

'Let's get him inside. Here, let me.'

Laura released contact with her father and stepped from the limousine. She saw Craig's muscles stretch the silk inlet of his waistcoat as he slid his arms under her father's thighs and inched him along the seat and lifted him out.

'Can I help, sir?' the chauffeur asked.

'Just make sure the doors are open,' Craig said.

Craig carried her father as if he were a baby, pausing only once to adjust the weight of the man. Laura followed, anxiously watching her father's face, tilted back against the doctor's shoulder, his arms hanging slackly.

The wind droned along the railings, scooping up leaves and paper trash and city dust in an abrasive cloud. Laura shivered and hurried on up the steps into the consulting rooms.

Robert Craig pulled the needle from Meredith's arm and stepped back a pace from the examination couch.

'No arguments, Ashley, please. The diamorphine injection should relax you and ease the discomfort a little. But it's hospital for you at once.'

'Craig . . . my . . . my daughter. Let me . . . talk.'

Certain aspects of Meredith's condition puzzled Craig. He was not given to make snap decisions but, in general, he had gained sufficient experience in practical medicine to anticipate diagnostic findings that came through more intensive hospital testing. Meredith's signs were classic, but the circumstances cast doubt.

'Laura,' Meredith gasped. 'I . . . must . . . talk to . . . Laura.'

'Very well,' Craig agreed. 'But don't move. Not a muscle. And don't, for God's sake, excite yourself.'

Crossing to the desk, Craig flicked on the intercom and spoke to his receptionist. 'Jane, ask Miss Meredith to come in, please. And connect me immediately with the emergency ambulance service.'

He lifted the receiver of the red telephone and tucked it against his jaw, pinning it with his shoulder. With Meredith newly returned from abroad there would probably be reports to draft and a good deal of follow-up. That would come later. The welfare of the patient was the most important concern.

The receptionist showed Laura Meredith into the room. Though she was deeply tanned, her fatigue was apparent. The room's chandelier cast planes of soft light upon her, yet the shadows were harsh, etching the drawn features.

On the couch, Meredith's head flopped towards his daughter.

'How is he, Dr. Craig?' the young woman asked.

Into the phone, Craig said, 'Ambulance, please. Immediate priority. I'm Dr. Robert Craig, 17 East Eaton Place. The patient is at this address. I require urgent transportation for him to the National Cardiac Surgery Hospital, Winston Street. Yes. Thank you.'

Craig hung up and turned to look at the young woman.

Meredith was listening, aware, attentive.

Craig said, 'He's seriously ill.'

'Is it his heart?'

'Yes, but frankly I don't understand it. I checked him over thoroughly shortly before you went abroad. Everything was functioning normally, his heart included. Now his heart's under critical strain from what appears to be a malfunctioning valve.'

'Will he be . . . all right?'

'In my opinion,' said Craig, warily, 'he'll require emergency cardiac surgery: a valve replacement. It's a comparatively simple operation these days, however. *If* we get him to the operating theatre in time.'

'Oh, God.' Tears swam in Laura's eyes again.

Craig gave his attention to the patient. Meredith's eyes were wide and oddly fixed, as if he held himself above discomfort sheerly by strength of will.

'L . . . Laura?'

Craig nodded. 'A word or two, no more.'

Kneeling by the couch, Laura covered her father's hand with her own.

'Tell . . . Upton,' Meredith gasped. 'Tell him . . . at . . . once.'

'Our work must wait until you're well again,' said Laura.

Meredith pumped himself up on his elbow, before Craig could prevent it. '*Promise me you'll tell Upton*?'

'Yes, father. Please rest,' said Laura. 'I'll tell him.'

The coughing bout smote Meredith suddenly again, hammering him flat on the couch. His grey ghoulish features contorted under the pressure of the racking spasm.

Craig reached for the oxygen trolley with its long torpedo-like cylinder clamped into the vices. Already fiddling with the gauge, he hauled the device across the room.

Meredith quivered and sagged, turned on his right shoulder.

Laura uttered an alarmed shout.

'It's all right. He's all right. Not dead,' Craig assured her. 'Cheyne-Stokes respiration. He's been breathing that way for the last five minutes. Here, this'll help.'

Brushing the young woman to one side, Craig fitted the mask across Meredith's face and tapped on the supply. He bent over the patient, peering, muttering, 'Where the bloody hell's that ambulance?'

A moment later, with relief, he heard the wail of the emergency siren and the yelp of brakes as the ambulance pulled up outside the house.

Holding the oxygen mask in place, Craig turned, 'You'd better come with us, Miss Meredith.'

'Yes, yes, of course.'

'To be perfectly frank, I'm afraid there's a possibility your father may not reach Winston Street alive.'

The chauffeur stood on the pavement watching the ambulance swing out of the square and down Pindar Street. The siren's wail sounded even more urgent as it diminished and was absorbed into the growl of traffic in the heart of the city. He watched it take the red lights at Lindisfarne Place and then vanish from sight.

The square seemed suddenly empty. Cars that stole round the Water Board barriers were cautious, as if they had passed a road accident. The wind drawled along the railings, swirling dust from the gutter. Dusk was congealing into darkness and the lights of the buildings were vivid. Under the lamps the trees in the gardens visibly shed their papery leaves. Quite soon it would be winter once more, the season of frosts and fogs and dangerous driving conditions. Alf looked at the limousine and, adjusting his hat and buttoning up the coat of his uniform, returned to it.

In his haste he had neglected to lock the doors. He was damned lucky that the Daimler was still where he had left it. Sneak thieves were rife in the city, opportunists to a man. He opened the passenger door and peered inside. Miss Meredith had taken her purse, but the piece of Antler hand-luggage was still propped against the seat where Meredith had asked Alf to put it before he became too sick to issue orders.

Alf redeemed the case. It weighed heavy. There had probably

been an argument at the baggage stall in Ankara about it, but knowing Meredith's type, he guessed that the Professor had stood adamantly on his rights as an English gentleman. They were all the same, the men of that generation, Alf thought; they invariably got what they wanted by being arrogant enough to insist on it. He admired that quality.

After checking the security of the boot, he locked the Daimler and, carrying the case, returned to Craig's consulting rooms. He took off his hat this time and tucked it deferentially under his left arm.

The receptionist's desk was at the corner of the hallway. The girl was young but glacial. Already she had begun to rearrange the appointments that Craig's hasty departure had thrown into disorder.

'Pardon me, miss.'

'Oh, you're the Meredith's chauffeur, aren't you?'

'Yes, miss. May I use your telephone?'

The girl gave the request careful consideration, then, deciding that Alf was closely enough involved in this medical emergency, nodded. 'You may use this one. Will it take long?'

'Coupler minutes.'

She turned her attention to the appointments book, pretending not to listen. Alf put his hat on the desk and planted the suitcase between his shins and the desk front. He did not require to consult the day's itinerary to discover where his boss would be. At this hour, Sir George would be at the Darwin Club, in Elam Street in Westminster.

Alf dialled the number and passed the message through one of the porters.

Seconds later Upton's eager voice asked, 'Alf? Are they safe home?'

'No, sir. There's been a complication.' Briefly Alf explained what had happened, adding, 'The Professor seemed anxious that you should be contacted. Perhaps the young lady'll remember, but . . .'

'Where did they take him, Alf?' Upton did not seem particularly dismayed.

'To the National Cardiac.'

'Yes, that's excellent. And the luggage?'

'I've secured the luggage, Sir George.'

'Including the documents?'

'I think that's what I've got right here.'

'Good chap,' Upton said. 'Don't let them out of your sight.'

'No fear of that, sir,' Alf said. 'Shall I pick you up at the club?'

'No, I'll go at once to the hospital.'

'With due respect, sir, I wouldn't hang about.'

'Is Meredith's condition that serious?'

'Yes, sir,' Alf said. 'If you was to ask me, he'll croak.'

'Meet me in the almoner's office of the National in twenty minutes,' Upton said. 'And bring the luggage with you.'

'Yes, sir,' Alf said.

The receptionist was staring at him as he put down the receiver. He gave her his most winning Cockney smile, thanked her for the use of the line and, with the suitcase firmly in his possession, hurried out into the raw night air.

WEDNESDAY
NEW YORK

In Central Manhattan, east of Madison, the 21-storey air-conditioned apartment block, Florissant House, snuggled on the flank of Murray Hill. It was a newish building, dwarfed by the towers of an enormous residential development that soared over a shopping plaza. High rentals limited the Florissant's tenant rating to upper-income singles and solid career people. But it was less friendly than most of the neighbouring blocks and boasted no match-making super or swingers union. Maybe twenty percent of the residents were engaged in 'executive' work that was points-off honest, and the remainder, discreetly vetted by the backroom clerks of Amadeus Management, knew how to keep themselves to themselves.

On the eighteenth floor, protected by the circumspect anonymity of his surroundings, Mr. Wing had established a secure New York base.

He took the call from Istanbul calmly, though the recent acceleration of events indicated that important, maybe crucial, deals were afoot within the organisation.

Sheng Kittegawa did most of the talking. Kittegawa spoke in a South China dialect that Mr. Wing clearly understood, though his own rendering of it was quaintly sing-song and plaintive.

Mr. Wing asked no questions, apart from a mandatory enquiry after his godfather's health. Naturally, he was given no specific instructions on how to conduct the operation. He needed none. He was a product of long training, a professional worth the hundred thousand bucks that, in one form or another, came his way every fiscal year.

When Mr. Wing finally put down the phone, he stood quite still for a couple of minutes, allowing his thoughts to settle; then he crossed to and entered the bedroom.

Dorothy was exactly as he had left her. She squatted on the bed, cross-legged like a tailor. Headphones were clamped to her skull and her expression was transcendental, the blue, blue eyes pure and remote. She was naked. The coarse patch of pubic hair seemed to increase the impression of ingenuousness. She paid no attention to Mr. Wing as he showered in the adjoining bathroom and changed, in the bedroom again, into a warm Brooks Brothers suit.

From past experience Mr. Wing knew that Dorothy was a captive to the music that spooled silently from one of the five tapes that she ran over and over – songs of innocence, not experience: Denver, the Dillards, Salt, the hymns of sensitive tow-headed boys for a gone world of natural awareness, a world that had never been. The participation mystique.

Though Mr. Wing considered his own soul to be quite secure, he often felt a little threatened by these products of the exploitable age. He could not even be sure that he fully understood Dorothy or that he had cured her of her slave-like devotion to a kill-crazy, none-too-intelligent Californian messiah, a revolutionary with no discernible cause and no valid motive to excuse his murderous attacks on society.

Mr. Wing had obtained a partial dossier on Dorothy. The facts were unappealing and, oddly, uninformative. He could not fathom the basic nature of her experiences and stood back from in-depth knowledge of the squalid permissiveness of her teenage trips, of the events of the six-year period that marked the interval between her flight from Scion, Kansas, and her coming into his ken. She was a product of hill camps, ranch communes, crash pads. She had also been the 'wife' of the infamous Robert Hoffman for three years. Foulness and perversion had made her what she was today, Mr. Wing assumed, bottling dreams of liberation into the five finger-length cassettes that she played endlessly, like mantras.

Her daring, her courage, even her intelligence stemmed from a lack of caring. But her skills were unique, a mimicry and a mockery of all that was best on the flip side of the American coin. Most important of all, she could freely penetrate community pockets where he, an Oriental, might be noticed and remembered. On the surface, Dorothy was an American everywoman, one of the programmed people. But even Mr. Wing, sufficiently secure of soul and psyche to consider himself a cynic, would not wish too many of her kind loosed upon the nation.

Groomed and neat, Mr. Wing reached over the base of the oval bed and dabbed the button to cut off the mind-absorbing flow of sound. The girl blinked, drifted back from her own private dominion and identified him. Obeying his signal, she tipped the huge Germanic headphones back from her ears.

'Dorothy,' said Mr. Wing, 'I must go out now. Stay here. I'll be back in time to take you to dinner, in three or four hours. Do you understand?'

'She nodded.

'Early tomorrow morning we will leave for England. Have you ever been in that country before?'

She shook her head.

'We will not be there long. Pack clothing for two days. I'll bring the Canadian passports. Is that clear to you?'

Dorothy nodded again, then asked, 'Who is it?'

'A man, not young. It should not prove difficult.'

'Okay.'

Mr. Wing dipped his fingers into his breast pocket and produced a stamp-sized envelope filled with fine white powder. She watched him intently, alert for the first time. He tossed her the envelope. She scrabbled on the bedsheet between her splayed knees, captured the sachet and held it protectively against her breast.

'Be good, Dorothy,' said Mr. Wing and left for Wall Street and the banker's offices.

High in the canyon wall, under fishscale reflections of the

Chase Manhattan's glassware, Phil Hickman, the Guthrie Tait Guaranty Trust's president, was suffering from nervous stomach.

Two, maybe three times a year, Frank Varese put in a personal appearance and leaned on Hickman a little. No storekeeper, no impious heavyweight would ever have recognised the amiable luncheons as pressure. But Phil Hickman felt the master's hand on those occasions, and Varese's visits left him shaken and temporarily depleted of energy.

This time, out of nowhere, Frank had rolled into the office and set up camp. Ross Paulsen was with him. Hickman was convinced that they had come expressly to breathe down his neck. Bank presidents didn't get that way without using a little juice, of course, and the inside of the Guthrie Tait had more juice than a Florida orange. Similarly, though, no bank president ever clung to his exhalted position without nerve, know-how and tact, and these three virtues Phil Hickman had in plenty. Only his stomach was nervous, not his manner.

He sat it out, asked no questions and tried to calculate just what the fuck Varese wanted. He counted off his petty dealings and all the little red guilts in his professional life, like rosary beads.

Phil Hickman, president of the Guthrie Tait, the syndicate's main New York piggy-bank, had no way of knowing that in nine other principal centres of finance across the United States, nine other presidents were suffering similar fits of paranoia. He would not have been soothed by the knowledge nor flattered by the fact that he, out of the ten, had inherited the attentions of the eastern seaboard's chief manager.

Frank Varese *was* New York, as far as syndicate dealings went. Ross Paulsen was back-up book-keeper for the territory.

Varese and Paulsen had spent four days now in the bank's precincts, mainly in the presidential office. They passed the hours staring up at the bank of monitor screens on the office's inner wall or down in the vault of the security detail, where closed-circuit tv controls were housed.

It occurred to Hickman that the guys might be expecting a rip off. But when he jocularly suggested this to Frank he was told, graciously, to mind his own business. Christ, the Guthrie Tait *was* his business. As the fourth day of the stake-out waned and he was still in the dark concerning Varese's purpose, Phil Hickman began to feel less persecuted than sore.

The presence of the big men had a disturbing influence on the staff. Senior tellers muttered among themselves, speculating on the kind of larceny that he, their president, had been caught at, doodling pictures on their blotters of the hideously old-fashioned fate that awaited him. Hickman had as good as told Collins, his managerial deputy, that the appearance of the two up-town executives had nothing to do with him. He pointed out the salient fact that they had not so much as opened a ledger or approached the computer, hadn't asked one single question concerning the fucking investment accounts or the private fiduciary funds: had they? Well, had they? Collins had grunted non-commitally. Hickman's stomach hurt some more.

It was mid-afternoon. The big men were drinking coffee. They were both wooden, like larger-than-life dummies expertly carved out of cedar and clothed for an F. R. Tripler window display. Even Varese's Edwardian-bordello moustache had a dark synthetic gloss that made it seem less than genuine. A decade younger than forty-four year old Varese, Paulsen had eyes like a dead beagle, eyes that seldom left the monitors.

From the president's office the pair commanded a view of the entire bank, tellers' stalls, main concourse, even the plush corridors that led clients to the consultants' offices. Who or what Varese and Paulsen were looking for, Hickman still did not know.

It was twenty minutes to afternoon closing, when Varese came for him. Hickman was in the small vice-presidential office dictating urgent mail when the interconnecting door clicked open and Frank Varese beckoned with one big thick cedarwood forefinger. Heart thudding, Hickman entered his own office and, at a wordless sign from Paulsen, turned to look up at the monitors.

'Window four,' Varese said.

The concourse was crowded. It took Hickman a moment's concentrated study to pick out the Oriental. Miss Bern was attending him.

The Oriental was small, compact, bland. He had a pronounced yellow colouration, not ochre like so many of the traders from New York's Chinatown. He was dressed like half the sharks of Wall Street, but just a little too conservatively, as if he copied the style from a catalogue five seasons out of date.

Varese was already in touch with the bank's security detail. An instant later three concourse cameras rotated and bored in on the

Chinese client, framing him in a corral of steel beams and glassy reflections.

'Do you know him?' Varese asked.

'No, Frank,' Hickman answered.

Paulsen pursed his lips. 'That's Wing.'

'They took some chance,' said Varese. 'I had a hunch they might fund from the cross-exchange account. But I was just beginning to think I'd figured it wrong.'

'Frank, what the hell is . . .?' Hickman began.

'I want Wing's accounts. I want the source and disposition of all his funds, under whatever name he happens to be using.'

'I don't even know if he banks with us, Frank.'

'Then find out.'

'Of course, Frank, of course; just as soon as he leaves the window.'

They watched the Oriental complete his transaction and move up the concourse towards the doors. A lintel-mounted camera zoomed in, and the three men watched Wing tuck documents into his pocket and then stroll out of vision range. Hickman was already on the phone to Miss Bern.

A minute later, he said, 'He's registered as James Shang. Established customer. He's maintained a feed account with us for almost seven years.'

'It's Wing,' said Paulsen again. 'I don't care what he calls himself. His real name is Wing.'

'What kind of business did he transact today?'

'He purchased a batch of travellers' cheques,' said Hickman. 'What are we looking for, exactly?'

'I want everything you can scratch up on James Shang – accounts, read-outs, everything, Phil.'

Hickman added, 'Tax shelters, subvention payments, back-to-back credit dealings?'

'I told you already – everything.'

Paulsen said, 'We should stake him out, you know, Frank. Obviously he's about to make a move.'

'Put three shift teams on it, Ross. The best watchers you've got.'

Paulsen lifted the phone and, covering the mouthpiece, said, 'Frank, there's no mystery about who pays his tab, is there?'

'It's not who pays him that matters,' Varese said. 'It's just how they do it that's important right now.'

'You're looking for a connection?' Paulsen said.

'I'm looking,' said Varese, 'for somebody to grab by the balls.'

Close to midnight, Frank Varese and Ross Paulsen were seated before the long oak desk in the Paulsen Company headquarters on Lexington Avenue. They were waiting for a return call to the company's unlisted number. They had been waiting almost three hours.

Only once Paulsen asked, 'You sure this guy'll come back to you?'

'He knows what's good for him,' Varese had answered.

At a couple of minutes to twelve, the phone rang. Varese motioned Paulsen from the room, then lifted the receiver.

'Mr. Varese, Mr. Frank Varese?'

'Yeah.'

'I,m returning your call. I don't believe I know you, however.'

'You know me,' Varese said.

'Listen, should we have this conversation on an open line?'

'Don't bullshit,' said Varese. 'You wouldn't call me on a tampered wire.'

'What about your end?'

'Safer than the White House,' said Varese.

A pause. 'Well, uh . . . what can I do for you?'

'You hold stock in Amadeus Management, right?'

'Amadeus . . . No, I don't honestly believe I . . .'

'You're a nominee shareholder.'

'Well, uh . . . I . . .'

'You know who controls Amadeus?'

'Of course, I . . .'

'You've said nothing about this holding before.'

'Look, Varese, I . . . uh, I'm not even supposed to *know* you.'

'I have another deal for you, Senator.'

'I'm worried about this line.'

'So talk faster,' said Varese.

A pause. 'What . . . uh . . . what do you want me to say?'

'Tell me what you held back.'

'Held back? I don't understand.'

'You slid something past us. Why?'

'Really, honestly, I don't . . .'

'What's your price for the information?'

'I don't like that kind of talk. I'm not on the market any more. I certainly can't condone any . . . uh . . . you know.'

'All right,' said Varese. 'I'll give you the offer. The offer is a nice tight lip on my part. No speakee. You understand?'

'That's *all*? Look, I can . . .'

'I wouldn't advise it,' said Frank Varese.

'I have sound personal reasons for this, you know.'

'Reasons like a side deal with a couple of pricks from Hong Kong?'

'I don't think I want to talk about it.'

'You talked about it to Kittegawa and Yu-lan.'

'Look, I don't want to involve them.'

'Would you rather "involve" us?'

A pause. 'What *do* you want?'

'The Chinese gentlemen are active. Why?'

'How would I know a thing like that . . . uh?'

'I can use other methods to get the information I need, Senator. You wouldn't want me to use other methods, would you?'

'I take it that you're referring to the project?'

'Maybe,' said Varese, carefully.

'I can't say what . . .'

'What sort of project?'

'The government probe into poppy cultivation. Research, like that.'

'Why are the Far East dealers so interested?'

'Obviously it might affect their interests.'

'What about our interests?'

'I honestly don't know what your . . . uh, interests are.'

'Who heads this government project?'

'I'm not sure that . . .'

Varese said nothing. Almost a minute went past. He waited, holding the phone out, looking at it.

The voice said, 'Two botanists: Gordon Rand and Ashley Meredith.'

'Where are they located?'

'Rand's from Stanford. But I believe he's in Washington at the present time.'

'And Meredith?'

'He's English: London, England.'

'More?'

'No, uh . . . honestly, that's all I've picked up so far.'

Varese said, 'Right. We'll talk again soon.'

'I can't talk to . . .'

Varese hung up.

He yelled, and Paulsen came back from the stenographer's office. Paulsen said, 'Is it serious, Frank?'

'Yeah, it's serious.' Varese pushed himself out of the chair. 'I should go see Sarsby.'

'Have you enough for that yet?'

'Fuck it, more than enough,' said Frank Varese. 'Those Chink mothers are trying to screw us, and I gotta find out how.'

THURSDAY 18 AUGUST
LONDON

Laura Meredith's hands trembled as she took the coffee cup from the nurse. The cup rattled on the saucer and a few drops of the steaming liquid spilled on the green rubber floor. Laura gripped the cup firmly and put it down on the half-moon desk of the nursing station.

The intensive care unit seemed weirdly familiar, like a sterile laboratory rather than a hospital ward. Meredith lay in bed on the far side of the ward. Laura did not dare approach him. The transformations that the disease had wrought upon him were too terrible to contemplate for long. In the nine hours since the onslaught of the first signs, her father had become like an imbecile, his body bloated, his head lolling limply.

In contrast, Sir Matthew Price, the National's chief cardiologist, was the epitome of urbanity. Arms crossed, he stood before the X-ray viewer. The red rose in his buttonhole was silvered by the unnatural light from the machine and seemed to match the sleek wings of hair brushed over his ears. When he spoke it was in a murmurous drawl that Laura considered more furtive than respectful.

She caught a few scattered phrases. 'Bacterial endocarditis. Pulmonary oedema.

The man by Price's side was younger and less austere. In her present state of nervous exhaustion, Laura imagined him releasing opinions as a goldfish releases bubbles, in little shivering columns. His eyes were magnified by huge horn-rimmed glasses, his forehead was bald, his lips thick. He looked ugly. Somehow, though, his ugliness made him seem more human.

Hours had passed since she had begun her vigil. She had no clear idea of the time now. The intense activity of the half hour after her father's admission had dwindled into a series of examinations and consultations that came to seem interminable and, latterly, pointless. Now the medical force had been reduced to two men. Two men to hold on to her father's life. They were unperturbed by the responsibility.

'That's settled then, Miles.' Price turned from the viewer. 'Put it forward just as soon as you can make all the necessary arrangements.'

As the men approached, Laura got unsteadily to her feet.

'Ah, Miss Meredith,' Price said, as if he were surprised to find her still there. 'I'd like you to meet Mr. Miles Harper, our specialist heart surgeon.'

Harper, Laura thought, was inordinately shy. He mouthed noises that did not quite form into words and then, poking his glasses deep into the flesh of his nose, stared at the green rubber with what seemed like a boyish embarrassment. Immediately, Laura doubted his competence.

Price said, 'Mr. Harper and I have carried out certain tests, Miss Meredith, a fairly extensive series. Alas, the results are not totally conclusive.'

'But,' said Harper, 'they do provide sufficient grounds to warrant immediate cardiac surgery.'

'What is wrong with my father?' Laura demanded.

'An infection in one of the heart valves,' Price told her.

'And you intend to replace this valve?'

'Yes, we do.'

'Will my father survive?'

'He has every chance of recovery,' Price declared.

'Every chance,' echoed Harper.

Laura did not hear the unit door opening. She was alerted by the sudden attention that the two doctors gave to the arrival. Turning, she found herself face to face with Sir George Upton.

Tonight she could not disguise her dislike of the man. It was

Upton who had persuaded her father to enter the bacterial field, who had strenuously promoted the Turkish trip and who, in that underhand way of his, had even managed to ignite her father's enthusiasm for the project. Even so, her father had never been wholly committed to Upton's scheme.

Without doubt, it *was* Upton's scheme. All of it. Foreboding clouded Laura's reason.

Upton's secrets seemed to swarm into the sterile room like black flies. Instinctively she stepped back to put herself between Upton and the hospital bed in which her father lay.

As a government adviser on scientific affairs, Upton was entitled to respect, she supposed. But the title applied to a role, not to a man. She had gathered that Upton was an entrepreneur, sinister, spontaneous, and highly influential: a perverse paradox. He had been at Cambridge with her father before the last world war. She had heard talk of that far-off period, rumours that Upton was too disdainful of inferior minds to be popular with his contemporaries. She did not believe that the leopard had changed his spots, only that he had become more subtle, more soft-footed. He hid his inbred intellectual arrogance behind an easy charm.

'Laura,' he said, 'I'm sorry. You have my sympathy. I'm sure that everything possible is being done.'

'How did you know?' she snapped.

'I've been waiting outside for hours,' Upton said, ignoring her question.

'Because you feel responsible for what's happened?'

'Certainly, Laura. I do feel responsible. I'm almost as anxious as you must be for your father's welfare.'

'Because you need him to do more dirty work for you?'

'Because I like him,' said Upton. 'Believe me, I'd no idea that he had an incipient heart weakness.'

'Would it have made any difference?'

Miles Harper intervened. 'To the best of my knowledge, Miss Meredith, there *was* no history of heart disease.'

Price said, 'On Sir George's instruction I personally carried out a complete physical examination on your father prior to your departure for Turkey. All the reports indicated . . .'

'What reports?' Laura interrupted.

Upton said, 'Do you suppose I would subject a man of your father's age to the stresses of foreign field work without having his health checked?'

'It seems that your reports were not thorough enough,' the young woman said.

Price said, 'Miss Meredith, I assure you that this is no common-or-garden heart attack. I doubt if the condition is stress-originated. I gather that your father went into pulmonary oedema secondary to an incompetent aortic valve with remarkable suddenness. According to your own statement, he showed no advance signs of valve failure.'

'I . . . No, none that I know of.'

Miles Harper said, 'Let me explain. Your father's heart valve is infected. The infection has eroded the surface of the aortic valve causing disruption in mechanical function. Operations for replacement of an aortic valve are very common nowadays.'

'Then he will recover?'

Price said, 'He has a chance, Miss Meredith. But there are some unusual complications. The replacement operation itself is commonplace. In your father's case, however, the risks of failure are somewhat increased by an attendant infection active in the body.'

Harper said, 'Really we've no idea what'll happen to the new replacement valve. It too might be attacked by the infection. If that does happen, well . . .'

'You blame my father's illness on infection? What sort of infection?'

'We'll treat it with antibiotics, of course,' said Harper.

To Upton, Laura said, 'What *is* this infection? What's the *cause* of it?'

'I've no idea,' Upton answered.

'Bacterium?' Laura demanded.

'Possibly,' Upton said.

'You provided my father with that . . .'

'Laura, please calm down,' Upton ordered.

'Did you know there was a chance of this happening? Is that why you asked for a preliminary medical report?' she persisted.

'Laura, believe me . . .'

'I *don't* believe you.'

'Laura, I'd like a word with you, in private, please,' Upton said firmly.

'No, I intend to stay with my father.'

'We must prepare your father for surgery,' Price told her. 'Mr. Harper will operate tomorrow morning.'

Laura turned helplessly to the bed. There were nurses in the room now. The unit seemed suddenly crowded, hostile. She stared at the face above the clean stiff sheet. Above the bed were instruments, oscilloscope, thermal recorder, an untidy tangle of tubing draped from a brushed steel clamp. She touched her fingers to his cheek, finding no warmth, no response to the contact. Weeping, she swung away and allowed Upton to lead her from the unit and along a short corridor into Price's office.

Even Upton's solicitousness was brisk. Anger calmed the young woman, an uncharacteristic bitterness that trained itself on Upton.

'You provided that bacterial culture. You must have known that it was dangerously virulent. Why did you choose my father? Because he was foolish enough to give in to your deceptions? Why did you persuade him to pass off the development as a product of our research?'

'Because of his impeccable record for scientific integrity,' said Upton.

'You may have killed him.'

He gripped her by the shoulders and pinned her back against the wall. Strangely, she found more comfort in his anger than in his sympathy.

'Laura, listen to me. I did not dupe your father. He agreed to do what I asked. He realised how important the deception was.'

Laura said, 'Important enough to risk his life?'

'Yes.'

'Simply to disrupt the world's opium traffic?'

'That,' said Upton, 'is only a minor part of it.'

'I thought you believed in the neutrality of science.'

Upton said, 'I pay lip service to it. But – as your father well understood – science is disorder, randomness. The scientific community is not impregnable. There is no perfect design to any piece of work, no single method.'

'What does this have to do with my father's illness?'

'Do you think I'm indifferent to what happens to my friends?' said Upton. 'I'm no automaton, Laura. But I *am* scientific enough to want to get to the root of whatever problem confronts me, even if I do not understand it.'

'Is that how you see my father's condition now, as a problem?'

'One part of a much larger problem,' Upton said. 'Your father and I are much more alike than you imagine. He would want you to do as I say.'

'What do you want of me?'

'I want you to stay here and rest until after the operation, then to return home. I want you to stay at home and talk to nobody.'

'But what if my father should . . .?'

Upton said, 'I want your promise, Laura.'

'Why?'

'I can't tell you, not yet.'

Laura hesitated, then asked, 'Does Gordon Rand know the truth? Does he know what you intend to do?'

'No,' Upton said. 'The less Rand knows the better for his safety.'

'You are vile,' she whispered.

'Will you do as I ask?'

'Yes, I'll do as you ask. But not for you, Sir George. For my father.'

'Come, Laura.' Upton released her. 'I'll find some place where you can lie down and rest.'

'Rest – like my father?'

'I hope not, said Upton.

'This,' said Miles Harper, 'reminds me of my internship. For almost a year I lived on such rare delicacies.' He contemplated the stale ham sandwich, then bit deeply into it. 'Ham, doughnuts, yogurt, cream soda, scoffed at all sorts of godawful hours. I'm amazed that my intestines remained intact. There's metabolic adaptability for you.'

'You were younger then, of course,' Price said. 'More coffee, George?'

'No thanks,' Upton said. 'How's the girl?'

'I gave her a sedative,' Price replied. 'She should sleep for four or five hours at least. She really has it in for you, George. What the devil are you up to now?'

Upton said, 'Government business.'

Harper groaned. He pushed the remainder of the sandwich into his mouth. He was sprawled on the long sofa that hugged the inner wall of Price's office. He seemed perfectly at ease as he reached for a doughnut from the plate balanced on his chest. 'Government business usually covers a multitude of sins.'

'What time will you operate on Meredith?' Upton asked.

'A rapid change of subject, I see,' said Harper. 'At ten a.m., that's the best we can do.'

'I hope that he survives the next eight hours.'

Price leaned back in the swivel chair. He smoked a thin brown cigar, holding it between his little finger and thumb in a manner that reminded Upton of the smoking habits of Kadish tribesmen, the fingers spread like a cockscomb, the inhalations made with deliberation. Price said, 'I gather from what the girl let out that Meredith was actually working with a new bacterial strain.'

'Yes.'

'Isn't he a botanist?' asked Harper.

'He is.'

'I take it that there's a possibility that the infection has been transferred from plant bacteria?' said Price.

'There is that chance,' Upton admitted.

Harper swung his feet to the floor and sat up. 'Oh-ho, so it's not just a funny foreign disease, then?'

'I don't quite know what it is,' said Upton, innocently.

Price squinted through the cigar smoke. 'How many scientists were involved in this Turkish trip?'

'Meredith, his daughter and an American, plus ten or twelve Turkish field workers.'

'I suppose it's already occurred to you, George, that if the disease is highly infectious, then Laura Meredith stands a considerable chance of catching it.'

'It had occurred to me, Matthew.'

'What about us?' asked Harper. 'Is the bug liable to be that virulent?'

'I doubt it.'

'Christ, you are comforting,' said Harper. 'A hush-hush bacterial strain that rampages through the system and gnaws away the aortic valve and you *doubt* if it's infectious.'

'At the moment,' said Upton, 'it's all conjecture.'

'I suppose we must keep a weather eye on the girl,' said Price. 'Can we pump her full of antibiotics?'

'Wait until morning,' said Upton. 'I may know a little more by then.'

'More about what?' asked Harper inquisitively.

Side-stepping the question, Upton asked Harper, 'Off-hand, whom would you list as the top cardiac surgeons in North America?'

Harper laid the plate on the floor and wiped his lips with his handkerchief. 'Top Americans? Let's see, there's Greenbush in Salt Lake City, for one. Da Ponte, the Italian, in Chicago. Armstrong of Johns Hopkins, though I've heard he's a little past it now. Walter Stein, and . . .'

'How does Stein rate?' asked Upton, casually.

'Do you know him?'

'We've met once or twice.'

'He's certainly the best technician on the West Coast,' said Harper. 'His figures are excellent, and he's attracted an enviable P.R. team to San Francisco. Yes, old Walter's about as good as they come, I suppose.'

'You aren't given to asking idle questions, George,' said Price. 'I assume you're concerned about the American botanist.'

'I am.'

'Is he at all aware that he might be at risk?'

'It's unlikely.'

'And the Turks?' said Harper. 'What about those Turks?'

'To hell with the Turks,' Upton said.

Harper swallowed the last of the doughnut, prodded his horn-rims onto his fleshy nose and, as Upton abruptly left the office, muttered, 'How bloody cold-blooded.'

THURSDAY
CLOUDSRIDGE COUNTRY CLUB

The chopper, a Bragg Gadfly, lifted Frank Varese at Los Angeles International and whisked him sixty miles through an acid morning haze to Cloudsridge Country Club. Somehow the sun had struggled through the smog that billowed over the freeways. Though it was still early and humidity was low, Varese's shirt was tacky with sweat before the Gadfly put down within the tall chainlink fence that protected the club's private heliport.

Varese made no move to disembark. He waited for the persimmon-coloured, discreetly armoured Dodge pick-up to glide across the tarmac and stop forty feet from the chopper.

The guard loped towards him, ducking under the limping blades, one hand on his cap, the other close to the black leather holster on his hip.

'Name?' the guard shouted.

'Frank Varese.'

Varese showed identification and told the guard that he had pre-arranged an appointment with Arnold Sarsby.

Clearance procedure was smooth, swift and thorough. The chopper pilot, though one of the Cloudsridge contract boys and known to both truck guards, was put through the same system and cleared too.

'How long will you be with Mr. Sarsby, Mr. Varese?'

'An hour, maybe an hour and a half.'

'Okay, we'll leave the chopper on the pad. Mr. Sarsby's on the golf course. I'll call him in,' the guard said.

'Is he playing two-ball or four-ball?' Varese asked.

'Just practising, with a caddy.'

'Can you get me out there?'

'No problem, Mr. Varese,' the guard said.

They drove him out of the heliport compound in the truck, past the guardpost at the gate and followed a cool road through eucalyptus trees on to the artificial ridge that overlooked the sprawling, green acres of the golf course. On his right Varese could make out the cream Spanish-style houses, the secluded community of the condominium, and the club's social facilities, including the long two-storey pavilion with its persimmon and lemon awnings belled over the breakfast terrace.

Six or eight golf carts already dotted the west course. Just below the tenth green, two snowy-haired gentlemen were locked in combat, each laying a psych-out barrage on the other before going forth to putt. The caddies, young and handsome, watched with no visible signs of boredom, really earning their gingerbread.

Cloudsridge was a paradise for rich games-players, all of whom were co-owners. Sarsby had once told him that several of the members never left the lush wooded estate, doing all their wheeling and dealing from secure office accommodation in the basement of the main block.

Varese liked Cloudsridge, though he did not otherwise covet Sarsby's life-style, his power or his resources. Sarsby had been born into and bred for it. A Harvard education and a five-year stretch in a Boston law firm had polished the pebble. Sarsby's old man and his four uncles, all into their eighties, were men of wealth and repute, games-players too but crude at it – more like Varese's own kind.

The Dodge halted by a stucco wall where a young black man tended a rank of golf carts. Behind the wall were flowerbeds, gaudy with late blossoms. Rotating sprinklers bathed the petals in fine golden rain. The perfume was too cloying for Varese. He was glad when the guard drove the cart down a grass ramp onto the turf by the fairway.

Sarsby was waiting on the seventh tee. He had sent his caddy off to rest in the shadow of one of the stately sycamores that gave the hole its reputation as a score buster. The fairway boomeranged left, a 510-yard par five, with a scrub below the dipping green and a crescent of deep water behind.

As Sarsby climbed from the cart and, sweating more profusely than ever, crossed to the tee, Varese came forward to greet his New York manager. Sarsby, Varese thought, looked more like a mature golf pro than the emperor of a multi-million dollar enterprise.

'Good to see you, Frank. Have you had breakfast?'

'I ate on the plane.'

'Shall we go on back to the pavilion?' The word was quaint, typical of the courteous affectations of the bluechip Cloudsridge members, none of whom, if pressed, would hesitate to go for the groin.

'No, this place is fine,' Varese said.

'What's the problem?' said Sarsby.

'That rumour you picked up in Washington,' Varese said. 'It had substance after all. I figure I've found out who's knocking.'

'Yu-lan and Kittegawa?'

'Right,' said Varese. 'I took a chance. I guessed that the White Tigers wouldn't be flexible enough to operate big in our territory without using an existing fund. We stack most of their U.S. hard currency in our banks. If they don't want to rock the boat, they've gotta use the interlink system. I put a stake-out on the banks.'

'And you got something?'

'I got Mr. Wing.'

'That's heavy,' said Sarsby. 'Wing's no ordinary butcherboy.'

'He still operates out of New York: Kittegawa's number one knife.'

'Wing's never crossed us before, except one time in Havanna, years ago, and that was accidental.'

'It could be that he's crossing us now?'

'We've known for years that Wing was on the payroll,' said Sarsby. 'What makes you think he's acting against our interests?'

'I had a hunch that they would use Wing if they wanted something done fast and neat,' said Varese. 'Turns out he has a money faucet in the Guthrie Tait. Paulsen identified him. Hickman dug up the financial statements.'

'If they're working him open like this,' said Sarsby, 'the Tigers must be pretty goddamned confident that we know nothing about what they're up to out there in the paddyfields.'

'I don't have too many hard facts yet, just enough to assure us that your tame Washington senator isn't lying.'

Sarsby laid the driver on the grass. He looked lean and raffish in flared pants, turtleneck shirt and calfskin shoes. He took a pack of Slims from his pocket, lit one and, motioning Varese to follow, walked to the brink of the tee and seated himself on the grass.

'Halveston never lies,' he said 'What more did you dredge up, Frank?'

'Wing has himself an apartment in New York, in the Florissant House. It's an Amadeus property. Yesterday afternoon he bought travellers' checks and tickets for a direct flight to London. Two tickets. He left late last night.'

'Two?'

'He's shacking up with some little fox.'

'Yeah, well, even Wing is entitled to some relaxation,' said Sarsby. 'Give me the connections, Frank.'

'Right,' said Varese. 'We analysed Wing's income sources. Basically he's paid through a property bond fund. Hickman squeezed confidential data from his old buddies in the Street. Wing is into Amadeus Management. He's more than just a tenant.'

'Tell me about Amadeus.'

'It's a realty-based investment corporate with another interesting client in the bag.'

'Back in the old days, so my father tells me, the syndicates paid their torpedoes with used bills left in a bowling bag in a Penn Station locker,' said Sarsby. 'I'm beginning to think the old system had its advantages. What client, Frank?'

'An agent who happens to have a straight connection with our Washington contact. Looks like Senator Halveston's selling news to the Chinese as well as to us.'

Sarsby glanced up quickly. 'The bastard. He promised us exclusive rights on all information.'

'I came across a bit old-fashioned with him, you know,' said Varese. 'He talked.'

'But did he talk the truth?'

'It smells genuine.'

'What does?'

'He told me that the Vice-Presidential committee *is* backing a special project, a strictly-secret high flier.'

'Jay Rainer may only be making noises to prove he's got balls,' said Sarsby. 'It's an unpleasant twitch some Vice-Presidents develop, especially new White House men who ride into office bare-assed.'

'But Rainer's making no noise at all. He can't be gunning for publicity when the narco committee's muffled up like a fucking CIA bid to annex Moscow.'

'Maybe Rainer's just picking his time to roll out the bandwagon.'

Varese shook his head. 'It's not executive song and dance, Arnold. He's funded a project.'

'What sort of project?'

'He set up a field experimental unit using a couple of botanists.'

'Botanists? Jesus Christ,' said Sarsby.

'Gordon Rand is the American whizz kid. He comes out of Vereker Laboratory of Plant Sciences in Stanford. The boss is an English guy, a Professor Ashley Meredith, from some government-backed institute in London.'

'What's with the English angle?'

'I can't figure it,' Varese admitted. 'Rank, yeah. If you're Jay Rainer and you're planning a narcotics witch-hunt at top level, then Rand's just the kind of solid academic you might want to have around to add a little tone to your press announcements. But this Meredith guy . . .' Varese shrugged.

'What's Meredith's speciality?'

'Plant virology.'

'Where was the field unit situated?'

'Turkey. Kahutshir, near Ayfon.'

Sarsby drew thinly on his cigarette, then ground it out on the base of his shoe and flicked the butt away. He stared towards the caddy who was sprawled on his back under the shady sycamore. 'And Wing's gone off to London?'

'Right.'

'All right, Frank, so what have we got so far?' Sarsby said. 'First we pick up a rumour that Yu-lan and Kittegawa have a substance that affects the poppy flower. Sounds like a junkie's nightmare but maybe there's some truth in it. You never know with the Tigers. Plus, there's an unusual amount of buying of high grade down in the Macao market, in a region where you can grow opium poppies in windowboxes.'

'Middlemen purchases for the spring sales of the first harvest came to two and a half million,' Varese said.

'That's hardly monopoly stockpiling,' said Sarsby. 'Besides, Macao buying doesn't hurt us at all. Our Mexican supply is bought already, in the ground. And the Chinese haven't attempted to mess with our trading in the Far East.'

'But then we find Jay Rainer has floated a Vice-Presidential campaign – *without* publicity – a campaign that leads pretty goddamned quick to a covert team being shipped down to Turkey about the time the late crop comes ripe.'

'An American and an Englishman,' said Sarsby.

'They sure were testing *something* down there in Kahutshir,' said Varese.

'But what?'

'I don't know. But we can be goddamned sure it's no coincidence that Mr. Wing left for London last night.'

'Whatever the Chinese are into, it isn't aimed at benefiting our end of the trade,' said Sarsby, 'If the U.S. government's into it too, then we're in deep trouble.'

'Mostly likely it's some chemical that kills off poppies.'

'Can't be,' said Sarsby. 'World Health organisations wouldn't stand for it. In any case, that kind of trick has been tried before. Defoliant crop spraying's too clumsy. We all know that. And risky. Christ, available supply for legitimate world demand fell critically low because of the Turkish treaty. That's why it didn't last. It can't be a simple poppy destroyer.'

'Whatever it is,' said Varese, 'not even Jay Rainer can expect the CIA to bully the major producing countries into letting him fly squadrons of USAF dusters all over their territory.'

'Have you heard of airborne viruses, Frank?'

'Some.'

'One virulent airborne virus could wipe out crops in most areas.'

'Yeah, but how would the government control it? Jay Rainer's not crazy enough to let that kind of thing loose.'

'Maybe – maybe not,' said Varese. 'Opium's a straight cash crop. Perhaps Rainer figures it could be produced on state or federal farms, under strict government control, carefully protected from the virus.'

'It's doubtful if the U.S. could grow enough under licence to meet medical demand,' said Sarsby. 'Besides, it's not likely the CIA could penetrate deep into the Chinese mainland.'

'Hand the Chinks a total monopoly on all illicit supplies?' Varese said. 'Jesus, the price would shoot to ten, twenty times the current rate.'

'That wouldn't do our market any good,' Sarsby said. 'Price control of the product is essential. The street shooter can't pay a ransom for every bag. We depend on the street corner bagman.'

'Yeah, there'd be more dead mackerel scattered across America than Rainer could justify, plus an inevitable increase in crime. Rainer's committee can't be aiming to put us right out of business. If he pushed in a killer virus to destroy even a few of the big poppy crops, then our whole network, *everybody's* network, would burn up in three, four months.'

'Not quite everybody's,' said Sarsby. 'Chen Yu-lan and Shen Kittegawa would be left sitting on top of the heap. At best we'd have to buy from them at their price – or starve.'

'They wouldn't sell to us,' said Varese. 'Jesus, they could auction to legitimate markets and still make a killing.'

'Whatever,' said Sarsby, 'we'd be out of business.'

'That's a very scary thought,' Varese said.

'What *is* this stuff the Chinks *and* the U.S. government have gotten their hands on?' said Sarsby.

'That's what we've got to find out.'

'I could put the arm on our Washington senator again.'

'He's not likely to know,' said Sarsby. 'Anything this important will have the lid screwed right down on it.'

'We can't just fuck around until the lid blows off.'

'I know,' Sarsby said. 'We've got to discover what this stuff is supposed to do and how it's going to be used.'

'So we ask somebody,' said Varese. 'Who?'

'The scientists that Wing's been programmed to eliminate,' said Sarsby.

'We don't know for sure Wing is on a contract.'

'Look, Frank, Wing's a killer. He's the best knife the Tigers have. If they ship him to London there can only be one possible target.'

'This Professor, this Meredith guy?'

'Who else? If the Tigers want Meredith silenced, you can be goddamned sure Meredith *knows* something *we* should know. Hard information, Frank. The government scientists already have hard information.'

Varese stared down at Sarsby who was studying the distant edge of the green. Rising above the protective rim of the hills that backed Cloudsridge to the east, the morning sun made the shadows long on the grass.

'Scientists,' said Varese, 'in the plural.'

'If Wing burns the Englishman today, who will he burn tomorrow?' Sarsby asked.

'Gordon Rand.'

'Right.'

'So we've got to get to him first?'

'Bring Rand in, Frank,' Sarsby said. 'All in one piece.'

THURSDAY
WASHINGTON, D.C.

Rand's relief when the big Pan-Am jet liner touched down at Dulles International was short lived. So much tension had built up in him during the journey out of Turkey that he had been unable to cat-nap. He was fatigued, irritable and consequently suspicious of official red-carpet civilities. Behind Jay Rainer's gesture of hospitality he detected obsessive pressure.

Rand was conducted from the airport in a black Lincoln Continental driven by a plainclothes officer from an indeterminate bureau. Ostensibly the officer's function was to smooth Rand's passage through customs and escort him to his apartment. Really, though, the aide was on hand to make goddamned sure that Rand didn't stop off to indulge in such luxuries as eating or sleeping en route to the Capitol building.

The officer – a bland young man who spoke little – drove the limo directly to Rand's apartment in Northwest Washington: 100 Waverley Street, near the Naval Observatory. The 18-storey, air-conditioned building had a 24-hour doorman, attended garage, basement laundry and master tv antenna. A view of Montrose Park was thrown in for good measure. Tenancy of the private apartment was one of the perks that Rainer had extended to Rand for the duration of the Meredith hitch. The implication – supposed to be flattering – was that Rand would spend much time in Washington, consorting with high-level politicians. So far, the botanist had only slept five nights in the apartment. He would have felt more at home in a hotel.

Even so, in the drab, rain-washed streets of Washington Rand might have found relief after the heat of Turkey, might have relaxed and pulled out of his grouch, if he hadn't noticed the baby-blue Chevette tailing the Lincoln. It was on the tip of his tongue to ask the aide if the Chevette was part of the official security detail. But he guessed by the slight frown on the aide's face in the rearview mirror and the almost imperceptible wrinkling of the odd-shaped scar on the young man's cheek that it was not. Rand said nothing. The aide did nothing to evade the follower. Unchecked, the Lincoln stole down into the lot below 100 Waverley Street. The two men took the elevator to the tenth floor.

The aide entered the apartment before Rand.

'What the hell is all this?' Rand demanded as soon as they were inside.

'Sir?'

'How long do I have?' Rand asked, sourly. Obviously he would ring no change out of the ice-man.

'Vice-President Rainer runs to a very tight schedule, sir,' the young man said. 'He has you slated for six, I believe.'

'So, how long do I have?'

'Ten minutes, sir.'

Rand dumped his hand luggage on the bedroom floor and kicked it under the bed. He showered, shaved and changed into warmer clothing; then, saying nothing, he allowed himself to be ushered out to the Lincoln again.

In gathering dusk, historical Washington buildings stood bone-white against contrasting pockets of autumn-leaf shadow. Floodlamps streaming onto or from national monuments added erstaz theatricality. Enclosed in the hushed interior of the Lincoln, Rand felt himself becoming more and more alienated, cut off from the real business of the city, the nation. Nothing that happened in the next hour increased his sense of reality. He blamed it all on Rainer, uncharitably ignoring the added factors of jet-lag and exhaustion.

He noticed that they'd shed the Chevette. Maybe it had never existed. Maybe he'd imagined it.

The Lincoln drew up among traffic by the steps of the Senate wing of the Capitol building. Now towards the day's end, the steps along the East Front were thronged with senators, secretaries and pressmen, a mobile of umbrellas, hats and mackinaws that, as the aide opened the Lincoln's door and Rand stepped out, seemed to seethe against the colonnades.

Rand blinked. He sucked in a welcome lungful of moist evening air. A young man, younger even than the aide, separated himself from the crowd and, with tilted umbrella, took over escort duty. Rand was left with no lasting impression of the boy or of the male secretary who took charge of him at the door of the Capitol.

He was led quickly through bustling corridors and the gilded splendour of the Senate Reception Room to the Vice-President's formal office. Here, under an over-ornate crystal chandelier, Jay Rainer waited behind his imposing desk.

The door of the office closed. Rand found himself staring into the surrealistic depths of a tall John Adams mirror above a marble fireplace. In the glass he could see Rainer's handsome profile: long straight nose with a fleshy tip, the thin-lipped mouth that could never make a smile seem natural, except to the eye of a tv camera.

Also reflected in the mirror he saw a stranger – himself – a grey, hollowed-eyed, surly, ursine creature whose scowl suggested peevish gaucheness. The unappealing image pulled him temporarily out of his evil mood. Deliberately, he forced a grin as Rainer heaved himself from his chair. With the stiff rolling gait of a tall ex-cowpoke – going back thirty-three years, of course – the Vice-President sauntered round to greet the botanist.

Rainer's handshake was firm.

'Gordon, you look terrible.'

'Tired, Mr. Vice-President, that's all.'

'Sit down. Drink?'

'No. Thank you, sir.'

Rainer returned to the chair behind the official desk. Flag and seal were to his right. He eased the heavy chair back as if to associate himself as closely as possible with the emblems of national prestige.

For no accountable reason, Rand continued to feel threatened. Maybe Rainer himself generated a faint aura of foreboding – or the accumulation of sinister secrets that had percolated through this office since the President had firmed up the post and graced it with a fresh declension of authority. In picking Rainer as a running mate, the Chief Executive had chosen a man of keen intelligence and independence. It was rumoured that Rainer was a ruthless manipulator. Just how calculating he could be remained, to Rand's knowledge, unproven.

Rainer elected to dispense with small-talk. His manner was unpatronising and informal. The guy, thought Rand, is anxious to be off and running and needs me to give him the gun.

'I take it the Turkish trip was pretty rough?'

'Yes, but not lacking in interest,' Rand answered.

'Just how interesting did it turn out?'

'Before I answer that, sir,' Rand said, 'I'd like to put a question of my own.'

'Sure,' Rainer said.

'I'd like to ask what you expect from me?'

'I don't understand, Gordon.'

'As you know, sir, I didn't angle for this assignment. I wasn't much flattered by the fact that the Narcotics Commission appointed me to monitor the Turkish project. Maybe I should have been – but I wasn't. I was puzzled right from the start. I'm even more puzzled now. Mr. Vice-President, you've been less than straight with me.'

Jay Rainer nodded. 'It's true, Gordon. But you must understand by now how important the project is and the reasons why my committee wants it kept under wraps.'

'Yes,' Rand agreed. 'That's fine, so long as my role is limited to providing analyses and reports. I don't want to be hauled into making assessments or donating advice on how this bacterium should be used.'

'Decisions of that nature won't be your concern, Gordon,' Rainer assured him. 'Once the botanical reports are completed, you'll be free to return to your work at Stanford.'

'So why are you guarding me?'

Rainer smiled. 'You mean Feldspar, the aide who met you at the airport?'

'And the rearguard protection.'

Rainer started. 'What rearguard protection?'

'A Chevette followed us from Dulles to Waverley Street. I thought it might be an additional security precaution.'

'No,' said Rainer. 'Unless the boys are acting on their own initiative. Did the driver, did Feldspar spot the tail too?'

'Yes.'

'Don't worry. It'll be handled.'

'It means somebody knows what we're on to, doesn't it?'

'It might.'

Rand said, 'You didn't need me in Turkey. The British could have conducted the experiment, with less risk to security, and presented their findings to us.'

'It was expedient to send you along,' Rainer said. 'The British don't have facilities for moving fast.'

'Please, Mr. Vice-President,' Rand said, 'I'm not stupid. You wanted the United States to be *visible* in its involvement.'

'I needed on-the-spot U.S. representation, that's all.'

'Enough to rouse interest, with a neat cover job to make it seem like we're trying to hide something.'

'*Are* we trying to hide something?' said Rainer. 'I think it's time you told me just how effective Meredith's bacterium really is.'

'I still don't know how Meredith came by the stuff,' said Rand. 'But I saw how it works. Believe me, sir, it eats through poppies.'

'By what process?'

'The bacterium produces a toxin that arrests the synthesis of the morphine molecule early in its metabolic pathway. It reduces the output of the morphine from the pod to less than five percent of normal expectation.'

'Without actually destroying the plant?'

'The plant remains absolutely undamaged. There's no way of telling that the plant is infected without detailed chromatogram analyses.'

'Fundamentally, that's all I need to know.'

'Not quite, sir,' said Rand. 'If – as I assume to be your intention – you wish to disseminate the bacterium into major producing areas and dry up illegal morphine supplies at source, I'd advise you to hold off awhile.'

'For how long, Gordon?'

'A year, at least.'

'Why?'

'To enable me to study the bacterium's reproduction kinetics, its mode of action, growth requirements and responses to variations in chemical and climatic conditions.'

'And that will take a whole year?'

'Ideally, two years.'

'Hasn't Meredith done preliminary work already?'

'Some. Not enough.'

Rainer hesitated. 'The use to which the bacterium will be put isn't your concern, Gordon. You said yourself that you don't want to be involved in that aspect of the work.'

'That's true,' said Rand. 'But you appointed me to monitor the Meredith experiment and, I suppose, to test results.'

'That won't take a year,' Rainer stated.

'Sir, I'm telling you the bacterium may turn out to have long-term side-effects that won't show in the first seeding. The Meredith bacterium might even be dangerous.'

'Have you any reason for making that statement, Gordon?'

'Nothing positive, but . . .'

'I'd like a "first findings" report, results of your observations in Turkey, in four weeks, Professor,' Rainer's voice hardened. 'I intend to summon a full meeting of the Commission in October. I'd like to have copies of your report circulated at least a month in advance of that date.'

'Mr. Vice-President, I can't be held responsible . . .'

Rainer got to his feet. 'In the meantime, I'll firm up that

security detail. No sense in taking chances.'

'Jesus Christ,' said Rand, under his breath. He figured he knew now what Rainer had dragged him into. The realisation sickened him. The poppy crop was a blind.

What Jay Rainer wanted was a bargaining weapon. Saying nothing, Rand got to his feet and shook hands with the Vice-President. There was no percentage in hotly arguing the case for long-term testing. He could tell by his attitude that Rainer would not delay. He'd been used by the U.S. government, like so many of his colleagues before him; used like an old Kleenex and then tossed away. Some other guy, some other scientist, would be vetted and given orders to adapt the bacterium. Meredith had tried to warn him of that eventuality. He had been naïve not to grasp the point before now.

Angrily, he stalked through the corridors of the Capitol building and followed the young male secretary back down to the waiting Lincoln. The aide opened the door for him. Rand thrust himself into the limousine's plush compartment.

'What are my orders now?' he growled.

'I've to take you home, sir,' Harold Feldspar said mildly.

'Home?' Rand immediately thought of Stanford.

'To your apartment in Waverley Street.'

The Lincoln moved away from the illuminated pillars. Christ, if only there were as much light in committee rooms and private Senate chambers as there was on the architecture, Rand thought furiously. He was dizzy with frustrated rage.

'You'll feel better after a night's sleep, sir,' Feldspar said, cocking his head to speak through the open glass partition.

'I doubt it.' Rand lit a cigarette. One puff made him feel nauseous. He stubbed it out in the ashtray. 'When do I get out of this miserable city?'

'In the morning,' Agent Feldspar told him. 'We have you booked for a direct flight to San Francisco. We leave your place at 07.15 hours. When shall I awaken you?'

'Around six,' Rand said. 'Are you my permanent security detail by any chance?'

'Part of it. I'm Agent Feldspar. FBI Agent Donohue will be working shift with me.'

'So I can sleep safe in the knowledge that Uncle Sam's looking out for my welfare?' said Rand, sarcastically.

'You've nothing to worry about, Professor,' Feldspar said. 'There will be no hitches, I'm sure; nothing Donohue and I can't cope with.'

For once Harold Feldspar was wrong.

The man behind the wheel of the baby blue Chevette drawn up adjacent to 100 Waverley Street was called Jimmy Hogarth. His name was the most memorable thing about him. Otherwise he was so nondescript as to be almost invisible, a talent he'd spent the last thirty years trying to eliminate.

Jimmy had been told that the break-in must take no longer than one hour and must be indetectable. The mark's name – Gordon Rand. Jimmy had been given a recent photograph to aid identification. Apart from that he had no notion who the guy was or why he rated a tail, let alone the use of a government limousine. Jimmy had been hit with the contract by Sam Smith, *aka* Sam Oregon. The fee was generous. It came with the strong hint that its originator was Frank Varese, a name that nobody in East Coast criminal circles took lightly.

The nine hours that Jimmy had spent hanging around Dulles did not bore him. He was used to prolonged stake-outs. He had served a lengthy apprenticeship in the eyeball trade. His successes included nine armed robberies, all of which had depended on exact scheduling of movements of money and personnel into and out of banks. Preliminaries for each job had taken upwards of a month. It was about the time of the sixth raid that Jimmy grew a stopwatch in his head.

Since then Jimmy had found himself compelled to clock up mentally the seconds, minutes, hours that the most trivial of chores cost – the eleven-minute breakfast, the eight-minute shower, the five-minute shave, and, in spite of best medical and psychiatric attention, the forty-four second ejaculation.

Jimmy, however, was calm and confident about the Waverley Street commission. An hour was a fucking eternity. And the building was a breeze.

Within three minutes of Gordon Rand's departure in the Lincoln – headed for the Capitol, though Hogarth didn't know it – Jimmy had crossed the street, descended into the back service area, opened the fire door to an inside staircase, put the dupe key back into his pocket and, toting his pouchette of equipment, had strolled up to the tenth floor.

Here the fire door was open. Some activity in the corridor: a husband and wife bickering at an apartment doorway. Jimmy waited until the husband stalked off, then went on along the corridor to the door of Rand's apartment. He picked both locks in the time it took him to deal three full hands of stud: one minute and thirty-seven seconds. Now he put on the fine, leather golfing gloves that he preferred for indoor work. He closed the apartment door, fitted the safety chain, crossed to the window, drew the drapes and switched on a table lamp.

The apartment was comfortable but impersonal. No homey little oddments lay around. Jimmy went into the bedroom, closed the drapes there too and, by an overhead light, checked out the closets. He found nothing. Nothing at all. The bathroom had been used recently. The shower stall was wet, the mirror above the basin misty. In the bedroom, on the bed lay a shirt, rumpled coat and pants. On the floor by the bed were socks and shoes. Under the bed, kicked in, was a scuffed black-leather attaché case.

Jimmy pulled out the case. Kneeling, he opened the two simple locks with a slender platignum wire that he extracted from behind his lapel.

The case contained two folders of manuscript notes and a box of eight one-hour tapes in cassette. Two tapes had been filled.

On a scribble pad Jimmy made a little pencil drawing of the placement of the objects in the case. Leaving the case open on the rug, the drawing beside it, he carried the files and the two cassettes through to the living room. He opened his equipment pouchette and took out a neat transcription device. The machine's modifications enabled it to record the one-hundred and eighteen minutes and eleven seconds of material on Rand's cassettes in four minutes and fifty-three seconds.

Deke, Jimmy's kid brother, had graduated into the information racket four years back. This last year or so Jimmy had been helping him out as a vacation from dark doorways, storefronts, rooftops and windy places. The transcription machine was Deke's invention, part of his essential equipment, like the Minox with which Jimmy photographed each page of the files.

All in all it took Jimmy Hogarth eighteen minutes and forty seconds to do what he had to do in the apartment. Then he reversed each action precisely. Files and tapes were returned to case, case pushed beneath the bed, doors, lights, drapes, chain, lock, corridor, and so on down to Waverley Street and the baby blue Chevette.

A breeze, a real breeze. Thirty-two minutes and twenty seconds remained on the hour that Oregon had allotted him. All he had to do now was brave the rush-hour traffic, haul himself over to the Islamic Centre on Massachusetts Avenue and deliver the goods to Sam Oregon who would be waiting on the sidewalk outside the main entrance to pay him his fee.

Though Jimmy didn't know it, he had plenty of time on hand. Forty-two minutes after Hogarth nosed the Chevette into the traffic Gordon Rand stepped from the limo in Waverley Street and crawled exhaustedly into the apartment building. So weary was Rand now, in fact, that he did not notice that the baby blue automobile was no longer parked across the street – or that his apartment had been entered and his private files rifled.

By that time, copies of the botanist's notes on the Meredith bacterium were on their way to Frank Varese and the one contracted employee in the whole of the syndicate who would be sure to understand them.

THURSDAY NIGHT
NEW YORK

Dr. Anthony Bulthius closed his eyes. His plump face relaxed, sagging with ecstasy like that of a classical music buff transported by the strains of a Mahler choral symphony. Bulthius, however, had tin ears. He couldn't distinguish a sharp from a flat or tell a minum from a quaver. He got his kicks from harmonies of a different kind, from the pleasing logic of chemical formulae.

Carbon compounds, amino acids and alkaloids hummed in Bulthius's head like low sweet chords. They had done so since his old man had first introduced him to chemistry some forty years ago and, at the age of seventeen, had shipped Tony out of the family druggists in Mitton County in up-state New York to be educated in England. In 1936 Tony Bulthius headed the honours list in organic chemistry at Oxford. A couple of years later, having seen firsthand what was brewing in Europe, he accepted a place as lecturer in Sorbell College of Pharmacy in Southern California and successfully avoided involvement in the war.

Girls were Bulthius's weakness. He had the pallor of a Transylvanian count, the moral scruples of a lycanthrope, and a passion for budding innocents that finally ran him foul of the law. In that pretohistorical era, smart Californian society did not consider twelve-year-old chicks fair game in the hunt for kicks, and Bulthius was fortunate to escape to Marseilles with his neck. He was also fortunate to have a couple of buddies with sufficient foresight to predict a post-war boom in narcotics and to hitch their waggons to that star. Now Balthius, founder father of fifty secret heroin processing plants plus several legitimate pharmaceutical businesses, was a big wheel in a white coat. He was rich, respected and almost – if not quite – sated with the prepubescent *belle dames* that one of Frank Varese's trusted lieutenants imported from safe stables in the sticks.

Success hadn't changed Tony much. He was still fascinated by chemistry in all of its manifestations and retained a humourous awareness of his own foibles that kept him from being patronising to dum-dums like Varese.

For the second time Bulthius was listening to Rand's tape. Varese knew better than to disturb him.

Detailed analysis of the enzyme kinetics, mass-spectra, electron-capture gas liquid chromatographic studies. Electron-photomicrographs still to be made. Seems bacterium produces factors capable of inducing lysosomal membrane disintegration and alosteric enzyme inhibition. Substances produced thus have multilevel site of action within plant cell. Very stable, and highly potent. When poppy cells grown in culture containing nanogram quantities of bacterial exotoxin, virtually all intermediary metabolities become undetectable.

The tape ran out. Without opening his eyes, Bulthius groped with his slender forefinger, found the button and depressed it. Smiling slightly, he rested his head on the armchair's squashy upholstery.

'Beautiful,' he said. 'Beautiful.'

Frank Varese stared across the twenty feet of Persian rug that separated him from the chemist and tried to look as if the gobbledegook had meant something to him.

Bulthius opened his eyes. They were pale brown, like cinnamon candy, crinkled at the corners with friendly lines that had developed through years of playing uncle.

Varese licked his bottom lip and asked, 'You mean it's a hype?'

'I mean, you've got problems, Francis.'

'This . . . this stuff . . .?'

Bulthius got up, crossed his living room to a mandarin cabinet and poured himself a glass of Spanish sherry and a shot of Glenlivet for the anxious Varese. Sipping wine, he brought the whisky to Varese and handed it to him.

Standing, serious now, he said, 'This is a government-backed project, Frank, is it not?'

'So far as we know, yeah.'

'Then you do have trouble,' Balthius said. 'It appears that the Englishman, Meredith, has discovered a germ that produces a potent plant toxin – a poison capable of penetrating plant cells.'

'But I can buy stuff like that in any dry goods store.'

'No, Frank,' said Bulthius. 'This is no common herbicide. I gather it confines its detrimental action to the poppy plant. What's more, it doesn't destroy the plant, doesn't shrivel it up like a weed, doesn't even prevent the plant reproducing itself. What it does do is reduce the morphine-bearing properties of the plant to approximately five percent of norm.'

'Tony, I gotta be *sure* that's true.'

Bulthius understood the implications better than Varese. Much better. He had gleaned a lot from the tapes, even more from the formulae on the files. Essential information was scant, however, and he did not have sufficient to figure out the actual chemical transformations.

Varese got to his feet. He swallowed the whisky in a gulp. Balthius took the glass from him. In the demurely elegant room, Frank Varese seemed coarse and out of place.

Bulthius said, 'I'm not bullshitting, Frank. It's all there. Rand's in the process of working out the mechanics. But, if he was called in as a helper or observer, he sure was convinced. They have it, Frank. It exists. A bacterium capable of drying out the poppy. It's how they plan to use it that's important now.'

'How far have the scientists got?'

'Not too far. Obviously the Turkish trip was a preliminary

experiment. Far enough, though, to give us cause for concern.'

'Look,' Varese asked, 'is there no chance this formula, whatever, is still secret?'

'You mean, if you steal it will that stop progress on experimentation?'

'Yeah.'

'Not a hope, Frank. It's not some code, you know. The stuff, the germ, exists. Too many people know about it already. Samples will be stored in several secret laboratories. You can bet on that.'

'So what's the answer?'

'Find a substance that will combat the germ's action.'

'What?'

'To put it simply, Frank, develop an antidote.'

'Can *you* do it?'

'Hey, now!' Bulthius was amused by such naïve confidence. 'I'm not quite in that league. Anyhow, no chemist in the world could work without more detailed knowledge of the construction of the primary bacterium. Only Rand and Meredith, maybe a couple of assistants, will have enough data to . . .'

'Yeah,' Varese interrupted. 'We need an expert.'

'There *are* only two experts.'

'We'll get Rand,' Varese said.

Bulthius smiled more widely still. 'He's your man – if you make him talk.'

'He'll talk.' Varese lifted the telephone.

'To me?' Bulthius asked.

'Before we're through Rand will talk to anyone,' Varese promised.

THURSDAY
LONDON

Mr. Wing did not much care for London. That chameleon city with its patchwork patterns of history, ancient and modern, and cracked carspace of contemporary elegance did, however, exert an appeal on Dorothy. Intended only as a diversion, he treated the girl to a one-hour taxi ride round the most famous sights. The effect upon his protégé was surprising: a gradual shucking off of the almost somnambulistic indifference that was her customary response to new places. Though he gave no outward sign of it, Mr. Wing was apprehensive in case this stimulation adversely affected her work.

It was a bright, brisk afternoon. Late summer sun brought out the unique tints of the old buildings and created the sort of atmosphere that seemed most fitting for England, a mellow fading, the most appropriate hue for the wistful flag of a crumbled empire.

Around five, the cab deposited the couple at Piccadilly Circus. Mr. Wing permitted the girl a run at the cheap arcades at the delta of Regent Street and Shaftesbury Avenue where she bought souvenirs like any first-time tourist. There was no hurry, no hurry at all. They would have ample time to do the work and catch the midnight jet back to New York.

Mr. Wing had checked in at the Pegasus Hotel, close to the airport. He had booked two single rooms. Working openly through the hotel switchboard, he had steered Dorothy through a series of calls and had, without too much difficulty, pinpointed the whereabouts of Ashley Meredith. The English were *so* trusting.

Adopting her most sympathetic voice, Dorothy had first called the Institute and, without pressing, received the news that Professor Meredith had been taken ill. More sympathy and an unchallenged lie soon elicited the name of the hospital – the National Cardiac Surgery. Prompted by Mr. Wing, Dorothy tackled the hospital next. That warm, breathless, plausible voice had once more gotten immediate information. It seemed that Meredith had suffered a heart attack, had undergone an emergency operation early that day and was presently in Intensive Care. Visitors were not permitted.

The unexpected development did not throw Mr. Wing in the least. Within minutes of receiving the information, he had adapted his plan and was, once more, in total control of the situation. In his experience, victims in hospitals were a gift.

Naturally, he had to establish that Meredith was, in fact, ill. Mr. Wing was not blind to the possibility that the British had set up a trap. He made one brief telephone call and then, lightheartedly, whisked Dorothy off into the heart of the city to pass the rest of the afternoon.

It was a little after seven in the evening when the couple

arrived, on foot, at Elsinore Court, in the Oxford Street pocket of Soho. Dorothy following dutifully, Mr. Wing climbed the stairs of a raddled office block. On the third floor, a card scotch-taped to a pebble-glass door announced the premises of Emperor Khan Film Distributors. Mr. Wing knocked and was admitted by a youthful Anglified Chinese entrepreneur, Huang Hain-chu, who traded in London under the alias James Nanking.

Nanking was delighted to reacquaint himself with Mr. Wing and to meet Miss Dorothy. Nanking spoke with an accent indistinguishable from that of a famous BBC newscaster. He wore Cordoba handout leather and Deliss ankle-length boots, and boasted of how he had turned *Emperor Khan* into a highly profitable venture in its own right. Politely, Mr. Wing evinced great interest in Nanking's bragging but refused tea, Scotch or vodka and, as soon as seemed courteous, brought the young man back to earth.

Leaving Dorothy in the outer office, Wing steered Nanking into the inner sanctum, a tiny closet of a room decorated with garish movie posters and meretricious oriental tat picked up on the stalls of the Portobello Road.

Out of the proximity of the girl, Nanking's manner changed. Soberly, he balanced himself on the edge of his miniature desk, folded his arms and said, 'The person you enquired about, Mr. Wing: yes, he is indeed a patient at the National Cardiac Surgery Hospital. I am advised that a heart valve replacement operation was conducted upon him this morning. No pronouncement upon his post-operative condition is available as yet.'

'I assume that he is in an intensive care unit?'

'He is.'

'Is it probable that he will die?'

'That I cannot say.'

'How did you obtain such information?'

'Without arousing suspicions, Mr. Wing.'

Wing had worked with Nanking before, once in Hong Kong and a couple of times in London. For all his gaudiness, the young man was a vessel of the proper shape, now fired by experience. He was entitled to protect his private sources; Wing respected that right.

'I have obtained a small chart of the interior of the hospital,' Nanking said. 'I cannot vouch that it is accurate in every tiny detail, however.'

'Does it show the location of entrances, exits, staff offices and the intensive care units?'

'It does.'

'Then it will serve.'

'I have also acquired sufficient documentation to ensure entry. It is not genuine but has all the appearances of being so.'

'And the rest?'

'I have obtained everything you requested.'

'May I see it?'

'By all means, Mr. Wing.'

Unlocking a cupboard in a corner of the office, Nanking produced a brown-paper parcel and a cardboard box. He handed the small box to Wing, who tugged off the lid and studied the hypodermic and soft plastic vial that the box contained.

'Is it exactly what I asked for?'

'Exactly. I admit that it was bothersome to acquire on such short notice,' said Nanking, 'but there it is.'

'You've done well.' Wing closed the box and slipped it into his overcoat pocket. 'Now?'

Smiling, Nanking tore open the parcel and, discarding the wrappings, shook out a nurse's uniform. 'It is perfectly authentic. All the appurtenances, correct in each detail. The fitting may require minor adjustment. I take it that it is not for you personally, Mr. Wing.'

Mr. Wing returned Nanking's smile. 'I do not have the figure for it.'

'The girl, your companion?'

'Yes, the girl.'

'May I ask how long the impersonation will be required to last?'

'Not long,' said Wing.

'Do you require further assistance from me?'

'No, Huang Hain-chu. You have done very well. The rest is my business – and Dorothy's.

Later, irrationally, Upton blamed the Prime Minister. He might as easily have blamed himself for failing to take the precaution of posting a Special Branch guard on Meredith's room.

But it did not occur to him – in the light of other developments – that Meredith was in any danger from external forces at that moment in time. When he finally tracked down the tiny clues that the assassin had left, Upton realised that he, not the Prime Minister, was at fault. He had made the killer's assignment very easy indeed. Even so, he tended to think that if he had not been summoned to Downing Street to squander valuable time re-assuring that vacillating little martinet, Ronald Hobson, that no threat to his position as leader of the party was posed by the Meredith project, he would have been at the National Cardiac in person and might have seen through the assassin's disguise.

As it was, during the twenty minutes it took Mr. Wing's helpmate to check into personnel and find her way to Meredith's room in the intensive care unit, Sir George Upton was on the carpet in front of the Queen's First Minister a half mile off in stunted Downing Street.

The decor of the domestic lounge had been chosen by Hobson's 'goodlady' and showed a shade more taste than Upton would have credited her with, considering her choice in hats and husbands: bottle-green silk wallpaper and curtains, a couple of Sheraton chairs and a strange wood-and-leather lounger that Hobson believed kept him free from back trouble.

The Prime Minister was installed in his 'special' chair. He wore the familiar cardigan and the familiar quilted slippers, and smoked the familiar curved briar pipe that, cruel gossips said, had been one of Harold Wilson's rejects, like half of Hobson's cabinet. The aroma in the lounge was of the sickly-sweet 'special' blend of weight in a shop in New Bond Street. On a broad walnut table close by his right hand were a glass of lager, a bowl of potato chips and a gallery of family photographs each identically framed in gilt. The impression was of confrontation with a whole up-coming dynasty of Hobsons, for his three sons, two sons-in-law and one of his daughters were all 'committed' to politics in one form or another. The most telling photograph of all, however, was one of Grandad Hobson holding a puffy-faced infant at arms-length, grinning at the baby's abject howls.

Hobson did not rise, making Upton come to him. He waved away a cloud of smoke and, leaning from the waist, offered Upton his hand. Across Hobson's ample lap lay a red-folder file.

'Sir George,' Hobson began, allowing Upton to find himself a seat, 'I am considerably . . . um, troubled by this . . . um, dossier that came my way yesterday.'

'What dossier is that, Mr Hobson?' Upton took his case from his pocket, extracted a cigarette and lit it. He looked round in vain for an ashtray. Hobson gave him no help.

'What's all this about you doin' a deal with the Americans?' Hobson went on.

'I'm afraid you'll have to be more specific,' Upton said.

'It seems that one of your lads has come up with some bug, a micro-organism, that's got our transatlantic friends' interest.'

'May I ask where you got your information, Mr. Hobson?'

'I have my sources. I have my . . . um, sources, just as you do, Sir George.' There was a smug, crowing note in Hobson's flat voice as he gave the answer.

'I trust, Mr. Hobson, that your sources are reliable?'

'That's what we'll soon find out.'

With a frosty smile, Upton said, 'And how may I help?'

'By answerin' a few questions.'

'Certainly.'

'How much . . . um, funding did you get for it from them?'

'Prime Minister, I'm not a market trader. As it happens . . .'

'As it happens, this is a British discovery, developed by means of a generous grant out of public funds.'

'That simply isn't true, Mr. Hobson.'

'No?' Hobson flipped open the red-folder file with the stem of his pipe, leaving a wet smear on the board. 'Over the past three years, unless my figures are wrong, you've got grants totalling ninety-thousand pounds out of the Science Development Fund to pay salaries of members of the Institute of Botanical Research.'

'Thirty thousand per annum is trifling, Mr. Hobson; a pitiful sum, in fact. At each Allocations Committee meeting I have . . .'

'Yes, yes, I know what you've done.'

'Well?' For once, Upton could not help being snappish. He deplored Hobson's niggardly attitude to any branch of science that did not promise an immediate return in 'industrial know-how'. Hobson's Victorianism went all through the present government, reaching down into the bureaucratic sub-structures on which the nation floated like the survivor of an ocean disaster on a papyrus raft. Simple funding procedures had grown so complex that for every bench scientist there were four administrators to record and direct his every movement, to veto his every request. This, not international skullduggery, was the heaviest cross that Upton had to bear. Hobson seemed to typify the national sickness, the old-fashioned reductionism that made a mockery of progress, a word that Ronald and his cohorts equated only with reducing the massive debts incurred by social programmes that took no account of human greed and idleness.

'What you have done, Sir George,' said Hobson, simpering out the accusation, 'is pump money from other sources into this so-called experiment. Now, now, now, now, no use denyin' it. I have it all down here in black and white.'

'And facts is facts, I suppose,' said Upton, thinly. 'Just *where* did you acquire the figures, if I may ask?'

'From the Institute.'

Upton nodded.

Hobson pointed with the pipe stem again, raising one untrimmed eyebrow. 'At least you didn't try to hide them, I'll say that for you.'

'There's nothing to hide.'

'What's this then?' Hobson dabbed with the pipe, spilling ash on the open pages of the dossier, a photostat copy of the master ledger from the Institute of Botanical Research. 'A hundred thousand pounds . . . um, crossed over from another project. What other project?'

'I cannot answer off-hand.'

'And this? Travel expenses for over three thousand pounds.'

'Prime Minister,' said Upton, very quietly, 'you are behaving like a tax inspector, not the leader of the country. I cannot believe that you really intend to live up to the *Josh* cartoon.'

The *Josh* cartoon had attained national prominence at the time of the Anglo-French atomic pile bungle. It showed Hobson in bed with a sexy Frency whore, Hobson complete with nightcap and curved briar, scattering banknotes right and left and saying, 'The Art of Good Government is the Art of Good Book-keeping.' The cartoon was surmounted by the bye-line, *The Impotent Accountant.* The insult had stuck. Though Hobson had somehow survived a general election and held a minority party in the House with all the determination of Custer making his last stand twice a night, every night, the reminder was enough to make the parliamentarian flush with anger.

'Right you are, right you are,' said Hobson. 'If that's the way of it, I'll be blunt with you, Sir George. What are the people of this country gettin' for their money?'

Upton thought quickly. He would have preferred to soothe Hobson by quoting some mythical pound figure there and then, but he had not been prepared for such a simplistic attack upon his authority. There were times when he felt like the last individual left in government affairs, and he protected that position zealously. He had no lie ready. He needed a minute or two to devise one. Hobson was waiting, puffing that infernal sickly mixture in the bent briar, smug and arch, like some neutered tomcat that knows he has found the fish.

Upton thought of President Fisher, or Vice-President Rainer. However much the American people suspected their leaders of deviousness and perhaps of hypocrisy, such men knew what power was for and how to use it to the benefit of the nation. In contrast, Hobson was a self-seeking amateur. Behind each platitude, each cliché about the Great British People was a cry for help for an ailing party. Nothing was to be gained by being subtle with this man.

On impulse, Upton played the one card he had never dared use before. He got to his feet and stared directly at Hobson.

'Mr. Prime Minister,' he said, evenly. 'I appreciate that you were landed with me, that I was not your choice of Scientific Projects Adviser and that if you could have found another person willing, let alone able, to fill the post then you would have replaced me at the time of your coming to office.'

'Now, Upton, I'm not complaining about your work. I . . . um.'

Upton went on. 'My success in the past – I imagine that even you, Mr. Hobson, would acknowledge that I have been successful – has depended upon freedom to act rapidly and, where necessary, upon my own initiative. I cannot function under the committee system.'

'Sir George, I meant no . . . um.'

'It seems, however, that you believe I have acted rashly and irresponsibly. Indeed, you've virtually accused me of misappropriation of government funds. I have no alternative but to offer you my resignation and request a full investigation into the serious allegations that you have lodged against me.'

'Now, now. Now, now.' Hobson pushed himself to his feet,

making placating gestures with his left hand.

'Good night, Prime Minister.'

Somehow Hobson reached the door before him, moving with a lightness of foot that must have stretched ligaments not used since his days as the Northern Ballroom Dance Champion in the 'thirties.

'Don't be hasty, George. Come back here and let's discuss this matter like sensible men.'

'My integrity has been questioned.'

'I . . . um . . . I find your unorthodox methods a little bit disconcerting, George, that's all. No need to fly off half-cocked. Come back here, and we'll thrash it out. At the end of the day, I'm sure you'll have done the right thing.'

Upton hesitated, then allowed Hobson, with a hand on his arm, to escort him back to the Sheraton chair. It was not good policy to let Ronald Hobson know that you have out-manoeuvred him. Despite his utter lack of charm, he was not without intelligence and was known to harbour grudges.

Upton settled himself on the edge of the chair. Hobson hovered uncertainly, then offered him a drink, which he politely refused.

Sucking on the briar for inspiration, Hobson said at length, 'I expressed myself badly, George. I admit it. But the doings of the scientific community concern me deeply, and I . . . um . . . tend to over-react. I'm sure you know what I mean?'

Upton understood perfectly. The organisation of society depended upon the control of the behaviour of its individuals. Hobson's whole philosophy was based on that credo. But he was an educated man and realised how inefficient and ineffective the implements of political control had become. There were areas of social life, however, where 'science' threatened to dominate, to bring the control of behaviour down to a level of precision that frightened men like Hobson. He had been burned by Scientific Projects, had lost face because of his tentative handling of them. Men like Upton, who seemed to understand everything, highlighted his own lack of perception.

Upton had Hobson in a defensive position; he intended to keep him there. He needed freedom to act. More importantly, he required the unquestioned use of certain government funds and departments. The early collapse of Ashley Meredith had changed the original plan, had made it much more complicated. Upton had to adapt to it – or lose out. Once he was over this hurdle, had Hobson's personal agreement, then he would move swiftly again.

He chose his words with care. 'I assume that you have heard of defoliant experimentation, Mr. Hobson, and the disturbing results that American botanical scientists have had with certain living substances used during the hostilities in South-East Asia?'

'I have. I . . . um, sanctioned experimentation in this field through the Defence Department at the beginning of my second term of office, didn't I?'

'And very opportunely, Prime Minister,' said Upton. 'In fact, it was out of those experiments at Radleigh Hall establishment, some twenty months ago, that the line developed.'

'Line?'

'A line of explorative experiment,' said Upton. The phrase had no real meaning, but it seemed to satisfy Hobson, who was an economist not a chemist by training. 'I deemed it advisable to split off one particular line and put it into a less obviously "secret" environment; in effect, to make it even more secret.'

'Meredith's work at the Institute?'

'In a nutshell, yes,' said Upton.

Warming a little, for the next fifteen minutes Upton fed Hobson a heady mixture of fact and fiction, censoring out all mention of the Narcotics Commission involvement, of the American criminal connection, of the Chinese, and of the distant clutch of scientists at Drayton Down who had laid the groundwork for this present drama. He made it seem simple, a question of refining a useful product – the Meredith bacterium.

Ronald Hobson listened attentively. When Upton had finished he asked a dozen or so questions, including the inevitable one: 'At what stage did you involve the Americans?'

'Quite recently, in the early spring.'

'But . . . um, why?'

'I had no choice,' said Upton. 'I heard a rumour that a professor of botany in Stanford was working along similar lines to Meredith, but with less satisfactory results.'

'You wanted Meredith to be first?'

'Yes, of course.'

Hobson stuck his tongue in his cheek. 'Might be a knighthood in this for Meredith, you know.'

Upton paused. 'I'm afraid Professor Meredith may not live long enough to collect the honour, Mr. Hobson. He was taken very seriously ill with a heart condition yesterday evening.'

'Good God.'

'Initially my reason for involving the Americans was simply to gain access to facilities that only they could offer. I was careful not to leak to them too much information concerning the nature of the bacterium. But I felt that we required their co-operation in the matter of finding a suitable site for testing. In addition to which, I wanted this Stanford professor involved. It's as well, in the light of Meredith's illness, that I did so.'

Hobson nodded.

Like many laymen, he accepted the old shopworn cliché about the 'lone scientist'. In effect, there were five or six able botanists in England who could have stepped into Meredith's shoes and assimilated the recorded data with ease. But Upton traded now on the accepted myth of the cabala of knowledge and implied that only Gordon Rand, the Stanford professor, had the training to grasp the intricacies of Meredith's discovery. A complete nonsense, of course.

Hobson continued to nod. 'What do you propose to do now, Sir George?'

'Bring Rand to the Institute.'

'Ah, what a good idea.'

'It may cost us money.'

'His salary, you mean?'

'Our offer must be generous.'

'Quite. Quite,' said Hobson, airily. 'Keep it in the country, though.'

'Rand will work with Meredith's chief assistant, his daughter, until such time as Meredith is able to take over the research in person again.'

'We will, though, have shared our knowledge.'

'That is very much in the principle of science,' said Upton. 'In addition, Prime Minister, you have a meeting scheduled with President Fisher in London in January.'

'That's correct.'

'You may take it from me that President Fisher will be thoroughly briefed on this situation.'

'And I can use the bacterium, perhaps, as a bargaining point?'

'In the scientific exchange talks, as a boost to our purchase of the Meton Pile Plant at a reasonable fee.'

Hobson smiled, his Cheshire smile. 'Yes, yes. If the Americans are really as keen as you say to have the Meredith bacterium, then I . . . um will certainly be able to do a bit of horse-trading.'

Upton said, 'I will be travelling to Washington in a day or so, Prime Minister. May I take it that I have your authority to set up this exchange as best I can?'

'Of course. Of course. I . . . um, never doubted your capability, Sir George. I ask only that you keep me personally informed of all developments.'

'Naturally, Prime Minister.'

Anxious now to be back about his real business, Upton got to his feet. He shook Hobson's hand and allowed the fellow to show him to the door.

'By the way,' asked Hobson, 'just what value will this defoliant bacterium have when all's said and done?'

'It will be a weapon,' said Upton. 'A deadly and insidious weapon.'

'Ah, yes,' said Hobson, nodding sagely. 'We can always get our price for that.'

'One way or another,' said Upton.

'My best wishes to Professor Meredith for a speedy recovery,' Hobson said, shaking Upton's hand again. 'You will tell him that, won't you?'

'I'll tell him, Prime Minister.'

But Upton had no opportunity to tell Ashley Meredith anything. Before he got back to the National Cardiac Surgery Hospital, Professor Meredith was dead.

'I'm sorry, truly sorry.'

Miles Harper's words seemed to have fallen on deaf ears. He tried not to look at the girl's face.

Laura and her father had been close, very close. They had worked together, lived in the same house, shared the same interests. In this bereavement there would be no trace of the faint sense of relief that some daughters feel when their fathers die, an easing of a relationship that had become, with age, burdensome.

Tears welled in Laura's eyes and rolled down each cheek.

'Wha . . . what happened?'

Harper put a hand on her shoulder. He tried to read her expression, to see which particular emotion would surface with grief – resignation, accusation, suspicion or fury.

Harper said, 'I really don't quite know, Miss Meredith. The operation went well. His post-operation progress was routine. No complications.'

'But he's . . . he's *dead*, isn't he?'

'Yes, his heart simply stopped beating. Resuscitation failed.'

It sounded lame; he had to admit that it sounded very lame indeed. Valve-replacement operations were hardly simple, but the death rate in immediate post-operative hours was low.

Nurses fussing, moving from one monitoring device to another, noting readings, milking the clear plastic drainage tubes that wormed from under the padded chest dressings into glass measuring cylinders: nurses murmuring to each other in a medley of accents – Irish, Australian, American.

And then the high frequency wail. The jagged irregular tracing on the oscilloscope above Meredith's bed. Nurses running. A nurse in a green gown sprinting down the corridors. A nurse with plump legs straddling the patient, pounding his naked chest with her fists, her jeans visible under the green theatre gown. Head nurse clipping out orders, not appearing to hurry. Compressing the black rubber bag connected to the tube that curved down Meredith's windpipe, forcing oxygen into the failing lungs. New solutions run into the veins. The oscilloscope showing a disorganised trace.

The only possible diagnosis – ventricular fibrillation. The fresh scars bleeding under the fists, padded dressings flung aside, like white flaps of dead flesh. *Shock him. Is the defibrillator charged?* Charge light glowing red, joule meter swinging up to 300 registration. Jelly-covered metal paddles with plastic handles gingerly placed on the chest. All stand back from the bed. Press the button on the paddle handle. Sparks leaping, the body convulsing, relaxing. The neutral oscilloscope. Nurses sweating now, panting. *Calcium*. Then four hundred joules shot into the corpse. Repeat shock. Nurse pounding, pounding on the bleeding chest until . . . great zipper of surgical stitches ripped and the red lipped wound opened, bleeding ever more copiously. Harper stopped it there.

He tightened his grip on Laura's shoulder. 'We did all we could, Miss Meredith. Absolutely everything.'

From the end of the corridor, Upton watched a senior staff nurse lead Laura Meredith away. He could tell at once by the young woman's slumped shoulders that her father was dead.

It was late now. That fool Hobson had delayed him far longer than was necessary. Striding, Upton reached the surgeon's office and, without knocking, pushed through into the room.

Miles Harper looked up, startled.

'Meredith's dead, isn't he?'

'He died twenty minutes ago,' Harper said, flushing as if Upton had directly accused him of negligence. He restrained himself from making yet another apologetic declaration of competence. He had nothing – nothing whatsoever – to blame himself for.

It was now approaching midnight.

Upton said, 'How was he when he left surgery?'

'As well as one could expect under the circumstances,' Harper replied. 'Look, Sir George, I don't know what happened. It could have been one of a dozen different things. He wasn't a young man, and the cause of the disease . . .'

'Suggest the most likely cause.'

'Pulmonary embolus, post-surgical clotting. A post-mortem will give us some clue.'

Upton said nothing for a moment, and Harper glanced conspicuously at his watch. He had been on his feet for eighteen hours now and he had several things to attend to before leaving for home. He was not unsympathetic. He regretted Meredith's death, of course, but patients *did* die, in spite of all the monitoring, all the care in the world.

'I'll require a copy of the post-mortem report just as soon as it's available,' Upton said.

'Of course.'

'In particular I wish the examination to include a serum potassium estimation.'

'Potassium . . .' Harper's eyes widened.

'How many nurses had access to Meredith in the immediate post-operative period?'

'Six – three each on two shifts.'

'Do you know them all?'

'No, not all. Good staff nurses are . . .'

'Harper,' said Upton. 'I want you to check the register of personnel, particularly the nurses.'

'You think somebody deliberately knobbled the old chap?'

'If, Harper, you wanted to make sure that somebody in Meredith's condition did *not* survive, how would you do it?'

Harper puffed out his cheeks and, furrowing his lips, blew out a long soundless whistle of air. 'Induce an asystole.'

'How?'

'An intravenous bolus of potassium chloride.'

'Will you make sure that death was due to entirely natural causes?'

'Indeed I will.'

Upton turned and put his hand on the knob of the door. 'You did your best, Harper. I think the error was mine.'

'This disease . . .'

'I'll have the post-mortem report collected tomorrow evening.'

'Sir George, listen . . .'

But Upton was gone.

The earliest commercial flight that Upton could find to carry him to Washington, D.C., left him five hours to catch up on a little sleep. He did not undress, however, but cat-napped in a comfortable armchair in the lounge of the Darwin, a small residential club in Elam Street, Westminster. He had notified Alf and, thanks to the head-porter of the club, acquired himself a cooked English breakfast at the ungodly hour of six a.m. Prompt at six-thirty, Alf brought the Daimler to the kerb outside the Darwin. Sir George was already waiting on the chilly, windswept pavement.

'London airport, Alf, please,' Upton said.

Alf glanced over his shoulder and skimmed the Daimler away from the kerb, accelerating past a milk-float at the mouth of Elam Mews and a Cortina containing a bibulous traveller from the north. The day was cloudy but a raw dawn wind kept the rain at bay. Alf had more sense than to flout traffic regulations. He would make up time when he got onto the motorway.

'Did you manage a bit of breakfast, sir?' he asked.

'I did, thanks,'

'There's a flask of coffee in the compartment, case you need wakin' up.'

Upton smiled. He drew down the lid of the picnic compartment, found the flask in its padded clip and the china cup, and poured himself a draught of the strong black Brazilian blend. He lit a cigarette. He would sleep again on the flight. At the moment he felt wide awake.

'Alf, Meredith's papers?'

'Safe in the black case in the boot, together with your travelling luggage. I packed for a week.'

'Yes,' Upton said. 'I have the feeling that there's no more to be done in England now. I may be gone for longer than a week, Alf.'

'Yer want me t'inform your good lady?'

'Please,' said Upton.

He took a notebook from his vest pocket and, with a ballpoint pen, jotted down three telephone numbers. He passed them through the open partition to his chauffeur.

'As soon as my flight leaves, Alf, will you place a person-to-person call to Henry Marks at the Washington number. It's unlisted but you should be able to reach him without too much difficulty. If that fails, call the second number. I require to be met at Dulles by Harold Feldspar. Nobody else, just Feldspar.'

'Right.'

'The third number will reach me. This afternoon I want you to collect a copy of the post-mortem report from Miles Harper at the National Cardiac Surgery Hospital. He expects you. Once you have the report, I will call you and have you read me the relative sections of the report.'

'Professor Meredith?' asked Alf, quietly.

'Yes.'

'What killed him, sir? The disease?'

'If it wasn't the disease, Alf, then I have made a serious error of judgement.'

Alf said, 'About the enemy?'

'Yes,' Upton said, more to himself than his chauffeur. 'I really thought they would go for Rand first.'

'Instead, they went for the Professor.'

Upton nodded, brooding over the coffee cup, watching the liquid lurch as the Daimler boomed out onto the flyover. 'And they killed him.'

'Now you think they'll kill your American?'

'I hope not,' said Upton, with a sigh. 'It's imperative that they take him alive.'

FRIDAY 19 AUGUST: WASHINGTON D.C.

It was difficult for Agent Harold Feldspar to avoid developing sympathy for Gordon Rand. After all, he felt as if he and Rand were old friends. Stored in Feldspar's memory were intimate details of Rand's birth, background and upbringing, school and college successes, career highs and lows, physical condition, psychological profile, even the names, habits and whereabouts of lovers, some of whom Rand himself had probably forgotten. For all that, Feldspar could not afford to let Rand intrude into his emotions. He must be friendly enough to do his job, no more. In fact, he would have found it much easier to defend Rand, to protect him from harm. He would have approached that duty with much more relish than he approached his present task.

By nature, Feldspar was devious. He had replaced his sense of humour – a handicap in the security community – by a wry cynicism that protected him from surprise at anything that anybody came up with. In his day, he had been party to all kinds of trivial dealings, some of which had ended in murder – and were rendered, somehow, all the more trivial for that. But Upton was the most cunning manipulator that Feldspar had ever encountered, and it had cost him considerable attention to absorb the strategy that the Englishman had cooked up. He had to admit that he could evolve no feasible alternative scheme. High stakes always called for risk and sacrifice, and, as Upton had made clear, the stakes were very high indeed.

For all that, Feldspar was glad that he had personally had no hand in administering the virus to Gordon Rand – or to Professor Meredith, for that matter, though he'd never met that gentleman.

Feldspar had read up some on bacteriology, but he would claim no more than a passing knowledge of the subject. This particular bug was one that Upton had produced from his big box of biomedical tricks, a brand-new infective agent processed for use at one or other of the secret establishments that Upton controlled. It had been 'on the shelf', as Upton put it, for some years now – V/811. Just that: V/811 – an innocent number for a lethal little weapon.

V/811 had apparently been used in a half-dozen quiet assassinations in Northern Ireland and in Africa, and had not been traced. That much Upton did impart. It had several advantages over conventional poisons, though its use was rather limited. Mainly, its importance as a killing aid lay in the fact that it was not infectious. Its action was confined within the parent body where it attacked the heart valve system, for reasons that, as yet, remained one of nature's many close-guarded secrets.

V/811 had grown out of research into aeortic heart disease, an interesting by-product of a programme of testing on certain anti-rejection serums intended for use in transplant surgery. Now it had found a place in the elaborate scheme that Upton had put together in meticulous detail, an interlocking series of apparently separate plots that would, with luck, make the mob a tool of the U.S. government and reverse the Chinese intention.

It did not occur to Feldspar, any more than it had occurred to Upton, that whole systems of morality were involved and that mathematical models proving that one life sacrificed was worth ten thousand saved were spurious and suspect at best. And, at worst, screened a kind of wickedness that was ethically indefensible.

How much of the truth Jay Rainer and Henry Marks and the other government wheels had been told, Feldspar could only surmise. It hardly mattered to them. They were far off in their smug offices, protected by secretaries, computers and a whole legion of 'buffermen', like him. Death was a file closed, an erasure on tape, a point lost or won. They didn't have to listen to the faint seething rasp in Gordon Rand's chest or watch the effort it cost him to make himself ready for departure for Dulles International.

At least Upton had made arrangements, of a sort, to pull Rand through. Rand and Meredith. At least, Upton had given them both a chance of survival. It all sounded so neat, so easy. Valve replacement. The thought of being dependent on a surgeon's skill did not comfort Feldspar. For four or five minutes in the cheerless apartment at 100 Waverley Street he felt guilty.

But it was soon to pass. It was soon to be brought home to him that by bullet or bacterium, death was a fact he had to live with in his profession. Paradoxically, death was the antidote to too much conscience, the placebo that relieved guilt.

Leaving breakfast untouched, Rand picked up his scuffed black-leather attaché case, refused Feldspar's offer to carry it down to the car for him and, complaining about the chest cold he had brought back from Turkey, moved after the agent out of the apartment.

Feldspar had already attended to the rest of Rand's luggage. It was packed away in the boot of the Corvair that FBI Agent Donohue had chosen in preference to the big Lincoln to transport the cargo safely and discreetly to Dulles. As far as Agent Donohue was concerned, this was merely routine escort duty: his function was to protect Gordon Rand. it was Feldspar's decision to play it that way, a decision he was soon to regret.

He hadn't counted on Varese's hirelings coming in old style, though he guessed that the snatch would be attempted somewhere along the route to Dulles. He figured he was ready, ready to ascertain that Gordon Rand was 'lost' in a fracas as convincingly as possible.

Feldspar sat in the back with Rand. Donohue scanned the underground parking lot, then climbed into the driver's seat and fixed the seat belt strap. He prowled the car along the line of slots and up towards the rectangle of daylight under the lip of the roof, easing it up the ramp and braking gently.

It was early, the morning still. A faint uncertain haze hung over the moist street. Trees in the parkland jutted beyond the soaring gable of the street's one major office development, the leaves pale and massed in the pearly August light as if washed in with watered inks. Feldspar craned forward. He could see nothing of the Georgetown Heights except five or six upright wafers of delicate yellow rising through the sepia-tinted mist. He was aware of the stillness, of the stealthy hiss of Rand's breathing beside him, the fluctuating purr of the Corvair's engine, the tiny creaking wrinkles of sound that Donohue's leather coat made against the upholstery.

Feldspar felt the lurch as the rear tyres cleared the hump of the parking lot. He was keyed-up, tuned, edgy, professionally sensitive. He saw and noted each of the seven vehicles parked right of the route, the five parked left. He even saw the big midnight-blue Volvo panel truck parked up aways, its bland rear to them. Saw the section's half-dozen pedestrians, including one good-looking black lady walking an afghan hound. Saw the coffee shop on the corner of Mayfield, the commercial bookstore next to it. He noticed every detail, his brain selecting and rejecting, sifting the banal from the potentially threatening. Dipping his head, he had just started to scan the windows along the route when Agent Donohue tramped on the gas and swept the Corvair out into Waverley, heading west.

Feldspar heard Donohue's sharp whoop of warning. The bulk of the Volvo panel truck loomed huge against the windshield and right-side windows, angles of blue-painted steel bolted onto the frame. He flung his right arm across Rand's chest and thrust him back. Still accelerating, the Corvair struck the reversing truck like running into a mountain.

The Volvo's steel edges sheared off headlamp and wing and then, as the Corvair slammed inwards, checked violently, buckled and bit into the body of the car. Still reversing, the Volvo thrust it back along its line of travel and, with all wheels locked, nosed it up like a hooked tuna.

At impact Feldspar was hurled forward. He had sense enough not to brace himself, though every reflex screamed at him to do so. His head snapped forward like a sunflower on a withered stalk. His brow struck Donohue's shoulder. Instantly his vision was blurred by a horde of bright vermillion pain – flies that swarmed into his brain like bees into a hive. Then he was flung back, body bowed, involuntarily arching himself away from the impact zone, from the prow-like butt of the truck. He figured that if Donohue had been as dazed as he was, then Donohue would not have gotten himself shot.

There were four guys on the assault squad. Knitted ski-masks, sea-green nylon overalls zipped up to their throats, thick leather welders' gloves. Two sets of metal cutters, torturers' tools. Two handguns. Magnums. The windshield had turned to crystal. Shapes. Feldspar shook his head. Bees buzzed furiously. He hauled himself from the well, reaching for the lock on the door. He thought he could smell gasoline. His head twisted. Seat felt spongy, giving no purchase. Light flooded in. Both sides of him.

He shook his head again. Got his legs working, thrusting, so that he wallowed round and, thrusting again, slumped out onto the sidewalk.

Cool morning air flushed his senses. He sucked it into his lungs. Propping himself on knees and elbows, he looked around.

Far along the pavement, the afghan hound was prancing on its lead. The svelte black lady was reining the dog in, her hair explosions of black around her face as she shouted and darted her head this way and that, seeking help. He saw an old guy in an apron peer out of the coffee shop. Then, as he struggled and rose to his feet, he brought into focus the four men, behind the wreckage of the Corvair and the abandoned Volvo. Four men running in a bunch with a fifth man, Rand, somewhere in the middle of the huddle.

His reaction was like a spasm. He had the gun out – because he had to – and, slapping right wrist into left hand, pitched forward and snapped off four shots. Aiming at nothing, he hit nothing. He rolled away from the returning fire. And saw Donohue charge.

He yelled. He yelled loudly. He thought that the top of his head would blow off like the cap of a volcano. He rolled again. He came up running and spun himself round behind the truck of the uptilted Corvair. Donohue was sprinting faster and faster.

Three men and Rand at the rear of the Granada. Fourth man stooped, legs spread, left arm crooked. The hole in the knitted mask gaped wide as he pointed the magnum. The shot seemed to pluck Donohue out of mid-air, snatching him from the diagonal that would have carried the agent into the deep bunker of the bookstore doorway.

Donohue's body corkscrewed. He flipped round and seemed to be still running, though maybe he was dead even then. His Luger .38 Special pumped shots down into the asphalt. He went at last into a long, slow-seeming dive and, in the end, lay straight and flat as a spear in the middle of the empty street.

Snarling, the Granada powered forward. The marksman skipped and groped at the wing of the open door. He was swallowed up as the car leapt over the kerb at the corner of Mayfield – and vanished.

Feldspar fired one last token shot. Token shot – shit. Orders notwithstanding, he was trying to gun the bastards down. He said nothing about that though when he summoned Rainer's emergency janitors through a payphone in the coffee shop and told them tersely to come out on the double to sweep up the mess.

FRIDAY EVENING
BERTRAM – WEST VIRGINIA

If Clark Halveston were nervous he gave no sign of it. Long ago he had acquired a steel-plated implacability that nothing could dent. In appearance he epitomised all Washington career attorneys. Before his entry into politics, he had been a member of an élite corps of legal aces. His elder brother, a former presidential candidate, held high office in the Justice Department. A younger brother and two brothers-in-law still operated the family firm of Halveston, Halveston & Shapes and were privvy to most of the capital's dirty secrets. They did not, of course, have a clue that Clark was a Judas.

Halveston had been recruited and operated exclusively by Henry Marks. Nobody put the iron grip on the senator. He could not explain to himself why he had accepted Marks's deal and cast himself in a traitor's role. Over the years, however, that role had become so natural that Halveston felt uncomfortable in the presence of men who actually trusted his integrity.

The senator's first assignment had been a simple piece of espionage, a covert head-to-head meeting with a mobster the FBI had locked up for arraignment. In those days co-operation between CIA and FBI had been minimal. Marks did not dare risk an open application, particularly as the mobster was supposed to be none of the CIA's concern and nobody, but nobody, wanted it leaked that Central Intelligence required muscle on the wrong side of the tracks. The complicated plots of that period had been more or less exposed; the Politics of Herion seemed old hat. But Halveston had proved so useful that Marks had pushed him into specialised forms of treachery, puppet-mastering criminal syndicates to further the national interest at home and abroad. Feedback – information that came Halveston's way – was anonymously passed by Marks through several intermediaries to the appropriate authority.

Seven years had thoroughly consolidated Halveston's cover. Marks handpicked his assignments, nothing more demanding than discreet calls and an occasional meeting with a hood. The senator received no direct payment for his work. Undercover deals reaped him fat profits, however, and, by a very special arrangement with the U.S. Treasury, Halveston was permitted to salt them away. Illicit money dumps were an essential part of his cover. The syndicates, who inevitably got wind of everything, were strengthened in their conviction that Clark Halveston remained their man on Capitol Hill.

Duplicity had become a way of life for Halveston. He was no longer scared out of his wits by contact with mob bosses. He once admitted to Marks that he got a charge out of double cross. Halveston's ancestors had been corporate brigands, his grandfather and father political corsairs. For that reason, perhaps, the senator found himself an affinity with the generals of organised crime. It was only men like George Upton, an English dilletante, that brought a prickle of sweat to his spine now.

The rendezvous was set in Marks's country place in the rugged hills of West Virginia. Convenient for Washington and Langley, the converted barn was perched on a bowsprit of land overlooking the Potomac near the hamlet of Bertram, only a few miles below the crossroads of Harper's Ferry. Since his wife's death six years before, Marks hadn't used the place much, though his daughter, her husband and four kids spent weekends there from time to time.

The main apartment was crowded with furniture: wicker armchairs with daffodil yellow cushions, long davenports in herringbone hessian. Pine tables supported baskets of leaf spray. Through sliding glass doors light spilled onto a dark sundeck and the wet leaves of the spruces that screened the frontage.

Upton wore a vested suit of Cotswold cloth. He had been asleep upstairs when Halveston arrived and looked rested and affable now. In contrast, Marks was dressed in a chunky sweater, jeans and sneakers. Examining his first reactions, Halveston found that his distrust of the Englishman had spread over to Marks. Perhaps that was due to an involuntary reaction to the mud-slinging that had gone on in the inner enclaves at the time of the Bream Commission investigation. Marks's sudden retirement from the director's post had shaken his faith in the old warrior. Halveston did not know Henry Marks well – well enough, however, to stiffen himself to resist the onslaught of the man's personality.

There was also a young man present. It surprised Halveston that Marks had chosen to reveal his identity to a low-echelon agent. The whole assignment was way below the waterline. Marks had no authority now, no position, no goddamned business really, to summon him at all.

Halveston accepted coffee. During the brief ritual of introductions and the dispensing of hospitality he studied Upton carefully. He was reminded of one of the great hucksters from the South, the kind of men who fuelled a natural charm with nuclear confidence and had minds like whittling knives. Sunk into himself, he became even more still and unresponsive as Upton spoke with Marks and Feldspar.

'What happened this morning, Feldspar?'

'I wasn't smart enough.' Feldspar looked drawn and defensive, Halveston thought. 'In hindsight, I figure we made an error in not briefing Donohue more fully.'

'Rand wasn't harmed?'

'I don't think so.'

Marks said, 'The FBI are howling for explanations.'

'I assume Jay Rainer is capable of staving them off,' said Upton. 'An inquiry could prove awkward at this stage.'

'Jay's an inventive guy,' said Marks. 'He'll spin them some cock-and-bull story. What's more important, he'll screw the lid down on the kidnapping, keep it out of the newspapers.'

Solicitously Upton said, 'Feldspar, are you all right?'

'Fine,' said the young man, grimly. 'I just didn't expect them to come in so . . . so crudely.'

'I think we may take that as a sign that our American colleagues are beginning to panic,' said Upton. 'After all, that's what we intended.'

'Donohue's widow would be comforted to hear you say that, Sir George,' Feldspar remarked.

'Yes,' Upton said, softly. 'However, I have another snippet of information that may not console Donohue's widow, Feldspar, but that might help *you* to understand the magnitude of this operation. I've just telephoned my aide in London and received the results of the post-mortem examination carried out on the body of Ashley Meredith. Meredith did not, repeat *not*, die of natural causes or post-operative complications. He was killed – murdered – by the injection of a small quantity of potassium chloride into his bloodstream. It is quite probable that the killing would not have been discovered at all in the circumstances. There is, however, no doubt that somebody – possibly an agent of the White Tigers – put Professor Meredith away.'

'Christ, George, it's beginning to take,' said Marks. 'I didn't think they'd bite. I really didn't.'

'I did not intend that Meredith should die.' Upton glanced at Halveston, allowing his eyes to linger on the senator. 'Five men dead and we have only just moved into the second phase. What do you think of that, Senator?'

'You're asking if I feel squeamish about fingering Meredith and Rand,' said Halveston. 'The answer is that I don't.'

Cautiously Marks said, 'We need your help again, Senator. Your connection with the syndicates is crucial to the success of the operation.'

'But,' Halveston said, 'you no longer direct the CIA, Henry. Is this an English assignment?'

'Come now, Senator,' said Upton. 'I have the feeling you've already done your arithmetic.'

Halveston said, 'Sarsby and Varese, the Chinese, Vice-Presidential involvement. My arithmetic is good, Sir George, but I don't have all the figures.'

Marks said, 'This will be your last assignment, Clark.'

'I thought as much,' Halveston said. 'I'm not ungrateful to you, Henry. You kept me clean when the Commission were leaning on you. You didn't have to do that.'

'It wasn't only for your sake, Clark,' Marks told him. 'I'd plenty of other reasons for bucking the Bream Commission.'

'Those other reasons don't concern me,' Halveston said. 'My gratitude is quite selfish. I figure it puts me in your debt. Just answer me one question, gentlemen: whose operation *is* this? And what's the objective?'

'Put at its most simple,' Upton began, 'it's our intention to persuade a Chinese opium syndicate, who trade as the White Tiger Pharmaceutical Company, to bring a certain scientist out of hiding in the Far East. The scientist's name is Conrad Vigson. His speciality is bacterial manipulation.'

'I know about Vigson,' said Halveston. 'I thought he died in a plane crash.'

'The crash was engineered,' said Marks, 'to throw the agencies off guard.'

'But it didn't throw you?'

'Yes,' Upton answered. 'Yes, we accepted the crash more or less with relief, and only a minimum of reserve. Just enough reserve, Henry and I, to keep a pot on the stove, in case Vigson ever returned from the dead.'

'And he did?' said Halveston.

'Alas, he did.' said Upton. 'To cut it short, Senator, Conrad Vigson was seduced by the White Tiger Company while in a state of total disillusionment with the scientific communities of the West.'

'What did the White Tigers want with him?'

'Vigson is a creative scientist,' said Upton. 'The Chinese were obviously aware of his value. I suspect – though I have little concrete proof – that they had a scheme in mind when they approached him. Throughout his career, Vigson's research findings were filched from him and put to military use. It was for reasons of conscience that Vigson and a colleague, Rafe Poggendorf, abandoned England in the early nineteen-fifties.'

'They applied for entry into the United States,' said Marks. 'We grabbed them quick. We set up Poggendorf in a laboratory of his own in Seattle and teamed Vigson with Chasson in Baltimore.'

'Baltimore? Why Baltimore?'

'To keep him out of the limelight.'

'Did you consider him a security risk, even then?'

'Vigson was an idealist,' said Upton. 'And idealists are notoriously malleable.'

'Poggendorf died in 'sixty-four.' said Marks. 'During his decade in the U.S. he achieved little of startling worth.'

Halveston smiled wryly. 'But Vigson gave you value. Wasn't he the "inventor", for want of a better word, of many of the defoliants used in Vietnam?'

'He did not *seek* to be a weapon-maker. he vigorously opposed the use of untested bacterial substances,' said Marks.

'But the Pentagon went right ahead,' said Halveston. 'I'm beginning to sympathise with Conrad Vigson. Maybe I should tell you that I was one of the select group that got to examine the scientific feedback from Vietnam. For my sins, I was one of a small number of senators permitted access to classified reports from areas where Vigson's bacterial defoliants had been used. Mutants, hideously crippled children, babies with . . .'

'Yeah, yeah,' Marks growled. 'That war is over.'

'But we're still living with it,' said Halveston. 'All right, you've given me the reasons for Vigson's defection. But you still haven't explained what the White Tigers want with him or how you hope to coax him back.'

Upton said, 'Some of what I'll tell you now, Senator, is based on concrete fact, some on unsubstantiated rumour, some on intimate knowledge of Vigson's lines of research, a little inspired guesswork.'

'We do know that Vigson is alive; that's fact,' said Marks. 'We also know that he's developed a bacterial substance that reduces the morphine-bearing properties of the opium poppy.'

'The rumour came my way through an agent in Hong Kong,' said Upton. 'I contacted Henry. He enlisted the formal aid of Jay Rainer. We . . . ah, didn't feel confident that the official intelligence units could cope with the White Tiger Company.'

'Particularly as I was perfectly placed to intervene,' said Halveston. 'Did you initially put me into a middleman position, Henry, with Vigson in mind?'

'Nope,' said Marks. 'That was coincidence, Clark. I may have been doubtful about Vigson's demise, but I'd no way of knowing he'd flown to the Orient or gotten mixed up with drug dealers.'

Upton continued, 'We – Henry and I – decided to structure the project ourselves; to use *ex-officio* sources, balanced with whatever services we could wring from the FBI through Jay Rainer's committees.'

'But this young man,' Halveston gestured in Feldspar's direction, 'is CIA, isn't he?'

'Research,' said Feldspar. 'Strictly research.'

'A favour to me from the Deputy,' said Marks, with a shrug.

'If it ever gets out . . .' said Halveston.

'Sure, all our heads will roll,' said Marks. 'But that never worried you in the past, Clark. Why should it worry you now?'

'I wasn't thinking of myself,' said Halveston.

'We're in too deep to pull out,' said Marks. 'It's neck or nothing as far as we're concerned.'

'My agent in Hong Kong succeeded in obtaining a culture of the bacterium Vigson had developed.' Upton said. 'At that time we had no real idea of what our friend was up to. Unfortunately my agent, Ballard, was discovered and eliminated before I could make person-to-person contact with him. I know only that he bribed a pilot to steal the culture – not directly from the White Tiger laboratory, from a salesman . . .'

'A salesman?' Halveston could not keep the surprise out of his voice. 'The White Tigers are *selling* the stuff?'

'The White Tigers are selling rather a lot of stuff,' said Upton. 'But the bacterium in question is the important one. From the little that Ballard did unearth, coupled with other information that has filtered to us, we can be fairly certain that the White Tigers are consolidating a massive deal with Peking.'

Halveston licked his botton lip. 'What sort of a deal?'

'Red China is low on bargaining power,' said Upton. 'So far they have no weapon to exert in the *economic* war that's being waged between the major producing nations. The Chinese have no spare workable oil reserves, no excess wheat, no highly-organised industrial structure. Clearly this lack of muscle concerns them. It's a matter of priority in policy circles in the Social Affairs Department. Liaison with the White Tigers is undoubtedly the prize scheme of an ambitious director of covert assignments. How much blessing it has in State Council, I have no way of knowing. I suspect it stems from the zeal of an inner corps, rather than the Central Committee as such.'

'Do you mean Peking's Secret Service are pushing the NPC into the arms race, by stockpiling biological weapons?'

'Not quite, Senator,' said Upton. 'It appears their intention is to devise an *economic* weapon to use at the bargaining tables.'

'Vigson's bacterium – the poppy killer?'

'The development of a bacterium capable of reducing the morphine-producing content of the opium poppy is a grave enough threat,' said Upton. 'That, however, is only half the story.'

Marks said, 'Four years back Conrad Vigson was obviously "on the turn". If the gentlemen in Peking wanted a scientist capable of leading – and training – a prime team, then Vigson was bound to be their choice. He wouldn't work for the Reds, though. Disgusted with military wheeler-dealers, he went along with the White Tiger Company as the most viable alternative.'

'But the White Tiger Company represent the interests of

Peking,' said Upton. 'They are entrepreneurs, middlemen. They will receive inconceivably huge benefits for their services.'

'From what?'

'From the monopoly that Peking intends to create in opium.'

'Yes,' said Halveston. 'I've got you all the way now, Sir George. It's a brilliant concept, rocking the opium market. Particularly in a country geared to intensive agriculture and collectivization. Opium, the most remunerative cash crop known to man. China, with a million square miles across the Tropic of Cancer. Dear God, about the only country in the world still crusading *against* a spread of opium production is the United States.'

'Europe's screaming for opiates,' said Marks. 'Representation's already been made to encourage China to become a licit exporter of opium. Only the pussyfooting attitude of the United Nations and a certain shyness on the part of the Chinese themselves have prevented it. Goddamn it, Jay Rainer's personal crusade against traffickers and addicts is really opposed to the wishes of the American pharmaceutical industry.'

'The problems of addiction and the protection of pharmaceutical supplies are often confused,' said Upton. 'I think we are all aware of the enormous threat that a drying up of opium sources would pose.'

'And the enormous profit a monopoly supplier would gain,' said Halveston. 'You said, Sir George, that the Vigson bacterium was only half the story. What's the other half?'

'Vigson's records indicate that his main interest has always been in increasing plant yield by bacterial intervention. There's nothing new in this. Vigson's methods, however, are original and adventurous. He has been sufficiently successful in the past to suggest that, given the right environment and freedom to operate as he wills, he might come up with even more startling developments.'

'Yes,' said Halveston again. 'A team of Vigson-trained scientists might develop satisfactory methods of increasing poppy-crop yield.'

'Two or three harvests a year,' said Marks, 'instead of one.'

'Bacterially-stimulated increase in the morphine-bearing properties of the poppy plant is another possibility,' added Upton. 'A reverse effect on the original bacterium.'

'To be used in the depths of Red China, with attendant processing plants and distribution centres,' said Halveston. 'How would the White Tiger Company fit into a Republican set-up like that?'

'The White Tigers have half a century of experience, both in licit and illicit drug trading. As far as the Tigers are concerned, they would be happy enough to act as negotiators, salesmen when the time comes, to cream off a percentage on every transaction. Bear in mind, Senator, that the price of opiates would be dictated by the Chinese. World buyers would *have* to stump up or starve.'

'The old commodity blackmail,' said Halveston. 'Dear God, opium instead of oil. Not a pleasant prospect. How far has Vigson progressed?'

'Phase one is complete: the bacterium exists,' said Upton. 'We have samples and preliminary reports on its effectiveness. Discreetly introduced into areas of intensive poppy cultivation – just a handful of rich-yield areas would do – opiate famine ensues.'

'The root of Red China's poison tree,' said Halveston.

'But when the root is established and the tree grows strong . . .' Upton did not complete the sentence.

'As of now,' said Marks, 'the plan's contained. And containable.'

'We must stop Conrad Vigson,' said Upton. 'That's the long and the short of it. We must prevent him from handing on his knowledge to Chinese scientists.'

'Hasn't he done so already?'

'In four years, no; that's hardly long enough,' said Upton. 'Particularly when we can be sure that Vigson's been busily engaged in research and development of the initial bacterium.'

'Can we – the CIA, I mean – reach him?' said Halveston.

'It's possible, of course,' Upton answered. 'But if the mission failed, the White Tigers would remove Vigson and hide him in the uplands of Red China, where Western agents would have no opportunity of reaching him.'

'What then?' said Halveston.

'So far dealings between the White Tigers and the Chinese Republic have been covert,' said Upton. 'The representatives of Peking's Social Affairs Department are treading warily. Elements of doubt and uncertainty remain. They are monitoring progress, evaluating Vigson's worth, keeping in the background

– and being very cautious in their contacts with the White Tigers. It's our intention to fan the flames of doubt, foster mistrust and hopefully force the White Tigers to bring Vigson out of hiding.'

'How?'

'By convincing them that the bacterium is unsafe,' Marks replied.

'The Tigers are not unaware that the bacterium is untested as to long-term side-effects,' Upton said. 'Vigson will have made that clear to them. He has bitter experience of unsuspected side-effects resulting from his products in the past. Red Chinese specialists will not embark on any sort of defoliant programme until they are completely convinced that the bacterium will do only what it is alleged to do – and nothing worse. It's possible that Vigson is presently seeking an antidote to the bacterium. Such a safeguard would surely give the Chinese clearance to begin defoliant procedures in easily-accessible cultivation areas.'

'And you hope to sell the Tigers the notion that Rand and Meredith have come up with just such an antidote?' asked Halveston.

'We hope to create doubts; no more than that,' said Upton. 'Doubts of all kinds.'

'*Is* the bacterium unsafe?' asked Halveston.

Upton hesitated. 'Bacterial substances are never *quite* stable, you know.'

Marks leaned back in the davenport, eyes closed, as if he had lost interest in the conversation. Only Feldspar, who had sucked in every word and processed it against the research he'd been obliged to undertake during the past months, remained obviously intent upon Upton. It was not his place to push. But he prayed that the senator would be quick enough to grasp the implications, to frame the proper question. Though Feldspar knew the truth, he wanted Upton to confess it in plain speech; a mild punishment, a sop to decency.

'*Is* the bacterium safe?' Halveston persisted.

'As far as we can tell, yes.'

'Then how do you intend to prove its instability and make a strong enough case to disrupt the White Tigers?'

'It's already been done,' said Upton.

'Meredith and Rand?' said Halveston.

'Only living proof will do the trick.'

'*You* tampered with them, didn't you?'

'Meredith was fully aware of the risks.'

'And Rand?'

'No.'

'What the hell *did* you do to him?'

'Really, Senator, it's best if you . . .'

'This is pretty sick already,' said Halveston. 'But I'm not squeamish, Sir George. Did *you* infect Gordon Rand with a secondary bacterium, unconnected with the Vigson product?'

'A virus, actually,' said Upton, softly. 'A man-made virus. We've had it in stock for several years. It's a most effective killing agent.'

'Go on.'

'It infects the aortic valves. We haven't yet discovered why its action is so highly confined. The . . . the patient suffers sudden cardiac symptoms.'

'And dies?'

'Valve replacement will save the patient's life.'

'Giving the poor bastard a fifty-fifty chance?'

'Rand will have better odds than that, I assure you.'

'When, how did you administer the virus?'

'During Rand's course of standard shots before the Turkish trip,' said Marks. 'Same thing was done for Meredith in England. Takes twenty-two to thirty days for the virus to attack. Depending on metabolic factors in the . . . the patient.'

'Don't you mean the victim, Henry?'

'With your help, Senator,' said Upton, abruptly, 'Gordon Rand will not die.'

'You put him down the pipeline knowing he was sick?' said Halveston. 'How do you propose to "save" him?'

'Sarsby has the same kind of mentality as Yu-lan and Kittegawa,' Upton said. 'Thanks to you, we've already "telegraphed" him that the White Tigers are planning a massive coup. Sarsby now has Rand. He'll trade with Rand. To do that, Sarsby must keep Rand alive.'

'I suppose a couple of his hoods will perform a valve replacement operation,' said Halveston scathingly.

'No, Senator,' said Upton. 'The best heart surgeon in America will perform the operation.'

'I see,' said Halveston. 'You're using Sarsby as a screen, same as you're using Jay Rainer's Narcotics Sub-committee. And you want me to feed Sarsby the information?'

'To suggest that he can protect his property – Rand – by doing a deal with us,' said Marks.

'Won't Rand truthfully deny that he has an antidote to the bacterium?' said Halveston.

'Of course he will,' said Upton. 'But Sarsby isn't likely to take his word for it. Besides, Sarsby will not remain in ignorance about Conrad Vigson for long. Sarsby will be as anxious to stop Vigson as we are.'

'So the two syndicates will deal,' explained Marks. 'They'll horse trade. They don't trust each other one inch. But they're both profit orientated. They'll sniff the kind of money that, even by their standards, is too big to pass up. Peking will put pressure on the Tigers to *prove* that the bacterium is harmless, so the Tigers will be required to verify that Gordon Rand is genuinely infected and to discover if the U.S. government really does have an antidote.'

'Only Vigson is capable of confirming such things,' said Upton. 'The syndicates will be forced to arrange a meeting between Rand and Vigson.'

'If Rand's still alive,' said Halveston.

'He'll be alive,' said Upton confidently, 'but too frail to risk on a trans-continental flight. We must be sure that the Tigers are left with no option but to smuggle Vigson into the U.S.A.'

'And that's when you'll nail him?'

'If we accurately pin-point the time and place of the meeting,' said Marks. 'Which is where you come in, Clark.'

Halveston thought seriously, then said, 'Now that Sarsby has Rand, he won't contact me again. After all, what can he possibly want from me?'

'Sarsby and Varese know you hold stock in Amadeus Management,' said Marks. 'They figure you've been peddling information to the Chinese . . .'

'Which I have,' said Halveston. 'Minor stuff.'

'Did you take payment in the form of stock in this East Coast management company?' asked Upton with interest.

'I did them a few small favours,' said Halveston. 'They paid me in stock. I don't have any real ingress into the Chinese syndicate, however.'

'Is Amadeus Management the Tigers only East Coast funding unit?' Upton asked.

'Yes,' said Halveston. 'I know of no other.'

Upton nodded, thoughtfully.

'Surely you don't expect me to lead the Chinese by the nose too?' said Halveston.

'No,' said Upton. 'But the fact that Sarsby knows you've been selling your wares elsewhere, Senator, gives you a feasible excuse for seeking to make amends.'

'Tomorrow, you'll call Varese and dish out some very hot news,' said Marks.

'Tell Varese more or less what the Chinese are up to. Tell him that Rand has an antidote for the bacterium *almost* perfected. And, most important of all, tell him that Rand is seriously ill.'

'Will Rand be ill?'

'Yes,' said Upton. 'He's a strong chap but the virus will certainly be making itself felt by now.'

Feldspar said, 'He was off-colour this morning; he put it down to a chest cold.'

'Suggest to Varese,' said Upton, 'that he deal with us.'

'He'll never buy that.'

'He has very little alternative,' said Upton.

'Not even Arnold Sarsby could rake together an operating team and all the equipment necessary to perform valve replacement surgery,' said Marks. 'He'll have to come to you for help in setting up some kind of a deal – an official deal. You got me?'

'I've got you all right, Henry,' said Halveston. 'I just hope Sarsby trusts me sufficiently to accept my advice.'

'There's a lot of heavy pressure on Varese right now,' said Marks. 'Tomorrow evening Jay Rainer will convene an emergency meeting of the Narcotics Sub-committee to break the news that Gordon Rand has been kidnapped; break it to the committee, that is, not to the public. That meeting will provide you with information to relay to Frank Varese.'

'Assuming,' said Upton, 'that you agree to help us, Senator.'

Halveston considered. The trade craft was nothing. He could handle that side of it with ease, to make Varese believe him. He would demand a high price, a piece of the action perhaps. But if something were to go wrong, if Upton's complicated plot went adrift, he could expect no mercy from the syndicate. He would collect a bullet in the head.

And all for what? That was the question he had to ask himself. His ancestors hadn't needed the excuse of patriotism to hype themselves up. He just hoped that he was acting with a modicum of honour, an obsolete virtue in the season of decline.

He'd meant what he said about sympathising with Vigson. The movie that the Senate sub-committee had been shown – and had unanimously elected to veto – had given him the horrors. Everything in it seemed so contrived, so removed from the world in which he lived and breathed: gnarled two-headed babes born to peasant women in the raped village of Tek; huts, grainstores standing in a gaunt wilderness, a sterile blot caused not by napalm but a substance like chalk dust – RA-KA-4440 (a college chant cadance – RA-KA-4440); a two-headed, purblind, drooling twenty-month-old kid that its mother fed with a splinter of wood until the medics took it away to hook it to life support-systems and study it until the little freak died. Four women in deep jungle; pariah – the cursed of the gods – suckling bloated hemaphrodite infants; a tiny tribe of pig-snouted toddlers cowering under the bole of a dead tree by the shores of a leaden river. That kind of reality was too strong for the folks back home, even senators.

His own survival was a relative issue.

'I'll do what I can,' Halveston said.

Feldspar, Marks and Upton ate a late dinner of steaks and green salad. The senator had returned to Washington. Upton required one more thing to make the plan complete. He edged the conversation round to the killing of Meredith.

Feldspar said, 'Hospitals are easy meat for a trained assassin. Was it a male or a female?'

'I'm not sure,' said Upton. 'I imagine it was a woman. The National Cardiac was staffed by agency nurses, holiday replacements. It would have been a simple matter for a stranger to slip in, provided she wore a uniform.'

'A Caucasian,' said Marks. 'A Chink would have been too noticeable.'

'Henry, what do you know of the White Tigers' strength in England?'

'They probably have a few contacts there, but, to the best of my knowledge, they aren't much of a force.'

'So there's a possibility that they imported a killer, or killers, to do the job.' Upton chewed thoughtfully. 'Henry, when you bought Halveston into Amadeus Management, you knew it was a funding pool for the White Tiger Company, didn't you?'

'Halveston came up with the idea himself,' said Marks. 'He had a low-rank contact in the drug-ring and thought he might exploit him.'

'But you approved it?'

'Sure. Amadeus is the bridge between the American syndicate and its oriental counterparts.'

Upton addressed Feldspar. 'Did you come across any material related to Amadeus Management in your research?'

'No, sir.'

'Tomorrow, Harold,' said Upton, 'I think you might apply yourself to gathering such material.'

'Looking for what, Sir George?'

'Mercenaries.'

'Specifically you mean Meredith's killer?'

'It's not improbable that the man or woman who does the Tiger's elimination work is funded through Amadeus,' Upton said.

'I assume you're not just tying up a loose end, sir,' said Feldspar.

'Mercenaries can sometimes be bought,' said Upton. 'Do a little digging, Feldspar. If it comes to naught, at least it'll keep you out of mischief until I need you in San Francisco.'

'How far do you want me to go?' Feldspar asked.

'As far as you judge prudent.'

'How long do I have?'

'Two or three days, I would guess,' said Upton.

'Until Sarsby makes his next move,' said Marks.

'What if I spook the Tigers in the process?' asked Feldspar.

'That,' said Upton, 'is all to the good. We've put pressure on friend Sarsby. Time, I think, to turn the screw on those inscrutible Chinese.'

SATURDAY 20 AUGUST
WASHINGTON, D.C.

Much to Feldspar's surprise, Upton's hunch paid off at the first pull of the lever. Feldspar was a shade too young, and too American, to understand the workings of a mind seasoned by forty years of deceit. He did, however, appreciate that Sir George was a master at improvisation and liked to keep his options open. In coping with the unexpected 'turn up for the book', the old man functioned at peak.

Dorothy Newhoff was a gift-wrapped surprise. Almost as soon as he stumbled across the lady, Feldspar knew that Upton's talent for synthesis would allow him to incorporate her into the unlikely collection of criminals, scientists and Capitol Hill cowboys that formed his guerrila squadron.

Through departmental heads and section bosses, Feldspar utilised his authority to plumb the facilities of the CIA's research divisions. Feldspar at work, though, was a different Feldspar from the odd-ball who devoted his free time to contemplation of the philosophy of espionage. He had gradually reached the conclusion that the final product of most clandestine operations did not add up to a sack of beans; it did not justify the vast expenditure in cash, energy and lives poured out on its acquisition. Seeking a personal rationale, Feldspar figured that the CIA served a more enduring purpose than that of protecting national security and stomping on the Red Menace whenever it shucked across the board.

Recently, Feldspar had come to regard the Agency as the warehouse of a wonderful collection of tales, the foundation of a great mythological system. On miles of tape and film, in hundreds of tons of written records, were storics that would give birth to the legend of the twentieth century and become, perhaps, the Matter of America. Usually, Feldspar was not a prey to fantasy, but the weird concept kept him sane and kept him admiring the gross organisation of which he was a part.

Marks had assembled his cast: a Judas senator, Brooks Brothers godfathers, a manipulated Vice-President. Upton had groomed his buddies, his botanists and surgeons. It was left to young Harold Feldspar to recruit the Princess. He felt quite proud of his contribution. At first.

Feldspar reached his office early, having driven down from Bertram where he had spent the night in a guest bedroom in the barn. Upton would soon be leaving for San Francisco. Marks had arranged a meeting with Jay Rainer to organise the surveillance teams – an odd mixture of FBI eyeballs and wiretappers boosted, if required, by state police. Feldspar was relieved not to be involved in the furtive administration. He preferred to work alone.

The office was one of a dozen large cubby-holes that opened from a third-floor corridor in the undistinguished special research building on the corner of Wynton and Proctor. The basement was off-limits, the lair of GRETA, the computer that stored all inter-unit connections and recorded holdings of all material up to Single A restriction. Using the high-clearance identification badge that Marks had finnagled for him, he checked through security.

In his narrow office, a third telephone had been added to the pair that flanked his desk. He had returned all his files to source before taking over the Rand detail. He crossed at once to the safe and, using a coded combination that he was ordered to change each month, opened it and hauled out four telephone books and a coded interservices directory. He also extracted a tubby ring-binder, his personal directory. It contained all the unlisted numbers he'd managed to acquire and kept up to date. The binder never left the office. On changing 'locations', Feldspar required specific clearance to take the directory with him. He would have been risking more than a rap on the knuckles to try to smuggle it from the premises.

In addition to the high-band telephone that Marks had had installed, Feldspar had been allocated a top-security clearance code. Use of the high-band in conjunction with the code gave him drawing power on most sources of classified information, as far as GRETA went. Marks had assured him, through an anonymous senior officer, that the code word *Poppy* would ensure him the immediate co-operation of departmental and section chiefs within the D.O.D. and several other unspecified intelligence sectors besides. The limit had never been defined. Feldspar so far had not reached it, and co-operation had been swift and thorough on all requests to date.

To mobilise personnel, Feldspar had a new extension number on an alphabetic grouping that he recognised as that of Directorate of Operations, Clandestine Services. Apparently, he was fully tuned to cut through the chainlink system of authority and command.

Henry Marks had always been an obsessive gamesman. Within the vast interdepartmental federation that radiated from the Pentagon, Marks's power had been circumscribed by political realities. Even so the old fox had managed to step over the tripwires that Senate and Congress had laid for him and kept his tracks open. Like Dulles, Hoover and at least one recent President, the guy could not resist utilising the sporting opportunities of his post, just for the hell of it.

One knee braced on the edge of the desk, Feldspar tipped back his chair and plunged into the task that Upton had allotted him. There was no brilliance, no fine deductive achievement behind what happened that day. He just got lucky – mainly because nobody had thought to emancipate the complete Amadeus Management file before.

No doubt, Marks had held so much material back that the Amadeus file seemed too thin and inconsequential to grade in a group that might attract the attention of a full-time digger.

Halveston interested Feldspar. He was intrigued by the psychology of this amateur traitor, who had no call to risk his neck, or his reputation, by trucking doctored information. In Feldspar's opinion, Halveston would have done more good for his country by administering a student travel foundation.

Vigson he could relate to. Scientists were the best quarry for spies to chase. But Feldspar could not believe that Vigson was *that* important. Trained to respond, however, he fixed himself upon Halveston and the structure of the funding company where double-agent met double-dealer in financial intimacy.

Checking through the latest directories, Feldspar extracted a basic extension number. Lifting the receiver of the new phone, he got himself through to switchboard and onto *Circuit 2*. He identified himself only by the code name *Poppy*. A shrill, impersonal voice asked him to repeat. Pursing his lips, Feldspar breathed seductively into the mouthpiece. Stony silence. He waited. Faint chirps, electronic scramblings, like stag beetles mating in the receiver.

A brisker and more interested voice asked him what service he required. Feldspar had no notion of where his contact lived, in what building, even. It might even have been GRETA speaking for all he knew. Naturally, there would be no personnel file on Clark Helveston. But Marks had put no embargo on Amadeus

Management. Feldspar requested an All Inclusive on the Amadeus Management Corporation.

'How urgent is your requirement?'

'It's urgent,' said Feldspar.

'One hour?'

'Fine. Will I collect?'

'We'll deliver.'

It happened: *Poppy* pulled that much weight. No questions asked. Rapid service. They didn't even make him walk for his files.

'To this number, please,' he said.

'Will do.'

Feldspar lowered the receiver.

He went out into the corridor, found a vending machine, bought coffee and a candy bar and returned to his office. He saw nobody. Nobody saw him. It was barely nine o'clock, ten hours before he was due to rendezvous with Halveston and monitor the senator's vital call to Frank Varese.

One hour later, almost to the minute, the couriers arrived: a tall good-looking black woman and a dumpy blonde. They were casually dressed. The blonde carried a canvas totebag with a dyestamp portrait of Emma Goldman on it. For all Feldspar knew they had travelled across the city by bus.

The blonde heaved the totebag onto the desk. Bending, she peered at the laminated badge on his lapel.

'Pardon me,' said the black woman. 'Do you happen to know my name?'

Feldspar said, 'Poppy, right?'

Unsmiling, the blonde tipped out the totebag and deposited upon the desk a collection of documents wrapped in plastic film. She hit him with a sealed inventory. He slit open the envelope and checked the listing against the contents of the totebag.

Though he asked for an All Inclusive, he hadn't expected GRETA to be quite so thorough in the space of an hour. He signed the inventory and returned the top copy to the blonde. Without another word, she led her companion from the room.

Eagerly, Feldspar settled down to ingest the fresh material. There were two unexpected items. First was an FBI digest of reports of shortspan surveillances in connection with a bungled assassination attempt on a New York lawyer, backed by an appendix of all witnesses questioned. Second was a catalogue of wiretap conversations that could be requisitioned, if required, from the State Department's Bureau of Intelligence and Research.

Feldspar read on. Soon it became apparent that Amadeus was a low-profile financial shelter for Chinese drug dealers splitting legitimate pharmaceutical trading with underground transactions. The structure of the corporation was not documented in detail. By comparing analyses from the Audits Department with a listing of tenants in Amadeus main properties, however, Feldspar sorted out eight possible stockholders. One of them – he had no means of knowing which – would be Halveston's 'broker'. He assumed that the others were either key employees payrolled through the corporation or regular buyers. He was impressed by Halveston's foresight in accepting stock as in lieu of cash payments. Infiltration of Amadeus certainly lent credibility to Halveston's cover and furnished the senator with on-going access to scraps of information about drug activity on the East Coast.

At first, Feldspar was puzzled by the inclusion of the FBI and State Department's BIR digests. He had done his preliminary research with both eyes wide open, however, and now recalled memoranda that had drifted his way during his months of random reading. The cross-references threw him until it dawned on him that nobody had ever pulled the material together before. He could check that conclusion against the drawing records; it was hardly necessary. Obviously, the office had pinned the sheaf together on the strength of an elementary name, subject or locational coding coughed out by GRETA.

Nobody had thought to spell out the motive behind the computer's cross coding. But the lovely GRETA, a fast lady, was always logical. Comparisons quickly brought GRETA's reasoning to the surface and – via the Tale of the New York Lawyer – led him directly to Dorothy Newhoff.

The lawyer went by the euphonious name of Wolfgang Wangler. He had been winged by a bullet fired at short range on the steps of the Malvern Racquet Club. The lawyer had been a minor participant in the Sperry-Bean spy trial which, as all the world knew, was one of the biggest mysteries in an age of big mysteries.

The Sperry-Bean case had generated its share of conspiracy theories. It was mooted that John Randolph Sperry and James Warden Bean were CIA double-agents abandoned by Daddy in their hour of need and persuaded to clam up by threats on their families. The truth was much more banal. Sperry and Bean had been nothing but a couple of Defence Contract engineers recruited by an ambitious two-bit Russian Embassy official. Piqued at the dishwater the pair doled out and with the KGB breathing down his neck on account of the thirty-four thousand bucks he'd chiselled from embassy contingency funds to purchase the product, the Russian sold the little spies to a hungry reporter on a New Jersey tabloid. And thus sparked off yet another national scandal.

Wolfgang Wangler was a member of an eight-man team of legal gumshoes commissioned by the Justice Department to aid the prosecution. His one claim to fame was a bullet in the buttock. It ruined his serve-volley game but, by way of compensation, got him incredible public exposure. A puckered butt did his career no harm at all.

One theory proposed that Wangler had stumbled across information that positively linked a high government official to the Sperry-Bean case and that the h.g.o. had put out a contract to prevent W.W. spilling the beans. That theory too was balls.

Mike Foner, the assassin, was a tow-headed, twenty-four year old dropout. After shakily discharging four slugs at the quailing Wangler, Foner had hotfooted it round the gable of the Racquet Club building and raced across Broadway out of West 14th Street. Here the kid made another mistake by firing the last three rounds from his Colt Combat .38 Super in the general direction of a prowl car that happened to be parked by a Sweet'n'Sour stall where two patrolmen were conning their supper out of the owner. The younger cop, Patrolman Donald Ebart, issued the mandatory warning in a loud, slightly hysterical voice. His senior colleague, Patrolman Lou Hinkle, fired once, killing Foner stone dead. Poor Patrolman Hinkle was thus responsible for tying the NYPD into the goddamned conspiracy theory and blighting his own career as an officer. Among witnesses questioned during the course of the investigation were thirteen girls known to Mike Foner, erstwhile residents of the ghetto crashpads that Foner called home.

Narco-related charges were brought against five males of the crashpad fraternity. But officially Foner was written off as a strungout junkie who'd muffed a desperate mugging. Wangler was dismissed as the unfortunate victim of coincidence. Only press and media heat kept scandal simmering.

The girl's name appeared only once. In the appendix. No details of the conversation that the investigating officer had had with her were set down on record, only a cryptic comment that Dorothy Newhoff's contact with Foner was tenuous and immaterial.

Dorothy Newhoff. Feldspar frowned. The name had a familiar ring. He couldn't quite bring the connection to mind. He went out for more coffee and another candy bar, then returned to delve into the State Department's BIR wiretap catalogue.

Its security grading was a low P.3. A general preparatory note explained what the guys from the Bureau had hoped to gain by monitoring Florissant House. Their interest was confined to a single tenant, known as Howard Ch'ung. Ch'ung, a former interpreter for a Peking Trade Delegation, had skipped and gone underground without seeking political asylum. A year later, in 1974, an unidentified source informed the State Department's BIR that Ch'ung had surfaced in Florissant House, New York City. Further prying indicated that Ch'ung might be involved in the purchase of large shipments of strategic arms for an unidentified group, believed to be politically subversive. Phone taps had been easy to arrange. Bugging the fabric of Florissant House had proved excessively awkward though. It had not been done with sufficient discretion. Alerted, Howard Ch'ung had flown the coop.

The yield of information from the Bureau had not been high. But even before he got to it, Feldspar sensed that the link between the FBI digest and the BRI catalogue would be the name Dorothy Newhoff.

And so it was. Dear Dorothy Newhoff was a tenant in Florissant House.

Feldspar now whipped out a call requesting all material held on Dorothy Newhoff, including full FBI and BRI holdings. The Voice gave him no argument. Documents would be delivered at six that evening, held for his personal collection at the third-floor desk.

Feldspar's second call was inspired. Checking through the New York book, he found a Manhattan listing for Wangler, under Wangler, Larkin, Mason & Reeve, attorneys at law. The call caught Wolfgang in the act of limping out to lunch.

Feldspar identified himself as a member of the State Department's Bureau of Research and Intelligence. He assumed that Bureau investigators had grilled Wangler at the time of the shooting.

'Mr. Wangler?'

'Yeah.'

'My name is Holcraft, William Holcraft; from the Records Section of the State Department.'

Trustingly, Wangler said, 'And what can I do for you, Mr. Holcraft?'

'I'd appreciate clarification on a minor point in connection with your involvement in the Foner shooting.'

Wangler sighed theatrically. 'What now?'

Self-effacingly, Feldspar said, 'I'm in the process of closing out your file. Your assistance would save me hours of work.'

'Sure, sure.' Wangler was probably grateful to the State Department, to everybody – including Foner – for making him a national figure. 'How can I help?'

'How long were you resident in New York before the night of the shooting?' Feldspar asked.

'Couple of years; twenty-two months to be precise.'

'And before coming to New York, where were you located?'

'Based in San Francisco.'

Feldspar nodded to himself. Not Newhoff: Hoffman.

Casually, he said, 'Worked on the Hoffman trial, right?'

'Hoffman trial, yeah. In a minor capacity. Traced five, six witnesses for State's Counsel, that's all.'

How in Christ's name had the Bureau failed to put the pieces together? Feldspar wondered. He resisted the temptation to pump Wangler further. He was afraid that his big fat theory would pop like a bubble. He thanked the attorney, broke the connection and reached for the high-band phone. The Voice didn't seem surprised to hear from him again so soon.

'What is it now?'

'I want the complete trial record of the Bobby Hoffman case; all the volumes, no matter how many.'

'Six o'clock collection?'

'Fine,' said Feldspar. 'Just fine.'

He hung up. Grinning at his own cleverness, he locked the files into the wall safe and checked himself out of the building to eat dinner before his rendezvous with Senator Halveston. Already he was convinced that he knew Dorothy Newhoff's true identity. It would be the next morning before he learned why she was shacked up in Florissant House with a gentleman named Wing.

THE ASSASSINS

SATURDAY 20 AUGUST
SAN FRANCISCO

Pacific breezes cooled the stifling August heat. The bay was flecked with white tops, the air fresh and invigorating. Upton left the Saint Francis Hotel feeling pretty chipper. He had no doubt that he would be able to persuade Walter Stein to 'join in the fun'. The phrase had an archaic ring to it – once it had been Kingsley Roach's personal invitation to enlist in the Special Mission team and risk one's life in the smouldering ruins of Europe.

During the ten-minute ride from Union Square to the Saint Augustine Cardiothoracic Hospital, Upton prepared his approach to the world-famous – and extremely wealthy – surgeon. A bluff, flush-faced, broad-shouldered bully of a kid whose hatred of Nazis was almost pathological, Stein had needed no second invitation to work with Special Mission. In fact, he had sought out the elusive Roach and begged to be signed on. Though Stein at that time was only four years out of medical school, he had flair beyond his years and quickly gained experience in conditions that would have made an established surgeon wince. He had performed surgery in all sorts of strange places, in basements and attics, under sagging tarpaulins, in deep forests, knee deep in debris in Munich and Hamburg. Later, in Berlin itself, he was employed to stitch together the defectors and captive scientists that Roach garnered in defiance of the conventions of war.

In particular, Upton recalled a dank cellar deep below the Neuverhoven prison in Liege during the wet spring of 1944. An elderly Belgian dentist was anaesthetist. Two gaunt Flemish women who spoke no English were theatre nurses, and a coarse red-haired Scots girl was the angel of aftercare. Stein had operated for twenty-one hours at a stretch, virtually resurrecting nine of the thirteen important prisoners that the Gestapo had left for dead. Allied rockets whumped overhead. Dust rained down on cots and operating table. The flagged floor trembled with the rumble of retreating German tanks. Rigby and Upton had guarded the barred door. Roach and a Yank named Beppo had been out scouring the city for S.S. General von Graebe, a two-headed spy who deserved every drop of sweat that Roach shed to bring him out of the war in one piece.

Since the war, Walter Stein had occasionally worked for U.S. intelligence, exercising his surgical skills upon patients whose very existence had to be kept secret. Upton, however, had had no hand in these domestic undercover activities. Once or twice every year he met up with Stein to reminisce about 'old times'. The last get-together had been in Paris where Stein was showing his latest wife the sights and Upton had been lying up after a verbal mauling from a French physicist he'd been sent abroad to bribe. The reunion had started out in a gutter club in Montparnasse and, by a nebulous route, had concluded some thirty-six hours later on a sun-drenched bridge hovering over the Yvette in Saint Remy-les-Chevreuse, with Upton soberly discoursing on the genius of Pascal and Stein eating snails from a paper plate and eying his pretty young bride who lay asleep on a mohair car rug on the grass nearby.

Upton always found it difficult to envisage Stein in his natural environment. The wealthy crust of American medicine was so different from its English counterpart. Soaring blocks of steel and glass, spacious wards and corridors, the ultra-modernity of its theatres – a surgeon of Stein's calibre was like a Saxon earl in his fortress, protected by thralls and vassals. Upton had thoughtfully notified Stein of his arrival in advance.

The Saint Augustine's entrance hall was roofed with glass-like material. Its whorled texture caught and blended natural and artificial light. Upton walked soundlessly across the rubberised floor. No crammed general hospital, no sawbone's front yard, the Saint Augustine had been founded with Catholic Church cash and raised to rare heights by the skills of its Jewish surgeon.

A blonde receptionist, just old enough to give confidence to new arrivals, asked Upton to repeat his name. Before her a panel of miniature tv screens fed administrative data from one of the hospital's three computers. The woman did not have to check on Upton. She placed a hand across her breast as if the pleasure of meeting a genuine English gentleman had robbed her of breath. '*Sir* Gaw'ge Upton?'

Upton bowed.

Dark-haired and svelte as a panther, another reception nurse glided up behind Upton.

'Mizz Daw'zn will show yuh the way.'

The bustle in the corridors was restrained. All the nurses seemed beautiful and elegant. The 'hospital' odour was replaced by a fragrance of flowers. Upton followed the girl into the south wing of the building and up a hanging staircase to an octagonal room – the theatre gallery.

Eerie dead-white light silvered walls and ceiling. A raked panel of thick plastic glass looked down into the theatre. On the walls of the octagonal gallery were framed photographs of medical hardware – the Stein Prosthetic Valve, the Stein Cold Light Illuminator, and similar esoteric items, all of them for sale. Echoing voices, sucked up from the theatre below, were relayed through speakers on the gallery wall.

The receptionist showed Upton to a padded bench. He thanked her and she left.

Hunched like eagles, three residents spectated. Two were smooth well-fed specimens; the third had a grubby, half-starved appearance and scribbled notes on a yellow-leaf pad on his lap. All three ignored Upton completely.

'. . . up there yet, Jack?' Stein's accent was still faintly Teutonic, tainted by argot that he picked up indiscriminately from his students.

'Yes, Walt,' the half-starved young man answered. Upton realised that this was the physician in charge of the case.

'You have been too gotdam quiet this morning, Jack. I thought maybe you stay in bed with the Nutmeg.'

'I've got too much respect for Mr. Killian,' Jack said.

'Uh?'

'I want to make sure you don't hack out his gallbladder by mistake.'

Stein laughed; the amplified sound was like a bull walrus summoning its mate.

'What've you found in there, Walt?' the physician asked.

'Gotdam congenital bicuspid aortic valve,' Stein replied. 'Lousy left ventricle. Like Danish blue. Worse than you indicated.'

'How will you tackle it?'

'Rapid prothesis. Slap on three coronary grafts and get to hell out.'

'I think Mr. Killian has problems.'

'Believe it, pal,' said Stein distantly.

'Circulation support, right?'

'Yap. Prep a pump team, Jack.' Stein was preoccupied. 'Look like your Mr. Killian also harbours an undiagnosed pulmonary stenosis.'

'Jesus Christ,' said Jack dolefully.

Stein's reply was lost in the clatter of technicians and anaesthetists at work, industriously tugging Mr. Killian back from the brink of the grave. An occasional cussword punctuated the babel. The residents watched, saying nothing.

After three or four minutes, Jack rose.

'Good luck, Walt.'

'Yap.' Stein's head was lowered over the shrouded figure on the table.

When the physician had left the gallery, Upton moved forward to the front bench. He was grateful for the opportunity of watching Stein at work.

After thirty years of specialised surgery, Stein's techniques had become so refined that they seemed almost casual. Unlike the popular image, Stein's hands were large, the fingers spatulate inside the gossamer gloves. 'Gotdam trenching tools,' Stein had called them once. In his manipulating the instruments and in probing the bloody cavities of Mr. Killian's chest, however, Stein's inimitible delicacy of touch was evident. A ten-fingered exercise, like card-sharping, each point, each broad tip, carried out the minute, fussy engineering procedures that coronary grafting demanded. He controlled his theatre staff firmly but called everyone, right down to the assistant swabnurse, by first name. He coaxed them into the crucial act by intimacy rather than command.

Fascinated, Upton did not notice time pass. He was startled when Stein's voice boomed from the speakers. 'George, you don't look a day older. How you do that, uh?'

Stein's fingers were webbed with thirty sutures, threaded down into his palms. His powerful thighs had straightened, his broad shoulders relaxed. Tension in the fabric of his theatre greens had visibly slackened. He glanced up at the viewing panel, bushy brows raised in welcome.

'Clean living and vintage port,' said Upton.

Stein barked once more.

'Will your patient pull through?'

'You betcha,' said Stein. 'Listen, George, if you have had enough blood'n'guts for one morning, step down to the lounge and Miss Dawson will pour you a shot. I be through here, twenty minutes or so.'

The residents squinted at Upton as he left the gallery, wondering if they had passed up an opportunity to ingratiate themselves with a close friend of the master.

Miss Dawson was waiting in the lounge, an elegantly appointed room that adjoined the surgeon's changing room. When he had turned the mundane part of the operation over to his chief assistant and had washed and shed his theatre clogs, gloves, mask and gown, Stein would join him here. Miss Dawson served Upton coffee, asked him about the weather in England and then left him.

It was close to one o'clock before Stein made his appearance. He wore a lightweight suit, styled too youthfully for his bulky frame. Damp from the shower, his hair was plastered thinly to his scalp. He showed no sign of the strain of performing intricate surgery.

'Finally made it,' he said. 'Had problems hauling the guy off bypass.'

He opened a cabinet by the wall and helped himself to a shot of scotch. He seated himself on a leather couch, drank the whiskey in a swallow, put down the glass and sat back.

'Social visit, George?'

'No.'

'Figured it wasn't.'

'Shall we dance, Walter?'

'You may take me straight to bed.' Another fragment of Roach jargon.

'Very well,' said Upton. 'I'll come directly to the point, Walter. I need your help.'

'Medically?'

'Yes. It's an unofficial game.'

'Who is the mastermind – you?'

'Henry Marks is involved. We have the . . . restrained blessing of Vice-President Rainer.

'Ach – Jay. You would not tell him whole truth? Is that right?'

'That's right, Walter,' said Upton. 'I'd like you to perform an operation.'

'Where?'

'Probably right here; quite "unofficially", however.'

'Patient?'

'Gordan Rand. Male, thirty-nine years old, strong constitution.'

'What's wrong with the man?'

'Cardiac disfunction. I imagine that he will require a replacement of the aortic valve.'

'Soon?'

'Probably within the week.'

'Moonlight work?'

'Yes,' said Upton. 'Very much moonlight work.'

'Who's has been handling Rand's case?'

'Nobody.'

'Then how you know he has . . .' Stein was suspicious. 'What in hell is this you bring me?'

'I've reason to believe the condition may be infective.'

'What gotdam disease has Rand got?' said Stein, mistrust deepening. 'Better you talk to me straight, George.'

Upton explained as much of the situation as he felt Stein needed to know. The surgeon did not interrupt, but his features were too mobile to hide his disbelief.

When Upton finished, he blurted out, 'Plant infection? Mutated? Pathogenic to humans? Rip-roaring bacterial endocarditis. *Bullshit.*'

'May I remind you, Walter,' said Upton mildly, 'that Rand's colleague in England suffered precisely the same disease. He was subjected to an aortic valve homograft replacement.'

'Who did the cutting?'

'Harper. Yes, the operation was successful,' said Upton.

'So you assume Rand is also infected?'

'It's a strong possibility.'

'And half Turkish nation, too huh?' said Stein. 'Some gotdam bacterium, so selective a mutation it attacks two guys. Knock it off, George. It is Walter Stein you got here. Thirty-three years wiser than I used to be. Induced bacterial endocarditis. That much I buy. Mutation? No gotdam sale.'

'The fact remains that Gordon Rand *will* need a valve replacement.'

'What you really want George? You want me to act like bait?

You put this son on the firing line, invite the hoods to hijack the guy. You know they got to come in from the cold, trade for survival operation.'

'Essentially, that's it,' said Upton.

'What you slip him, George? Pill, powder, doctored highball? Where you buy that heart infection? Could not be Drayton Down, could it?'

For a long moment Upton studied the toes of his shoes. 'I might have known you were too downy a bird to fool, even for a little while,' he said at length. 'Yes, I fed Rand the infection. It's a virus we've had in stock for some years. It *isn't* infective; you and your team are in no danger. It's a strange little monster, though. We don't understand its habits; why, for instance, it localises its destructive action in the aortic valve. There's just no *reason*, in our knowledge of the behaviour of viruses, for that kind of selectivity.'

'Meredith, he survived after surgery?'

'He survived long enough to be murdered.'

'So?' Stein was not surprised.

'When Sarsby brings Rand here, you will perform the operation in secret. Can you keep the identity of the patient from your team?'

'Yap, easy.'

'By that time Sarsby will suspect that we have set him up. He'll wriggle and squirm to gain control of the deal again. He'll try to double-cross us.'

'How?'

'It's my guess he'll smuggle Rand out of here before the appointed time.'

'Could kill him?'

'Sarsby will be aware of the risks. But he daren't stand idle and allow the U.S. government, or any member of it, to steal his thunder. He won't trust us any more than we trust him. He'll take precautions. And we'll be ready for him.'

'You mean, George, he will take me too?'

'Rand will be your pateint, Walter. Sarsby needs you. He'll have no fear of bringing the police down on his neck. Provided he keeps Rand alive long enough to meet with Vigson.'

'You want *me* to kill Vigson?'

Upton raised his head quickly. 'Would you?'

'No opiates – a medical nightmare! Yap, I would kill such a dangerous man.'

Upton said, 'Someone must.'

'But not if it means my gotdam ass gets shot off.'

'Quite,' said Upton. 'For that reason, Walter, I would prefer to use you merely as a tool for pinpointing the location; that is, Sarsby's hideout. You will make it very clear to Sarsby or his representatives that Rand must not be subjected to an air flight. If my judgement is correct, Sarsby will put Rand to bed somewhere in California, a safe hideout not too far from here.'

'With Stein to nursemaid?'

'Yes.'

'Me and my liddle radio transmitter?'

'Yes.'

'They will search me.'

'My boffins have provided me with a miniature bleeper, a tiny coil that can be implanted beneath the skin of your heel. It has an effective pick-up range of fifteen miles and is strong enough to resist constant pounding.'

Stein nodded. 'How you manage to cover for me?'

'Can I leave that to you, Walter? I suggest you send Julie out of the country, at least to somewhere safe.'

'Precaution?' said Stein.

'Just in case,' said Upton.

Stein said, 'Sarsby brings Rand to Stein. I operate. Sarsby hijacks Rand and Stein. Hides us out. Chinese bring Vigson into country for meeting?'

'In theory, yes.'

'In practice,' said Stein, 'the Chinese are not going to sit around. They will have protection. That meeting, a potential bloodbath.'

'I know.'

'Stein and Rand, in the middle?'

'You've always had a remarkable gift for self-preservation, Walter. Just look after your patient, that's all I ask.'

'Chessboard tactics again,' said Stein. 'Interpretation, prediction of opponent's moves, forcing strategy, sacrifice for eventual gain.'

'Will you do it, Walter?'

'Not for you, George. I come in on this sizzle for Gordon Rand.

I am his one gotdam chance, is that right?'

'More or less,' said Upton.

'You are still a bastard, George.'

Upton did not deny it. He did not wish to encourage the surgeon to prod at his guilt feelings; nor did he feel that Stein was entitled to a holier-than-thou attitude. In his own way, Stein was as merciless as he was.

He said, 'I know Conrad Vigson. I know enough of the trade that the White Tiger Company are involved in to realise that it must be stopped. Stopped *now*, while it's still in embryo.'

'Because you help to give birth to plague bugs?'

'Ah, the moral argument,' said Upton. 'Fact hasn't quite caught up with fiction yet. Nothing has been manufactured that isn't under strict control.'

'Only Vigson got loose, huh?'

'I won't take all the blame for Vigson.'

'Maybe you should, George. Maybe you should.' Stein rose and poured another measure of scotch. He drank it straight, tilting his head back. 'How long before Vigson comes in?'

'We've forced the issue, put the machinery in motion. Because of Rand's illness, Sarsby will push very swiftly from now on.'

'It occurs to you, George – Rand may not make it?'

'You must ensure that he does.'

'Otherwise,' Stein laid a forefinger across his gullet. '*Shiiiiick.*'

'For all of us,' said Upton.

'Yap,' said Stein. 'This is one gotdam patient I better not bury.'

SATURDAY NIGHT
WASHINGTON, D.C.

'Is this how you always do it?' Feldspar asked. 'Call the same New York number, leave a coded message and wait for Varese to call you back?'

'It's one system,' said Halveston grudgingly. He did not see why he should be saddled with the young agent. Did Marks not trust him to shade the information correctly? He had managed satisfactorily for seven years without some boy breathing down his neck.

The men were alone in the main suite of a stockbroker block on the better side of 15th Street, a scarred brownstone that had been almost devoured by deteriorating residential zones around it. From this office, half a century ago, the Halvestons had started out. It was retained – the whole block – as a secondary seat of business. Rental of offices in the block brought in a healthy income for Clark's spinster sister who spent most of the year in Florida.

Halveston relented a little. Gesturing at the eight black phones that roved across the desk like toy tanks, he said, 'All fixed to a scrambler. Safe.'

And old domed tickertape machine, kept out of sentiment and no longer used, stood by the draped window under a conch-shaped wall lamp that illuminated it with dramatic effect. A fussy beaded desk lamp gave Halveston all the light he required.

'You wouldn't believe the thieving that went on when recession gripped the market,' he said. 'Decent, honourable brokers were transformed into ravening wolves. Stop at nothing to protect their private portfolios.'

'I'd believe it,' said Feldspar. 'Senator, have you ever met Frank Varese?'

'Never.'

'Sarsby?'

'One time, by accident, at a convention in Los Angeles.'

'Did he give any sign of recognition?'

'He offered me a cigar,' Halveston said, flatly.

One hour after Halveston's original call, Varese got back to him. Feldspar listened carefully to the senator's performance. It was a humble, greasy, shrewd, anxious, greedy act that manifested itself not only vocally but in a change of mannerisms. Bert Lahr, Feldspar thought, in a Beckett play; chilling subservience.

In contrast, Varese's voice was rich and deeply masculine and revealed nothing.

Feldspar held the earpiece extension to his cheek. His admiration for Halveston grew as the conversation limped on. Varese's pitch rose about half an octave as, with seeming reluctance, Halveston coaxed the Italian to drag everything out of him, grain by grain, while still ensuring that every gobbet of information was disgorged.

Halveston: 'Look, it isn't my place to tell you what to do.'

And Varese: 'Listen, is he sick, *is he*?'

'How would I know. Nobody knows.'

'You told me Rainer said . . .'

'Please, no names like that,' said Halveston.

'The other guy, the Englishman, he was sick?'

'There's no doubt about that.'

'He died though?'

'Look, I can only tell you what Rainer told the committee. There isn't any doubt. The Englishman was sick, was operated on, successfully, and was recovering when he was murdered. I mean, he *was* murdered; that's an established fact.'

'Okay; okay. Why're they covering up on Rand?'

'Come now,' said Halveston. 'Use your brain. How would it look if that got out? Particularly as he may be infectious.'

'Jesus. Listen, I didn't admit that we had anything to do with Rand.'

'Well, if you did – handle with care, that's my advice.'

'That other stuff? Is that true? The Chinese have this guy, this Conrad Vigson, in hiding in the Far East?'

'Every single thing I've told you is as true as I can make it,' said Halveston. 'It was presented in all good faith by Rainer to the committee.'

'This bacterium, is it really dangerous?'

'Well, Rainer had a heart specialist standing by just in case Rand went down.'

'What's wrong with the bacterium?'

'It's changed.'

'Don't talk to me like a fucking kid.'

'All right, if you must have the technical details. Vigson's bacterium has mutated, has become pathogenic to humans. It's rare but not entirely unknown with unstable biogenic material. Rainer's experts are in a state of trauma.'

'So Rand's a walking epidemic?'

'Not exactly; it seems that the bacterium in mutated form is self-confining. Do you understand me?'

'Yeah.'

'But Rand is probably infected and will suffer a severe heart condition within the next thirty-six or forty-eight hours.'

Varese was silent.

Halveston said, 'Does it matter to you if Rand dies?'

'Shit, yeah. Rainer had a surgical team standing by?'

'I told you twice, yes.'

'What surgeon?'

'No, no, Frank; this fellow can't be bought.'

'What fucking surgeon?'

'Walter Stein.'

'The big wheel in San Francisco?'

'Yes.'

'If he . . . he put in this valve, whatever, would Rand live?'

'That's the general consensus of medical opinion. You can see why Rainer's so dreadfully concerned now that Rand's been kidnapped.'

'Supposing we did have him? Hey, no, listen, do they have any clue who's taken Rand off?'

'The assumption is that it's a top syndicate concerned about the poppy bacterium,' said Halveston. 'Sarsby's name was mentioned, among others. I introduced the idea that it might be the Chinese.'

'Yeah, good for you.'

'I think that's enough. At least, until we talk money.'

'Money?'

'I'm not doing this because I approve of your outfit. I don't want to lose out on the profits.'

'We're talking about a man's fucking life, Jesus!'

'You could always dump him.'

'I could dump you too, Senator.'

'That wouldn't be prudent at this moment in time.'

'I could spill to your Chinese buddies, let them . . .'

A trace of angry resolve grated in Halveston's voice now. 'Look, I want an agreed sum, a fee. On the deal.'

'Deal – there *is* no fucking deal.'

'But there will be. I think you intend to co-operate with the Chinese. Rand is your ace. Vigson is their ace. It's obvious.'

'Nothing is fucking obvious. You know nothing about what we want with fucking Rand.'

'He's of no value to you, to the Chinese, to anyone, if he dies,' said Halveston. 'So, before we go any further on this, I want a fee.'

'Fifty thousand.'

'Don't be insulting,' said Halveston. 'I'm as aware as you are what Rand is worth, alive. More aware, perhaps.'

'What's that supposed to mean?'

'All I'm saying is that you can *sell* Rand, alive, to the Chinese. They'd pay the earth, sky and stars to get him.'

'Why?'

'My fee is two-hundred thousand dollars, in cash. Paid to me tomorrow.'

'You must be fucking crazy, think we'll shell out two hundred grand on a promise.'

'It will be worth every cent, I assure you.'

'Rand can be made to talk, for nothing.'

'Certainly – if you wish to risk killing him in the process.'

'Yeah, and I suppose you can guarantee to keep him alive.'

'Not guarantee,' said Halveston. 'But Rainer can shorten the odds. Rainer will arrange it.'

'And cut us out. I don't deal with the White House.'

'Deal with me, then. At least you know my price. For two hundred thousand dollars I'll tell you why Gordon Rand is such a hot property, and I'll act as intermediary in the deal you'll have to do with Rainer, like it or not.'

'If you're fucking screwing . . .'

'Varese, I'm the only person that can set up the deal.' Halveston spoke firmly now. 'I'll arrange to have Rand operated on by Walter Stein, in California, without Rand leaving your tender care for too long.'

'We'll get shafted by every cop, every agent . . .'

'Rainer will agree to your terms. He *must* keep Rand alive.'

'You can't do this without blowing your connections.'

'I think I can manoeuvre within the system,' said Halveston. 'It's no deep secret that I'm a member of Rainer's committee. It's plausible that you'd contact me to make the offer. From your point of view, Varese, the advantage is that I'm already on your side. It's a question of trusting me – or of watching Rand die.'

'Senator, you're a fucking leech.'

'A trusted friend of mine – who, incidentally, knows nothing of Rand or Vigson – will be waiting outside the Corcoran Art Gallery tomorrow at one o'clock . . .'

'Forget it,' Varese snapped. 'I need twenty-four hours at least. I want to be sure that Rand really is sick.'

'All right,' Halveston said. 'Ten a.m. Monday, at the steps of the Corcoran Art Gallery on 17th North West. My friend will carry a brand new black leather attaché case. It'll be empty, of course. Your man will carry a similar attaché case, with two hundred thousand in large denomination bills in it. I think we can leave it to them to make the transfer discreetly. Have you got all that?'

'I'll get back to you,' said Varese. 'My boss may not want to buy.'

'That's up to you and your boss,' said Halveston. 'Just bear in mind that the White Tiger Company have it in their power to bust you; and that means a million a month down the tubes and you go out of business rather swiftly.'

'How much of this did you get from the horse's mouth?'

'I don't understand.'

'From your Chinese pals?'

'Just be thankful, Varese, that I did do a little bit of sideline selling of information,' said Halveston. 'Otherwise, I wouldn't be talking to you now.'

'Right, all right.'

'I'll call you Monday – after I get the payment.'

'*If* you get the fucking payment.'

'Two hundred thousand. Cash. Monday.'

'Maybe.' Varese broke the connection.

Gently Halveston lowered the receiver. Dabbing his brow with a handkerchief, he glanced at Feldspar. 'I think he'll buy it, don't you?'

'Uh-huh.'

'Now what?' said Halveston.

'I go buy myself a brand new black leather attaché case,' Feldspar said.

Feldspar held a finger in the pages of the fourth volume of the trial transcript and jammed the telephone receiver against his shoulder. The office was silent, except for the low purr of the air-conditioning. Down the corridor, the duty janitor would be setting himself up in his glass-walled cage for the wee small hours of Sunday morning, his salami-on-rye, flask of coffee and the bulky wad of the newspapers laid on his counter. Apart from floor janitors and basic security staff, there were unlikely to be any other bodies toiling in the offices at that hour of the weekend. Even the switchboard operator had sounded unusually dull and drowsy.

Feldspar had delivered a phoned report on Halveston's bilking of Varese. He concluded, 'Varese will report to Sarsby and they'll check out Rand's physical condition; then, I imagine, they'll buy the package.'

'They have very little choice,' said Upton.

'Sir George, why didn't we put a tag on Frank Varese?'

'Do you know where he is?'

'No, but . . .'

'There's nothing really to be gained by spooking that gentleman.'

'Is it worthwhile spooking the Tigers?' said Feldspar.

'Why do you ask?'

'I think I may have turned up Meredith's assassin.'

'That was bloody quick,' said Upton.

Feldspar explained the logic behind his deductions, picking out salient points from the evidence he had gathered.

'Tell me about Wing's mistress,' said Upton.

'Dorothy Newhoff, formerly Dorothy Hoffmann. If my guess is accurate, she's the mate of Robert Hoffmann, the so-called cult leader now incarcerated in Barbary Point prison serving ninety-nine years.'

'I've heard of Hoffmann,' said Upton. 'Similar type to Manson.'

'Not really so similar,' said Feldspar. 'Hoffmann killed for profit and revenge. Maybe he's crazy by our definition, but there was no hint of demonic attraction in his leadership, though the drug influence was strong.'

'Where is Barbary Point prison?'

'California. Not too far from San Francisco as it happens. It's high-security. Hoffmann's still considered dangerous. He took the whole rap himself. None of his followers were convicted. At the time of Hoffmann's arrest they vanished into the woodwork; didn't hang around; didn't squat on the courthouse steps. He was convicted on four counts of first-degree murder, acquitted on a bunch of lesser charges for lack of concrete evidence. The murders were savage, but a profit motive could be ascribed to each of them. Hoffmann was into several nasty rackets, drugs and extortion mostly. He had decided to knock off the competition.'

'Go on.'

'Hoffmann's woman, his commonlaw wife, came of the proceedings smelling like a rose.'

'Strange.'

'Very strange,' Feldspar agreed. 'She was a drifter Hoffmann picked up along with a group of other girls. He appears to have treated her differently, with . . . well, respect. He kept her apart from the gang, stashed her away in a trim little cottage in Sacramento.'

'Home is where the heart is,' said Upton. 'The wife, the woman, did she remain in Sacramento after Hoffmann's conviction?'

'Within twenty-four hours of the jury bringing in its verdict, the wife vanished, disappeared from the face of the earth.'

'And the rest of Hoffmann's associates?'

'Some were kept under surveillance, for a while. Oddly, three died within the next half year.'

'Not from natural causes, I assume?'

'Drug overdose in all three cases.'

'Do you think that the missing wife had a hand in the killings?'

'That's my guess. It'll take some time to track down the evidence, piece it together from root sources, and . . .'

'Keep guessing, Feldspar,' said Upton. 'Guesswork will have to do for now.'

'Hoffmann didn't put up much of a case for himself. It wasn't one of those knock-down, drag 'em out trials. No circus. It was all over in eighteen days. The appeal came to nothing. I gather from the transcript, Hoffmann gave the defence lawyers nothing to work with. He sung dumb. In fact, he comes over as vague, stupid and petty in the printed account.'

'Ah-hah,' said Upton. 'The power behind the throne was the commonlaw wife, is that what you're driving at?'

'Dorothy, yes. I figured Hoffmann took the fall to protect her.'

'Ninety-nine years is a very long time?'

'Perhaps he trusted Dorothy's promise to shorten his sentence.'

'Or take revenge on the folk who put him away?'

'Or both.' Feldspar tugged his notes from behind the legal tome and read out cryptic points to Upton.

When the agent had finished, Upton asked, 'How did she team up with Wing?'

'God knows,' said Feldspar. 'Her motives are pretty obvious.'

'She needed a . . . what's the word – sugardaddy?'

'Quaint, Sir George, but accurate,' said Feldspar. 'She probably needed a reliable feeder to keep her happy on heroin. Wing was the ideal person to increase her sphere of influence, to enable her to build up a bankroll and lay long-term plans to retrieve her "husband".'

'Rather heavy on the conjecture, Feldspar?'

'Perhaps. What is hard fact, however, is that this girl's a tenant in Florissant House, the Amadeus property in New York. She's the "constant companion", shall we say, of Wing, a gentleman who fills the bill as the Chinese number one contract artist.'

'Did Wing, and/or the girl, leave the country in the past week?'

'No way of knowing.'

'What do you propose to do, Feldspar?'

'Boldly go,' said Feldspar, 'and interview Miss Newhoff.'

'An arrest or a surveillance?'

'Neither.'

'Lean on the Chinese, you mean.'

'In my own inimitable manner. Do I have your approval, Sir George?'

'Yes,' Upton said. 'Fire ahead. But Feldspar, be careful.'

SATURDAY EVENING
THE PAIUTE RANCH – CALIFORNIA

Rand had no memory of his flight across America. He had a hazy, dream-like recollection of waking once and seeing the curved skin of the airplane – a Cessna twelve-seater – above his head, of the straps that held him to the stretcher and of being filled, for his few brief moments of consciousness, with a sense of raging helplessness. He did not feel the prick of the needle and had drifted to sleep again with a sensation of drowning.

When next he recovered consciousness, he was propped more or less upright between two burly men. He opened his eyes. Splinters of light pierced his brain, bringing pain. He groaned and cramped forward. A gentle arm lifted him back. His head ached, his mouth was foul, his bladder felt achingly full. He groaned once more.

Fingers lifted his right eyelid. 'Dr. Rand?'

He had no will to resist.

'Dr. Rand?'

'Where . . . ?' Lips blubbery, words so slurred that he could barely decipher them himself. 'Where . . . ?'

'Don't worry, Doctor.' The voice was calm, educated. 'You are suffering nothing more permanent than a hangover.'

'Where . . . am . . . ?'

'The journey is almost over. Rest and natural sleep will refresh you,' the voice told him. 'If it's any comfort, may I say that I'm experienced in administering barbiturates. You have received a controlled dosage of amylobarbitone sodium, boosted with chlorpromazine. Your discomfort will soon pass off.'

Rand strove to take in everything that the voice said, to relate it to his fragmented memory of the kidnapping, the gunplay, and all that had gone before.

'Who . . . are . . . ?'

'Call me Tony. My close friends call me Tony.'

Pieces were clicking into place.

The pressure in his bladder was agonising. However, the effort of will required to keep himself from voiding urine seemed to hasten his recovery. An ache in his chest and shooting pains in neck and head diminished slightly, replaced by heart palpitations. He did not dare open his eyes again, afraid of the bright, brittle light.

The vehicle bounced and swayed over rough surfaces.

He embarked on the process of deduction and interpretation.

'Dr. Rand? I would appreciate a few words from you.'

'I . . . I need to pee.'

'Of course you do. I ask you to restrain yourself for five more minutes, that's all. Can you hold on?'

Rand opened his eyes. The light was fiery. Shapes of the driver and the occupant of the passenger seat were like cutouts in the foreground of a distinct focal place. It was like peering through a mailbox at a Martian landscape. Rand struggled to make relationships, squinting at the inhospitable country.

Nevada? New Mexico? Vast, semi-desert waste. Beige dust billowed from the wings of the vehicle and crested back along the windows in a gritty rolling cloud. Deliberately Rand blotted out the men and concentrated on the land. Blue-grey mountains.

Burnt-brown foothills. Air clear. No trees visible. No meadows. No farmsteads. Rough riding.

Rand clenched his fists and squeezed them down into his lap. His head was splitting and the palpitations continued, *thud-thud-thud*, like a Congolese drum, inside his chest. He blinked and shifted his attention to the interior of the wagon. A Chevrolet Blazer, new model. Radio viced to the dashboard. The driver wore wash-leather gloves, like a rodeo cowboy, and had hairy arms and a shirt of dark blue towelling material. A clean-shaven jaw was beaded with sweat in spite of the full blast of the air-conditioning.

'No, Dr. Rand, it certainly isn't Washington.'

The man – Tony – smiled. He was plump, smooth and urbane, in city duds. He had the kind of languid sophistication that suggested he might be a homosexual.

'Then it must be . . . New York,' said Rand.

Tony laughed appreciatively at his prisoner's witticism.

Rand felt the intoxication ease, though the pain in his chest was still there, throbbing. He screwed his fists deeper into his lap. He figured the men to be representatives of the gang that Meredith had feared, hoods, mobsters. Chinese, American, Turkish? Almost certainly American.

'How do you feel now, Dr. Rand?'

'Still need to pee.'

'Soon, very soon.'

The driver glanced over his shoulder and nosed the Blazer up a curving incline. Outside, Rand glimpsed a fence, a phantom of perspective. Then his attention was caught by thirty or forty sturdy mustangs thundering through the dust cloud. The run of the herd paralleled the Blazer's course, four, five hundred yards out from it. The animals were the colour of the earth, with streaming manes and heaving flanks.

The torpedo on Rand's left leaned across him, agog. 'Man, look't dem ponies go.'

The herd sheered off and vanished back along the trail.

'Up ahead, Dr. Rand,' Tony said, 'is our destination.'

The building reminded Rand of a resort lodge – only there was no ocean, no ski slopes or green golf course close to it. It crouched above the valley on a spike of rocky ground at the mouth of a shallow arroyo that ran almost vertically into the foothills. A ranch. A dude ranch, Rand thought; run down. Bulging corral below the main building. Adobe cabins scattered round an artificial pond, flat and brown as a biscuit below the dry throat of the draw. Main block had a pitched roof; two storeys; a balcony under deep projecting eaves; tiny windows, most of them shuttered with weathered boards.

The Blazer sped on, skipping and bucketing onto a hard surface that broadened to surround the complex inside patchwork fences. The whole place had burned up, except for a small area by the cabins where shrubs and small trees sprouted from tubs, and trailing flowers made a splash of colour.

'It's not so uncomfortable as it appears, Dr. Rand,' Tony told him. 'You'll be well cared for and able to enjoy a breath of desert air between sessions.'

'Sessions?'

'Exchanging information.'

'Yeah,' said Rand.

The Blazer slowed, swung and halted adjacent to steps that lead up to a patio that in turn cornered the block. Two men stood there. Caretakers. They had the leathery dessicated appearance of desert dwellers and wore faded cowboy rig unselfconsciously. One in levis and plaid shirt. Older man in denim overalls, bib latched over the top of a union suit. Two slat-sided pick-up trucks were parked in the yard. A buckboard, tilted on its side, made a barricade between the house and the path to the cabins. The height of the foothills and mountains had deceived Rand; the building cluster was tighter than it looked.

Tony helped him from the hatch. Rand's legs, like latex, would hardly bear his weight. He stumbled.

'Let me help you.' Tony lead Rand to the nearest corral post. Rand braced himself, fumbled with his zip and emptied his bladder while his guardian politely studied the sky.

The grogginess was passing. Rand found that he was able to disregard the pain in his chest and temples. He needed some kind of an early edge over these guys – if he could find one. Christ, he needed to know where he was, for a start. He was more angry than afraid.

Resting his brow on the rail, he took several deep breaths of thin mountain air and peered back along the trail that wandered along the narrow valley. Seeing the mountains all of a piece, dry, tall and jagged, Rand suddenly reckoned he knew where they'd brought him.

Six years back he'd been hired by the Pacific Crest Task Force, a powerful ecological group concerned about despoilation of the Owens Valley Region. The L.A. Water Department was a traditional enemy, unscrupulously tapping not only lakes and surface catchments – which they'd been doing for fifty years – but also claiming underground water rights in their quest for water to squander on the expanding city. Rand had teamed with a geologist to prepare a report on the fragile ecology of Mono Lake, to submit a survey of the botanical significance of the entire rift valley from the Mojave to the flanks of the Yosemite.

He had been fascinated by the rare species to be found in the area, particularly the bristlecone pine. He had devoted many weekends to expanding the study and had come to know the Owens Valley wilderness pretty well. Well enough to identify the ridges of the Inyo Mountains that enclosed the ranch.

Cautiously he lifted his head. Tony still had his back turned. Guards were unpacking cartons of supplies from the Blazer. He noticed a couple of fleece coats being toted up the steps into the living quarters. The caretakers were motionless, lazy, giving him the hard eye from a distance.

'Finished?' Tony's sympathy had a sinister quality.

'Give me a couple of minutes to breathe.'

'Take all the time you need, Dr. Rand.'

Rand kept his head down, draping his arms on the rail. Canyon dog-legged on a south-west diagonal. He hadn't visited this particular sprig. He figured it lay west of the Westgard Pass where the White Mountains heaved into the Inyo, south of the river along the barren stretch between Big Pine and Independence. A track forked out of the hamlet of Liberon across the sturdy old Bloodworth Bridge, a track that headed into nowhere. Many such tracks webbed the wilderness, running to deserted ranches. Some had been converted into motels or ski and trek lodges. But many had been built too early to catch the wilderness tourist boom, had failed and been sold off for a quick ten cents on the dollar by their power baron owners.

Tony's hand on his shoulder caused Rand to start. His nervous system was inflamed. The shock of the man's touch made him tremble and his knees go weak. He scanned the towering mountains as his captor guided him across the yard towards the block.

Faint dusting of snow on the summits, matching the alkaline smudges on the canyon floor. No alfalfa, no sheep, no cattle. Only mustangs, refugees from the original ranch herd maybe, or imports from Arizona or Nevada to add cowboy colour? How many miles from habitation, from a telephone? Liberon must be fifteen, twenty miles away across the hostile ridge. How far by the exposed, bonewhite road? Thirty?

Christ, he was a prisoner in his own home state. Three hours out from L.A.; four, five from San Francisco; yet he could hardly have been more cut off if the bastards had flown him back to the Turkish uplands or all the way to China.

For a moment anger was red and raw in him. His body responded weakly to the emotion, trembling again. He *must* discover who they were and why they'd snatched him.

Leaning on Tony's shoulder – catching a whiff of expensive male cologne – he was guided along the porch and into the cool umber interior of the block. Neglect was not evident within. Anyone of Hollywood's perennial cattle barons would have felt right at home. The decor was overwhelmingly masculine. Huge longhorns were mounted over a stone hearth – creased leather chairs and settles, paintings of warpath redskins, prancing cavalry. The largest Navaho blanket he'd ever seen covered half the floor of the vast living room.

It was erstaz as hell, of course. The Owens history was one of peaceful agricultural takeover by the settlers of Paiute lands, followed by the rape, in 1910, of prosperous pastures by the L.A. Department of Water and Power. No troopers had galloped past this arroyo, only official Angelenos in search of pools to tap to sprinkle the lawns of Beverley Hills.

From the corridor that ran under the heavy staircase, Rand heard guards stocking away provisions.

'Very habitable, you see.' Tony drew him to a pinewood door at the rear of the living room. 'Your private quarters, Dr. Rand.'

Cream walls, a bed, a chair, washstand with jug and basin, plasic trailer toilet; like a cell. One square window, fitted with an iron grid, let in warm light.

A pitcher of water stood on the washstand, also a bowl of icecubes.

'You're thirsty?'

'Yeah.'

'Prolonged sedation always has that effect,' Tony said. 'Drink as much water as you wish, but sip it slowly.'

Rand reached for the glass and dashed ice into it. He poured from the pitcher, spilling water everywhere. The man did not offer to assist him.

'You aren't *that* unwell, Dr. Rand,' Tony said.

Rand gulped the water. He filled the glass again and sank back into the bed with it, gasping. The guy was right, though. Apart from the tightness in his chest and throbbing head, he was beginning to feel almost human again.

Tony stood in the doorway. 'Rest now, Dr. Rand.'

'Wait! Listen, I . . .'

'I assume that you know where you are?'

'How the hell would I know that? Last thing I remember I was in Washington.'

'Tut, tut!' Anthony Bulthius chided. 'You're not much of a liar, Dr. Rand. Anyhow, I read your contribution to the Pacific Crest Report. Became quite incensed, did you not?'

Rand busied himself with the water pitcher again to hide his irritation.

'In about an hour you'll be hungry,' Bulthius said. 'I'll arrange for food to be brought in.'

'How long do you intend to keep me in this room?'

'Until you've recovered.'

'And then?'

'I'm not your interrogator, Dr. Rand.'

'Who is?'

'You'll meet him in the morning.'

'Listen . . .' Rand waved his arm, splashing water on the bed. 'I don't know what you expect to get from me, but . . .'

'No noise, Doctor. No excitement,' said Bulthius. 'You'll have plenty of opportunity to make a noise tomorrow.'

The door closed; a bolt rattled.

Rand lay back, sipping water, sweating now, and trembling again.

Jay Rainer had dropped him straight into a goddamned cesspool. Now he had to work out just what the mobsters wanted from him – so that he could give it up at once.

Fuck the government. It had never been his fight.

SATURDAY NIGHT
NEW YORK

Head pressed back on heels, her body was arched like a bow. Incredible tautness flattened her belly, made her breasts stand out from her ribcage like pinons. Sexual ecstasy and sculptured abandon – a well-rehearsed act, of course. Mr. Wing enjoyed it nonetheless.

All life, said an ancient philosopher, was a precarious ritual of balancing duty and desire, good and evil, need and necessity. Bangkok dancers mimed the conflict perfectly, though no better than the nude corps-de-ballet, three girls and a boy whose gyrations he'd watched through an aquarium-like window in a nightspot in Los Angeles.

Mr. Wing was not repressed. He could deliberately let go. The girl's ability to excite him mattered on such occasions, not her merits as an assassin.

He mated as a snake does, gratified that he had finally found a cold-blooded female with whom to copulate. Nature demanded such harmony. Wing achieved domination by withholding the hypo until she sweated, twitched and writhed in need of him. He laughed like a cooing dove, without a trace of sardonic distaste, as she begged him to put it into her, shoot it into her.

All a matter of chemistry. Even a tumescent penis and quivering nerve-ends were the results of chemistry. Tonight, however, he did not speculate on the mysteries of man and woman. Sentiment softened the proceedings. He was taking a temporary farewell. The great provider had been summoned away.

Naked, he thrust upon her, hairless body weaving. He placed his hand upon the petals, pressing them wide to accommodate his knuckles. She rose higher still from the sheet, so high that he expected her vertebrae to crack.

Mr. Wing lowered his head. In lovemaking, he believed himself to be languid, non-aggressive. But his style was patterned to include a tiny bit of cruelty, for Dorothy's pleasure more than his own.

Though she was no great beauty, she was large, flaxen and young. Mr. Wing had never relished the attentions of professionals, Western or Oriental. They were to unctuous for his tastes. Dorothy cared not at all for intercourse. As the result of excess beyond his imaginings, she had dried out. Even so, she performed well, indulged him. Mr. Wing was a slave to chemistry like any other male, whatever the colour of his skin.

Finally, after checking his watch, he climbed aboard and balled the girl from the top all the way to satisfaction. She supported him like a mare, grunting, bucking until Wing slid sleekly from her. She sank promptly back into the bed. Her fingers clawed at the sheet. She hissed, 'Give it to me now.'

Wing padded into the shower.

She rolled her head. 'Please, Wing. *Give it to me.*'

He made her wait. Exercises for the will were beneficial to young girls. Besides, she was just a weeny bit stubborn. Delay would increase her awareness of her reliance on him.

After five minutes, he emerged from the bathroom. His loins were draped in soft blue towels, like a youthful Sumo wrestler. Dorothy's eyes trailed him as he crossed to a walnut cabinet, unlocked it, brought out the glissane envelope and carried it between finger and thumb to the foot of the bed.

She waited. She knew what he wanted, what he would do. She was racked okay. But not suffering, not *really* suffering.

He edged the envelope into her, with a cooing chuckle. She held herself immobile until, shaking his head, Wing returned to the bathroom. Then and only then she plucked out the packet, bit it open, hauled open the drawer of the night-table and dragged out the gear.

Quickly, but with care, she hit the fix. Cleaned the spoon, broke the hypo and wrapped both in tissue. Slid the tissue into the box to dispose of later, then, luxuriating, rolled onto her side. And thought of Bobby. Roberto. And how she would free him soon.

Wing seemed far away, in the tunnel between bedroom and living room. Dressed in topcoat and cashmere scarf, though a heatwave was moving in to the coast and humidity in the streets was high. The stupid black fedora made him look like Mr. Moto or a son of Charlie Chan. A large suitcase was by his side.

She took it all in with idle attention, before mild panic spurted through her rational mind. She sat up abruptly.

'Dorothy, I must leave you now.'

'You didn't tell me.'

'There was no need to tell you.'

'How long you be gone?'

'I'm uncertain; five or six days, I expect.'

As he approached the bed, he was so relaxed that he seemed to float across the carpet. His fingers on her cheek like the wings of moths. 'You must take care of yourself until I return.'

'But Wing! Jesus . . . I mean.'

'In the cabinet. One week's supply. Pure and cut accordingly. But don't become so bored that you throw a party. Two sachets would kill even you, Dorothy.'

'Seven bags. What if you don't . . . ?'

'I'll send a friend with more.'

'Wing? Wing?'

At the door, the suitcase in his hand, he paused.

'You *are* coming back?' she asked.

'Yes, Dorothy. You will be here when I return, won't you?'

'Where else've I got to go?'

Already she was thinking in beautiful colours. Stained-glass colours. California. Home. Home. Home. She might ride the Greyhound across the country. She had money put away. And an emergency supply plus the seven good bags that Wing'd left. She might go see Bobby. Not in the flesh. But look up from the highway at the hill, at Barbary Point stuck out on the baked earth like a butte. Just gaze at the walls, count the windows, speculate on which one was his cell. Maybe she'd do just that, while Wing was away.

On the other hand, she could make more bread staying in New York. She had a couple of scores to settle yet, scores that had been shelved during her time with the Chink, personal matters that Wing knew nothing about. One bag per day would juice her. The progress of her life, her *real* life, would be forward.

Her eyelids were heavy.

'Bye, Wing. Bye, bye.'

He had already gone.

Next thing Dorothy knew, the cop was leaning on the foot of the bed with the gun trained on her cunt. The long dream of the night was over and her life had twisted around.

SUNDAY 21 AUGUST
THE PAIUTE RANCH

Frank Varese's Uncle Guido had played the banjo with Al Capone in the Roman Catholic Church of Alcatraz in the dogdays of the big fellow's career. Later, in New York, Uncle Guido had imparted the philosophy of the hoodlum to his nephew, indoctrinating the lad in the unexpurgated wisdom of the bandits who ruled the streets through the 'twenties and 'thirties. But Frank was no punk, no zip-gun carrier. Thanks to his mother, he was brought up smart. Respect for the good management of money was hammered into him.

A product of tenement society, polished by his terms as a business school student, Frank was an ideal candidate to become Sarsby's aide. He had known Sarsby for many years. They'd met in a Blue Moon club on the Strip during the year that Frank was seeking the sun as a cure for the patch on his lung that kept him out of the army. They'd shared booze and an occasional broad and, by the rating of the crooks with whom they associated, were a circumspect and thrifty pair: Frank, the muscle; Arnold, the brain. Together they scaled the heights of organised crime without being caught in Sicilian landslides or falling off the edge of the law.

Inwards, however, Frank was a little unsure of himself. During the past half dozen years Sarsby's deals had become more and more complex and esoteric. Sometimes Varese felt he was being left behind. Where he scored over Arnold was in his attitude to travel. He did not regard New York as his patch. He was broad-minded enough to make the world his oyster. On the other hand, Sarsby hated airplanes, boats and automobiles. In that single respect he retained the mentality of the whitehaired boys of the Boulevard whose horizons stretched only from Long Beach to Santa Monica. Varese, the legs; Sarsby, the tongue.

From New York, Frank Varese had hitched a ride on the West Coast shuttle. He arrived with the other nightriders in the velvet dawn that wrapped Los Angeles. He made his exit north-east across the Soledad Pass on Highway 6, travelling fast in the Turbo Porsche he'd had sent from the Burbank Autorama that was one of his lesser holdings in the state. He had toyed with the idea of leasing a chopper again. But he disliked the trip over the mountains.

Between townships he pushed the Porsche hard, hoping to make the ranch before the temperature soared.

The Paiute had been an early investment. It didn't worry Sarsby that the ranch failed to draw tourists. Its value lay in the vast cellars beneath the stables, cellars easily converted into a refining plant for the raw opium that was smuggled up from Mexico. Four years back the Feds had become so aggressive that Sarsby had decided to close the refinery and transfer activities to the Baja where smugglers worked by the boatland.

As he powered the Porsche over the Bloodworth Bridge into the Pronghorn canyon, Varese cleared his mind of respect for Rand's position. Balthius would handle the technical angle. Halveston's data would furnish him with opening gambits to add weight to his strong right arm. He'd always had the ability to frighten people into co-operation. If that tactic failed, he would turn Balthius loose on the poor sonuvabitch, let Tony stick him full of needles. Tony would know if Rand's health were failing.

In the back of his mind, Varese was terrified of the strange disease. He tried to convince himself that Halveston was lying. Trouble was, he trusted the fucking senator. Halveston had been checked and re-checked. He was greedy, selfish and shrewd enough to be honest. Any senator who sold out his position *had* to be clever enough to split his interests. When it came to the wire, though, Halveston would side with Sarsby, not with some goddamned Chink outfit.

The sun inched over the eastern rim of the mountains. Blue-denim shadows were shrinking as Varese slewed the Porsche into the yard and braked to a standstill by the corral. He felt himself threatened worse than ever, like a pearl-diver confronted by a lagoon in which lurked unknown creatures. Gathering his courage, Varese hurried up the steps and into the living room of the block. He ignored Balthius's startled greeting.

'Where's Rand?'

'There.'

He strode across the room, shot back the bolt and flung open the bedroom door. Rand was seated at the table, head on hand, picking listlessly at the steak and eggs on the plate before him. He wore an undervest and had a two-day stubble and bruised bags under his eyes. His pallor caused Varese to stop on the threshhold. Sick-white waxy skin made Rand's lips seem purple, like an old wino's.

Varese and Rand stared mutely at each other. Egg yolk dripped from Rand's fork onto his vest. Quickly Varese stepped back, closed the door and snapped the bolt. Turning, he found Balthius close behind him.

'Is *he* sick?' Varese demanded.

'It's an ab-reaction to the drugs I gave him.'

'Balthius, you're supposed to be a fucking chemical expert.'

'Rand's metabolism . . .'

'*He's sick.*'

'Frank, it's quite safe to question him. He isn't that sick, you know. He's playing it up.'

'Yeah? Supposing I told you Rand's liable to die on us.'

'Poison?' asked Balthius.

'Heart disease – a fucking *infectious* heart disease.'

'Impossible!'

'Look at him, for Chrissakes.'

'Frank, he's displaying perfectly natural symptoms of shock and accumulated fatigue. Remember, he only got home from Turkey couple of days ago. Plus the sodium . . .'

'The English botanist,' said Varese, 'contracted the same disease. They had to operate on him to save his goddamned life. In London. Know where he picked up the disease? From that fucking bacterium.'

'Oh, then why aren't the Chinese . . . ?'

'*How the fuck would I know?*' Varese shouted.

'Who told you this, Frank?'

'It's authentic information. Government had a surgeon primed, ready to operate on Rand when we took him.'

'What effect does the disease have?'

'Christ, Bulthius, I just told you – heart. *Heart.*'

'So, you've been lead to believe that Rand's a walking germ-factory. Is that why you're so up-tight?'

Varese controlled his fury. 'It's possible, isn't it?'

'Frank, my friend, I think you've been conned.'

'Then you get on in there, Bulthius, and examine him.'

'I suppose I *could* check his pulse-rate, breathing, chest signs.

Basic routines. I don't have equipment to run a blood or urine test.

'*Check him out, Tony.*'

'Frank, this disease *can't* be contagious, whatever else it is.'

'I don't want him dying on me during interrogation.'

'Ah, yes, of course,' said Bulthius diplomatically. 'We do rather want to keep the good doctor alive, don't we?'

Bulthius fetched a brown bag from an upstairs room. He glanced at Varese, who was drinking hot coffee. Varese imagined derision in that look, as if the chemist were humouring a scared kid.

Bulthius went into the bedroom cell, closing the door behind him. For twenty minutes, Varese was obliged to cool his heels. Then Bulthius slipped out of the bedroom again.

'Well?' Varese snapped.

'Rand is sick, and it's genuine.'

'Christ!'

'I don't understand it.'

'What's wrong with him, exactly?'

'Frank, I'm no doctor.'

'Bulthius,' said Varese threateningly.

'Well, his respiration *is* very irregular. Blood pressure's up. I can't interpret the sounds in his heart. Chest sounds congested.'

'Try.'

'Murmurs, loud and obvious. May signify nothing very serious.'

'Or?'

'A valve defect.'

'How soon can you tell beyond doubt?'

Bulthius shrugged. 'We'd require a full examination: EKG, X-rays, blood work-up. I can't do that here. Anyhow, I don't have the knowledge.'

Varese placed a palm across his mouth and stroked his fleshy nose with forefinger and thumb.

'Can I talk to the guy? Is he conscious?'

'Yes, he's conscious. But don't . . . you know, don't pressure him, Frank. Not until we're sure that the condition's . . .'

'Open the fucking door,' Varese said.

Crossing himself devoutly, he stepped into the sunlit cell.

SUNDAY MORNING
NEW YORK

'Move a muscle, kid, and you're dead.'

She came up with the sheet draped round her, like something from the grave, eyes clicking open, mouth opening wide.

Drapes were still drawn against the muggy dawn that struggled up over New York. Sunday morning in the city, a time of hang-overs, remorse and sticky summer itch; a dead time in the sour August heat. The girl was so much part of it – an expensive apartment in an underworld hang-out; B-movie stuff, grainy and steeply-lighted.

The sheet seemed to peel away from her body in slow motion. The swollen silencer on the Python .357 Magnum, one of two handguns that Feldspar had checked out of his personal armoury, was pointed directly at her flaxen belly. She looked leonine in her nakedness, with firm oval breasts and young plum-coloured nipples that, for some reason, were erect. Her flanks were slightly downed with blonde hair. Muscular thighs; a handsome athletic animal, Feldspar thought, all grace and cunning. No cosmetics; a natural force.

The blue eyes blinked once. She rolled, hips first, then shoulders. Faster than he would have believed possible for a girl, let alone a junkie.

The knife was an ancient Boone Huntsman with a taped handle. She had it stashed under a corner of the mattress, where some kids kept a crucifix, a treasured locket or a college pin.

It was all over in a split-second. Feldspar thanked his stars that he was still keyed-up from a stealthy approach to the building and a soft ascent to the apartment. He pushed himself left, pivoting away from her. Bending his left knee, he flicked out his right foot. The shoe heel snapped against her forearm. The weapon skit-tered to the carpet. She uttered no sound at all, rolled once more. Thrusting away from the bedtable, she charged him.

Balanced and prepared, Feldspar blocked with his right thigh. He tapped the butt of the Python against the side of her jaw. Her hands groped for his groin. He caught her hair and pulled her on down, dropped his weight on her, knees pinning her shoulders, forearm pressing hard on the nape of her neck.

Prick marks peppered her arms. The veins were like blue wool threads. To his surprise, Feldspar felt no revulsion, only a kind of release, admiration for her agility and the fact that she'd responded, not surrendered, to the drop. Deep down, the agent experienced an odd quality of exultation. It reminded him of his youth, his vigour, a stimulating assurance that combat was not a matter of committees, dead letter drops, codes, documents and disembodied voices.

He jabbed the silencer against her pelvis and leaned closer to her hair. Beads of perspiration dewed her spine. He could smell her body. It was not unpleasant.

'Where's the man?' he said. 'Come on, kid. Where's your Chinaman?'

She was breathing deeply, ribs heaving. Hyper-ventilating.

Jesus, Feldspar thought, she's a wild one all right. She's not quitting. She's gathering to try me again. He was less gentle, settling his weight, crushing all possibility of movement.

'Wing?' he said. 'Where is he?'

'You won't find him.'

'I know he isn't here. So where is he?'

'What's your fucking problem, mack?' she said.

He had got to her; gotten a response, slit the protective professional layer that she'd wrapped around herself. Though Feldspar had no means of knowing it, he was talking to Dorothy Newhoff, Bobby's woman, not to Wing's helpmate, Wing's automated lover.

'Not juice, kid,' said Feldspar. 'I'm not interested in your stock of juice. Just tell me about Wing?'

'Or what?'

'I'll kick your ass all over this apartment.'

She laughed, scornfully.

'Shit, you're no hardnosed narco,' she said.

'Good guess.'

'Going to ride on my back all day?'

'Maybe I won't kick you around this apartment,' said Feldspar. 'Not with all those little yellow ears to hear you yell your head off. Think I'll take you to a nice quiet place and let you dry out slowly. How about that?'

'Suit yourself.'

It had not occurred to Feldspar that he would effect entry to the Florissant so easily or that he would find the girl alone. He had come in like a bull, horns lowered, prepared to take out the assassin if he had to. Upton had virtually given him *carte blanche*. To cop the girl was even better. That would shake the Tigers' topgun for sure. As he lifted himself carefully from her, he wondered just how much she did know about the Tigers' business and how much she could be made to reveal. Probably, given time, she would spill everything just for one shot of H. He had her typed already. Maintained addiction. She was getting it regularly without having to hustle. No signs of emaciation; just tattooed scars over the veins and constricted pupils.

He had other problems to cope with, however; more practical things to think about. How to get her out of the Florissant building for starters. He had burgled his way in from the laundry room in the basement. Expertise in the use of various tools had been a part of his training. He was good at it, dexterous. He had a holy horror, though, of running into Wing on the exit route. No way he could handle the dynamite chick and a Chinese professional short of shooting anything that moved.

'Get dressed.'

'Don't you like me the way I am.'

'For Chrissakes, kid,' said Feldspar, 'put your clothes on.' He stood well back from her, holding the Python steady. He didn't take his eyes off her, not for an instant, following her to the sliding-door closet as she took out a shirt and underwear, jeans and shoes. She glanced round at him. 'You want me formal?'

'I don't care.'

He studied her while she slipped on panties and bra, back to him. He kept watching her hands, forcing his attention away from her body. It surprised him that he found her desirable. Even in that tense situation, he was hungry for her. An aspect of his character he hadn't suspected was surfacing; Feldspar didn't much care for it.

'Listen,' he said. 'I'm going to let you pack a bag.'

'How kind,' she said, mocking him.

Trailing through the apartment, he watched her fill a totebag with spare clothing, keeping a bead on her gut every time she opened a drawer or closet. For all he could tell, she had a shiv in every nook and a gun in every cranny. It was that kind of an apartment. She was that kind of girl.

'You going to let me go to the john?'

Feldspar sighed, considered, shook his head.

'I gotta.' Baby-voiced, pleading.

'Move it out, Dorothy,' he told her.

'Mister, you'll never make it.'

But he did make it; along the deserted corridor, down the back staircase into the basement and out through the door he'd wedged open into the clean concrete service bay and the short alley that led to Patterson Street. He kept her ahead of him, gun in his left hand, his senses aching with alertness.

Why she didn't scream or yell during the walk away was more than he could figure. Perhaps she had more respect for the Python Magnum than she had for him. Perhaps she was too proud to make the kind of scene that would bring tenants of the Florissant to her rescue.

The little red Bobcat was slotted into the curb at the corner of the alley. Patterson Street was still fast asleep. Stores shuttered, swell apartment blocks looking tall and somnolent above the quiet thoroughfare at Borden and Cheyne. Heavy August heat was building up again on the eastern seaboard. Sunday in New York: six-fifty-seven.

He clipped her across the nape of her neck with his right hand and caught her in his arms as she sagged towards the sidewalk. She was heavy. It made him sweat, the effort of lugging her the last few yards to the Bobcat and stuffing her into the passenger seat. He took two pairs of Mainwaring manacles from under a plaid travelling rug, clipped a pair to her ankles and another to her wrists, looped a length of cord through the ankle manacle and knotted it to the harness attachment. He did the same with the wrists. She was twisted but the position looked fairly natural; a night owl sleeping it off. He tucked the plaid rug around her, hiding the cuffs, slid into the driving seat, checked the gas, and tooled slowly out into Patterson heading for the loop that would swing him onto the New Jersey Turnpike.

By noon, or shortly after, he would have her stowed away safe and sound in Henry Marks's barn in Bertram. After that, Upton would decide how best to use her.

Feldspar glanced to his right. The Bobcat ran smoothly. Sun streamed in hazy golden shafts down the canyons of New York, then came clear in, falling on the prisoner's flaxen hair, her wide mouth. She reminded him of a girl he had once dated, in his hometown of Tasman, Connecticut, before he recruited into the Agency. Cinnamon cake and eggnog, two sets of footprints in the powdery snow of a quiet tree-lined avenue.

He remembered the knife; the knife made it different. And goddamned exciting.

'Two of a kind, kid,' said Feldspar, arrogantly aware that, for the time being, he had the upper hand.

SUNDAY MORNING
THE PAIUTE RANCH

Now that he had been backed to the wall, Rand's lazy indifference to everything that did not contribute to his personal or professional comfort was replaced by a kind of annoyance. He was rational enough to realise that his life had been laid on the line for a cause, a purpose, that had been kept from him.

It intrigued him that the Italian-American was scared. He had interpreted the signs at first glance. He pushed the breakfast plate away, lifted the coffee cup in both hands and brought it to his lips, scowling. He was prepared for rough treatment and had worked out a story that might contain enough of the truth to satisfy his captors.

'How do you feel?'

'What?'

'Come on, Rand, don't act the dummy. How do you feel, I said?'

'Does it matter how I feel?'

They knew something they were reluctant to impart, something about his condition. He had spent a lousy night. The symptoms were so constant and obvious that he was obliged to acknowledge that he was ill. Somehow that development was mixed into the puzzle, maybe a crucial part of it. If only Meredith had been straight with him. If only the professor had demonstrated the kind of honesty expected between scientists and not tossed his lot in with government agents.

In the plant world, in the architecture of life forms, there was always a definable pattern, a series of causes for every effect.

Elaborate theories were founded on logical probability. Rand tried to apply the principles to his present situation, to ignore not only his pain but the Dick Tracy elements that had gotten into it through Rainer's baiting of the syndicates.

Throughout the long gritty hours of the night, Rand had struggled not only for breath but to accumulate into a logical whole all the pieces of the puzzle. Inevitably, he was drawn back to his first instinctive conclusion. The government was taking him for a ride. He was Rainer's guinea-pig, a laboratory rat.

If he were important enough to kidnap, then he'd be important enough to protect. But the security arrangements had been laughably inadequate. The baby-blue Chevette had only been the tip of an iceberg; Rainer had known as much. Now the mob, organisation, syndicate, whatever, now they had him at their mercy in a hideout in California.

And he was sick. And they were scared of his sickness. Therefore, the sickness was part of it; an unforeseen circumstance the hoods hadn't bargained on but had heard enough about to examine him. He didn't have to scratch deep to come up with an answer to find the link. The Meredith bacterium.

Coffee ran down his gullet like mercury and lay in his chest, cold and heavy, clogging his breathing.

'Look, Rand, just answer me a few questions, will you?' the Italian-American said. He was trying to come on hard but anxiety ruined his act. 'We know about your trip to Turkey. What happened there?'

Rand spelled out an answer. He told his interrogator everything that had happened – about the Meredith bacterium, its effects on the poppy plants. He co-operated, gaspingly, but without weakness. He tried to give the impression that he was indifferent, not cowed. The guy was still over by the door, ten paces away, standing. Rand had the feeling that if he got to his feet and approached him, the man would back out of the cell like somebody presented with a live grenade.

'The Englishman, Meredith, he invented this bacterium?'

'You don't invent bacterium; you discover them, and their specific properties, by a process of trial and error. You can also change the process – the way bacteria work – by breeding particular strains, combing the hereditary blueprints and combining them to form a *new* bacterium.'

'Yeah, right,' the interrogator said. 'A new bacterium. Meredith did this?'

'So did another scientist, in the field we're talking about.'

'A Chinese?'

'A bacteriologist named Vigson. He was into bacterial manipulation way back. But Vigson's dead. Killed in a plane crash three, four years ago. Maybe some Chinese got hold of his . . .'

'The bacterium takes the morphine out of poppies?'

'Yes.'

'What else does it do?'

'Isn't that enough?' said Rand.

'What other kinds of things can it infect?'

Rand sucked in air. He hung onto the implication behind the question. Outside was the expert, probably a trained chemist. If he strung the interrogator along with lies, they'd better be good ones. He had to be of more use to the hoods than this. Obviously they hadn't snatched him just to find out about the Meredith bacterium. Hell, they seemed to know as much about it as he did.

'Meredith's bacterium,' Rand said, 'triggers specific inhibitory mechanisms in the synthesis of enzymes in the poppy plant.'

'And in . . . people? How about people?'

So he wasn't alone. There were others. Maybe hundreds of others, suffering the same symptoms. He thought about the results of the testing. They couldn't be questioned. The bacterium did what it was touted to do – changed the master-reaction in specific plant growth and development. It could not be pathogenic to humans. *It couldn't, could it*?

Bacteria were weird entities. Not *too* much was known about the ability of the bacterial cell to revert to normal chromosome content after the breeding of cross strains. Feeding and breeding in the Meredith bacterium had been inculcated through dependence on the natural biochemical process of the opium poppy. It had not yet been tested on other systems, in strange environments. Could it have undergone a mutation? Could it have been *designed* to mutate? Another biological missile for the stockpile? Guinea-pig; laboratory rat? Victim? What was he? The interrogator's fear insidiously transferred itself to Rand. Accident, or design? How unpredictable was the bacterium?

Christ, it didn't matter. He fought mounting panic. Even if it weren't true and he were suffering nothing worse than a pleural condition that simple antibiotic treatment would clear up in a few days, he could – he must – exploit the doubt.

'Yeah, it's . . . it's possible.'

'Why did the English bring in Jay Rainer?'

'They needed U.S. expertise – and cash.'

'Gimme the real reason?'

'Me. They wanted my help.'

'For what?'

Rand did not have to feign nausea to gain time to invent the lie.

'Develop an antidote,' he said.

The Italian's features sagged into shape, tension going briefly out of the muscles.

'And did you? the interrogator asked.

'Coming . . . close,' said Rand.

'How close?'

'We . . . have it. Haven't tested it thoroughly.'

Rand was thinking fast now, designing a model in his mind, something just credible enough to pass muster with the chemist, Tony. That was his first hurdle, to establish his value in their eyes. It *had* to be an antidote; that was all they could really want from him. He forestalled the next question.

He said, 'Don't . . . know how it'll affect the . . . the mutant strain, if . . . if . . . if that's what you want to know.'

'You mean, if it'll cure you?'

Rand shook his head. He could hardly breathe.

'Won't . . . won't "cure" me. Not possible. Need . . . need medical help.'

'All right, all right.' The interrogator held up his hands, palms raised as if to ward off infection. 'First you gotta tell me what this antidote is. I need enough facts about it to make certain you're not lying. Do that, I'll find you a doctor.'

Rand said, 'Synthetic counter bacterium cultured from corn endosperm. Not . . . not difficult to do. Simple intervention by new strain bacteria on . . . on natural auxin, IAA – indole-3-acetic acid. Simple. Creates synthetic auxin reaction that reverses inhibitory specialised effect of . . . of original bacterium in poppy plant. Used Indian corn.'

'All right, all right. How come the Chinese expert didn't discover this simple stuff?'

'He'd have to run through thousands . . . thousands of substances to find base. We . . . we took Indian corn early, grew culture from endosperm and egg albumin,' Rand panted. 'Luck, chance.'

'You were supposed to work *with* Meredith, right?

'Vereker Laboratory well equipped; more . . . more Meredith's province than mine, bacteria.'

'Yeah, Dr. Rand. Well, you have the field to yourself now,' the interrogator said, giving no clue as to whether he had swallowed Rand's inventions or not. 'We'll get you back in shape, then we'll introduce you to the Chinese expert.'

'What expert?'

'Name of Vigson.'

'Can't be . . . be Vigson; dead.'

'Conrad Vigson. And he's alive.'

Rand lolled in the chair, supporting his ailing body on his forearms. He was spent, his strength giving out. His mind could not grasp the new factor in the equation. It had all become too complicated.

'It's Vigson you'll have to convince,' the Italian said.

'If,' Rand said, 'I live that long.'

'Make the effort, Rand,' the interrogator said, from the open doorway. 'We got too much riding on your survival to wanna lose you now.'

SUNDAY AFTERNOON
CLOUDSRIDGE COUNTRY CLUB

Varese ate lunch. He had a healthy appetite and filled a large oval plate from the Danish buffet laid out in the cool dining room, carrying it to the quiet table at the west corner of the terrace. Under the shade of the awning Sarsby had already begun eating. The table was decently removed from the other members who, with their women, were spread out along the terrace. They recognised business when they saw it, however, and left Arnold and his guest to themselves.

As he ate, Varese talked. Sarsby listened, interjecting a question now and again. By the time Varese had returned with second helpings and a schooner of beer drawn from the keg by the buffet table, Sarsby had made decisions.

First, he asked, 'Did Bulthius swallow Rand's story about the antidote?'

'Yeah. He's sceptical about the whole thing. But he figures Rand and Meredith between them picked the right approach – so far as he can follow.'

Sarsby helped himself to a sip from the schooner, dabbed froth from his upper lip with a linen napkin. 'Frank, we're being manipulated,' he said.

'I figured as much.'

'Rainer's gotten to Halveston.'

'I don't know about that.'

'Rainer's not scalphunting. He wants Rand back, in one functioning piece. He has to deal straight. Otherwise, Rainer carries the cross for a world famine in opium. Our interests are basically the same.'

'You're gonna take up his offer?'

'First I'm going to pow-wow with the Tigers, not minions. Yu-lan and Kittegawa. They're not far away, I'll bet. They know we're stringing it out now, and at least one, maybe both, of the dealers will be close to the scène of the action. I'll make contact through the Tigers' agent in San Diego. He'll pass the word along.'

'Arnold, it's urgent,' said Varese. 'If we accept Halveston's word, Rand will flake out in a day or so.'

'I'll move on it,' Sarsby promised. 'Your job is to pay Halvęston his two hundred thousand. Pull it from the emergency fund in the Guthrie Tait. Do it just like Halveston says – in case he's still honest, you understand. Give the pick-up man a couple of hours to feed back the cash, then talk with Halveston. During those two hours, Frank, you'll also talk person-to-person with Jay Rainer.'

'Shit, that's risky.'

'Not at all, Frank. Rainer already knows we're involved. As I say, perhaps he even hopes to use us. We go to the table with the Tigers, we also go to the table with Rainer. If Rand dies, we lose everything; the Tigers have it clear.'

'Unless Rand's left details of the antidote . . .'

'Immaterial,' said Sarsby. 'The Tigers will shoot first. They have the loaded gun. We're still filling the chamber. No, Frank, we make all the deals we can. We got to lay hands on Vigson.'

'Rainer won't let you crate Rand and whip him off again after surgery.'

'He will – if we have a hostage.'

'Hostage? Who?'

'Senator Clark Halveston.'

Varese grinned. 'Arnold, I like it,' he said.

SUNDAY AFTERNOON
SAN FRANCISCO

Guarded respect was the keynote of the relationship between Michael Lassiter, Chief of the FBI Narcotics Bureau, and the governor of the state of California. It was through the governor that Lassiter received his 'invitation' to participate in the round-up of the Sarsby network. The governor was a plausible fellow and flattered Lassiter in such a way that Lassiter was committed before he found out that it was not his coup at all, that it involved certain factions in and out of government that had no right to interfere in Bureau business.

Lassiter, however, was an employee, a public servant. With his bosses ranged against him – thanks to a Vice-Presidential appeal – he had no choice but to go along with the private war and provide necessary back-up of manpower and machines. He consoled himself that Sarsby was a prize worth winning. He had lamped the Sarsby syndicate for years now, put the lever into its minor works whenever he could. But he was acutely aware that heavy bread was being made under his nose and that vast quantities of drugs of the heroin/morphine variety were pouring through the Sarsby plants into his territory. He had had meetings with area chiefs, Bureau analysers, east, west, north and south, endeavouring to plot the routes that Sarsby used. None of them came up with much that was fundamentally detrimental to the syndicate supermarket. Through courts of law, Lassiter attacked the licensing bodies that braced the legitimate architecture of Sarsby's empire. But the dealer's backing was too influential, greased by payola, bolstered by the ultimate law, that of supply and demand. Lassiter's innings had been disasters, humiliating in their frequency.

Though he didn't appreciate being reduced to the status of stage manager, Lassiter was eager to scotch Sarsby any old how. Consequently he muffled his suspicion of the Englishman and his irritation at the stern commands that floated down off Capitol Hill through the governor's office.

Mike Lassiter was a squat, bull-headed, forty-seven years-old careerist. He had run through three wives and fathered four sons, none of them currently resident in California. He had a mistress in the Bureau, though they got to spend very little time together as Mike sternly refused to cut back on his work load. He wore single-breasted, dark blue suits and expensive silk shirts and walked with a stiff cocky roll, like somebody with a steel pin through one hip joint.

Lassiter and Upton met in the formal surroundings of the Bureau office on Lancaster Boulevard with its view out over the Southern Pacific Depot and the clutter of highliner land freight warehouses that ate into the famous old residential area. Below the office, at street level, were garish stores selling liquor and coffee and fruit. The steps to the Bureau doorway were littered with peel and the heels of discarded pastries.

The office was painted plain spring green with two used desks and angular modern chairs that had fallen off the end of a requisition last year.

Upton, Lassiter thought, looked scrubbed and fragile like an English gentleman should. The Bureau chieftain had been fed much of the requirement, and his grilling of Upton – for that's what it amounted to – was smart and unpredictable.

'Let me get this straight,' Lassiter said. 'You want me to find a hospital that has facilities for big scale surgery and that can be guarded like Fort Knox?'

'The surgeon will have some say in the matter.'

Lassiter ignored the interruption. 'Sarsby's bunch will bring in your scientist, Rand, dump him, and drive off unchallenged.'

'Yes.'

'They kidnapped Rand, didn't they?'

'For reasons of security,' said Upton, 'we prefer to disregard that fact for the moment.'

Lassiter said, 'Rand receives medical attention. Two or three days later, Sarsby collects the merchandise and drives off with him again.'

'Sarsby will send in a task force,' said Upton. 'He will come for Rand earlier than any date we agree upon.'

'You want that?'

'Of course. He'll also take the surgeon, Walter Stein.'

'You play it for real, don't you?'

'It's important that Sarsby feels he has an edge and some freedom of action,' said Upton. 'We must do all that we can to foster that feeling. There will be no gunplay.'

Lassiter said, 'Stein will be mine?'

'Yes.'

'We track Stein, find out where he's located and prepare a task force.'

'And wait.'

'How long?'

'I've no idea; not too long, I wouldn't think.'

'When the Chinese bring in their boy, we strike.'

'Yes.'

'I should warn you, sir,' said Lassiter, 'that I can't guarantee a bloodless strike at the rendezvous.'

'I understand that,' said Upton. 'Stein will be aware of the situation and of the inherent risks. He'll do what he can to protect Gordon Rand.'

'I've gotta ask – who is this guy the Chinese are bringing in? It's all for him, isn't it? Rainer, Marks, Stein and me?'

'All for his benefit,' said Upton. 'His name would mean nothing to you, Mr. Lassiter.'

'You don't wanna tell me?'

'I'd rather not'

'Who's the co-ordinator? You?'

'Henry Marks, acting on behalf of Vice-President Rainer.'

'And that stupid committee of his.'

'I sympathise with your scorn for political amateurs,' said Upton. 'Would it appease your professional conscience, Mr. Lassiter, if I told you that the Vice-Presidential committee is only a piece of scenery as far as this operation is concerned?'

Lassiter smiled. 'I get the strange feeling that it's *all* your production, sir. Agency, Bureau . . .'

'I believe that the end justifies the means,' said Upton. 'It's not a popular philosophy these days, in your country or in mine.

Smacks of a lack of respect for democracy. If my hands were tied by reliance on a single system, CIA or FBI, that system would bind us in red-tape. This, Mr. Lassiter, is not a matter of law, of security, or international politics. It's a matter of the gravest importance, and it centres on one man.'

'The scientist the Chinese will bring to the rendezvous?'

'Precisely.'

'I . . . can't do anything illegal.'

Upton snorted. 'Of course you can. I'm sure that your men frequently do things that are against the letter of the law, otherwise there would be no justice at all. Am I not right, Mr. Lassiter?'

'I'm afraid you are,' Lassiter conceded.

'In the long run, it comes down to the individual.'

'You, you mean?'

'And you too, Mr. Lassiter. Men, not the system.'

'Hell, you don't just want my co-operation, you want my approval.'

'Not necessarily approval,' said Upton. 'But no grudges.'

'Let me ask you one question, sir,' said Mike Lassiter. 'Will this weird operation net me Arnold Sarsby?'

'Is that your particular price?'

'Yeah, it is.'

'Sarsby's yours for the taking,' Upton said.

'Then leave the details to me,' said Lassiter.

SUNDAY NIGHT
BERTRAM – WEST VIRGINIA

The john below stairs was an unfurnished wedge with toilet, miniature washbasin and no windows. Feldspar let the girl use it shen she asked. He checked it beforehand, and afterwards, ignoring her ribald comments and her angry abuse when he pat-searched her too. Throughout the afternoon and evening he kept her wrists and ankles cuffed. He took no chances. He unlocked the manacles to allow her to eat the soup and club sandwiches he prepared around six. Between whiles he served Coke and Carlsberg, sitting by her side on the davenport in the warm sunshine, holding the cans while she sucked the liquid through straws.

Dorothy wasn't grateful for his civilised treatment. To while away the hours and perhaps win her confidence a little, Feldspar told her about another prisoner he'd guarded, down in Tampico, a Cuban who'd worked a funny money turnaround with six sugar-cane agents. It had been Feldspar's duty to hold the guy safe for nineteen hours until a special squad could collect. It seemed like a simple assignment, but the details were tricky.

Between supper and dusk, Dorothy slept, huddled uncomfortably in a corner of the davenport. Feldspar wondered how long it would take Marks to rake up a collection detail and prepare a safe place in which to break the lassie down. Marks had been less than enthusiastic about this piece of the plan and had growled some at Feldspar for exceeding his authority. Feldspar pointed out that it was Upton's idea and that he'd only followed orders.

'What's she like?' Marks had asked.

'Young – and tough.'

'Will she break, Feldspar?'

'In my opinion,' Feldspar had said, 'no chance.'

Naturally Feldspar had tested out the girl's willingness to fink on her daddy. He conversationally dangled carrots before her throughout the day, hinting that he knew *all* about her. What surprised him more than her reluctance to talk about the Tigers, or anything else of importance, was her utter lack of interest in who *he* was and what particular group he represented.

Her psychology, however, was primitive; a kind of grasping fatalism, perhaps, or the dedicated belief that the law could not hold her. If she feared anything, she gave no hint of it to Feldspar. In fact, she treated him like one big joke.

In response, Feldspar persisted in his gentle probing, more intrigued than ever. At the back of his mind was the assurance that, when the alkaloids in her bloodstream were absorbed, she would crack. He had boned up on the clinical characteristics of addiction. The girl was suspended in a state of physical dependence on heroin. Whatever she was using, it was no substitute for adaptive behaviour. She did not appear to need to seek refuge in the drug. On the other hand, around dusk she became increasingly animated. Feldspar figured she was a 'nightcapper'. Maintained addiction: tolerance. Just how long would it take to break that kind of chemical hold?

Certainly, she was no somnabulist, not like some of the freaks he'd encountered. She didn't look malnourished and wolfed down the soup and sandwich with appetite. Only when he happened to mention Bobby Hoffmann did he get the kind of response that seemed to go with the naked figure squirming out of the bed that morning, with the Boone Huntsman, and her barbarous case history.

'You smooth mother fucker,' she hissed, slanting the blue eyes and lipping up her mouth. 'You think you can trap me. Keep your shit, cowboy. I never heard of Bobby Hoffmann.'

'Sure you have,' said Feldspar.

It was still mid-afternoon then, and he was bored, wary of the kind of things that boredom let slide into his mind.

'You remember Bobby – two-bit little creep down in San Francisco. Supposed to have killed four people. I don't believe it. I think he was to weak to kill. Too stupid to sidestep the rap,' Feldspar said.

She lunged, using the thigh muscles for thrust and dove at him where he sat along the davenport from her, his profile indistinct against the pretty freckled leaves of the vase arrangement.

'Kid.' Feldspar caught a fistful of her hair and dragged her down, pinning her easily with his elbow. 'I know you were Bobby Hoffmann's woman.'

'*Wife*, you fucker. I was his *wife*: not *was* either. *Is*. I'm his fucking wife.'

'See,' said Feldspar. 'I had it right.'

His arrogance was a cover up. He was consumed by a fire of emotion. Impatience to be shot of her was uppermost, licking yellow around the periphery of his control. Below it, red hot, was a centre of obscene desire that Feldspar hated. He had experienced it once or twice in the past. Then it had manifest itself as hatred; now it wasn't hate but a variety of lust that made him suspicious of his own gestures and movements, made him doubt the wisdom of having involved himself with this girl at all.

It was about dusk, while she slept, that the true reason for his anxious passion came to him. She was his. For this period, he *owned* her. She had put herself way beyond the accepted code of behaviour. If only half the tales were true, Dorothy Newhoff was the devil's chattel; and once you'd consorted with the devil, you carried the mark forever.

How many guys would have envied him? Feldspar thought. He

had run into state police here and there in the course of Agency assignments who saw nothing wrong in groping a female suspect, in needless strip searches, even in taking a suspect into the bushes to let her 'co-operate': always hippies, dropouts, the ones who'd put themselves out of reach of sympathy with society. The same with agents, field agents in particular: the user begged also to be used.

Feldspar had never met Rigby or Meredith so he couldn't bleed for the old men. He could find no moral connecting point, no anchor, in that lazy, bee-somnulent barn deep in the Virginia woods. If she protested that he'd raped her, who'd believe her? Who, in God's name, would take her word against his, particularly if she were snivelling and dribbling and pleading for a shot? Who'd believe her anyhow? She had put herself beyond all that.

Three buttons on the shirt undone. He could see the brassiere cup and the soft girl flesh of her breasts. He imagined her nakedness again. Hurriedly he got up, made coffee, came back and stood by the telephone uncertain who he should call to speed up collection. Snoring slightly, she slept, oblivious to his torment.

Torment: Jesus, she would suffer worse than this before the 'treatment' was through, before Upton got what he required. Feldspar did not even know what Upton expected from such a pathetic child.

He was still standing by the telephone with the coffee cup in his hand when she awakened. She was in trouble. It had come on much more rapidly than he had anticipated. *Where the hell were they*? Mucus ran from her nose. Her eyes looked a little gummy.

'Is that coffee?'

'Yes.'

'Gimme a drink.'

He had checked her totebag, knew the kit was there, plus the glissane envelope that, he assumed, contained her nightly dose. She'd only brought one. Enough to satisfy a booking officer, if it came to a police desk – which, of course, it wouldn't. As if she had predicted the delay, she had brought one bag.

'Is it really a drink you need?' he asked.

'Drop it.'

'Drop what?'

'The fucking subject.'

'I'm not the law; I'm no narco officer. It means nothing to me to let you shoot up.'

'Jesus!'

'Kid, don't you even want to know who's got you?'

'I know who you are. You're government. Obvious. Pig! You're a shadow, man. I know your kind. I've seen your kind before.'

'Government?'

'You wouldn't really let me shoot, would you?'

'That depends?'

'You want . . . mouth?'

'Of course not,' said Feldspar. 'Three or four answers, that's all.'

'The old fucking routine.' She seemed disgusted by his lack of originality.

Feldspar finished coffee and put the cup down. The Python was over on the long table. He put his hands on his hips and looked at the girl. She was still lying back, hands in her lap, comfortable enough in spite of the cuffs. She had large hands, practical hands; square nails.

'Will you talk about Hoffmann?'

'Fuck off! Pig!'

'It isn't my business,' Feldspar shrugged. 'You *will* talk, Dorothy. My superiors will wring everything they want to know out of you, inch by inch. Don't get me wrong; they won't lay a finger on you. No abuse. They'll simply shut you in a padded room and walk away. In two days, or three, you'll be willing to co-operate.'

'Usual fucking routine, yeah.' She was defiant, scornful, and without apprehension. It came naturally to her. It wasn't applied the way it would have been by a street delinquent.

'Dorothy, we're not interested in Bobby Hoffmann,' said Feldspar. 'It's 'husband' number two that concerns us. Your yellow sugardaddy. Wing.'

'Let me take the shot; then I'll give you anything you want.'

'Information?'

'Head: I give the best head you ever had.'

When she curled her tongue over her upper lip, Feldspar tried to think of her scarred arms and wasted inner tubing. He didn't quite make it. It wasn't his fault that he was caught in this kind of trap. Marks was to blame. They should have been here hours ago. What scared Feldspar most of all was the prospect of having a raving junkie on his hands. He could cope with it, of course; but he didn't want to have to.

He found her totebag, took out the envelope and white box with the fresh hypo and spoon in it and laid them on the coffee table. He lifted the Python and slipped it into his pocket. She did not look at the kit.

Feldspar said, 'Let's bargain, Dorothy. Two straight answers and you can shoot up. Be the last fix you'll have for some time. May as well seize your chance.'

'What answers?'

'How long will Wing be gone?'

'Week.'

'Fine; that's fine,' said Feldspar. 'Question two: were you with him in London?'

'Yeah.'

The key for the cuffs was on a ring. The girl's gaze was fixed hungrily on the glissane envelope. She seemed to have gone into a trance of expectation. Feldspar brought the kit over and placed it on the arm of the davenport. Her head turned to follow the journey of the heroin packet. Feldspar inserted the key in the lock of the manacles. The spring clicked.

She brought her head round and up, driving with her elbows. The crown of her head struck Feldspar full on the nose. At the same moment, she lashed up with her feet and drove them straight into his groin.

Dazzled by the first blow, Feldspar had just sufficient sense to jacknife. Her heels missed his privates but struck his belly, exploding breath from him. He crumpled.

The key-ring flipped onto the rug.

She leapt, knees pounding into Feldspar's chest, the Mainwaring cuffs dangling from her left wrist. Feldspar curled into a ball, covered his face with his forearm, and tried to roll away. She plucked up the key-ring and scrabbled over him. Hobbled at the ankles, she used her elbows to haul herself away from him. Feldspar could see little. Blood streamed from his nose. His eyes watered. He fought to draw breath. In the order of things, she could have killed him there and then. But she went for the keys. Not for the junk kit or the agent.

Using the pine table, Feldspar clawed himself up, fumbling in his pocket for the gun.

She was running already.

Feldspar rubbed his face with his sleeve. He tottered after her. She'd gone on down the corridor, past the john under the stairs. She was faster than a jackrabbit. On the key-ring was the ignition key for the Bobcat slotted into the bay under the sundeck.

Stumbling into milky waves of pain, Feldspar crashed open the sliding doors to the deck. The night air was warm. He could hear insects purring, and one jeering bird. Far down on the turnpike were glimpses of headlights between dense trees. He slung himself over the rail, hanging on with his left hand, gun in his right fist. He swung free of the deck and dropped to the flagged area in front of the carport.

He landed heavily, taking the spill on his buttock and left shoulder. A fluorescent cube at the corner of the steps by the root of the barn gave light. She came into it, springing softly down the steps.

Feldspar fired once, high and wide.

She feinted left then sheered off right, vaulting the step-like concrete ballustrade. Reviving, Feldspar went after her into the trees.

Fury swept him along, fury with himself. It strengthened him, charged him up. Some goddamned weekend this had turned out to be. The steepening slope hauled him down into underbrush. He caroomed off trunks, was slapped by stinging branches and finally skidded to a halt on his ass and elbows. He lay motionless, panting, listening. Faint radiance from the barn above him gave definition to the hem of the woodland. He picked up a sound, distinct, not stealthy.

She was a runner, an escaper, a survivor. Her every instinct would be homed in on getting out of the trees. He figured it swiftly. She had fifty, maybe sixty feet of descent on him. She wouldn't risk the long black drop through the forest. She would hook back to the drive and trail it down to the turnpike. If he guessed wrong and she went on down, then he'd lose her.

Moving more cautiously, Feldspar picked his way across the slope towards the tarmac avenue that wended up to the house. He had an advantage over her; he knew the terrain. All she would remember was the lie of the road. He should have blindfolded the bitch or coldcocked her again when she came round. His face felt like chopped liver. His gut ached where she'd kicked him. Three inches lower and he would be splayed out on the rug in the living room, and she could have danced a jig on his head for all he could do about it. Coldness came over him, hunger for revenge.

He stepped softly over the shoulder onto the tarmac. The barn was lit behind him. Below was seamless darkness, intensified by the pale glow of Bertram. Walking fast on the balls of his feet, he went down the centre of the drive, stopping every twenty paces to listen. She was still with him, still down there. He'd guessed right.

The jeering bird came up loud; an owl probably. It skimmed low over the drive, screeching twice before it vanished into the silent branches. A little breeze from the Potomac basin stroked the hillside, stirring leaves, drowning out the telltales. Feldspar was breathing through his mouth. He could taste blood.

Round the curve, a farmstead on high ground across the valley showed its shape against the sky. Further, forty paces, the drive rolled out straight at last, the turnpike below. Feldspar halted and crouched. He could see well enough – satin tarmac, the whip of headlights on the pike a quarter of a mile below – well enough to put a bullet in her back if she emerged below him. He lifted his collar over his cheeks and turtled his head down.

He saw her before he heard her, hugging the inside edge of the drive, walking just the way he'd walked, fast, on the balls of her feet. Her shirt was distinct against the trees. She glanced behind her from time to time, coming on down. Holding his breath, tongue arched against the roof of his mouth to prevent the sluggish trickle of blood making him cough, he waited. If she saw him, he would shoot.

The full width of the drive separated them. She spotted him only when he rose. He took her in a flying tackle, real stylish, just as she swayed to plunge again into the forest. Yielding she went before him, her body buffering his fall as they dove from the tarmac into shelving underbrush. He gave her no chance, crushing her beneath him, left hand and arm under her crotch, ramming her deep into the leaf mat, the muzzle of the magnum jammed against her carotid artery.

Sprawled on her, he sucked the plug of congealed blood into his mouth and spat it out. Then he put his mouth against hers, his thumb on her pubic bone through the denim. Her tongue shot into his mouth. Feldspar felt a throbbing langour in the wake of the tension, then he jerked his head away.

He could barely make her out. Pale hair against the pine mat. The smell of her perspiration mingled with his own, with the heavy loamy odour of the forest floor. Feldspar felt her thighs open beneath him, hips arch into his hand. His forefinger tightened on the trigger of the magnum. He might have blown her head off if the big jerking beams of the ambulance hadn't flitted across the branches at that moment.

He got to his feet, reached down, grabbed her by the belt of her jeans and yanked her to her knees. Dragging her, he scrambled over the edge of the tarmac. In the blinding light of the ambulance, he saw her face, scratched and bloody, her eyes amused.

The ambulance rocked to a halt. Two whitecoated attendants got out.

'You Feldspar?'

'Yes.'

'That the patient?'

'Yes.'

'Jesus. You gotta busted nose?'

'Get her out of here, will you?'

'Come on, kid.'

They were large men, about Feldspar's age, not cynical like general hospital staff.

'Where's Marks?' Feldspar asked, as he gave Dorothy over to the two janitors.

'Who?'

He followed them as they opened the rear of the vehicle and hoisted the girl inside.

'You wanna ride, fellah?'

'No, thanks,' said Feldspar. 'Where are you taking her?'

'Washington. You sure you don't wanna ride along?'

'Charlie, he's had enough.'

'Strap her down,' Feldspar said. 'I mean it.'

'Yeah, we'll do that.'

Feldspar glanced into the interior of the vehicle as the attendant closed the doors. Dorothy was seated on the stretcher with her hands on her knees, her head turned to look out at him.

She grinned wickedly. 'See you around, mother fucker.'

The door slammed.

'The Meriweather Clinic; near the Walter Reed, the attendant told him. 'You know it?'

'No.'

'Swing east off Missouri Avenue; small place at 488 Belmont.'

'I'll find it.'

'Fellah, is she that tough?'

'Rawhide,' said Feldspar.

'Wait 'til tomorrow,' said the attendant. 'Come see her then.'

'Maybe I will,' Feldspar said and, wheeling away, began the long weary walk back up the drive to the barn.

SUNDAY NIGHT
SAN FRANCISCO

Dragons artistically carved on the skin of a melon did not impress Frank Varese. He was tired now, his nerves rasped by hopping from city to city. He had no patience with the simpering ritual of dining with the White Tigers. He was in the mood for prime steak and mashed potatoes, not lotus seeds, shark's fin and rose syrup, though the barbecued lamb, when they finally got around to it, appeased him somewhat.

The Emperor of China was an elegant spot. But it lay too close to the heart of Chinatown for Varese's liking. The pigtail architecture, nineteenth-century cable cars, pagodas picked out in coloured bulbs and fretwork lanterns were top dressing for tourists. Beneath was an active culture of wealth, power and calculated violence. In spite of claims to the contrary, Tongs and criminal syndicates remained dominant, creaming soldiers from seasoned veterans of the gang wars that frequently tore holes in the garish oriental facade.

Sarsby was too urbane to show tension. He had agreed to the meeting place without quibble, familiar with how such things were done. His call to the Tiger's agent in San Diego had been returned within the hour. He had spoken directly with Chen Yulan, an affable five-minute chat that culminated in an invitation to dinner in San Francisco. Varese had driven him from Cloudsridge to a private airstrip at San Cremona, and, following the route that Jake McGuire, the syndicate's transport manager, had set up, he reached the intersection of Grant Avenue and California in the back of a chauffeured Toyota Crown.

The alacrity with which Yu-lan had responded and his suggestion of a meeting place indicated that Sarsby's assessment had been accurate. The Tigers were on the doorstep – and growling.

The White Tigers strength in America centred on the Chinese sections of San Francisco and Los Angeles. Their connections with Sarsby on the West Coast were much more tenuous than back East where a cautious unity of purpose existed. It was three years since Sarsby had sat at table with either of the chief Tigers. In all, during eight or nine years of detente, he had met Yu-lan and Kittegawa only four times. The fifth man at the table, Mr. Wing, he had never actually seen before, though he understood the reason for having him present. Wing was the unsheathed sword, the covert threat that violence might be necessary in this particular deal.

Throughout the progress of the dinner, Wing said nothing. Varese too kept his mouth shut and tried to appear relaxed. There was nothing in the conversation to get up tight about, anyhow not for an hour or more. Only when the clutter of tiny plates and painted bowls had been cleared away and Shen Kittegawa had flouted tradition by ordering brandy did the dialogue take a subtle shift, and suddenly they were talking turkey. It was too indirect for Varese. But Sarsby was an expert and adopted the sly manner and gracious doubletalk. At first he gave nothing away.

The state of the markets, increasing demands of the legitimate buyers, ineffectual controls, monopolies, he played each subject like a Mah-Jongg tile. Yu-lan and Kittegawa responded with careful generalisations. Then, with another click, abruptly Sarsby was talking about Vigson, Meredith and Gordon Rand.

There was no change in the demeanour of the Chinese. They continued to smile and nod courteously, agreeing with each particular point that Sarsby raised, confidently telling him that he was correct, that the White Tiger Company *did* intend to capture the world market as Sarsby suggested.

It went on and on.

Varese drank bitter black coffee to stimulate his concentration. He could no longer quite follow who was telling who what, or what the fuck kind of deal they were moving towards. He tried to emulate Wing, to be utterly still and relaxed. But he came from the wrong ethnic group for that kind of act and chewed a cigar instead. It was like trying to read a badly printed oriental pillow book, sensing sensational material but not comprehending the detail. Only at the end, like a dozen graphic prints at the top of the page, did the statements become totally meaningful to Varese.

'Is there, then, a medical report on Dr. Rand that we may be permitted to look at?' Kittegawa asked.

'There is no such report,' said Sarsby. 'It would serve no purpose, would it, my friend? You'd hardly be likely to take such a report at face value.'

'Is Dr. Rand under professional care?'

'Not yet,' said Sarsby. 'I'm making arrangements.'

Kittegawa's finger and thumb on the bulge of the brandy glass seemed to fascinate his partner, Yu-lan. Varese watched for signals. There were none that he could read.

After a pause, Yu-lan said, 'It would be of interest to us to see Dr. Rand.'

'You mean, examine him?' said Sarsby.

'A few simple questions.'

'One of you,' said Sarsby, 'may see him.'

'One?'

'Bring a doctor, if you wish.'

'One?'

'Either one of you, and a doctor.'

'I will see Dr. Rand,' said Chen Yu-lan. 'Mr. Wing would also be interested.'

'The hell he would,' murmured Varese.

'Mr. Yu-lan, Mr. Wing and a doctor. A three-man delegation, will that satisfy you? said Sarsby.

'It will,' said Kittegawa.

Another pause. Yu-lan said, 'How can we be sure that Dr. Rand is suffering from an illness brought about by that substance?'

'You can't,' said Sarsby. 'But the Englishman, Meredith . . . Is the coincidence not a little bit too much? Apart from that, there's the question of the antidote.'

'Ah, yes, the antidote,' Kittegawa said. 'It is difficult for us to believe that Dr. Rand, even with Dr. Meredith's help, stumbled upon an antidote so very rapidly.'

Sarsby said, 'I don't feel it would be prudent to discuss details of the antidote with you, gentlemen. For obvious reasons, I'm reluctant to divulge anything about it.'

'Westerners are notorious for bluffing,' said Yu-lan. 'It is a distressing characteristic in some of your countrymen, Arnold.'

'Is my government bluffing?' said Sarsby, winningly.

'How can we be sure that they are not?'

'May I ask,' said Sarsby, 'if your organisation in the Far East is totally secure?'

Kittegawa's forefinger tapped the brandy glass twice. Neither of the Tigers answered the question. It was tacitly understood that their organisation had *not* been totally secure. Varese had gotten onto their wavelength. His grin was genuine now. He even winked at Mr. Wing, who pretended he didn't see.

Sarsby said, 'It's also a Western fault to speak forthrightly. You'll excuse my bluntness, gentlemen. You have a volatile bacterium that can be used to create an opium monopoly. Before you dare put it to use, you must be sure that it can be controlled. Looks like it's not so stable as you imagined. How unstable remains to be seen.'

'We have only your word that it is unstable, Arnold,' said Yu-lan.

'I'll give you all the proof I have,' said Sarsby, 'tomorrow morning.'

Yu-lan and Kittegawa both nodded.

'If you are *inclined* to believe Rand is a victim of your bacterium, in mutated form, then the development of an antidote to the original bacterium becomes of prime importance.'

'Arnold, how can we take your word?' said Kittegawa apologetically.

'I'll undertake to keep Rand alive, to cure him,' said Sarsby.

'By using the antidote?' said Yu-lan.

'No. Seems the mutated strain of the bacterium will require research. But I'll cure Rand; I'll keep him alive and fit enough to meet with your expert . . ."

'That is not possible,' Yu-lan interrupted.

'If it's not possible,' said Sarsby, 'then we'd all better change our businesses.'

'You exaggerate, Arnold.'

'Do I, Sheng?'

'Expert to expert,' said Yu-lan. 'It is very difficult for us.'

'I'm sure you can arrange it.'

'Let Rand come with us,' said Kittegawa. 'We will take care of him.'

Sarsby laughed, politely.

'Anyhow, what can be gained from such a meeting?' said Yu-lan.

'Assurance that Rand, and the government, do have the antidote,' said Sarsby. 'Assurance that the bacterium *your* boy developed isn't going to run wild and mow down half the population. It's a marvellous little bug, I agree, but none of us, not even you, would want to let it loose to start a plague.'

In unison, Yu-lan and Kittegawa sighed.

Kittegawa said, 'Will your Dr. Rand talk with our man?'

'As soon as he's fit to do so.'

'And if our man is satisfied that Rand is genuine, what then?'

'We'll package the deal and divide the profits,' said Sarsby, flatly.

Kittegawa finished his brandy, bowed from the waist, and got to his feet.

Sarsby rose too. 'It's a large package, Sheng. You were greedy to try to keep it all for yourself. There's more than enough for both of us.'

Kittegawa extended his hand. 'Tomorrow Chen will see Dr. Rand, and then we will talk again. I hope you have enjoyed your dinner?'

'Very much,' said Sarsby and, with Varese following close, threaded his way out through the tables into the hot streets of Chinatown.

Kittegawa filled the brandy bowl with a half measure and dispensed a larger drop for Yu-lan. Wing drank jasmine tea and ate almond cakes, one after another like crackerjack.

'Is Sarsby telling the truth?' said Yu-lan.

'He believes that he is,' said Kittegawa.

'If Peking hears of this . . .'

'They *must* hear of it, and from our lips,' said Kittegawa. 'We do not dare sell them such a dangerous thing. If we crossed Peking our business, our lives, would be worth nothing. We would be extinguished immediately.'

'Sarsby does not know of Peking's interest.'

'No, it would seem not,' said Kittegawa.

'Tomorrow, we will be face to face with this Rand. Mr. Wing could . . .?'

'Chen, how can you be so stupid,' said Kittegawa gently. 'Until we know the truth, we can do nothing but comply with Sarsby's arrangement. If it is as he says, then we must bring Vigson out of Tang Mang Mu and put him together with Rand. We must "acquire" Rand, if we can. But not yet, not now.'

'Sarsby will demand half.'

'Half of our sales,' said Kittegawa. 'Peking will not condone taking on an American partner. It has become very complex. We must tread slowly and softly and adjust our plans as we go along.'

'Tomorrow, what about tomorrow?'

'Call Dr. Chung. Comply with Sarsby's plan. Make no trouble. Do exactly as they say.'

'I do not like it, Sheng,' said Yu-lan.

'Console yourself, Chen; it may be a bluff.'

'And if not?'

'We have for sale a weapon of immeasurable worth.'

Mr. Wing polished off the last almond cake, smiling to himself. He could have told his mentors that startling fact an hour ago.

Varese sank into the leather of the Toyota Crown and let the air-conditioning dry the sweat on his neck and chest.

'I'm bushed, Arnold. Bushed.'

'You can rest tomorrow, Frank.'

'Yeah, I know. Back to Washington.'

'McGuire will arrange to ferry the Chinese to the ranch.'

'You think they'll buy it?'

'They've no choice,' said Sarsby. 'And we've no choice.'

'Make the deal with Jay Rainer?'

'With Halveston as hostage.'

Varese glanced at his watch. 'If you drop me at the airport, Arnold, I'll just make the midnight shuttle.'

MONDAY 22 AUGUST
WASHINGTON, D.C.

The Meriweather had no connection with the Walter Reed Army

Medical Centre, whose formidable reputation as one of the country's great medical institutions was not impugned by involvement in the sordid little affairs that bobbed like jetsam in the wake of the ship of state. The Walter Reed's buildings were set in beautiful landscaped grounds, the fringes of which were just visible as Feldspar made the turn from the Confederate Loop and headed up into the long cul-de-sac of Belmont.

The clinic at 488 was a decaying gothic mansion in a couple of acres of garden given over to close-packed poplars backed by rhododendron shrubs. The Meriweather even had wrought-iron gates with a little red brick lodge inside. Inside the lodge lived an elderly black man with a fat belly and a withered hand. He wore no uniform, just slacks, terry shirt and thong sandals.

Feldspar left the Bobcat, walked to the gate and pushed his ID badge through the iron curliques. The black man inspected it, nodded, returned to the lodge and operated some out-of-character electronic device that opened the gates. Feldspar drove through.

The approach to the mansion was like riding into a movie lot dressed for a scenario about demonism. The sweltering night had barely eased into dawn. The sky was banded with peculiarly artificial clouds, like strands of copper wire hammered flat against pink cardboard. Looming trees shadowed the bulk of the mansion. Only the turrets were etched sharp. There were no visible outbuildings. The parking lot was gravel, unraked and speared by a variety of weeds. Half a dozen autos stood there, including two ambulances and an unmarked '71 Dodge pick-up. There was also a dark blue '74 Skyhawk with Henry Marks leaning his elbows on its roof.

It was Marks's call to the barn that had awakened Feldspar and Marks's summons that had brought him here at this ungodly hour of the morning. He was stiff and aching. His nose had swollen so that he felt as if he were peeking at the world from behind a pumpkin. Three cups of black coffee, grabbed while he showered and shaved, had partly dispelled his exhaustion. For all that he had driven carefully from Bertram in case he nodded off at the wheel.

Five hours sleep had not punctuated the events of Sunday and separated them from that strange arrival. Feldspar was still strung out on the heavy sexual action with the girl. He was not at all sure that he wanted to be here, to witness the inevitable breaking of her spirit. There was an illogical sentimentality in his attitude. He felt as if he had been responsible for capturing a wild beast and, in spite of what had happened, had admired her resistance. Anywhere in the jungle, she would cut it, would survive and dominate. But not now, not here.

'Christ,' Marks said. 'What happened to you?'

'She made a break for it.'

'*She* did that to you?'

Feldspar said, 'I've a chore to do at eleven, sir, in Washington. I don't have too much time.'

Still leaning on the car roof, Marks said, 'I talked with Upton. He told me what he wants from this kid. Personally, I think it's crazy. I know her type. She won't crumble and co-operate. Junkie or not, we won't ever be able to trust her.'

'I take it you have background, sir?'

'Enough,' said Marks.

'What else did Sir George say?'

'To me – not much. He's briefed the head honcho – Willis Greer.'

'So this is where Greer hangs out,' said Feldspar. 'The lair of the magus.'

'How'd you get to hear about Greer?' said Marks.

'Nasty rumours,' said Feldspar, vaguely.

Marks turned towards the door. 'How long's Greer had her?'

'Seven, eight hours.'

'Well, she asked for it, I suppose.' Marks mounted the worn steps ahead of Feldspar and pressed a tiny metal pad set into the lefthand doorpost.

Feldspar had heard enough of the fabled Dr. Greer to pity Dorothy Newhoff. Greer was the ultimate backroom boy. Nobody had ever met up with him. His reputation rested on results. A specialist in persuasion. His methods were direct and fast-acting. Chemotherapy, a variety of different forms of hypnosis, brain wave stimulation and depression; not torture, manipulation. His early failures were buried in departmental psycho wards all across the country. His successes worked for U.S. intelligence services all across the globe.

Marks knew a little more about the legend. The Meriweather was one unit that no sub-committee or investigative board had dared to examine in depth. Greer ran the Meriweather on a shoestring, with a staff of eleven and an annual budget of less than 140,000 dollars. He handled a maximum of four patients at a time and, to give him credit, had brought more than one important Humpty-Dumpty agency executive together again after a nervous illness. He also had a way with broken field agents and treated their psychic wounds gently, wholeheartedly sharing in their paranoid reality while he glued their minds back together.

As far as Dr. Willis Greer was concerned, Miss Dorothy Newhoff was sugar candy.

He opened the door in person. He wore a tweed hacking jacket with leather patches on the sleeves and pea-green bedford cords. He was small, younger than Feldspar had imagined, not much over forty. His hair was bushy brown. His moustache sickled over to link with his sideburns, giving him a large-headed, top-heavy appearance. He had tiny hands, like a possum's paws, and wore two rings on each forefinger and one on each pinkie. He carried a hand-towel, and rims of soap on his sideburns suggested he had been disturbed at his toilet.

'Mr. Marks, good to see you. And you must be Agent Feldspar.'

Nobody ever used that term, *agent.*

Feldspar shook the small paw and wondered how the hell a guy like this had gotten laughter-lines around his cheerful cinnamon-coloured eyes.

Greer tossed the towel to the floor behind him and admitted the callers to a beamed, wood-panelled hall. They were now embedded in a Hitchcock movie. A dozen doors opened from the hall, each separated from its neighbour by an ebony pedestal topped by a vase or a piece of plaster statuary. If the patients weren't nutty when they came in here, they would surely be nutty when they left, Feldspar thought, as he followed the doctor and Marks down the length of the hall and through the last of the eight doors on the west side.

An angelic-looking woman in her sixties was seated at a switchboard combing her hair sleepily while a man in his fifties with a centurian hair-do and a sweet simpering smile flushed out a metal coffeepot at a sink in the corner.

'Morning, morning,' Greer said, breezing on through the office into another corridor.

'*Good* morning to *you* folks,' the man said, like a singing commercial.

The door closed behind Feldspar. Now no sound nor resemblance to an ersatz Hollywood shocker remained. He was in the treatment zone, a cross between a prison and a hospital. Sliding shutters on doors, and feeder slots. Cool air, strip lighting, an open lavatory, white shiny tile and copper plumbing, an open shower stall with a red plastic duckboard and taps on the outside wall.

The duty nurse was secured behind a heavy mesh grid at the corridor's blind end. He got up slowly from his armchair and put the novel he'd been reading down on the desk; something intellectual, in French.

The duty nurse looked like Roz Russell playing a mother superior. Ten tournament chess stepclocks were arranged on the desk. One had a Disneyland ornament, Goofy the Polevaulter, placed upon it.

The nurse consulted this clock and, stepping to the grid, said, 'You're early, Doctor Greer.'

'How is she?'

'She's fine.'

As Feldspar came closer, he saw four tv monitor screens tilted above the grid, facing down towards the desk. He could not make out the images from that angle.

'Denis is making coffee,' Greer said. 'If you ask him nicely, Karl, perhaps he'll make some for you.

Karl unlocked the office door and, with a friendly smile at Marks and Feldspar, sashayed off up the corridor.

'Come on in.' Greer ushered Marks and Feldspar into the office.

A drug cabinet in brushed steel occupied the entire outer wall, four logbooks on a sloping shelf before it. No other file depositories, no key board. The monitors were controlled from a neat hand unit that lay on the seat of the armchair. On one screen, Feldspar glimpsed a swaddled shape lying in a corner of an empty room. Greer killed that shot, leaving the adjacent image intact.

Dorothy was strapped by wrists, ankles and waist to a padded massage table. The light was dim. She appeared to be sleeping, head turned away from the camera.

Greer pressed a button and a second camera picked up her

face. Her eyes were open. She stared vacantly at the wall. A rivulet of saliva clung to her bottom lip. She was nude and belly down.

Greer said, 'Did the lady do that to you, Agent Feldspar?'

'What? Yeah.'

'Reminds me of a cat I used to have when I lived in Wisconsin. Delicate black-and-white tabby. Usual feline instinct but unusual responses. Whenever she was threatened, she attacked. Didn't matter the size or shape or degree of ferocity of the threatening agent, she unsheathed her claws and went for it. And if that didn't work, in heat or out of it, she rolled over and played sexy. Mostly, though, she attacked. Went for a neighbour's German shepherd once. Scared the shit out of the brute. He could have killed her with his paw. But he backed off, then ran yowling out of the gate. Funny little creature, that cat. Fear response triggered fight, never flight. Freud didn't recognise the fear response, of course. Classified it as anxiety.'

Feldspar said, 'Do you know who the girl is, Dr. Greer?'

'Yep. She's Robert Hoffmann's woman. In fact, an on-the-spot assessment indicates that's *all* she is.'

'Uh?' Marks appeared to be out of his depth. Feldspar doubted if that were true.

'How long do I have her for?' Greer asked.

Feldspar answered. 'Four days, five at the outside.'

'I assume you don't want a detailed profile, in that case,' said Greer.

'Didn't Upton talk with you?' Marks enquired.

'Yep. He wants her co-operation. He wants me to find out what makes her tick and then reprogramme her psychological defences so that she'll work for us.'

'Can that be done?' Marks asked. 'I mean, in four days?'

'She's a heroin addict,' said Greer.

Dorothy was still staring blankly at the wall. Apart from the rise and fall of her ribs, she was motionless. Feldspar did not look at her. He concentrated on Greer.

'Don't have much background,' Greer said. 'It won't matter under the circumstances. It's not a difficult case. Quite rare. But not difficult. Actually, you're asking me to re-channel self-generated internalised obsession. Classically, the psycho-pathology of obsessional neuroses rotates round regressions of one sort and another. I'm no Freudian, really. Point is that her personality is based on alienation; alienation from emotion. Strong defence. Naturally, heroin dependence is part of it. But that's not it all. Hoffmann is the lynchpin of her defensive system. I suspect a manic element, possibly fundamental, in her make-up. Denial of guilt, fear and depression, utilised by her ego when the non-specific obsessional techniques falter and fail to cope.'

Greer clapped his hands as if to summon himself back from a verbal trek into professional deserts too inhospitable for laymen. 'However, you don't want analysis or cure.'

'We need her . . . vitality,' said Feldspar.

'Yep. Psychomotor acceleration. Hypomania – appropriate word.' Greer hadn't taken his eyes off the gray screen. 'Tell you what I'll do, when the neuphretalomen injection I gave her an hour ago wears off – that'll be in a couple more hours – I'll pump her full of the old kickapoo joy juice – a little cocktail of my own devising. Never fails. One question, she's not an acid freak, too, by any chance?'

'I think,' said Feldspar, 'she has a regular supply of quality heroin. Is she likely to cut it with acid?'

'Highly unlikely,' said Greer. 'We'll risk it.'

Marks said, 'What does the cocktail do?'

'Markedly accelerates withdrawal symptoms.'

'How bad will it be for her?' said Feldspar.

Greer gave him a speculative glance, debating whether Feldspar wanted revenge or was concerned for the girl's welfare. It wasn't part of Greer's instruction to coddle agents.

'Bad,' Greer said. 'But she'll survive it. I know exactly what I'm doing. Chemotherapeutic balancing acts are my speciality. It's easy with opiate dependence, physical and emotional. I've got to dam her responses. In the lady's case, heroin is the substitute for normal adaptive behaviour processes. Below that, at a deeper level, is the transference of *all* emotional dependence onto Bobby Hoffmann. I don't mean that she *loves* the guy, the way we'd acknowledge love. He's no Christ figure, no Jehovah either. Perhaps – and this is just top-of-the-head theory – she's obsessed with the dream conceptualisation of dominence; "in love", if you like, with Hoffmann because he's the only guy she's found who was as pliant as a doll. Anyhow, Upton tells me you want her back in her natural habitat but working for you. If I can rechannel her present loyalty, wherever that lies, quite apart from tampering with her dependence on either heroin *or* Hoffmann, then I can give you what you want.'

'What do we want?' Marks asked.

'An operative in the field programmed to make decisions and generally act towards the ends you allocate.'

To Feldspar's surprise, Marks growled, 'Will she kill for us?'

'If she's killed before – yes.'

'That's what she is,' Marks said. 'She's a killer.'

'You sound as if you think you're telling me something I don't know already,' Greer said. 'I can't shift her alliegence into a vacuum. I need a controller. Who's it to be? You, Mr. Marks; or Upton?'

'Me,' Feldspar said. 'I'll be her controller.'

'Mr. Marks?' Greer asked.

'Sure, why not?' Marks said. 'After all, she must like you some, Feldspar. She almost broke your goddamned nose, didn't she?'

Feldspar said, 'You think I can handle it, Dr. Greer?'

'If you keep your head and do as I tell you.'

'All right,' Feldspar agreed.

'Come back around midnight,' Greer said. 'She'll be coherent by then.'

'Coherent?'

'She'll have told me all I need to know.'

'About what?' asked Feldspar.

'Bobby Hoffmann. Heroin. Her life and loves. And about you, Agent Feldspar. I'll find out how she feels about you.'

'Want to back out, Feldspar?' Marks asked.

'No, sir,' said Feldspar hastily. 'I guess I'll see it through.'

Marks jerked his thumb at the screen. Suddenly, Feldspar recognised bitterness in the former director, an unpleasant scorn for the instruments of his revenge against the system that had rejected him. 'With an ass like that, Feldspar, I don't blame you for grabbing the assignment.'

'Yes, sir,' Feldspar said, coldly. But he did not look at the screen.

MONDAY MORNING
THE PAIUTE RANCH/SAN FRANCISCO

Four of Sarsby's best soldiers ferried Chen Yu-lan, Mr. Wing and Dr. Chung from San Francisco to the Paiute in a ten-seater Adcock helicopter with the windows of the passenger section painted black. In addition, the Chinese were obliged to wear Ladysware Soundslumber Nitemasks. Blue velvet with sequin edging made them look ridiculous. Dr. Chung was a venerable, very yellow fellow with large brown teeth. He fell asleep beneath the mask.

The chopper set them down on the pad behind the Paiute. The blindfolded men were helped out and led to the main block. Only when the door was closed and drapes drawn were the masks removed.

Showing the Tigers every courtesy, as Sarsby had instructed him to do, Anthony Bulthius admitted Yu-lan and Dr. Chung to Rand's bedroom. The botanist was in pyjamas, stretched out on the bed. Even Yu-lan could tell after a moment's inspection that it was no act; also, that Rand was certainly in no condition to be questioned, even if Bulthius would permit it.

Dr. Chung opened his bag of tricks and proceeded with a full physical examination. Rand had no fever symptoms. His mind seemed clear enough. He did not struggle or protest as Chung subjected him to a series of medical tests. Nothing was said, apart from Chung's curt questions to the patient. In all, it took ten minutes. Chung and Yu-lan stepped out into the living room once more.

Mr. Wing had been given coffee and scrambled eggs. He ate with the plate balanced on his knee, four soldiers strategically ranged around him.

Bulthius did not offer breakfast to the other two Chinese, nor did he quiz the doctor. He watched as the men were once more fitted with the masks and walked after them onto the porch. Two soldiers guided Wing; Chung and Yu-lan had one guide each.

The Adcock took off. Three hours and twenty minutes later it touched down on the private pad near Brisbane. The Tigers' own limousine carried them back by the Bayshore Freeway into San

Francisco.

In a suite in the tiny luxury hotel, the Singapore, Dr. Chung delivered his verdict to Sheng Kittegawa and Chen Yu-lan. The doctor was paid five one hundred dollar bills and dismissed.

Kittegawa asked, 'Where do they have him?'

Wing answered, 'In the desert. Three or four hundred miles south-east. It was hot, dry and silent. That is all I know.'

Yu-lan said, 'They were very careful, Sheng.'

Kittegawa said, 'Are you convinced?'

'I am sufficiently convinced,' said Yu-lan, 'to be anxious.'

'If Sarsby fulfils his promise to keep Rand alive, then we must bring our friend from Tang Mang Wu to the meeting.'

'I am still in doubt about the wisdom of such a thing.'

'Have no doubts, Chen,' said Kittegawa. 'Sarsby's greed will enable us to obtain Gordon Rand.'

'I do not understand how that may be done.'

'Sarsby has not yet realised that we no longer need an American connection.'

Deprecatingly, Mr. Wing suggested, 'We will prepare for the day of the meeting. We will arrange to strike first, and thoroughly. Is that how it will be?'

'Leaving nothing behind,' said Kittegawa.

'Nothing alive,' said Wing.

'However it falls, we will retain the upper hand,' said Kittegawa.

'Then America must come to us with the begging bowl,' said Mr. Wing. 'Is that not so?'

'That is so, Wing,' Kittegawa said.

'But what if Sarsby's boast is hollow. What if Rand dies?'

'We will still have a weapon, will we not?' said Kittegawa.

'The new bacterium?'

'To sell to the highest bidder.' Kittegawa said.

'It is . . . deadly, Sheng; very deadly.'

'But valuable to those who know how to use it.'

'Peking?'

'Peking,' said Kittegawa. 'A suitable recompense.'

MONDAY
WASHINGTON, D.C.

Washington was airless and crowded. Half of Europe seemed to be on the prowl through its national shrines and museums. Flocks of packaged tourists were shepherded into and out of the fine buildings. Fortunately the Corcoran Gallery on New York Avenue at 17th Street N.W. was closed Mondays. Feldspar had no problem making the switch. The delivery boy was a smart-looking young Italian who seemed impatient with the precautions that Feldspar wanted to take. He was oblivious to the ambience of the place, the proximity of thousands of government officials and the fact that any one of the pedestrians might have been an agent.

He came up the pavement at a fast lick, listing to one side with the weight of the attaché case, and dumped it by the almost identical – empty – case that Feldspar had by his foot.

'Hey, is that for me?'

'That depends on who you are?' Feldspar said.

'I'm not fucking Western Union.'

'You remind me of a guy called Frank Varese,' said Feldspar.

'And you remind me of a Capitol Hill shit.'

'You got me,' said Feldspar, giving up the charade.

He reached down, picked up the heavy case, stepped round the delivery boy and walked off into the broil of pedestrians at the corner. He glanced behind him once. But the Italian had taken the empty case and departed, presumably in the opposite direction.

Feldspar caught a bus on 18th Street and rode it all the way up to the Dupont Circle with the case on his knee. Parking was impossible in the vicinity of the White House and he was in no mood to fight traffic congestion.

He walked from the Dupont Circle to the Talisman Club on Chester French Street and picked up the Bobcat from the parking lot there. First thing he did was plug a pocket detector into the cigar lighter and check out the case for boobytraps. Satisfied, he opened the case and looked down at taped wads of high denomination bills. He had made a few cash drops in his time but he had never seen so much loot in such small bulk before. It gave him no particular thrill. He drove back to the stockbroking office where Halveston waited, carried the case up three flights of stairs, knocked, entered, put the case on the desk and clicked open the lid.

'Two hundred thousand bucks, Senator.'

'You counted it?'

'It's your money, sir, you count it.'

Briskly, Halveston got to his feet and snapped the attaché case shut again. He opened a huge old-fashioned floor safe in a corner of the office, dumped the case inside, thudded the door shut and spun the combination lock.

'And that's it,' said Feldspar.

'Until Varese calls me,' said Halveston.

'Do you want me to hang around?'

'Have you other pressing business?'

'I thought I might catch up on some sleep.'

'You look as if you could use it, Feldspar,' Halveston said.

'If you need me for anything, you know how to get in touch.'

'I won't need you,' said Halveston. 'I can handle Varese.'

But at that precise moment, Senator Halveston was in the process of being outsmarted. He never did receive a call from Frank Varese. Instead, he was summoned to an urgent meeting by Vice-President Rainer.

Jay Rainer had no idea what he had gotten himself into. The perils of his post were legion. For all that, he had never doubted his capacity to walk a line between duty and ambition and still keep his patrician nose clean. He had sense enough to realise that only tragedy, another killing, could project him into the highest office in the land. He wanted no part of that promotion.

The debts he had accumulated during his rise to power had been honest and above board. He would not be snared by them. Perversely, he had embarked on the Marks-Upton project with a sense of relish, never imagining that it would mount so rapidly that his entire programme would be disrupted and that he would be committed to begging a United States senator to put his life in jeopardy.

There wasn't even a file or a docket to lean on. No half-pound of paper to scan to give him the facts. He had to make the decision immediately, in cold blood. It was too late to consult President Fisher, to go through the torturous process of explaining why he'd become involved in the shady project in the first place, why he had neglected to table discussion in any semi-open committee. The whole of the Vice-Presidential agenda would come under suspicion and the scrutiny of the House would focus upon his every move. He'd be hog-tied if he'd let that happen. He'd have to go with it, win himself a prize to justify his crass impetuosity.

But if he put Halveston in jeopardy and Halveston were iced, if it ever became known that he had entered into a private treaty with a criminal cartel, then he was finished. The press would wipe the floor with him. He'd be lucky to find himself a job this side of the Rio Grande.

In the wake of the person-to-person call from Frank Varese, Rainer covered his tracks as best he could. It was a clumsy manoeuvre but might be effective if the thing blew up. Apart from that, he did have a legitimate alibi: the trip to the conference in Geneva had been arranged months ago. He would travel one day early, that's all. His aides, his secretaries and official entourage would wall up his tracks. He could depend on at least half the members of his specially convened narco committee backing him in case of dire emergency.

The meeting was arranged at short notice. A USAF jet brought Upton from San Francisco. Halveston and Marks were both in Washington. The four men met shortly after six o'clock in an office that Rainer had 'borrowed' from the Department of the Environment, a modern building six blocks from the Museum of Natural History where several smaller departments had annexes.

Rainer did not try to disguise his destination. He went by car, accompanied by a male aide and two secret servicemen who were left to cool their heels in the building's cafeteria. Upton, Marks and Halveston arrived independently. No more than three people knew that Vice-President Rainer, Senator Halveston, the ex-director of the CIA, and an Englishman had come together that sultry August evening.

Behind Rainer, who took the tall swivel chair behind the desk, was a huge coloured map of industrial development in Louisiana, flanked by strip film of negro workers. The office had the atmosphere of a place where much work was done.

'I'll come right to the point, gentlemen,' said Rainer. 'Late this morning I received a person-to-person call from Frank Varese. Need I explain Varese's position in the Sarsby syndicate? No? Senator Halveston?'

'I know who Varese is,' Halveston said.

'You've been at the meetings, Clark,' Rainer went on. 'I think you're as familiar with what's going on as I am.'

'Probably, Mr. Vice-President.'

'Gordon Rand is a prisoner of the Sarsby syndicate. Rand is ill. He requires urgent surgical attention. We are willing to offer the services of Walter Stein. But Sarsby and Varese quite naturally don't trust us as far as they can piss. They want a hostage in Rand's place.'

'Yeah, yeah,' murmured Marks. 'We should have figured.'

'Anyone in particular?' Upton asked.'

'They want a senator, a member of my narcotics committee. They want Clark Halveston.'

'Did they indicate why they'd picked on me, Mr. Vice-President?'

'No,' said Rainer. 'Apparently they have need of Gordon Rand's professional expertise – we can imagine just what they require from him, can't we? – therefore must make a deal with us. We provide the surgical team and an operating theatre in the San Francisco or Los Angeles area. They'll bring Rand to the hospital and take Halveston in exchange. Clark, I'm sorry that you've been dragged into this.'

Upton said, 'We can't allow Rand to die, sir.'

Halveston said, 'I appreciate Rand's importance.'

Upton said, 'When Rand is sufficiently recovered, Sarsby will collect him and Halveston will be released; is that the idea?'

'Yes,' said Rainer. 'My first inclination, I admit, was to tell Varese to go fuck himself. But then I thought of Rand. I helped get him into this. I suppose . . .' He shrugged.

'Senator Halveston?' Marks said.

'Out of the committee room and into the fire,' Halveston said.

'You'll do it, Clark?' Rainer asked.

Halveston was not one to be easily caught.

He said, 'If you wish it, Mr. Vice-President.'

Rainer said, 'Hell!'

Upton said, 'Without surgery, Gordon Rand will surely die.'

'And with surgery?' said Halveston.
'He has a fifty-fifty chance.'
'Very well, gentlemen,' Halveston said. 'You leave me little choice but to volunteer.'
Rainer pushed himself from the chair. 'Henry, it's your show. Make the arrangements.'
'But I've no authority to . . .' Marks protested.
'Goddamn it, Marks. You've plundered my authority all along. Don't think I don't know it. You used me, and now you'll use the senator. As for you, Sir George, I'm not even certain where you fit into all this. It's gotten out of control.'
'No, sir,' Upton said calmly. 'It's working out quite well as it happens.'
'Will Sarsby buckle?' asked Rainer.
'Very soon now,' said Upton.
'Before I return from Geneva?' said Rainer.
'When are you leaving?'
'Early tomorrow, for nine days.'
'Unless I'm mistaken,' said Upton. 'We'll have what we want by then?'
'What *do* we want?'
'Sarsby, the White Tigers, and the safe return of Gordon Rand,' said Upton.
'And Senator Halveston, I hope.'
'Ah, yes,' Upton said. 'And Senator Halveston back safe and sound.'

After Rainer had left, the three men lingered in the office.
'It's clever,' said Halveston. 'I've got to admit it. Bloody clever.'
Marks said, 'We might be handing you over to the enemy, Clark. I mean, Jesus, what if they've tumbled to your act?'
'I question if that's the case,' said Upton.
'It doesn't matter much,' said Halveston. 'As I see it, Sarsby's aready done his deal with Yu-lan and Kittegawa. It's moving on just like you planned. My part's not so important. They only want me to ensure that you'll hand back Rand. It's clever, asking for a hostage who can't raise any kind of squeal.'
'Two hundred thousand bucks worth of co-operation, Clark,'

said Marks. 'They really paid through the nose for you.'

'Imagine the kind of cover-up job Rainer will have to do if anything goes adrift,' Halveston said.

'Varese will be left with no choice but to accept me as the organiser,' said Marks. 'When do we go into action, George?'

'Tomorrow night. Stein will be ready by then.'

'What if Rand dies on that operating table?' Halveston asked.

Upton grimaced. 'That just doesn't bear thinking about.'

'Agent Feldspar,' Greer said. 'What precisely *do* you want the girl to do for your people?'

'Take out an agent at a rendezvous,' said Feldspar.

'In that case,' said Greer, 'wheel and deal yourself. You don't need me.'

'You mean, you can't break her down?' said Feldspar, glumly.

They were together in the office in the wing of the Meriweather Clinic. Feldspar had spent late afternoon and early evening in bed in his apartment in the Maybury, one of two inexpensive establishments that he maintained. He felt better now, more able to cope with Dorothy.

'Oh, sure, yep, I can break her. Might take a week to melt through her indifference.'

'Indifference?'

'Just what *do* you know about this chickie?'

'Not too much,' Feldspar admitted.

'Classic, the early part of her story,' said Greer. 'Born into a repressive religious home in Arith, Kansas – an only child. Mother committed suicide when Dorothy was nine or thereabouts. Father sank to the bottom. Dumped the kid with a mad old grandma in Oklahoma City and lit out to convert Alaska to Jesus. The mad old grandma let the kid run so wild that the law got interested, and local school authorities were roused. Care and attention were foisted on Dorothy. Fosterling syndrome. Attempts to trace Dad failed. Grandma died. Dorothy bridged the gap into womanhood, then at the age of fourteen slid off into the wide blue.'

'How did she make out?'

'Not in the manner you might imagine,' said Greer. 'She became a thief, not a hooker. She took decent jobs, cleverly bided her time, stole cash money, and moved on. She worked in the Prince Royal Hotel in Galveston for a while and got off with a fat bundle one night. She had prepared for the strike, had a car, bought and paid for, laid up in a back-alley garage. She was out of the state before the theft was discovered. She graduated eventually to California.'

'All on her own?'

'Yep.'

'Did she tell you all this freely,' Dr. Greer?'

'With just a little "encouragement". She's proud of her ability to make out. She thinks her innate loneliness is her strength. Maybe it used to be. It's a fine protection, of course, and works well for drifters and grafters. While she was working in an hotel in central L.A. she met up with Bobby Hoffmann. A weakling.'

'Bonny and Clyde?'

'Well, you know, it *is* kind of romantic,' said Greer. 'She set Hoffmann up. She took his name, lived with him, constantly egged him on. Her name before she met Hoffmann was Webster, by the way.'

'Why did she put up with Hoffmann's harem? I'd have thought she'd have wanted to keep the adored one to herself?'

'She was sure of him. Casual sexual connections didn't matter. They were part of an obsessional defiance, bonding between Bobby and Dorothy. They were deep into drugs, into supplying. They exploited the poor little psychic exiles that floated in the Southern Cal sludge. She wouldn't tell me how the system worked. She kept herself "clean". Calculated and clever manipulation. In the long run, her foresight saved her from conviction, from any real involvement in the Hoffmann trial.'

'Bobby took the whole rap,' Feldspar stated.

'She promised she'd get him out.'

'Hoffmann believed her?'

'She'd never let him down before, had she?'

'So that's what she's doing with the Chinese?'

'Earning big bread,' said Greer. 'I tell you, Feldspar, your little chickie is pretty damned smart. She's not going to wave pistols at governors and demand Hoffmann's release. She's not going to highjack some airliner. She's building a fat bankroll.'

'Plus eliminating some of the men who put Hoffmann behind bars.'

'Yep, that's her smoke signal to Bobby that she hasn't forgotten him. The grapevine in the Barbary is, one assumes, efficient. Every time someone gets knocked off, Bobby believes that Dorothy still loves him.'

'Wing must know about this?'

'Probably knows enough to make him appreciate her worth. She's about as close as you can get to a handforged weapon. She'll do anything to keep her habit cosy – and fatten that bankroll. When she has enough money,' Greer said, 'she'll go hell for leather to spring Bobby. How? Blackmail, bribery, buy a professional team to break him out. Have the case reopened, maybe. No, come to think of it, I doubt if she'll go the legal route.'

'What makes her so efficient?'

'Her obsessional neurosis: Hoffmann. Plus her background. Plus the fact that she's indifferent to her own being. And I mean *being*. It's a form of amorality even I haven't encountered before, and I've met my share of purely evil sonsabitches.'

'I think I understand what you're saying, Dr. Greer. She'll turn against Wing without a qualm provided it appears to be advantageous to her personal purpose.'

'That purpose is simplicity itself. It's the interior monologue – dialogue – she has with Bobby that keeps her going.'

'And the heroin? The habit?'

'Maintains function. Helps things along. Oils the psyche's wheels.'

'But she is hooked?'

'Like a fish.'

'What did you do to her?'

'Not much. Twilight sleep with a butyraphenont cocktail, that put her into a mild stupor, talked to her for a while, then hit her with some i.v. methadrine before giving her a small shot of pure heroin.'

'The chemical juggling act, Dr. Greer?'

'Yep.' Greer switched on the tv monitor.

To Feldspar's astonishment, he saw Dorothy seated at a folding bridge table, eating supper. She was dressed in the clothing he'd picked her up in, but it had been laundered and looked fresh and neat. The girl ate heartily, concentrating on the food. She swabbed up gravy with a pinch of bread, pushed the plate away, and reached for the big dish of peppermint icecream that waited on the tray.

'What did you expect, Feldspar? To find her on the rack?'

'How can you be sure she isn't stringing you along?'

'Because she *believes*. She *has* faith – Lordie, Lordie! I convinced her that you can do for her what she can't do for herself – the one thing Wing can't do.'

'Uh-oh!' said Feldspar.

'Break Bobby Hoffmann from Barbary Point.'

'Hell, I can't do that.'

'Yep, yep. I know. I know.' said Greer. 'But Dorothy is willing to suspend credulity on the strength of a promise. Perhaps she's grown impatient. Perhaps she has an awareness of finality.'

'Now or never?' said Feldspar. 'Is that what you mean?'

'Soft, soft,' said Greer, putting his forefinger to his lips. 'This can't be love.'

'*What*?'

'Four years gone, Feldspar. Do you think Hoffmann is real for her now? I told you, she has no *being*. That's why she can kill without a qualm. It is a pleasure, like shooting shit. Superficial stimulation. Dependence. All for Bobby.'

'Did you suggest that I might help spring Hoffmann if she cooperates?'

'In many respects, she's naïve. She believes the CIA can do anything it wants to do. She regards it as the ultimate law. It's a replacement for religious mystique, I think. FBI – pigs! Law enforcement agents of any kind – motherfuckers! But she connects the amorphous world of the Central Intelligence Agency with her own internalised character. Interesting! I wish I had more time with her.'

'You're not helping me, Doctor,' said Feldspar.

Dorothy scraped the icecream dish, poured black coffee from a Cona bowl, helped herself to a cigarette from a new pack and sat back, satisfied. She explored the cell, found the eye of the monitor camera and blew an imperfect smoke ring at it.

'Clever girl,' said Greer. 'You see, Feldspar, it's all functioning for her again. Life instinct has once more satisfactorily become the object of her death instinct.'

'What do I say? What do I do?'

'You lie to her, Feldspar. Convince her that you can and will do what she imagines she wants done. She will deny you nothing while you seem to be inherent to the stability of her dreams.'

'How can I convince her?'

'Feldspar, she's *already* convinced. Just keep her that way. But remember this, never ignore the salient fact that Dorothy isn't working for you, nor even for Hoffmann. She has developed her own particular idiom, a unique one, for dealing with the destructive forces that shaped her young life. Clarity of motive is an illusion with Dorothy, as it is in the Agency she identifies with.'

Feldspar blew out his cheeks. 'All right! So I shore up her belief that I'm the CIA beast incarnate. Can I feed her direct instructions? Can I actually deal with her?'

'Yep, that's no problem. It's nothing new you're asking of her.'

'Does she . . . like me?'

'Who knows?' said Greer. 'How can I define that word in the context. She doesn't *have* to *like* you, my friend. Only to do what you ask of her.'

'That's true,' said Feldspar. 'Will you take her back in here – afterwards?'

Greer was surprised. He blinked several times and patted his tiny hands together. 'Afterwards? Do you think she'll pull through?'

'I . . . I can't say. Certainly, we'll make every effort to . . .'

'The illusion of the beast,' Greer said.

'I'm no nutcase,' Feldspar snapped.

'Of course not,' said Greer, soothingly. 'Go in now. Go ahead. Go talk to her. Convince her, Agent Feldspar. I don't think you'll have too much bother on that score.'

'Hi, kid!'

'CIA – huh? I thought you guys didn't get the horn.'

'We're human too.'

'The doc tells me you have a deal.'

Feldspar had expected to go through several rounds of sparring.

'It means crossing your partner, Wing,' he said.

'Wing. That yellow mother. What's your offer, your *official* offer.'

Feldspar was daunted by the magnitude of the lies he had to tell. He wasn't merely perverting truth now. He had descended into melodrama. Greer's warnings troubled him.

'Do you know what Wing's doing right now?'

'No, I don't.'

'Will he come back for you?'

'Sure. If there's work to be done.'

'Are you his only . . . assistant?'

'Assistant? Jesus, you're just like I thought you'd be.'

'Are you?'

'He knows he can depend on me.'

'Good,' said Feldspar. 'All right: my offer. My official offer. We can't pardon Hoffmann. No way. Not even my . . . not even the CIA can meddle that much with justice. Anyhow, it would reveal too much. It would expose you to . . . to an excess of scrutiny.'

'An excess of scrutiny. I like that, Feldspar. What's your first name?'

Her exuberance was unfeigned. It was also unnatural. He pressed the thought deep into the plastic areas of his brain.

'Harold.'

'They call you Harry?'

'You . . . you can call me Harry,' Feldspar said.

'No, I'll call you Harold. It's better. Harold. Excess of scrutiny, Harold. You wanna protect me?'

Batyraphenonts: methadrine: Christ, in eighteen hours Greer and his hypodermic had given the kid a whole new personality. Released a personality, that was it. In a week, a month, what could not be achieved? Feldspar hung in there, gripping tight to an authority that he did not possess.

'I . . . I want to protect you. But in good faith, I can't promise you a pardon for Bobby Hoffmann.'

'I figured that.'

'On the other hand,' Feldspar steeled himself for the whoppers, 'I can set up a jail break.'

'The CIA?'

'Yes.'

'Can do anything, can't it?'

'Some things legal, most anything illegal.'

'I always figured that.'

'How about it, Dorothy? A rigged jailbreak in exchange for some inside help.'

'Not so fast, Feldspar. Harold. I'm no daisy. I want proof.'

'Proof?'

'I want to be sure you won't run out.'

'How about . . . How about, you talk this over with Bobby? No taps. No hacks. Just you and Bobby alone together in a quiet spot in the Barbary?'

'Talk it . . . with . . .' He had thrown her. He thought fast.

'And cash, hard cash, a down payment,' he added.

Her eyes glittered, very blue. Cash was smart.

'How much?'

'Two hundred thousand dollars, in bills.'

'You're snowing me.'

'I'll get you two hundred thousand dollars in cash to prove our good faith,' said Feldspar. 'Then we go see Bobby.'

'Two hundred grand up front, and a break to follow?'

'It's about the best I can do.'

'When?'

'Tonight. We'll do it right away.'

'Because you gotta get me back into the Florissant before Wing finds out I've been gone?'

Feldspar hadn't thought it through that far yet. He was moving with a sluggishness that emphasised her hypomanic mental agility.

'Tonight. I'll take you with me. We go collect the money, then we get on a flight for San Francisco and see Bobby tomorrow.'

'That's some deal, Harold.'

'Best I can do, kid; really.'

'I'll take it.'

'You don't know what I . . . we want in exchange.'

'Doesn't matter. Kill Wing?'

'I'll explain while we travel. You feel up to travel?'

'Just get me out of here.'

Feldspar looked round at the monitor camera. There would be sound recording too. Doctor Greer would have heard it all. A faint clucking sound indicated that the heavy door had been unlocked. Feldspar tried the handle bolted to the metal sheeting, pushing gently. The door opened ahead of him. Greer waited in the corridor.

Going out, Feldspar kept his back to the girl and mouthed, 'Okay?'

Smiling like a Christmas gnome, Greer nodded, then beckoned Dorothy from the cell. The doctor escorted the couple out of the Meriweather. He even rode down to the gate with them in Feldspar's Bobcat just to make sure that the illusion was maintained and that Harris, the black night duty guard, didn't get sassy and spoil young Feldspar's image of omnipotence.

TUESDAY 23 AUGUST
WASHINGTON, D.C.

It was four o'clock in the wee small hours. The noisy plumbing of the old brownstone office building made Feldspar nervous, though he gave no sign of it as he lifted the typewriter from the desk and pulled the felt mat from under the machine. Like a helmeted sentinel, by the window the domed tickertape glinted in the beam of the pencil torch.

By the door, Dorothy stood motionless, hand resting on the oval brass knob. Thief's instinct Feldspar supposed. God, if he teamed up with Dorothy Newhoff they could steal themselves a fortune and retire to laze on Mexican beaches. Impossible! The company wouldn't rest until it tracked him down, and he would never be able to trust her not to shiv him in the back.

For the time being, though, he was safe. He would remain safe as long as he could maintain the omnipotent stance of a CIA agent – Dorothy's version. He hadn't bothered to explain that he would be guillotined if he were caught burglarising a stocker-brokers' office without official sanction. If Dorothy insisted that he behave like a technicolour kook, he mustn't disappoint her. Besides, he needed the money in short order. Even Marks couldn't conjure up two hundred thousand bucks in the middle of the night. At least, that was Feldspar's excuse for relieving Halveston of his mouth fee.

From the Meriweather, Feldspar had driven to his appartment. Leaving Dorothy in the car, he'd galloped upstairs, raked trade tools from the closet, stuffed them into a tennis holdall, raced back down to the Bobcat and headed for the offices of Halveston, Halveston and Shapes.

Reconnaissance was brief but thorough. Using rope and grapple, he shinned up from an alley onto the rusty firewalk. He brought the girl up after him. The alarm system was a hoot, a Greenboro clanger with external cabling. He doped it with secateurs and masking tape before cutting out a pane of the third-floor toilet window. With some contortion he reached in and eased back the safety bolt. Five minutes later he led Dorothy into the stockbrokers' main office.

Ridiculously easy. Also insane. The crazziness of it filled Feldspar with daring. After all, robbing a U.S. senator of two hundred grand acquired by peddling secrets to the mob was no more outlandish than many of his past assignments.

Dorothy was intrigued; that's what mattered. Later, when the vaudeville act was over, she would accept orders from him and obey.

Halveston's safe was like something left over from a Wells Fargo rummage sale: a head-high free-standing Morland Norris with a tumbler lock the size of a skillet and one huge handle. Kneeling on the typewriter mat, Feldspar wrapped the pencil torch in a Kleenex and nikked it between his teeth. He pulled a doctor's stethoscope from the holdall, plugged it into his ears and patiently set about cracking the old monster.

It took him fifty fussy minutes. During the operation, the girl did not speak. Finally, Feldspar got stiffly to his feet, dropped the instrument back into the holdall, depressed the handle and heaved open the safe door.

He beckoned. Treading like a fawn on ice, Dorothy approached. He could tell she was mighty impressed by his performance. Her blue eyes were round, her tongue touched her upper lip.

Feldspar drew out the suitcase, lowered it to the floor and, kneeling again, flung open the lid.

'*Voila*,' he whispered. 'Two hundred Gees.'

'Jesus!'

'Go ahead, kid, examine it. I assure you it's genuine.'

'Jesus!'

'Satisfied?'

'Yeah. Yeah, sure.'

'Come hell or high water, it's all yours.'

'Good,' she said. 'Now I wanna talk to Bobby.'

'Where are you at present?' Upton asked.

'My apartment,' Feldspar answered.

'What time is it in Washington?' Upton sounded sleepy, as if Feldspar's call had awakened him.

'Quarter to six.'

'Is the girl still in your custody?'

'She's cooking breakfast.'

Upton had not enquired as to her mental state. Perhaps he had been in touch with Greer.

'The Senator and Henry are flying west by USAF transport. The aircraft will leave Trent Base at nine-thirty.'

'Will there be room aboard for both of us?' Feldspar said.

'Room to shave.'

'The prison visit,' Feldspar glanced at the kitchen door. 'Are you *really* in a position to arrange that, Sir George?'

'Yes, I believe so.'

'Sir George, let me ask you, is she worth all this trouble?'

'What's your opinion, Feldspar?'

'I think we can use her.'

'Very well. Keep your prisoner happy.'

'To do that, Sir George, I'll need a street bag.'

'What's a street bag?' Upton enquired.

'Heroin.'

'Ah, yes. I'll find one.'

'And the meeting with Hoffmann?'

'Tonight.'

Trent Air Force Base lay across the Anacostia on the Suitland Parkway, indistinguishable from the other naval and air force installations that sprawled over the area. Feldspar had a little trouble finding it. But he had allowed for that and finally nosed the Bobcat under the pillared arch and brought the fender to rest over menacing yellow lines painted on the black macadam. Between low blocks ahead, he could see runways.

A sergeant stepped from the guardhouse door. Feldspar cranked down the side window. The sergeant was a big blond mountain boy toting a sidearm and sporting the white webbing and gloves of Special Militia. He was discreetly supported by two other SM non-coms, left and right of the barricade.

Feldspar had always been leery of inflexible military minds. He had come unstuck before on the barbed wire of 'regulations and procedure'. He prayed that Sir George had gotten on the horn to Henry and that Henry had gotten on the horn to Rainer's staff man delegated to pull wires.

Feldspar presented his plastic I/D disc. The sergeant inspected it critically, stooped and peered across Feldspar at the girl. She smiled at the blond mountain boy.

The sergeant drew slowly back.

Feldspar said, 'My instructions are to . . .'

The sergeant called to his buddy. His buddy went into the guardhouse and returned with a clipboard roster. The pair huddled over the clipboard while three long minutes ticked away. Feldspar scanned the sky over the blocks. He almost expected to see a jet climb from the strip, Marks's face scowling at him from a window. He sweated and caught the back taste of waffles and maple syrup in his gullet.

The sergeant lumbered over, returned the I/D.

'What about your vehicle, sir?'

Rainer's staff man obviously hadn't futzed around. Feldspar wondered why it couldn't always be this straightforward.

'What?' he said.

'The senator's waiting by the lot. You can park your vehicle indefinitely in Section C Zone, if you wish.'

'Fine, that's fine,' said Feldspar.

With a sudden punching motion that made Feldspar flinch, the blond mountain man slapped a sticker onto the windshield and shouted, 'Straight on, turn left at the sign. Your party's on Strip Three.'

The barrier rose. Feldspar eased the Bobcat into the avenue. Scrupulously obeying traffic signs, he crawled up to Strip Three, Section C Zone. By his side, Dorothy slumped in the seat, knees pressed against the dash. She was clearly impressed. She despised uniforms; all piggies, whatever the shade of the cloth. But Feldspar had power over them. Maybe she'd be a CIA undercover agent when she grew up. She was sure she'd be great at it.

Feldspar said, 'It isn't always like that, kid. For instance, we're about to meet up with two men who'll probably ignore you. Don't worry about it. Just be polite. Say nothing about the suitcase. I'll do all the talking.'

Since he was travelling in Halveston's company, Feldspar had carefully transferred the two hundred thousand dollars to a scuffed piece of luggage of his own. It bulged on both sides like a pregnant cow and the straps creaked against the buckles, but he had a convincing lie ready if Halveston or Marks got curious about the suitcase's contents.

Marks waited by a concrete bib that separated the strip from the lot. Out on the strip a sleek Lear Jet in USAF colours waited. The two-man crew loitered by the wing. The sky looked huge and flat, as if the airforce had painted it fresh during the night.

Feldspar got out of the Bobcat. Dorothy got out too. Marks watched. He seemed to be furious, and hard, holding himself tight.

Behind him, Halveston maintained an implacable indifference to the arrivals. He exuded a stiff-necked, Washington dignity that Feldspar could not relate to the crawling Judas who'd sold out his secrets for fat cash. It occurred to Feldspar then that it was senatorial power that had cleared the way for him.

Feldspar opened the trunk and took out two overnight bags and a suitcase. Neither Marks nor Halveston betrayed the slightest interest, then or later. In fact, Marks said nothing to him all during the flight. His welcome was hardly friendly.

'Is that Upton's goddamned secret weapon?' he hissed, jerking his thumb at the girl.

'That's her, sir.'

'I hope to Christ George knows what he's doing.'

'I hope so too, sir.'

'All right, let's shove off.'

At nine-thirty a.m., Washington time, the Lear's wheels left the strip. Up front, six clear seats away, Marks and Halveston relaxed.

In back, Feldspar and his little piece of pariah glanced at each other and grinned. He was relieved that the administration hadn't let him down and ruined his image. She was happy because she was coming round to believing the crazy agent. She figured all she had to do to free Bobby was to play along. And maybe kill a few guys.

Feldspar asked, 'How do you feel?'

Dorothy answered, 'Terrific.'

TUESDAY
SAN FRANCISCO

Mike Lassiter took the latest request more calmly than Upton had anticipated. The FBI chief had worked a graveyard shift to organise personnel and acquire use of facilities at the Fort Shaffer Military Hospital. Stein had suggested the Shaffer. It suited Lassiter, being south of the city in the Servetus Bay area, with a single arterial approach road.

Stein and he had inspected theatre and I.C. wards late Monday night, and Lassiter had stayed on, working with Colonel Jewel of Army Intelligence. Jewel was still under the impression that the show was an FBI undercover coup instigated by Rainer; another of those quiet calls from the Vice-Presidential aide had confirmed his supposition. Lassiter did not disillusion the colonel. He put an iron of his own on the fire by stationing four three-man teams at strategic points along the Servetus Bay freeway. He thought of using choppers, but he was shy of scaring off the quarry.

It was a little after nine a.m. when Upton was admitted to Lassiter's office. The FBI chief was fatigued. He had eaten a substantial breakfast at a diner down the street and, caught in a lull in activities, was re-scheduling his casebook to give himself several clear days.

Upton explained his latest requirement. Even Lassiter's phlegmatic temperament was incapable of accepting this request without some reaction.

'Who is the girl?' he asked.

'Dorothy Newhoff, also known as Hoffmann.'

'Bobby's wife,' said Lassiter. 'How the hell did you track her down?'

Upton said, 'Do you know her?'

'I've heard about her.'

Upton asked, 'Is she really Hoffmann's wife?'

'Shit, no. As far as I know they were married by a ju-ju man during a week-long debauch in Winslow. That's a hippie-junkie hang out below Big Sur.'

'Has she the right to visit Hoffmann?'

'You mean, can I get her into Barbary Point?' said Lassiter.

'Yes.'

'Yeah, I can do that. But I need a reason,' Lassiter said.

'The girl is closely linked with the Chinese crowd,' said Upton. 'I've every reason to believe she will be part of the bodyguard that the White Tigers will take to the rendezvous.'

'And her price is a meeting with Hoffmann,' said Upton. 'An untaped half hour's conversation.'

'For what?' said Lassiter suspiciously.

'Presumably to talk over the deal we've offered her.'

'Holy shit!' Lassiter rubbed his face with his hands, then looked up sourly at Upton. 'Barbary Point isn't any old prison. Sure, it has a Guidance Centre and a Division of Care and Treatment. But it's the Custody Division that holds all the power. In the struggle between the guards and medics, the guards always win. No outsiders are allowed to get themselves a top-hold in the administration to ferment the left-wing radical and racist elements. There's no insurgent activity *at all.* Warden Withers has developed the finest disturbance control system in the whole country – and I don't just mean the state. Barbary Point, Mr. Upton, is the *big* big slam.'

'If we require a district court judge's order, I . . .'

'No, no,' said Lassiter. 'I can do it off the record. I hear Hoffmann's a pussycat anyhow; a thumb-sucker.'

Upton said, 'The girl will arrive this afternoon. If possible, I'd like the visit made early this evening so she can be out of California and on her way home very quickly.'

Lassiter said, 'In case you'd forgotten, Mr. Upton, you asked me to manage a show for you tonight. Fort Shaffer's sixty miles from the Barbary. I can't be both places.'

'I have a man with her. A nursemaid. An agent of Central Intelligence. He has high security clearance. He can accompany her.'

Lassiter massaged the back of his neck with his right fist. His left hand drummed lightly on the desk. He squinted at Upton. 'Anything else while we're at it, Mr. Upton?'

'No thank you, Chief. I think that will be all.'

They sat at a small table on an apron of salty beams overlooking Fisherman's Wharf, eating crab cakes and Fracastoro oyster stew. The mixture was just a little rich for Upton but it seemed to be to Walter Stein's taste. Overhead gulls squealed and circled. Along the packed harbour, Italian fishermen were camping it up for tourists and lunch-hour visitors, in the baking sun. The scene reminded Upton of Naples.

'How's your neck?' Upton asked, pushing the last crab cake in Stein's direction.

The surgeon speared it onto his fork. He dipped it in oyster gravy, expertly cut it and pushed half into his mouth. 'Throbs, gotdam it.'

'But only when you laugh, Walter?' Upton said, wryly.

'I could have done a better job with this fork.'

Smaller than a cent, the transmitter coil had been inserted under the skin at the nape of Stein's neck. The operation had hardly been major, but Stein was a bad patient. During the insertion procedure, he had carped about the discomfort – even he could hardly call it pain – and the 'technique' of the surgeon, a practitioner from the San Francisco office who had considerable experience in anatomical plants. Upton speculated on how Stein would have reacted to one of the outdated rectal transmitters that had been all the rage ten years ago. Because of their size, they had tended to leave a permanent fistula in the delicate tissues. The latest 'bug' was powerful and virtually indetectable to anything but the most detailed physical search. Only a pinhead of raised flesh showed where the coil had been slipped in – and that would heal within a couple of days.

Upton asked, 'Is the Fort Shaffer theatre completely equipped, Walter? Will it do?'

Stein said, 'Yah, it's okay. I ship in what special stuff I need. I haf a good team.'

'Any of them worked with you before, on secret stitching?'

'All of them.'

'More wine?'

'You think I was condemned, the way you feed me, George.'

'Walter, we know each other well enough for me to say . . .'

Interrupting, Stein flapped his hand, 'Your Agincourt speech, goot got! Yah, yah, Georgie! I know how important it is, save Rand's life.'

'It's also exceedingly dangerous, Walter.'

'Rand stays alive, Walter Stein stays alive?'

'Basically, yes.'

'Can't set odds until I examine him. But I done hundreds of valve replacements, George. Got, I do them in my sleep. It's not like transplant; mechanics. I worry about this virus, though. Metabollic failure, like that.'

'What's your surgical schedule, Walter?'

'I get him tonight, say, ten o'clock. We do all tests, stock up on blood, get anaesthesia, look him over. We go in at six, maybe seven, tomorrow morning.'

'I suspect Rand may be failing,' Upton said.

'I cannot cut and come again,' said Stein. 'Can't go in for exploration.'

'I know.'

Overhead gulls squawked and dove from the ridge of the restaurant as fishing craft churned in from the bay. A Mercedes Sports Coupé trolled past, stereo belting out a Dean Martin evergreen. A big yellow tour bus braked with a noise like a Boeing touching down. A breeze rippled the checkered cloth and linen napkins and rolled the wine cork on its plate.

Stein put down the fork, the remains of the last crab cake squashed on its tines. He held out his hands.

'You want my hands to be your conscience, George?'

Upton was a little taken aback. 'That never occurred to me, Walter.'

Stein lowered his hands, found the fork and put the food into his mouth, still looking at Upton.

'Should haf,' he said. 'It sure should haf, Georgie. I think you been in this game too long. Time you gave up, retired.'

Upton watched the birds flock thickly on the oily water. Loners on the mast tops, one gull to each, they were alert and watchful.

'Yes,' he said, softly. 'Perhaps you're right.'

The pay-phone stood in solitary seediness on the open corner of Tempest and Anglada. Airforce personnel had recorded comments against numbers scraped into the paintwork. The printing had been done with a meticulousness that suggested concentration and seriousness of purpose, a sexual grapevine into which any man in blue might plug himself. Without superciliousness, Halveston read what Marla would do, how generous

Betty Lou could be, and where the 'big boys' met each night. Some prig had scrawled *Turn Ye Again to God* in wax crayon across the side glass. Through the large virtuous O in the final word, Halveston studied the four door Lincoln sedan in which Upton and the FBI chief waited.

It was hot in the glass booth. The ocean glinted like metal across the flats beyond the edge of the runways. He sweated even in his lightweight suit. He hoped that he would have leisure to bathe and change before Sarsby came for him.

He turned his head. The other FBI sedan, with Marks, Feldspar and the weird wild child girl in it, was parked by the side of a disused cold storage warehouse. He hadn't enquired about the girl. At this stage, he figured the less he knew the better about Upton's plans.

Eleven eternal minutes after he'd spoken to the New York contact, the phone rang. He lifted the receiver and heard Varese snap, 'Where the fuck are you?'

Nerves twanged at the graceless voice. His temper rose. He let it. 'You, Varese, get to *fuck* off the line. I talk with your *boss*, with *Sarsby,* or *I don't talk* at all.'

'Listen, Halveston, I . . .'

'*You* listen. I'm sick of being shoved around. Selling me to Rainer as a hostage wasn't your bright idea, sonny boy. That was Sarsby's brainwave. You haven't got the wit to dream up a manoeuvre like that. So – I deal with Sarsby now, or I don't deal at all, and you can kiss Rand goodbye. Get me Sarsby.'

A long pause; a hand over the mouthpiece; Varese was an interstate sandflea, but with the clans gathering in California Halveston figured he'd be at Sarsby's side.

If they'd finally figured out that the Judas senator had been making them dance for the past seven years, at least it hadn't cost them a nickel or a night in jail. He'd always delivered useful information; Marks had seen to that. Whatever Marks had gained in return, Halveston couldn't be sure. Anyway, it was water under the bridge. Sarsby was a different type from Frank Varese. Sarsby would hold no grudges.

Sarsby's smooth voice said, 'Senator, you want to talk to me.'

'Right now,' Halveston said, 'I'm not feeling too friendly, Sarsby.'

'You must admit it was poetic justice,' Sarsby said. 'Calling you out like that.'

'I'm here. In California. I flew down by USAF jet,' Halveston said, still clipped and angry. 'You spoke to Rainer, didn't you? He told you of the arrangement?'

'Not the where and when.'

'Listen carefully. I'm not wasting loose change on you,' Halveston said. 'You've no room for negotiation. It's take it or leave it.'

'Who's arguing.'

'How ill is Gordon Rand?'

'His condition's not so good.'

'The Fort Shaffer Military Hospital in San Francisco is the where. Walter Stein will assemble a full crew of medical experts there tonight. Bring Rand at ten o'clock, precisely. Leave him *inside* the gate. You get me in exchange. Depending on Rand's condition and the extent of surgery required, Stein figures it'll be next Saturday week at the earliest before he'll let Rand go. That's only if things go well. Stein also wants me to ascertain that you have trained medical personnel on tap, somebody with surgical experience.'

'Aftercare?' said Sarsby. 'We can handle it.'

'Rand won't be well for a month or more. Complications might arise over the next ten days.'

'Just when will Stein know if Rand will make it?'

'Twenty-four hours, minimum, after Rand regains consciousness.'

'All being well, we collect Rand again Saturday week? Where?'

'Fort Shaffer. Same as before, but with the procedures reversed. You hand me over, you get Rand in return.'

'No,' Sarsby said. 'We get Rand first.'

'Agreed,' said Halveston, without hesitation.

'Tonight, ten o'clock, at Fort Shaffer.'

'That's it.'

'We'll have him there.'

Halveston was trembling slightly. His head ached in the raw glare from the Pacific, a glare that seemed to reflect off the sky. He collected himself. He wiped his face and hands on a handkerchief, then walked across the street to Upton's car. He opened the rear door and got in.

'It's all arranged,' he said. 'I spoke directly to Sarsby.'

'Did he quibble?'

'Only about exchanging me in return for Rand. He wants Rand first.'

'Will Sarsby do you any harm, Senator?'

'Improbable,' said Halveston.

Lassiter was driving. He said, 'What do we do first, Mr. Upton?'

'Circle round and tell Mr. Marks.'

Lincoln came abreast of Lincoln in the centre of the empty street. Upton rolled down the window and looked across at Marks.

'It's on,' he said.

'All systems?' said Marks.

'Yes, all systems.'

'Good luck, George.'

'Good luck to you, Henry.'

In opposite directions the sedans moved off into the shimmering heat of the August afternoon.

At the end of an interminable walk, Agent Harold Feldspar and Miss Dorothy Newhoff reached the concrete heart of Barbary Point High Security Prison. They were flanked by two senior guards and Deputy Warden Brabenham. At the second of three checkgates they were joined by two younger guards who walked behind the party. After curt introductions, no words were spoken. The gentlemen of Custody Division patently disapproved of the visit.

Barbary Point was on an unprepossessing plain of scrub-oak and chaparral, raised four hundred feet like a huge burial mound. The prison's outer wall was a concrete hexagonal topped by towers – not the old-fashioned 'lighthouse' kind but tinted glass excrescences with stepped balustrades. Menacing and geometrically perfect, the towers overlooked every inch of ground, leaving no blindspots. There were no raking searchlights, only ribbed strips of neon on a fretwork of metal gantries that poured down light the colour of pus. Within the towered enclosure was a second wall: behind it, the blocks of Detention and Correction lay like shoeboxes.

Feldspar had visited correctional institutions, but none like the Barbary. Though only an hour or so after dusk, its interior was silent. Feldspar picked up no human sounds or odours, no indications that four hundred men were shut up there.

Beside him, Dorothy's face was pale as milk. Her litheness had deserted her, that insolent feminine athletic gait had stiffened. She seemed to have to force herself forward in little spasms, as if the guards at her back were driving her through rubbery membranes of dread.

Brabenham had read them no regulations, made no pompous speeches. The curators of Barbary Point felt no need to take extra precautions. Feldspar could understand why the penal code had no application here. Every man in the Barbary would be broken in time, ingrained sociopathic traits squeezed out by ugliness and isolation, by the utter lack of hope.

The group came at last to a fifth guarded gate. At Brabenham's signal, it too was opened. The 'visitors' entourage passed through into a yard the size of a basketball court.

Sheer walls were smeared with neon from gantry lights. Two steel doors fed into the yard; rows of unlit windows high on the end walls; a flagged floor, swept absolutely clean. Above the lights, the sky was so black and heavy that it might have been welded to the roofs. Penology at its most ruthless, its most efficient. Even prison-bred babies would not be happy here.

Brabenham nodded. A guard detached himself from the group and muttered a three-word message into a hand radio.

Dorothy was shaking. She blinked incessantly. Her mouth had pinched to a brittle line. Feldspar put his hand on her elbow. In reflex, she clutched his wrist. One of the guards gripped her tightly, fist against the base of her neck.

Across the yard the steel door swung inwards. A wafer of brilliant steelblue light; four figures against it; a cluttered silhouette, out of which the prisoner solidified. The guard continued to restrain Dorothy. Brabenham turned to her. Face close, he said, 'You meet that end of the yard. You have fifteen minutes, girl.'

She didn't argue. She didn't appeal to Feldspar to wave the magic CIA wand. Whatever she'd imagined, dreamed of, it had not been this, not remotely like this.

'Listen, Warden . . .' Feldspar began.

He was nudged from behind. 'Out there.' They parted.

Dorothy, alone, wandered left. Feldspar went right with Brabenham and two guards. Across the quadrangle the guards there had also detached themselves. Hoffmann stood alone and uncertain, immobilised by terror or suspicion, confused by this unexpected break in grindingly dull routine.

As far as Feldspar was concerned, the conning of Dorothy Newhoff was blown to the winds. Gone, after his careful groundwork in building himself an infallible image.

Hoffmann was small and stooped. Dressed in prison denims, he looked like a dirt farmer bemused by a disastrous crop blight. He shuffled left from the closing door, sneaking backward glances, cricking his head up and round to take in the sky. No delight, no moment of freedom, though; only apprehension, as if he expected new torments to descend on him from the leaden darkness.

'*Bobby*?' She was fifteen yards from him when she spoke his name. Still moving across the far corner of the yard, Feldspar heard her clearly. '*Bobby, it's me.*'

Hoffmann dragged to a halt, head way to one side, chin against the sweatshirt that showed under his throat. Like a man rehearsing a hanging, Feldspar thought.

Brabenham stopped the agent. 'Here.'

They were in a central position against the base of the west wall. There they stayed, facing down the length of the yard, vigilant yet somehow disinterested. The four guards standing mute by his side, Brabenham checked his wristwatch carefully. He was a medium tall man of forty or so in a tight brown suit. His hairline was receding.

Feldspar cleared his throat. 'What's wrong with him?'

'Hoffmann's gone,' Brabenham said.

'Gone?'

'Skulled out.'

'Has he had medical attention?'

'Sure; he was gone when he arrived.'

'But . . .'

'Don't talk, Mr. Feldspar, please.'

'Shit!' Feldspar leaned his back on the wall and slid down until he was seated on the warm flagstones, knees raised. He lit a cigarette, put his hands on his knees, and watched the pathetic courtship ritual at the far end of the yard.

She didn't touch him. Not once. Not a finger. Not an embrace. Not a kiss on the brow. They stood a couple of feet apart, face to face. As far as Feldspar could make out, Dorothy did all the talking. Hoffmann's head was still down, furtively.

What the hell was she saying to him? He strained his ears but could hear nothing.

Brabenham said, 'She's got six minutes.'

'Shit,' said Feldspar again, dragging on the cigarette.

'Bobby? Listen, Bobby, you okay? You don't look so good, I admit. It's me, Bobby. It's Dorothy. Don't you recognise me? Sure, you do. You shouldn't be surprised to see me. Listen, I told you I'd get you out, didn't I? Didn't you get the messages? Jesus, I thought you'd understand. Didn't you hear about . . .' She glanced at the group by the distant wall, then right at blank concrete, then, in a low, urgent tone continued, 'about Hepple and Syd Cliffords and Hershcorn. Wangler. We didn't get Wangler. But we will. Maybe you can get him yourself. Yeah. Jesus. That's what it's all about.'

Bobby smiled. He popped up his head like a marmot. She realised he's been somewhere else and had just gotten round to making connections.

Barbary Point was not the Garden of Allah. She could see what it would do to a guy like Bobby. She'd need to get him out of here soon. She'd hoped to talk it over with him like she used to do. But that was impossible. He was in a mood. She didn't mind that too much. She knew from past experience he could absorb everything she required him to know, would do what she told him to do.

He went on smiling, shy-like. Dorothy closed her hands into fists and folded her arms over her breasts.

'Come on, Bobby Hoffmann. They don't treat you *that* bad. Piggies, yeah. But you can handle piggies, can't you? Bobby, I went to a lotta trouble to get in here, I haven't got more than five minutes left. So you *listen*. I'm gettin' you out.'

'Dorothy?' he spoke under his breath. 'They got you too?'

'No chance, Bobby. I'm working for the motherfuckers. Yeah, the *government*. I got in with the CIA. Terrific, huh? I got us a deal. I'll get you out.'

Bobby Hoffmann, the weak-kneed child of her youth, the pinion, the only person she'd ever managed to dominate, the walking orgasm, mind-to-mind lover, her tool, her husband – Bobby said, 'Out of here?'

'I got no time to explain the details, Bobby. Just listen. I did a deal. Not with the pigs. With the government. The CIA can do it. Jesus, they don't care about four dead dealers four years back. I got over two hundred thousand dollars from the government already. They want me to kill a guy; maybe more than one. For that I got paid – cash in advance. Afterwards, they'll help get you out. I trust them. I mean, just *them*: the CIA. *Not the pigs.*'

'Where'd . . . where'd I got to go to?'

Hoffmann had been twelve hours in a maximum-security cell away from his 'room'. He didn't know why he'd been tossed in a special unit that morning, and he'd anticipated a long, long stay. They'd promised him a long stay. But he didn't know why he was being punished and that always depressed him. He had quit thinking about Dorothy a long, long, long time ago. He liked best to be alone. But not if it meant he'd been bad.

'Bobby, please. I mean it. I'll spring you. Soon. I do this job for the government, they gotta do what I ask or I'll yell to the *New York Times*. They think they're conning me. Jesus, I'm conning them. Two hundred thousand. We can go anywhere on that. I'll get papers. Passports an' stuff. I'll get whatever we need. They treat me like I'm a peasant. But I'll use them the way they think they're using me. I promise, Bobby. I'll have you back with me, no time at all.'

'Way t'go,' Hoffmann said, dredging the phrase up from the sump of his memory. He grinned at her; that always pleased folk like Doc O'Riordan and Guard Wallis. When he was grinning he wasn't expected to talk.

His voice sounded rusty. 'How's . . . how's Sacramento?'

'*What*? God *Jesus*, Bobby! *Just listen.*'

But he had heard enough. He could no longer buy the dream. She had always extolled the system. The system was there to be plundered like some long rumbling freight train. But the only part of the system she'd ever admired had been the government – she meant the CIA. Grinning still, Bobby Hoffmann put a few wires together in his head. 'You made it, darlin'.'

'What? Oh, Bobby. I thought . . .'

'The big top.'

'Yeah. But only so I can get you out. There's *no* other way. I couldn't *buy* a bust from this mountain, Bobby. When we get out we'll hide from *everybody* for a while, and . . .'

'In Sacramento?'

'Mexico.'

'I wanna go back to Sacramento.'

'Okay, yeah, all right. But you've *got* to glue it together, Bobby. It'll be the best organised bust you've *ever* seen. I *promise* you. *Do you believe me*?'

'I . . . I . . .'

'Bobby, you've *gotta* believe me.'

'You gettin' it regular, darlin'?'

'Like a cuckoo clock.'

'That's crazy!'

'Here they come. Fuck them. I *hate* them. *You wait*. We'll get them all. I promise. You believe me?'

'I . . .'

'It's straight.'

'I don' much feel like it, tell the truth.'

'*Wake up. Wake up*.'

The pig deputy gave a wet little laugh. The pig guards pulled Bobby back from her, like a sack of maize.

She felt a gulf opening, her self falling down into it; then she saw Feldspar, concerned and sympathetic. She hung over the gulf, like a gull, waiting. Feldspar winked. Man, she needed that wink more than she needed a nightcapper.

'Let's get out of this hell hole, kid,' the agent said.

She went with him gladly. Stepping back into the protection of the big sanity, the government design.

Eight miles out of Barbary Point, Feldspar drew the rented sedan up by the verge and gave her a brand new shooting kit that Upton had slipped him on arrival at the air base. There was only one bag. He hoped the strength was right. Sudden distrust of Upton enveloped him. But he had opened the kit and she was greedy for it. She was wrung out. Like he was.

She rolled over into the rear seat – modest with it – and prepared and administered the fix. He heard her sigh. He waited, smoking, while heroin filtered through her. Then he retrieved the needle, empty bag and ampoule of distilled water. He opened the door of the sedan and stepped out.

The air was dry. Behind he could make out the stain of the prison on the hem of the sky. He broke the glass under his heel, scooped the shards carefully into his palms, and threw them side-arm into the scrub. He tossed the bag into the wind. When he got back into the car, Dorothy was seated in the passenger seat again, head resting against the side window.

Feldspar said nothing. He had to sweat it out. He could not push, prompt her. After all, he didn't know what Hoffmann had said. It had surprised him that the guy had spoken at all. Perhaps it was all a ruse, some skilful acting to throw him off track.

She had buttoned her sleeve. She looked sleepy. Feldspar fired the engine and pulled the sedan out onto the crown of the back road.

Pick up at San Francisco's Angalada Base was scheduled for midnight. Plenty of time. They would be back in New York by morning. Back at the Florissant House. There, he would have to trust her – or hand her over to the FBI.

'I gotta get him out, Harold.'

'If that's what you want.'

'They're killing him.'

Feldspar said, 'It won't be easy, kid. You saw what it's like.'

'But it can be done, can't it?'

'I told you,' said Feldspar evenly. 'We can do anything.'

'You're the power, man.' She laughed, sadly. Obsession had weakened in the wake of the fix. In the wake of the brutal reality of Barbary Point. 'What do you want me to do?'

'I'll tell you on the plane.'

'Will this mean I'm legit?'

'Pardon?' Feldspar was caught unaware.

'Legit, working for the government; for the CIA?'

Feldspar hesitated only for a moment.

'That's what it means, Dorothy,' he lied.

Imperialist gateposts in beautiful red brick flanked the entrance to Fort Shaffer Military Hospital. Though there was a guardhouse it was discreetly camouflaged in the same red brick style. There was no barrier across the curving driveway that led in from Susquehanna Avenue and carried sedately up through parkland grounds to the medical and residential blocks. Swan-necked lamp standards lit the approach. The light was yellow and fat, in keeping with the tranquil, unmilitary atmosphere.

In the centre of the drive, thirty yards inside the gates, stood four men – Upton, Marks, Halveston and Lassiter. Back of them another twenty yards, drawn to the left verge, was an Army Express Ambulance, sidelights lit. Stein waited by the ambulance, chatting quietly to the three-man crew.

At a minute to ten o'clock, a Dodge transit van turned slowly in from Susquehanna Avenue and passed unchecked through the gates. It came to a gradual halt ten yards from the waiting men. Stein tossed away his cigarette and strode purposefully towards it. He wore a waistlength white jacket and carried a white kidskin bag.

The Dodge's side door opened. A man climbed out. He approached the group.

Upton said, 'Go with him, Walt. Our patient's in the back of the van.'

'You come too, Senator,' the man said.

The man's name was Gollings. He was the leader of a special four-person detail of trusted lieutenants that Sarsby had flown up from Mexico City to handle the exchanges. One of them, Janette Kaminsky, was a registered nurse who had found her niche in Sarsby's Mexican office where she looked after the health and welfare of eighty executives. Like Gollings and the others, she was clean as a whistle. She supervised the unloading of the patient who was strapped under a blanket on a rolling stretcher. When the stretcher was laid on the drive, nurse Kaminsky got down on one knee beside it.

'One moment, Senator.' Gollings was a cute little man with chubby cheeks and a pert mustache, affable rather than cool.

'What is it?' Halveston growled.

'I'd like it understood that you are accompanying us of your own free will and volition, under no duress.'

Halveston glanced at Upton, who nodded.

'Jesus Christ!' said Marks under his breath.

'Yes,' Halveston said.

'Just a mite louder, please, Senator,' Gollings suggested.

'Yes. I'm accompanying you without duress, of my own free

will.'

'Thank you, Senator,' said Gollings. 'This way please.'

'They've guessed it's a deal. They know we'll protect them,' said Marks quietly.

Upton nodded again. He was watching Stein. The surgeon knelt by the nurse's side.

'A sedative was administered,' she said. 'Ten milligramme morphine, and three 80 milligramme doses of frusemidt during the past eighteen hours.'

'The last?' Stein stripped the blanket back from the patient's chest.

'Two hours forty minutes ago.'

Halveston had climbed inside the cabin of the Dodge. Stein looked round and motioned to Upton who came over.

'Is this Gordon Rand?' Stein asked.

'Yes,' said Upton.

Miss Kaminsky said, 'He's only been in my charge since noon. Deterioration has been very pronounced since then.'

'Thank you,' said Stein automatically.

Rand's skin was ashen gray, his breathing fast and shallow. Even as Stein brought the stethoscope from the bag, Rand emitted a deep hollow cough. Nurse Kaminsky wiped flecks of mucus from his lips with a tissue.

Swiftly Stein made an initial examination. Pulse rate 120, volume poor. Through the diaphragm of the stethoscope he tuned in on a rapid cardiac rhythm and instantly discerned the big moist sigh that punctuated the usually silent pause between heartbeats. He tracked the diaphragm along the left border of Rand's breatstbone, picking up disruption in each cardiac cycle; like a subway train passing through an empty station at high speed, a rumbling *swoosh*. Gross incompetence of the main aortic valve. No mystery. Severe left heart failure. He would require to check out the clinical judgement by catheter findings, but he had no doubt that the clinical results would confirm his diagnosis.

He looked up at Upton again. 'Serious. Aortic valve. Signal the wagon.'

Nurse Kaminsky, with Gollings at her shoulder now, said apologetically, 'We've got to leave you.'

'Yah,' Stein said. 'Go.'

Upton signalled the Army Express to approach. Even as it

gunned its motor, the Dodge backed slowly away. Nurse Kaminsky hardly had time to scramble into the rear. Upton watched the van back out onto Susquehanna Avenue and swing right, then left again. Stein paid it no attention. He was rapping out commands. 'Get him to receiving ward. Dr. Clayton will take cine-aortagram. Twelve lead EKG. Blood profile too. Everything is ready. Make it all gotdam fast.'

The rolling stretcher hustled into the Army Express. Within seconds Rand was whisked away up the drive, the quarter mile to the emergency wing set aside for the team's exclusive use.

Upton moved to Stein's side.

'How serious, Walter?'

'Serious.'

'But have we got him in time?'

'Ask me tomorrow night,' Stein snapped and, turning on his heel, walked away from the Englishman. It had just come home to him in all its enormity what had been done to Gordon Rand and what his role in the heinous affair must be. He wanted no more of Upton or his hypocritical solicitude; not that night, not ever.

The open jeep came up behind him.

'Ride, sir?' asked the young lieutenant.

'Yah. Emergency wing.'

Stein paused, a foot into the jeep, then stood up and yelled back down the driveway. 'No gotdam kibitzers. My patient. You all leave him to me.'

His voice left a faint echo in the parkland darkness and Upton's reply, if there were one, was lost in the roar of the jeep's engine.

Upton walked back to Marks and Lassiter, his face a mask, betraying nothing.

Marks said, 'Temperamental sonuvabitch, always was.'

'Yes,' Upton said. 'But very positive. Gentlemen, I think we might as well go home to bed.'

'What about the senator?' Lassiter asked.

'Oh, the senator, like the patient, is in the very best of hands,' Upton said. 'Rest easy, Mr. Lassiter, there's no more we can do tonight.'

The egg-shaped pool lay under floods, very blue, backed by

Lombardy poplars. The girl on the diving board was a robust fifteen. She carried a little bit of puppy-fat in the pouches of her small bikini. Splashing and laughing in the water were two other girls, friends of the diver, about the same age. A remarkably beautiful woman sat on a lounger, like a lifeguard, watching the bathers. A thick scarlet robe was draped over her shoulders. Between the pool and the terrace was an area of soft summer darkness where the lights did not reach. It separated the two men from the four girls.

The house was somewhere on the coastal hills, south-west of the city above Highway 1. The terrace roof was supported by six pillars in classical style. Fibreglass, Sarsby explained, costing only a couple of hundred dollars each. The floor, though, was Italian tile; it had set him back over ten thousand. The table and chairs had been imported from France. A hole-in-the-wall fire made a bright spot, and against its glow moths and other insects danced like tiny stars. Steaks sizzled on a portable barbeque. There was salad in a wooden bowl, wine and imported strawberries.

Halveston was more relaxed than he had been in weeks. Deceit was Arnold Sarsby's natural medium; he breathed it like air. Halveston had nothing to hide; they were, he supposed, creatures of the same species. Now that Varese had gone, the obvious vulgar threat had been removed from their relationship.

'Usually she doesn't stay up so late,' Sarsby gestured at the girl on the diving board. 'But she was thrilled at the idea of a real live U.S. senator visiting. Besides, a little late night pool party does no harm in vacation time.'

'Your daughters?' said Halveston.

'Anna. My wife too. I have four girls.'

'Is this your home?'

'One of them. My wife lives here. I don't get to see enough of my family, Senator. You know how it is in business.'

'Yes,' Halveston said.

They moved to the barbecue table. Sarsby dished his guest steak and salad and rough brown bread. They returned with plates and glasses to the pine table. All three girls were on the board now, shiny and slippery as seals, giggling, glancing over at the famous U.S. senator. Halveston waved, and the girls waved back, giggling some more.

Sarsby said, 'It's all business, Senator, isn't it?'

Halveston said, 'Turning a buck? Yes, that's what's behind it.'

'It's in the lap of the gods now.'

'Rand?' said Halveston. 'Rand's life?'

'And other things,' said Sarsby. 'I figure we should work on the assumption that Rand will pull through.'

'I'm not sure I follow you.'

'Sure you do. Let's not be coy, Senator. Do you really think I shelled out two hundred thousand dollars for next to nothing?'

'I delivered information worth more than that.'

'No,' said Sarsby. 'You handed me a scare. Incidentally, Senator, I think the Chinese have accepted that mess of lies.'

Halveston felt more relaxed than ever. It comforted him to realise that organised crime was in the hands of such civilised men. Shrewd anyhow. If you were smart, you maintained equilibrium. You didn't reach for the blackjack and the gun. You played the word game – and the money game – like now.

Sarsby said, 'I admit you told me what the White Tigers were at. I suppose that's worth all the dough we paid you – over the past seven years.'

'Go on.'

'I gained more than I lost, Senator,' Sarsby said. 'And all I'm going to lose this time is you.'

Halveston laughed and ate steak. 'I can't believe you intend to dump me in the Bay.'

'Of course not. It would wreck my deal with the government,' said Sarsby. 'That's what I paid good money for, a deal with the government. I think it's time we put it on the table, Senator. You used my organisation long enough.'

Halveston said, 'When did you find out?'

'I had doubts for a couple of years,' said Sarsby. 'But I only figured it out when this bacterium thing blew up. Two hundred thousand dollars and your "participation" gave me a binding contract with the government. What's the service? Is it of mutual benefit?'

'Everything I told you is the truth,' said Halveston.

'And Rainer's addled narcotics bust? How "true" is that?'

'The Vice-President has "national interests" at heart,' said Halveston, with obvious sarcasm.

'Rainer's only a front. Who am I working with? The CIA?'

'You're working with me,' Halveston said. 'I represent the national interest.'

'Glad to hear it, Senator,' Sarsby said. 'It means I'm not going to come out of this thing with my ass in a sling. I've gotten protection for my syndicate. All this activity will have no backlash at all. Isn't that right?'

'Kidnapping charges? I doubt if the FBI will be permitted to press.'

'All right, Senator, roll it out for me. How far can I go? Give me the word from the mountain. What's the end of all this?'

'*Status quo*.'

'Suits me.'

'Tell me,' said Halveston, 'what did you demand from the Tigers?'

'Share of their monopoly market.'

'Don't you still want that?'

'There won't be a monopoly market,' said Sarsby. 'It was a pipedream all along. Christ, not even your lunatic analysts could have come up with a scheme like that and made it work.'

'Peking might have.'

'Peking wouldn't kill a couple of billion people?' said Sarsby. 'Look, Senator, I grab off my handful of dirty money. You know that. But I also keep the feedlines open. Sixty-four percent of my dealing is legitimate. It's a big pyramid. But it isn't solid. It teeters, sways, could tumble down. All right, so I funnel opiates to street addicts and make fat profits. I could slice off that side of my business tomorrow and still turn over thirty million a year from licensed pharmaceutical contracts.'

'Why don't you?'

'Because I got . . .' Sarsby pinged his fingernail against the wine glass, '. . . responsibilities. I built the machine, the supply machine. It isn't clean all through. I don't just mean the selling end, I mean crop purchase, processing, distribution. Look, Senator, if twenty percent of world opium crops, licit and illicit together, didn't come home, do you think the AMA would keep *its* hands clean for long? The drug corporates would be first to feel pressure. Profits would soar – then plummet. The so-called health of the western world depends on a network of suspect suppliers. Produce under licence? Controlled state-owned cultivation? You think that could ever be made to work? The

French tried it and look what happened. World health authorities would go crazy if opiate-based products became scarce.'

'You get no argument from me,' said Halveston.

'The world is full of pain,' said Sarsby. 'Opium alkaloids in a thousand different preparations relieve that pain. Synthetic narcotics don't rate; ask any heroin addict. Heroin, morphine – those we need. *Need*, Senator. We're no longer able to endure pain with fortitude. Relief from all kinds of suffering has become the *right* of every John and Jane Doe.'

'What if that right is denied them?'

'The medical establishment won't let that happen. The junkies, the corner bagmen, the big international rings – they're the dirty end of the market. But it's the lady in Oakland with a persistent cough, the guy in Camden with a broken foot, the kid in Duquesne with rotten teeth, the migraine in Omaha, a broken heart in Cheyenne, rheumatics in Little Rock, terminal cancer in Kansas City. They all depend on the seed of the opium poppy. All right, so everybody wants to scrub things up some. But the medical pundits, economists, and bloody-minded down home folks, they crave *their* share.'

'Good excuse, Sarsby,' said Halveston. 'But it wouldn't hold water in a court of law.'

'The operators, the really powerful financial rings, how often *do* they come to court? Sweep up a few chisellers and grafters; get the dogs off the street. But multi-million dollar suppliers, above and below the watermark, never suffer.'

Halveston finished the steak and put his plate down on the tiles. The girls had gone now, though the blue surface of the pool still rippled. He glimpsed them passing up a path through the Lombardy poplars towards the far side of the sprawling house, like rare antelopes, treading delicately, long-legged and shy. The woman followed them, her scarlet robe like a splash of blood against the dark trees.

'You want coffee?'

'The wine will be fine,' said Halveston.

The conversation had excited Sarsby. Perhaps he didn't get to talk much to men he could trust. Ironies were everywhere, Halveston thought, like tripwires in a minefield. It gave him a refreshing sense of dangers ahead. It didn't disturb him in the least that Sarsby had pegged him as a CIA puppetmaster.

Cooling his desire to impress the senator, Sarsby lit a cigarette and leaned his shoulder against the surround of the fire. He looked lean and raffish by the firelight. Maybe success in business had begun to bore him too.

Halveston said, 'You're absolutely right. It's the poison tree that drops the sweetest apples. We can't allow it to be chopped down.'

'Or fenced around,' said Sarsby. 'This one time the government bureaus and the syndicates have a one hundred per-cent common interest.'

'But you can't engage in open warfare with the White Tiger Company and hope to do their organisation any lasting damage. Is that assessment correct?'

'You're right. We could nip off their American contacts, shed a little blood, maybe. But that wouldn't really harm them. They'd withdraw to their own territories and we can't touch them there.'

Halveston considered his next statement, then said, 'If I told you that the White Tiger Company *are* working for Peking, would that explain my interest?'

'Peking? The Tigers?' Sarsby pushed him forward. 'Now that really would be a fat market. I mean with the cultivation areas the Red Chinese could command. My God, Halveston, are you snowing me again?'

'No. The ramifications of such a union are distressing.' Halveston hesitated again, then said, 'You're right, Sarsby. You *do* have government protection against obvious criminal charges. The whitewash is mixed, ready to be slapped all over this affair. The cover-up isn't for your benefit, of course. The Central Intelligence Agency isn't "officially" involved with you in any way.'

'It's their board though,' said Sarsby. 'What's my role?'

'Make the transaction. Persuade the Tigers to bring their expert out of hiding and into America. That's all we ask.'

'You could have asked outright.'

'Would you have trusted us? Co-operated with some stealthy agent, representing Capitol Hill?'

'Maybe not,' Sarsby admitted. 'Anyhow, from bitter experience, that kind of approach would have taken time. And time's something we don't have too much of. If I fix a meeting with Vigson, what happens then?'

'Vigson will be assassinated.'

'You want me to . . . ?'

'Emphatically not,' said Halveston. 'We want it kept low. Leave Vigson to us.'

'Don't imagine I'm going to telegraph the time and place of the meeting?' said Sarsby. 'Christ, Senator Halveston, that's too much trust you're asking. I got a roomful of suspicious Chinese and two scientists, one crippled, and you think I'm going to *invite* a raid. No, sir. That's not in the contract.'

'We thought it wouldn't be, actually,' said Halveston. 'That's why we'll nail Vigson elsewhere.'

'And the Tigers will try for Rand. You've got two goats tied to the same stake.'

'Rand's safety is secondary.'

'You'd trade that poor bastard for Vigson?'

'Only in an emergency situation,' said Halveston. 'If you do as we ask, go along with the plan you've set up, be assured that we'll look out for Rand. And make sure Vigson is removed.'

'Will that stop the Tigers?'

'It'll stop them long enough to allow us to develop an antidote to that damned bacterium. That's what we all want, isn't it?'

Sarsby said, '*Status quo*. Yeah, that's worth the risks.'

Halveston said, 'And afterwards, your organisation remains intact. I'm sure you can cope with minor retaliation from the Far East.'

'What if something goes adrift – with Rand, say?'

'You won't be held to blame.'

'So there is an antidote?'

'Yes.'

'And a mutation in the Vigson's bacterium?'

'So it would seem.'

'A weapon the Tigers could sell if they lost the bigger and better deal with Peking?'

'Probably. It's enough to get them off the hook.'

'More than one fucking poison tree, Senator, is growing here.'

'I'm afraid so.'

'You're laying it all on the line, aren't you?'

'Absolutely straight on the line.'

'I aim the gun,' Sarsby said.

'And we pull the trigger,' said Halveston.

Sarsby lifted his wine glass from the edge of the table. He held it up. 'God Bless America.'

'Yes,' said Halveston, ruefully. 'I'll drink to that,'

WEDNESDAY 24 AUGUST

The twelve lead EKG's wavy black lines showed evidence of rapid rate and distressed left main chamber. In the cold light illuminator the X-ray photograph of Gordon Rand's chest confirmed beyond doubt Stein's snap diagnosis – a classic picture: dilated heart, progressive failure. A bat's wing-shaped blizzard of minute feathery blotches virtually occluded the lungs. Stein was surprised that Rand could take oxygen into the blood at all, so obliterated with fluid were the lungs. He could not possibly live more than twenty-four hours without surgical intervention. Rand was drowning in his own secretions.

The aortagram projections were equally informative. On screen, Stein saw the fine catheter that fed up from the patient's groin. The catheter passed up the aorta and snaked around the left side of the heart. Injected into the main blood vessel above the heart, dye clearly depicted a gross backflow totally different from the norm. The heart was pumping blood into the main artery but an incompetent valve allowed the flow to fall back into the chambers.

Stein gave his orders. The cardio-pulmonary by-pass team, pump technicians, blood bank staff and anaesthetists were mustered and briefed. Again Stein filled Rand with anti-failure treatment in an attempt to stimulate the kidneys into flushing a portion of the fluid from the lungs. He selected plastic valves from the case he'd brought with him from the Saint Augustine and sent four for sterilization. With Rand's condition visibly worsening, he scheduled surgery to begin at six a.m.

The theatre team was composed of the best men and women available from the staff of the Saint Augustine, the Tempest Institute and the Greenwater Cardiothoracic Teaching Hospital. Like Upton, Stein had his buddies, disciples only too eager to repay debts, real or imagined. All of the persons had worked with him before on 'secret' surgery and would ask no awkward questions.

Rand regained consciousness for a brief period. Stein put no pressure on the patient. He gave him the grand 'welcome home' treatment and told him only that he was slated for surgery in a few hours. Oddly, Rand did not seem surprised.

He volunteered one piece of information. 'Listen; get . . . get a message to . . . a message; they kept me on a . . . a ranch, Inyo County area, near . . . near Liberon, I . . . I think.'

'Don't talk.'

'Chinese involved.'

'Relax; it's not important.'

'Want . . . want antidote to the Meredith, Vigson bacterium.'

'Sure, sure.'

'Told . . . told them . . . lies.'

'I'll report,' Stein promised. 'Now, you rest, gotdam it.'

Because it depended on a large team, open heart surgery was more subject to mishap than any other type of treatment. Aortic valve rupture was a bitch, even without a pressure situation.

Rand was comatose before the anaesthetist administered the initial injection. He was responding poorly to stimuli. His breath was coming in staccato bursts that caused Stein to revise his estimate of Rand's survival period; not twenty-four hours, more like five or six.

Though the anaesthetist had loaded his syringe with 500 mg of Pentothal, only a tenth of that normal dosage had been required to commence the anaesthetic procedure. During the two hours immediately prior to surgery, Rand's blood pressure slipped from a moderately safe 110/70 to 80/50. Regular recordings mapped a continuing decline in blood pressure and an increased heart rate; compensation for diminished efficiency. In the final hour, the rate rose from 90 to 130. Gordon Rand's flesh was the colour of an autopsy room cadaver.

The anaesthetist deftly inserted a tube down Rand's windpipe, inflated a pressure cup at the tip of the tube to ensure a close fit, and then began ventilation by oxygen catheter. When that stage had been reached, Stein entered the surgeons' changing room and quickly pulled on his theatre greens. The chief theatre nurse, who had worked with Stein on thousands of similar operations, was already dressed in her shapeless white paper robe. She knew Stein to be a garrulous man, not like some surgeons who contained their nervousness in silence.

She gave him the chance to talk. 'Will the infection make any difference to procedures?'

Glumly, Stein said, 'It is advanced, the degree of left ventricular failure. No perfusion of peripheral organs. How can we measure shock, Janie? It may be irreversible. The infection? Ach, Got knows. We may be unable to prevent the new valve becoming infected.'

The door of the surgeons' room flapped open. The assistant anaesthetist was recognisable by the horn-rimmed glasses that protruded from above his theatre mask. 'He's gone into a ventricular tachycardia with virtually no output.'

'Femoral pulses?' Stein demanded.

'None.'

'Put him on by-pass. *Now.*'

Stein followed the anaesthetist into the brilliantly lit service area of the theatre. Through a glass wall, Rand was visible, laid out in readiness on the table.

The men went on into the theatre itself. Stein consulted the heart monitor screen. As he watched, the anaesthetist thumped Rand on the breastbone and the monitor flickered. Rand's heart resumed its previous rhythm for a moment or two, then became weakly irregular.

'Get him onto by-pass state,' Stein said. 'While I scrub, you, Len, dissect out the femoral artery. Can't wait to get into the chest to establish the arterial feed. We use femoral feed. Janie, make sure you got the pneumatic bone saw handy. I go inside very fast.'

Stein hurried back to the scrubbing area and squirted a dark brown iodine soap preparation onto his hands and forearms. He thought of the ramifications of the operation and its possible aftermath were blotted from his mind. He washed rapidly, scowling at his hands as if warning them to behave.

Heart muscle starved of oxygenated blood was like an engine running out of gasoline; it might stagger and splutter on for a while and then quite abruptly stop. Once the stoppage occurred, irreversible changes would soon take place in muscle cells and brain. Five minutes, maybe ten, after – no hope of resuscitation would remain.

Stein knocked off the taps with his elbows and crossed to the trolley that supported sterile towels and gown. In the theatre he could see Leonard Johnson stooped over Rand's groin. A nurse fastened the tapes of his gown and mask. He sprinkled talc on his hands, snapped on surgical gloves and re-entered the theatre, ready to do battle.

The pump technician was seated on a stool by his machine. Coils of transparent plastic tubing primed with blood and physiological saline solution entered the DeBakey roller pump that ensured a continuous flow of oxygenated blood back into Rand's system through the insertion in the femoral artery. The technician, Masterman from the Greenwater, constantly checked the connections.

Johnson, Stein's first assistant, Looked up. 'Femoral's ready.'

Resolutely, Stein walked around the table to stand on Rand's right. It was his favoured stance; he felt most comfortable there.

'Can I begin?' Stein asked the anaesthetist, Leavitts.

'Yep.'

The nurse handed Stein a rotating saw. Seemingly at random, Stein tapped it against the broad area of exposed and prepared flesh and unceremoniously began to rip his way through Rand's sternum. A vacuum nozzle sucked away bone debris. Within minutes he had bisected the long flattish bone, inserted a retractor to wedge the halves apart and exposed the chest cavity.

Routine. He could work fast and deftly through familiar procedures. His fingers exposed the great veins that carried blood back to the heart. Using clamps laid across his demanding hand, he pinched the veins off and connected them to the machine that would function as heart and lungs for Rand during the course of the operation.

'Begin cooling.'

Blood now flowed steadily from the veins in Rand's chest into a Lillehei-de-Wall bubble oxygenator, into a heart exchanger and through the DeBakey pump before re-entering the body by the opened femoral artery, the intricate short circuit system that maintained blood flow to the vital organs and made open heart surgery possible. The heat exchanger captured the warmth of the blood and cooled it before its return. The gauge of the temperature control monitor, recorded by a thermocouple planted in Rand's throat, showed a marked fall. When the temperature had gotten down to 30°C, the heart's feeble pulse ceased. Stein waited, doing nothing, until the gauge showed an exact 20°C, then he started work in earnest.

Without being asked, chief theatre nurse Marnie Sumner bent and tapped the surgeon's ankle. Stein smiled under the mask and lifted one foot and then the other, allowing the woman to slip a foam rubber cushion under his clogs. He never asked for, but always got, that little concession to age. The cushion protected him from aching arches and low back pain during extended surgical programmes. Apart from that, it paid to be comfortable. He relaxed slightly. The territory was familiar, the team alert and well-tried.

The showpiece of the operation progressed smoothly. He pre-selected a plastic valve of appropriate size from the four on the paper napkin. He cut out the tattered shreds of Rand's rotten valve and sutured the replacement in at the mouth of the aorta. All relatively easy. He had performed over three thousand homografts; the techniques were almost automatic. Problem was to wean the patient off the heart/lung machine. If the heart had been too severely starved of oxygen, the weaning process would become a desperate debacle and, experience told him, Rand wouldn't leave the table alive.

It was that moment that surgeons worked towards; that moment that all surgeons and teams dreaded. Nimbly, Stein drove on towards the proving. Some of his colleagues, though none of the top guns that he'd worked with, slowed appreciably as this part of the operation approached. They seemed to flinch from it, to resist the ultimate challenge, the testing of their skill. Skill? Shit! It was partly just luck, a composite of factors that could not be monitored in advance. He had seen perfect, gotdam *perfect* technical replacements give up the ghost as soon as the transfer from the support system began. No real reason could be found. It was the essential secret, the kernel of the mystery that no surgeon, no man, had ever picked out; the fulcrum between the living and dying.

'How long has he been on by-pass?'

'Fifty minutes.'

'Start reheating.'

Fifty minutes: maybe too long. The greater the length of time the patient was dependent on the heart/lung machine, the more stubborn the body's resistance to doing it's own work; the more difficult it became to staunch bleeding.

Stein stabbed the apex of the heart neatly and lifted the organ gently on the point of the instrument. It was his particular method for encouraging the heart to refill with blood and to coax gravity to remove every tiny bubble of air from the cavities. Air bubbles released into the circulation caused irreparable harm; an embolism was often fatal. The heart accumulated blood. Finally blood spurted from the minute stab wound and Stein slid his left hand beneath the organ and massaged it; a strange tender sensuous motion, rolling the heel of the palm, forcing air out of the chambers.

'Temperature?'

'Thirty-three, rising steadily,' Leavitts, the anaesthetist, answered calmly.

The surfaces of the heart muscle rippled with an oceanic shimmer in the brilliant light.

'Defibrillation paddles.' Stein spoke over his shoulder to the nearest theatre nurse.

Instantly she handed him the small chrome-coated paddles. From each plastic handle a wire projected. The wires were entangled and had to be unwound; it took fifteen seconds.

Stein clamped his teeth together. He wanted to bawl the girl out. But he needed all his nervous energy intact. Besides, the team was pulling well and he didn't want to set them on edge. They were on the verge of the crucial moment.

The girl connected the wires to the terminals of the defibrillator and stuck the handles into Stein's fists. Stein placed the face of the paddles one on each side of the heart muscle and said, 'Jag it.'

With a loud *cluck,* current shot into the heart muscle, a tiny sizzling spark showing under one of the paddle faces. Rand's heart continued in its discordant contraction.

'*Fock*,' said Stein. 'Juice it up.'

The nurse fiddled with the defibrillator control.

'Jag it.'

Cluck.

The heart did not respond.

'*Fock*,' Stein repeated hollowly. 'Try calcium.'

Marnie Sumner put the needle into the vein cluster. Almost before the tip was withdrawn, Stein was cocking his wrists and laying the paddle faces on the muscle once more.

'Jag it, please.'

Cluck; another miscroscope spark.

There was a pause, agonising to the surgeon and his team; then, as if in reward for their services, the heart gave a shrug that changed into a concerted contraction that sent a fresh spurt of blood from the puncture wound in the apex.

'Allah,' said Stein, 'be praised.'

He raised his aching neck six inches and observed over the rim of the mask as the heart elected to support itself and assumed a steady unaided rhythm.

A nurse placed the suture needle in Stein's fingers and he inserted a single stitch in the puncture wound, sealing the organ up again completely.

Stein lifted his wrists and the nurse removed the needle. Marnie dabbed his brow and the bridge of his nose.

Stein was sorely tempted to complete the mechanical process of sewing up the chest. But that would have slighted Len Johnson, who was an accomplished surgeon in his own right and more than capable of such mundane work.

'Zip him up, Len, please,' Stein said, stepping back.

Johnson walked round the base of the table and instantly set about the tailoring.

Stein stepped back again, his eyes on the green oscilloscope of the heart monitor. The simultaneous display of the heart's rhythm on the electrographic recording and the visual of blood pressure were gratifyingly steady.

Stein turned and walked out of the operating room. Looked like he had saved Gordon Rand after all. But for what? To die again, maybe, at a more propitious time. Not if he could help it. By got, to take out the patient, they would have to take out the doctor first. In spite of his angry scepticism, he was committed now to protecting Gordon Rand against all comers, including Upton.

WEDNESDAY MORNING
NEW YORK

The Bobcat was parked three blocks away from Florissant House. The sun was growing fierce now towards mid-morning. Traffic snarled. Crowds brawled on the sidewalk. Two blacks, naked to the waist, and a young white kid in a Bermuda shirt, squatted against the wall of Murray's Meat Mart where cold air vented up from a grid. They were a little out of character for the neighbourhood. But at this time of day, in this heat, nobody cared. Two fat women in cartwheel hats dragged past, sweating and complaining. Another woman in a halter top and beach pants was arguing with a taxi driver in front of Delano's Photographic Studios.

The interior of the Bobcat was cool and insular. He held her left hand in his, his right hand on her shoulder, both their shoulders turned to the windshield, their backs to the doors.

'What if he's up there?' Feldspar said.

'He won't be.'

'What if he is?'

'I'll tell him I've been out.'

'Won't he ask where?'

'Jesus, Feldspar, he's not my keeper.'

'Big things are brewing, kid. Wing'll be nervous too.'

'That prick hasn't a nerve in his body.'

'Whatever,' said Feldspar. 'I'll wait outside for ten minutes or so.'

'You'll never find parking.'

'Leave that to me. Any problems upstairs, open a window.'

'Fat chance,' said Dorothy. 'Listen, I can take care of Wing, I have to.'

'I believe you,' said Feldspar.

He was pronouncing his vowels very properly and speaking at half his normal speed as if she were a child. He still could not believe that the meeting with Bobby Hoffmann hadn't been traumatic for her, that it had left no wounds. Didn't seem so, however. If anything, she was calmer than before. Amazingly calm and assured. But she *was* connected, of that he was certain. He had to remind himself that this girl had a *successful* criminal career stretching back six or seven years. Her absorbsion rate must be high; she must be taking it all in.

He went on, 'Are you sure you can stall Wing?'

'Probably won't have to.'

'All right,' Feldspar sighed. 'Dorothy, we won't see each other until it's all over. After it's over, I'll whisk you away and hide you out, and . . .'

'The CIA?'

'Yes, the CIA will hide you out.'

'Will you be with me?'

'If that's what you want.'

'Sure. I get along with you. Sure.'

Her attitude towards him had changed in the past twenty-four hours. He wondered exactly what she'd told Greer about him. She no longer wanted to devour him – or so it seemed. Had he – God help us – taken over a part of the role in her life that Hoffmann had relinquished?

'All right,' Feldspar said. 'I'll personally get you out, kid, stash you away until such time as I . . . as we can arrange to bust Bobby from the Barbary.'

'That's goin' to be tricky?'

'We have the means,' said Feldspar casually. 'I admit it's one hell of a fortress. But if I . . . if *we* promise, then we'll deliver.'

'Yeah.'

'The cash.' He glanced at the rear seat where the suitcase was. 'Can you put it in a safe place?' I mean, do you have somewhere . . .?'

'Yeah, sure.' She was curt on this point. He figured that was the reason she wanted dropped three blocks from the Florissant. Perhaps she had contacts in New York. Almost certainly, she had contacts that he didn't know anything about, that Wing didn't know anything about. However she intended to do it, she didn't trust him enough to hold the two hundred thousand for her. That was her signing fee, and no doubt she already planned for its security.

He said, 'You don't want me around at all right now, do you?'

'Nothing personal.'

'I understand.'

'Right.' She smiled at him. Partners.

Her fingers were cool. They had crammed so much shared experience into two days that their relationship had that dense impacted quality that vacation romances sometimes take on. He speculated on whether the girl was aware of it, or if she were used to living at such a pitch.

He took her hand from his shoulder. 'The victim's name is Vigson, Conrad Vigson. You must be quite sure that you have the right man. The White Tigers will bring him in; Wing's bosses. They may try to fob us off with the wrong guy, a fake, a substitute. Sarsby will be alert for that. Don't . . . don't move too fast, kid. As I explained . . .'

'Wing only goes over it once.'

She'd rapped his knuckles. This nutty junkie had reprimanded him for over-anxiousness.

Feldspar apologised. 'Suppose you tell me,' he went on. 'Briefly.'

'The Tigers are bringing this scientist Conrad Vigson out of South-East Asia, or where-ever. Wing and me, we're bound to be involved in the deal all the way along. Vigson'll be taken to a secret place to meet with an American professor, Gordon Rand. *After* that meeting, you figure Wing will try to make a move against Rand, and Sarsby; maybe them all.'

'Is that how Wing operates?'

'Depends on his instructions,' Dorothy said. 'It's then I take out Vigson, when Wing makes his move.'

'That's it in a nutshell.'

'Cotton candy.'

'What?'

'Used to say that when I was a kid – easy as eating cotton candy. Cotton candy. This operation is cotton candy, Feldspar. I can do it.'

A delicate order. Feldspar said, 'Whatever happens, Dorothy, the man called Gordon Rand must not be hurt.'

'Got you.'

'If Wing *doesn't* include you in his plans, you call me.'

'I'll persuade him.'

'Don't seem too eager.'

'I know how to make him.'

'Yes,' said Feldspar. 'All right. But *if* he doesn't include you, call me at the number I gave you. Leave the coded message.'

'The bird has flown alone.'

'That's it. That's all.'

'And what'll happen then?'

She was thinking laterally, a new innovation. Feldspar doubted if she would have thought that far ahead forty-eight hours ago. She'd have played the whole concerto by ear, never doubting. Now she had a future, not a nebulous cloud of fantasies. Was that, in Dorothy's case, progress or regression?

Feldspar said, 'What'll happen then, you mean, if Wing doesn't take you and it all falls apart?'

'Yeah.'

'You've got the money; you keep it.'

'And Bobby?'

Feldspar thought quickly. He touched her shoulder again. 'We'll find you another job, another assignment.'

'Promise.'

Oh brother! Feldspar said, 'Yes, you have my word; the . . . *we* won't let you down.'

She leaned forward and kissed him with the wide faintly-smiling mouth. Why the hell did she look so innocent? No, not innocent – rueful. Did she know that it was all just one big pink-ribbon dream, a dream with ragged red edges? Unbidden, he suddenly remembered a phrase from a long-ago training lecture: *The conceptualization of a covert project takes account of need, not practicality. Idea inseminates method. Thus in the scheming mind, nothing becomes impossible.*

Dream merchants and myth-makers run the show. *My* show, kid, as well as yours.

She drew her face back from his, leaving her lower lip against his mouth for an instant longer.

'Later, Feldspar,' she murmured.

'Yes; we . . . we'll have all the time in the world – later.'

'Until Bobby gets out.'

'Of course.'

She slid from the Bobcat. Feldspar pushed out the suitcase. She swept it from the seat as if it were weightless; a strong, confident young woman. She gave him a finger sign, rude and cheerful; the lodge, the brotherhood, the camaraderie. He had just asked her to kill a man. He made a clipped salute by way of reply.

He doubted he would ever see her alive again. He couldn't figure why that prospect made him grieve. She was a victim born.

She walked fast along the pavement, tilted a little to one side by the burden of the case, then she rounded the corner under the striped awning of a druggist's out of Feldspar's sight. The agent leaned his forearms on the wheel, staring after her, staring into the milling crowd that waited for the lights, staring bleakly long after Miss Dorothy Newhoff had gone.

WEDNESDAY EVENING
SAN FRANCISCO

Nothing looked sicker than Gordon Rand in the recovery room of the Fort Shaffer Military Hospital. Stein might have pointed out that the RR and IC units in the Shaffer were paradise compared to similar rooms in larger surgical hospitals where patients had precious little privacy and post-operative psychoses often made the joint jump like bedlam. Rand, however, was not one to vent his spleen loudly or aggressively in his recovery trauma. He was truculent, surly as a bear brought out of hibernation, glaring through the forest of tubes and wires that surrounded his bed. His chest was padded with bandages and painted a vile colour, like tobacco spit. He was remarkably *compos mentis* when it came to parrying Upton's simple questions.

'How do you feel, Dr. Rand?'

'Too sick to talk to you, you Limey bastard.'

'Do you know where you are?'

'Turkey?' He meant it.

'You're in a military hospital close to San Francisco,' Upton explained. 'Don't you remember being brought here, talking to the surgeon, to Walter Stein?'

'I . . . How the hell did you get me back? Did you trade?'

'Yes,' said Upton. 'Yes, we traded.'

'That's enough for now,' said Stein. 'Give him a chance to come round.'

Rand stirred. Anxiety more than temper made him grab at the Englishman's sleeve. 'What'd you do to me?'

Stein answered, 'Replaced your aortic valve.'

'God.' Rand slumped back, left hand moving to touch the padded chest. 'My heart. You . . .'

Stein said, 'The operation was successful. Your heart as good as new.'

'I feel hellish, hellish,' murmured Rand.

'I look after you,' Stein said. 'You'll be A-okay in three, four days.'

'My . . .'

'Button the lip, Dr. Rand,' said Stein, wagging his finger.

'Take it easy. You got nothing to worry about while Stein's around.'

Drawing Upton back from the bedside, Stein allowed a nurse to move in to make Rand comfortable, more particularly to offer him the reassurance that was so essential to the well-being of patients at this stage in the post-operative process.

Upton and Stein moved out into the corridor.

Two U.S. Marine Corps privates stood guard at each end of the long corridor. Far down at the tee-junction of the wing and the main block, Upton could see the business of the hospital going on – another world, another dimension. Marks waited outside the unit door.

'How's he doing?' he asked.

Stein said, 'He's strong as oxen. I did a good job; pretty quick. But the infection worries me, George. Now you better had tell me, will it still be in the system?'

'Apparently its dispersal rate is high. The attack on the heart valve is its final locus of action. To the best of our knowledge, it will have been passed out of the system via the kidneys in the urine and alimentary tract, in the faeces.'

'You sure?' Stein had thawed a little in his attitude to Upton. He needed the man's faculties and had called a truce. 'You got tested results?'

'Enough to be ninety percent certain,' said Upton. 'It's the truth, Walter. I wouldn't have used that virus at all except for the fact that it was perfect for the bluff. It has such a specialised and predictable effect on the metabolism of the victim.'

'But your underworld buddies, they don't know that,' said Stein.

'Of course not. We must make sure that they are kept in a state of "suspense", right to the bitter end.'

Marks said, 'What about Rand? What kind of life will he have?'

Stein shrugged. 'Close to normal, if he pulls through.'

Marks said, 'You think there's a chance he won't?'

Stein shrugged again. 'Next twelve hours will tell. Possibly intramediastinal bleeding around the heart leading to tampanadt, or a cardiac rhythm malfunction and consequent low output state.'

'An opinion, please, Walter?' said Upton.

'Rand's heart was not unduly weakened by prolonged illness,' said Stein. 'He should accept and adjust quickly. Arrhythmia is only serious danger, I can see. Irregular beating. I'm prepared for that.'

'How long until he's fit to travel?' said Marks.

The question was not one that Upton would have been bold enough to ask at that juncture. He was too sensitive to Stein's dislike of the situation and not unsympathetic to the surgeon's fear that he had saved a man's life only to watch that man die in the near future.

Stein said, 'If he was patient at Saint Augustine's, I'd probably discharge him seven days from now, if no complications crop up.'

'When can we talk to him?' Marks was pushing.

'Tomorrow night, earliest,' said Stein.

Now, thought Upton, he's playing the surgeon. Rand would be out of it by morning. He said nothing, however. He did not anticipate that Rand would be able to tell them much more than they already knew. Perhaps his information would assist in further pinpointing the location of the hide-out. But there was no guarantee that Sarsby would use the same hide-out for the rendezvous. Indeed, the probability was that he would change it.

'Sarsby'll have to sweat it out for another twenty-four hours,' said Marks. 'We don't call him until we talk to Rand.'

'Tomorrow night,' Stein repeated, threateningly.

'What's the earliest Rand could be moved without positive harm?' Upton asked.

'A week, I tell you.'

'Now, now, Walt, you know what I mean; a week's too long.'

'If they take him out of here inside seventy-two hours, they will kill him, sure.'

'That takes us through to Saturday morning,' said Upton. 'I imagine that Sarsby will have acquired accurate information on your previous post-operative procedures, Walt. I feel convinced that he'll come in on Saturday.'

'What's his rush?' said Marks.

'We've forced him to move quickly. He'll sustain that impetus. If he can get Rand back into his custody by the weekend, all in one piece, then he'll have enough of a drop on us – or so he'll suppose – to arrange the meeting with the Tigers to suit his best purposes.'

'Put him off, gotdam it,' said Stein.

'No, Walt. I can't.'

'You can stop him entering this hospital.'

'And risk bloodshed – and Halveston's neck,' said Marks.

'You're not worried about Halveston, or Rand, or Stein,' the surgeon said scathingly. 'You worry only about Conrad Vigson. You can't wait to lay hands on Vigson.'

'Look, Stein,' said Marks, 'I appreciate all you're doing for us, but that gives you no right to treat George and me like a couple of bullies. We never deceived you. You've no complaint. There's more than Rand involved.'

'Yah. Yah.' Stein flapped his hand in disdain. 'Big deal all through. I heard you right first time. I got work to do now. You excuse me.'

'Walt,' said Upton sharply, as the surgeon turned away. 'There's no latitude for argument. Unless Rand suffers a relapse, it'll be Saturday. That's when we'll let him go.'

Stein hesitated, his forearm against the panel of the recovery room door. He scowled and then his features hardened, becoming more Teutonic, almost cruel.

'I'll be ready,' he said harshly. 'I'll be ready for them.'

THURSDAY 25 AUGUST
SAN FRANCISCO

Neither Chen Yu-lan or Mr. Wing were aware that the White Tiger Pharmaceutical Company would not meet again before Conrad Vigson was brought out of Tang Mang Wu. The decision was Kittegawa's, his alone. His mind had been made up even before the telephone call from Arnold Sarsby confirmed the success of the surgical operation. Sarsby admitted that it was surgery, not some pretentious antidote. The crux of the matter, however, was that Rand was alive, the progress of his mysterious malady stopped.

The checkers game continued. From the present disposition of counters an infinite variety of moves opened up; not, alas, for the White Tiger Company but for Sarsby. The syndicate may – or may not – have forged a link with the U.S. authorities just as he and Yu-lan had done with the gentlemen from Peking.

An infinite variety of moves; most of them were based on

threat and not the realisation of threat. Kittegawa was more intelligent than his friend and partner, Yu-lan. Both tacitly acknowledged his superior intellect. But Kittegawa was wary of offending Yu-lan and did not present his decision as an ultimatum.

The three Chinese had been installed in a dainty four-roomed suite in the upper floor of an elegant town-house in the Chinatown district. The town-house belonged to a food importer named Robert Han, an American-born Eurasian who had built his business on muscle and unlimited credit supplied by the First Provincial Bank of Kowloon. Robert Han was on one of his frequent trips to Paris, where the best oriental food was to be found. Han's domicile was at the Tiger's disposal; in particular the upper floor, mellow, oriental, deeply luxurious – and quite private.

Mr. Wing was eating spare ribs with his fingers. As usual, he appeared indifferent to the laid back squabble in the sing-song dialect that was going on between his fathers. He had spent the previous night with two separate women. One milky-skinned beauty he had hired from a pimp in Costello Street; she had passed out shortly after midnight. The second, a local Chinese girl, had taken all night to respond and had finally lost all her self-control, much to Mr. Wing's satisfaction. Even so, he pined a little for Dorothy and wished now that he had left a limited supply of heroin to make her the more eager for his return.

Though he said nothing, Mr. Wing guessed that Sheng would soon bring the matter to a conclusion by arranging a head-to-head confrontation with Sarsby and Varese. He guessed also that the White Tiger Company would retreat from it's outposts and would abandon its American network, such as it was, and that he would be brought closer to his fathers. He had not yet devised a plan for dealing with Dorothy. Perhaps he would be permitted to take her with him on his return to Asia. Perhaps he would be ordered to dispose of her. Certainly, sentiment excluded, the latter course was safest and cleanest. But he did not wish to be rid of her yet. Perhaps he might persuade Sheng that she could be of use to them in the Orient; besides it would be easier to dispose of her there.

She would enjoy Hong Kong. He thought of a house in Kowloon that he might buy for her, where she might make a home for him. He had servants he could trust in the organisation, men too wily even for Dorothy; men who would ensure that she did not create inconvenience for the White Tigers.

Wing cracked the rib in his teeth and sucked silently on the juices of the marrow. He listened.

'Sarsby assures us that Gordon Rand is no longer in imminent danger of dying,' Kittegawa said. 'If that is the case, Rand is a threat to us.'

'Where is Rand?' said Yu-lan.

'Sarsby did not say.'

'But he is well again?'

'There was surgery. He will be well enough to talk in a week.'

'I do not trust Sarsby,' said Yu-lan.

'Chen, I feel that I must return to Tang Mang Wu to discuss the matter with Conrad Vigson.'

'Do you mean to persuade him to attend a meeting with Rand?'

Kittegawa said, 'I will not use force, Chen. I will not insist upon it.'

'Vigson will not come.'

'He may be curious. He may feel that the little we have gleaned is sufficient to indicate that the Americans possess an antidote or the key to the development of such a thing.'

'And the mutation, Sheng?' How will Vigson respond to that?'

'He will be unhappy. He still has the vestiges of a conscience.'

'Do you understand, Sheng, that we may lose Vigson?'

'I understand, Chen, that we may gain Rand.'

'The burden will be laid on our backs,' said Yu-lan. 'It will be a question of shaking it off.'

'I am wise to that fact,' said Kittegawa. 'To be blunt, we will require to outsmart Arnold Sarsby in his own territory.'

'Could we not arrange a substitute for Vigson?'

'No, that would not serve our purpose. Only Vigson will be able to interpret Rand's information.'

'There are an excessive number of imponderables, Sheng.'

'We have said little about the government.'

'Ah-hah. That is yet another imponderable.'

'Have you a proposal, Chen? I would like to listen to it.'

Disgruntled, Yu-lan said, 'It is too late for my proposal. I would have had Rand killed as we killed Meredith.'

'That would only throw a cloak over the affair.'

'I am aware of that,' said Yu-lan. 'But it would have exposed the bluff.'

'In the long term, it would have destroyed us.'

Yu-lan was too polite and too upset to disagree.

Kittegawa said, 'I will make the arrangement with Vigson. We will bring him into America with caution and in our own time. With your assistance, Chen, Mr. Wing will make the arrangements here.'

'What manner of arrangements?' said Yu-lan.

Wing said, 'Plans to protect ourselves. I will prepare several methods, to cover every eventuality. If we had knowledge of the place of the rendezvous, that would be to our advantage.'

'I feel that we will not have that,' said Kittegawa.

'I will prepare to blank out Arnold Sarsby and all his people,' said Wing. 'I will do it at the meeting.'

'Alone?' asked Kittegawa.

'With permission, I will use the American girl.'

'That is unwise,' said Yu-lan.

Kittegawa said, 'If matters were so arranged that the American girl could be brought to the place of the meeting without arousing Sarsby's suspicion, that would greatly assist you, Wing, would it not?'

'It would.'

'I feel, Chen, that Wing's young woman might be so used.'

'If that is your considered opinion, Sheng, I will agree to it.'

'Now, Wing,' said Kittegawa, smiling with paternal fondness at his protégé, 'what, in essence, will be the plan?'

'Kill everyone,' said Wing, 'and fly away.'

'Words come easily, Wing,' said Yu-lan.

'Deeds will follow, father,' Wing said. 'I will send for the girl tonight.'

All in all Rand felt better than he had done in weeks. Crinkling pains around the wound were minor discomforts compared to the suffering he had gone through before the operation. He was still unclear as to what had occurred. Fragments of information that had come his way in the desert hide-out had not been properly assimilated.

From Upton that Thursday night he learned who had kidnapped him and why. He also learned that the decay of his heart valve was connected with a mutation in the Vigson bacterium. This part of the explanation Rand refused to swallow. But he kept his doubts to himself. When he was fit again and back in circulation, he would do a little investigating on his own account. And if he came up with proof that he'd been deliberately infected, then, by God, he would roast the establishment. He would feed the media every scrap of information he could find about the project.

Conversations in the intensive care unit of the Shaffer were limp and ragged. Primary data was exchanged between patient and surgeon. That part of it was terse and factual. Rand, however, refused to indulge in conjecture. He declared himself unfit to make evaluations of his kidnappers' intentions. He was not impervious to the embarrassment that the conversations caused the Englishman, Henry Marks and, perhaps most of all, Walter Stein. Just why the surgeon should be disconcerted by his patient's questions was more than Rand could fathom. But tension was infectious, and fifteen minutes of cross-talk was all he could put up with before his body rebelled. He wanted the nurses back, Nurse Sheridan or Nurse Peters. Their soft, inconsequential chit-chat soothed him and gave him hope that everything would soon return to normal – except that he now had a piece of fucking plastic embedded in his heart. He would have to live with it for the next thirty or forty years. For that, Mr. Vice-President, gentlemen, much thanks.

It was at the end of Upton's second visit, after Rand had rested up and had managed to eat a little soup, that it occurred to him that they required more of him yet.

'Wait a minute,' he said. 'You mean you want me to *continue* working with that bullshit bacterium?'

'You're the expert now, Dr. Rand,' said Upton.

'Jesus Christ! What if it's still infectious?'

'There's no danger in it now – for you,' said Upton.

'That's what you said before.'

'I said nothing before; not to you, Dr. Rand, nor to Ashley Meredith,' Upton told him. 'In fact, it came as a complete surprise to me that Vigson's bacterium turned out to be unstable.'

'There are two things going on here,' said Rand. 'Everybody and his wife wants that bacterium tamed. The Italians, Varese and Bulthius – that their names?' – they want an antidote. The government wants an antidote. What do the Chinese want?'

'The same thing,' said Upton. 'The Chinese, however, are disturbed by your illness, by the fact that the bacterium has lethal properties that Conrad Vigson did not predict.'

Rand kept his mouth shut about his suspicions.

Upton said, 'There's some urgency, Dr. Rand. I think it fair to warn you that the two "elements", shall we say, are still very much interested in you.'

Rand raised himself a little in bed. 'Then it's up to you to make goddamned sure they don't get another chance.'

'We will,' said Upton. 'But this is not a full-scale operation. We are circumscribed by the need for secrecy.'

'Just what are you trying to tell me?'

'Nothing, said Upton. 'Nor do I wish to impose any further stress on you, Dr. Rand. I merely wish to be honest. There's an outside chance that some attempt to kidnap you may be made again.'

'I feel like a fucking hockey puck,' said Rand. 'Will they – Varese or the Chinese – try to exterminate me? Is that what you mean?'

'You've played along very intelligently so far,' said Upton. 'You've given them reason to believe that you're close to making a breakthrough in the discovery of an antidote. Provided that illusion is sustained, you are much more valuable alive than dead.'

'But what about you? How does my stock stand?'

'Oh, we'll look after you.'

'Like you did in Washington.'

'Rainer underestimated the opposition. It won't happen again.'

'It better not,' said Rand. 'If it does.'

'Hm?' said Upton, suddenly alert.

'If it does, I'll blow the whole works,' said Rand. 'I'll tell them everything.'

'That would be very foolish,' said Upton.

'Are you deliberately setting me up for a second time?' said Rand.

'How can we?' said Upton. 'You're still very sick.'

'Yeah,' said Rand. 'I feel it.'

'Don't worry, Doctor. I'm merely being alarmist. Nobody can reach you here.'

'Only you, Upton,' Rand said. 'Only you.'

SATURDAY 27 AUGUST
SAN FRANCISCO

Fort Shaffer Military Hospital had no valuable weapons and no top secret documents on its premises. It was a medical centre, a patch 'em up and toss 'em out corner of the Pentagon's empire, not lashed down by security measures. Maybe that had been in the back of Mike Lassiter's mind when he had made his deal with the army. Of all the suggestions and eccentric demands that Upton had pushed at Lassiter, the only one the FBI chief was willing to adopt as his personal motto was *No Bloodshed.*

Somehow he had to balance the need to convince Sarsby that the authorities had been taken for suckers against the necessity of ensuring that nobody on the right side of the fence got hurt. From official sources in Washington he had culled a little inside information on the Rand kidnapping fiasco. He hadn't known FBI Agent Donohue, of course, but he regarded any honest Bureau artisan as a blood brother and Donohue's death by mischance stuck in his craw like a fishbone.

Ivy League Feldspar's arrival in Lassiter's office didn't make the FBI chief any less jaundiced. He quizzed the agent carefully about the Washington affair to see what he could learn from it. Feldspar's only contribution was to repeat that Sarsby had 'come on rough'. Holy shit! What did the idiot expect? Kid gloves from the syndicate? What were they recruiting for Langley these days? The mysterious and highly fraught angle involving the psycho in Barbary High was probably more Feldspar's cup of java than active engagements with a ruthless enemy.

Whatever, Lassiter was inured to carrying out orders of which he did not approve. In recent years he had learned to sidestep the pitfalls of the law, to bring criminals to justice in such a way that bleeding-heart judges and smartass lawyers couldn't have the animals back on the streets again in a couple of months. If he'd had the case, he'd have investigated Marks so thoroughly that the director wouldn't have been able to hide; and, so Lassiter privately believed, he would have wound up in Leavenworth for illegal misappropriation of public funds. They were all at it in the intelligence community. Every last one of the mothers. It was an old beef of FBI diehards. Lassiter found nothing in the present assignment to alter his fixed opinion of the national security organisations.

He knew what *he* had to do – make sure Sarsby's monkeys got away with kidnapping, redeemed Rand, hijacked Stein, and released the senator; trace the Sarsby hideaway and lay an invisible force of FBI commandos around it, all without scaring Sarsby or the Chinese. When the time came, he would have to rush that force in fast enough to save the necks of the thumbsucking agents that Upton had planted in addition to Rand and Stein.

But he would have compensation; he would have Varese and Sarsby. By Jesus, if he couldn't get them cold on fine fat charges, he would get them cold in coffins. The last way would be the best way – then no cottonmouth from a government agency could issue him with an edict demanding their release for security reasons. Over guys like Sarsby, Frank Varese and Tony Bulthius, he just wouldn't bargain.

Fortunately, the Englishman had warned him to be prepared for Sarsby's raid. Otherwise, Lassiter would probably have missed the crunch, at such an unexpectedly early hour on Saturday morning. As it was he spent the night at the radio post army engineers had obligingly set up for him in a small office in the Shaffer's surgical wing. Feldspar hung around like a spare prick in a whorehouse. But Upton and Marks were civil enough not to interfere; they left him to get on with his job.

The raid itself was sudden and dramatic. Sarsby had decided to show his teeth, not to risk insinuation or an approach to the bosses.

No trade would have been considered before Wednesday. Arnold couldn't wait that long. Sarsby himself would be out in his big 'Frisco pad with his nominal family, his wife and daughters, pretending he was a man of honour and reputation, a regular reader of the *Saturday Evening Post* and *Good Housekeeping*, a model father. For Lassiter, though, it was just as if Sarsby were driving the lead pick-up, a scarred Dodge with plates wrapped in burlap and a grid fitted over its windshield.

Behind the Dodge were two vans, customised jobs but lacking the brash paintwork of road cruisers. One was the troop ship, the other the ambulance.

It was, as Feldspar said, rough; like an armed assault. Three men in the Dodge, six more in the first van; a medical crew, complete with theatre greens and surgical masks, in the second vehicle. The crew numbered four, plus two more monkeys with assault rifles. All the men were dressed in high-button denim overalls and Adidas sneakers and wore blue kerchiefs over their mouths and noses. They were well drilled, professional underworld soldiers signed on for the job.

The army guards at the garrison post put up no resistance as the Dodge unloaded its force. The gatehouse was instantly mobilised. The watch had been warned to expect intruders, warned not to be heroic, warned that any serious retaliation would put the whole six-man squad in the stockade.

The Dodge's crew took possession of the gate area. The two vans sped on up the driveway to the surgical wing. They parked neatly in the slots by Stein's Camaro. The medics, backed by the four tallest troops, walked in through the door that led to the secondary reception area.

Making no fuss at all – the main blocks of the hospital were not roused – the reception desk, telephones and intercom devices were knocked out by the simple presence of a couple of armed men.

The remaining two troops, followed by the medics, silently rounded the corner into the corridor of the IC units. The Marine Corps duty guards were caught in conversation at the coffee vendor.

One shot fired by the Marines drew an immediate reply from the leading storm trooper. He dropped full-length and pumped a gas cannister from an interesting sling-shot device – Japanese patent, as it happened. As the greyish coils burst outward like foliage from the tiny charge in the gullet of the cannister, he rolled to the base of the wall. His buddy wore a rubber mask under his kerchief. He whipped down goggles from his brow and dashed into the acidic murk, a blackjack in his right hand and a monstrous Luger in the other. He fired one .22 Long Rifle Standard into the chest of the burly Marine at forty paces and, rather to his surprise, stopped the big guard dead, bowling him over completely, sending him sprawling to the floor.

The trooper had been instructed to use only .22 standard cartridges; the Marine had been issued with a light bullet-proof garment that covered every vital organ in his body. He went down because he figured that was the best way to avoid getting blasted between the eyes.

Avoid any kind of retaliation; an order to be obeyed. The other guard was not so lucky. He had taken a mouthful of gas and had lost his sense of direction as a result. Blundering, he ran slap into the trooper who promptly zapped him across the side of the neck.

Two male medics stooped and dragged the unconscious Marine to the corridor's end, heaving him forward like a carcass in a butcher's trough. The other two male medics, peering through gasmasks, plucked up the ostensibly wounded guard by the armpits and slid him to join his buddy at the corridor's end; safe out of range of the worst of the gas and, more importantly, clear of the wheels of the roller stretcher that the ladies, God bless 'em, had sledded in from the van.

Though the third phase of the raid seemed chaotic, in effect it went smoothly. There was much shouting and waving of rifles and handguns, brandishing of blackjacks. The grizzled surgeon punched a couple of heads until he was pinned from behind and frog-marched out of IC. With a gloved hand squeezed over his eyes and nostrils, he was steered through the worst of the gas and across the foyer, out into the air, into the rear of the ambulance.

Stein's nurses had hidden out in the nursing station. One of them was seated crosslegged on the floor under the desk with the phone in her lap, frantically dialling the Red Alert code. In the rest room, three duty doctors, also members of Stein's team, stood behind the door while the appointed one among them reported to Lassiter on a walkie-talkie that everything seemed to be popping and that he'd heard only four shots but smelled tear gas.

'Holy shit. They used gas,' Lassiter said.

Leaning his forearms on the radio table, Feldspar said, 'Yes, well, so long as they remember to give Rand a breathing mask.'

Cumbersome bottles and drip-tubes tinkled and swayed. Still connected to basic systems, Rand was lifted from the hospital bed and transferred to the stretcher. Medics supported the bottles. Strangely Rand put up no complaint. He did not struggle, not even when one of the women clapped a mask across his face and the stretcher was bumped out of the unit into the corridor. Rand lay back and tried to relax. He folded his hands across his chest to protect the wound. He could see little through the sockets of the mask. But he'd recognised one of the nurses, the stocky, jovial one called Jan who'd been part of the detail that had brought him in to the Shaffer.

When the stretcher cleared the corridor, Jan took the mask away. Rand watched the roof go by, then saw the dawn sky. He'd been drowsing when they'd burst in and it was all rather like a dream. He found it amusing, really. It was as if his subconscious mind had invented the entire charade. What the hell did this have to do with anything as important as bacteriology? It was the game again. Had to be a fucking game, lugging a man with a plastic heart out of slumberland at the crack of dawn and racing him through the pearly light surrounded by gun-toting gangsters. Italians. His old friends from the desert ranch. Refusing to become excited or angry, Rand accepted the irrefutable fact that Upton had traded him back to the enemy.

Everybody had plans. Everybody was running around crazy. From all that activity, he was mercifully exempt. All he had to do was just lie there and heal.

They slid him into the ambulance and slammed the doors. The nurse was there, crouched, and a large man with a bandit's kerchief and a functional-looking handgun.

And Stein. The surgeon came down on his knees by the stretcher.

'How you feeling?' Stein asked.

'All right.'

So they'd brought Stein along. Well, Rand thought, at least they weren't skimping on medical attention. He would have the sole attention of California's leading surgeon during his recuperation. Provided the valve worked. Provided the bacterium didn't elect to have a chew at some other organ. Provided the Chinks weren't planning on dropping forty half-naked warriors from a gigantic box kite over MacArthur Boulevard. Provided Upton didn't intend to swap him for Conrad Vigson.

Stein had his hand on the nurse's shoulder. His features were gnarled with anger. 'Who are you?' What the hell you want with my patient? This man is sick.'

'Take it easy, sir.' the nurse said. 'You remember me?'

'Yah, I'll remember you, lady. And all the others. I see you all in the penitentiary for kidnapping. You know who I am.'

'My apologies, Dr. Stein,' the nurse said. 'But we need to keep your patient alive. Now, what can we give him?'

'What you got?'

The nurse opened a brushed steel case, like a Coty saleslady, and displayed an armoury of ampoules. 'Practically everything.'

'How long a journey?' said Stein.

'Three, four hours.'

'You're not to take him by air?' The horror in the surgeon's voice caused the nurse to be equally aghast, as if the suggestion offended her sense of professionalism.

'Of course not.'

'Then,' said Stein, 'I'll give him a little Digitoxin.'

'I'll do it.'

'Listen, woman. *I do it.* Nobody else puts a needle *near* this man.'

Rand turned his head on the pillow and grinned at Stein. He felt light-headed, almost intoxicated.

'You tell 'em, Doc,' he said.

The ambulance had passed unchecked through the gates of the Fort Shaffer Military Hospital. Token resistance was focused on the last vehicle, the Dodge pick-up.

The marksman Lassiter had secreted in the shrubs successfully planted four high-volocity bullets into the metal load-carrier, doing no damage. At that stage it would have been embarrassing to bring the pick-up to a halt, to force a shoot-out with the armed men. The Dodge, travelling fast, swooped away into the grey dawn, trailing the two vans.

From his radio control centre, Mike Lassiter released the two Special Police jeeps that would give chase for a while before 'losing' the Sarsby convoy. Lassiter also alerted the mobile tracking station – a hundred thousand dollars worth of equipment built into a scruffy Volkswagen camper – that was positioned at the mouth of the loop west of Fort Shaffer's domestic suburb. He backed up the Volkeswagen with two traffic control choppers charted in advance on arc flightpaths, just in case the transmitter in Stein's neck failed or the crew of the camper ran into some unforeseen snag.

Nine minutes after the ambulance squealed through the gates, the FBI agent in charge of the mobile tracking station reported in.

'Violet to Mary. Coming loud and clear. We've got him. Loud and clear.'

'Mary to Violet. Mary to Violet. Give broad co-ordinates. We will chart.'

'Violet to Mary. Co-ordinates will follow. Looks like the mountains.'

'The mountains,' said Lassiter. 'That's possible.'

Feldspar had been joined by Upton and Marks. All three stood anxiously behind the FBI chief and his assistant engineers. Throughout the next five hours, they followed the progress of Sarsby's raiders and the ambulance through the radio.

One change was made, at an auto dealers in Oakland. Sarsby was taking no chances. The Dodge and the van were left there. The first ambulance was replaced by another which continued unescorted. 'Violet' had conducted enough tracking surveillances to read the signals. The Volkswagen was held on the limit of transmitter range. The helicopters were pulled out.

The bug in Stein's neck was pulsing out strong signals. Even a strip search of surgeon and patient had no effect upon it; it remained undiscovered by Anthony Bulthius who had joined the group at the Oakland Autorama.

After that stopover, the pace became sedate. Stein and Rand rode comfortably enough in a curtained Ford Cruiser.

It was twenty-one minutes to noon when 'Violet' brought home the bacon.

'Violet to Mary, do you read?'

'Mary reads Violet.'

'Gone to ground, Mary. They've gone to ground.'

'Where?'

'The Pronghorn Valley, off the Owens.'

'Where are you?'

'The nearest town, Liberon.'

'Got you, Violet. Set up a base watch?'

'Right.'

Lassiter pushed the table microphone away from him and reached for the carton of stale coffee that stood by his elbow. He drank, then lit himself a cigarette. He looked round at Marks and Upton.

'Looks like they've settled. The Pronghorn Valley.'

'What's it like, Chief?' Marks asked.

'Bleak, an asshole canyon.' Lassiter took the cigarette from his lips and blew smoke noisily. 'Rand figured correctly. I reckon that's the place all right. Sarsby has property up thata way, a ranch. It ain't coincidence.'

'Good,' said Upton. 'It's better that it's out of the way.'

Lassiter got to his feet and stretched. 'Now I suppose we wait?'

'Yes,' Upton said. 'Position your squad and wait.'

'Do you mind telling me what we're waiting for?'

'A gentleman from the Far East,' said Upton.

'A Chink?'

'No,' Upton said. 'His name is Conrad Vigson, and the Tigers are bringing him home.'

THE AGENT

SUNDAY 28 AUGUST
TANG MANG WU

Miss Jackie Kyoto set about her perparations as carefully as she would have arranged a laboratory experiment. She returned to her quarters, bathed and perfumed her body, brushed her lustrous black hair and clothed herself in an ankle length *samang* of lemon yellow silk. She wore no undergarments and the sheath dress clung to her like a second skin.

She was gone from Vigson's room about an hour. During that period Sheng Kittegawa kept vigil by the bedside. Drugged to the eyeballs, Vigson slept peacefully, chin slack, lips slightly parted.

On returning, Miss Kyoto sent Rose Lips to the servants' compound to spend the night with the cooks; then she dispatched two houseboys to the greenhouses to bring back blooms. These she arranged in a vase on the inlaid table beneath the window. She opened the shutters and silently lowered the insect screen. Pale fabric diffused the moonlight and the faint glow from the compound, and let in the sounds and scents of the night. From the bookcase by the bed she selected the anthology of Chinese poetry, a volume finely bound in umber calf. She opened it at a familiar poem and laid the book on the walnut table by the chair under the shaded lamp.

Kittegawa watched in fascination.

'He will wake soon,' Miss Kyoto said.

'Do you wish me to leave?'

'I prefer to be alone with him.'

Kittegawa said, 'Is it your intention to seduce him?'

'He is already seduced,' Jackie Kyoto said.

Kittegawa said, 'Jackie, what *is* possible, concerning the bacterium?'

The woman considered her answer. She stood in profile by the veiled window, one finger hooking up a corner of the screen so that she could look down into the valley. Kittegawa had never seen anyone more beautiful. He felt no more desire for her than he would for a daughter; only pride, an intense sentimental satisfaction in the knowledge that his people could produce women who were not only breathtakingly beautiful but also intelligent.

Miss Kyoto said, 'From what you have told me, Sheng, I am unconvinced. No, I am "unsure" – that is the proper word. If the United States government sponsors a research project, then it is not fanciful to suppose that they may have developed an antidote.'

'From Indian corn?' said Kittegawa.

'From any one of a thousand substances,' said Miss Kyoto. 'The *precise* mechanism of auxins is, as yet, an unsolved mystery.'

'But the American may have invented the story, using auxins to make it seem plausible.'

'That is possible,' said Jackie Kyoto. 'But did he invent the bacterial mutation that infects his body?'

'Is such a mutation known to you?'

'It is a process of natural selection.' Jackie Kyoto turned her head and frowned across the semi-darkened room. 'We are all afraid of blind chance, Sheng. It is the interaction of blind chance operating within the bacterium with unspecified external forces that causes mutation. A bacterium has no ambition, no objective. We cannot be certain that the selective process will not programme changes in structure and effect. We do not know what the Americans *did* to the bacterium; they may not know themselves what minor incident sparked the change.'

'Will Conrad be able to discover the truth from the American?'

'The truth will fascinate Conrad, as it fascinates us all.' Miss Kyoto came from the window and seated herself in the chair by the unlit lamp. She took the open book and placed it on her lap. 'You have your games, Sheng, your enterprises. But they are as nothing compared to the games that we play, we botanists.' She paused, tilting her head so that her hair fell in a musky curtain across her eye and cheekbone. 'Physics has claimed the limelight. Nuclear fission is visibly concerned with power and the terrible consequences of power. Botany, in contrast, appears to be no more than the art of recognising flowers.'

'I am not so naïve as to believe that, Jackie.'

'One molecular type,' the woman said, 'can be so versatile that all growth and control development in plant forms hinge on it. In our ignorance we tamper with organisms capable of altering the metabolic processes on which differentiation depends. The cell is as dangerous as the atom. In our present state of knowledge, it is more mysterious. Conrad will put himself to one side. His fears will take second place to his curiosity. He will be impelled to see for himself, to examine the possibility that he has helped create yet another change in natural patterns, not synthetically but by accident.'

'He is very afraid of this man, Upton.'

'You heard how he raved, Sheng. Upton only is a ghost from his past.'

'What if that ghost still waits for him?'

Jackie Kyoto hesitated. 'I am ready, Sheng. I can continue Conrad's work without his direction.'

'That is what I wished to learn.'

'But not here.'

'I do not understand, Jackie.'

'If Conrad does not return, Tang Mang Wu will no longer be safe. I will go into China and continue my work there.'

'Yes,' said Kittegawa softly. 'Yes, that would be a wise course.'

'I will be your peace offering, instead of Conrad.'

'Conrad will return,' said Kittegawa. 'We will make sure of it. If all goes well, we will bring Gordon Rand here too.'

'If not, Sheng, am I free to leave?'

'You are free.'

Jackie Kyoto nodded. They had made terms.

'See,' she whispered. 'He's waking. Leave us now.'

'Will I keep the helicopter waiting?'

'Yes,' Miss Kyoto said. 'Conrad will depart with you come morning.'

'Because you ask it of him?'

'I will ask him to search for and bring me the truth.'

Sheng Kittegawa left the bedroom, silently closing the door behind him.

A breeze stirred the leaves of the teak plantation and brought an earthy scent into the room.

Vigson's eyes opened. He groaned, drily.

Miss Kyoto switched on the lamp.

The drugs had left Vigson temporarily dopy. But the woman was experienced in weaning. She made him shower and change into loose pyjamas and a robe. She ordered shirred eggs and toast and weak coffee and served them to him on a tray that sat neatly across his thighs as he propped himself up in bed.

As he ate, she engaged him in easy conversation. In his

memory was stamped the image she had created during his waking moments when she sat in the chair with the open book on her knee, one long leg exposed, her hair loose, her expression contemplative and concerned.

Nerves tranquillised by chemicals, his mind was soon sedated by Miss Kyoto's physical presence. Her voice seemed richer and more soothing than ever, like a sweet dark wine. She was not distant and objective like most of the psychiatrists he'd consulted during the Baltimore years. Her sympathy induced him to talk of his inner life, to unburden his soul of guilt and the trivial pettishness that, in some ways, was harder to bear than guilt. Gradually, she persuaded him to expose his terror of returning to America and convinced him that it was no more than a soap bubble, a shape without weight or substance. She forced him to admit that his past failures did not extend to his work, that he had not been responsible for the actions of bureaucrats – Upton, for example.

He spoke of Upton then, beginning not with the espionage community but with a woman, an English beauty, Clare. Clare was the first woman he had ever truly loved. Her reserve had been skin-deep, her passion fierce, her loyalty to him undiminished by the secrecy with which he was obliged to surround himself. War time: Clare was married to a serving officer of the Royal Engineers. The captain returned. Loyalties were divided. Duty prevailed. They had loved nobly and parted honourably. But sometimes when he closed his eyes he could still see Clare as she was on that last afternoon, in the room in the Kensington hotel, by the tumbled bed, her slender body racked by tears.

Loss of his own choosing left a healed scar. Loss imposed upon him festered still.

And Upton? Drayton Down: rain and barbed wire, identity cards in celluloid holders, boiled potatoes and greasy mutton, beer in pewter tankards. He was impatient with the pedestrian attitude of his colleagues, their refusal to question the work they were ordered to do. Upton? Charming, youthful, an *eminence grise* who faded into and out of the dull Drayton Down routine. He was always there when needed, staving off crises, allaying suspicions, ready for a 'cosy chat'. He was brimful of plausible and seemingly logical explanations for every regulation, every 'new rule', every subtle change in the direction of the experiments.

After a year or so, he had seen right through George Upton.

He had learned to keep his mouth shut, to wrap up his conscience, hide it from prying eyes. He spoke of his fears to nobody except Rafe Poggendorf, a fellow exile, of like mind but opposed temperament. Rafe was gruff, militant and quite mad.

The only decent thing Upton had ever done was to release them from their obligations, to arrange that Rafe and he leave England and travel unimpeded to the United States of America.

But they were not free of Upton. Upton was no longer a person. Upton was a system, a state of mind. In Baltimore there were many Uptons, Upton-like doppelgangers; not least his wife, Amelia.

'Did she look like an English gentleman?' Jackie asked.

Blueblood, strikingly handsome, influential, very wealthy; Vigson confessed with shame that he had hoped that his marriage might enable him to gain influence in political circles. But he inherited no influence at all from his domineering wife. He could not satisfy her – other than by 'meekness' and abject conformity. He waded deeper into his work. In the laboratory – not in the drawingroom or bedroom nor at the dinner table – he laboured to find the means of altering an unacceptable society.

His experiences at that period were terrifying and irrational. In his concepts, he knew himself to be alone. He might create new organisms, tamper with cells, rearrange molecules, stimulate plant growths, alter the genetic coding of simple living species – but he could not change the world or even reorganise the particles of his own personality. His work was conducted in desperation, in profane awareness of his own inadequacy. He was nothing but a bondserf in the fields of the scientific estate.

The masters would not permit him to be a moral aristocrat; as such, he might threaten one of the many mansions of technocratic power. Reason failed him. In using the functional products of his work, without comprehending its true meaning, his masters denied him the purity of vision that he sought, a perfect plenitude of being, the *mysterium fascinans* of frontier biology.

They, the Uptons, made filth of it. They wanted only certified realists, servants who spoke the language of the times, who would parrot the jargon of war without questioning its meaning.

He could not change it; so he must change himself.

Worst of all, perhaps, he had been too long deprived of comfort.

'Yes, my dearest, of comfort of the body as well as the spirit,' Vigson said. 'I had no place in the world.'

Miss Jackie Kyoto sat on the edge of the bed. She caught his animated hands, making them still. He saw the curve of her beautiful body under silk, generous flanks, full belly, the heavy swell of her breasts. He smelled her hair.

'Conrad, I understand.'

He believed that she did. He was right to believe her. The Eurasian woman did not lie on that count. She too was one of the dispossessed. Her sympathy contained elements of calculation but her understanding was unfeigned.

'Truly, I understand.'

'If I journey to America, I might get lost again,' he said.

'How can you get lost when you have this valley to return to?'

She placed her body against him, her breast pressing into his hands. He felt no desire for penetration, only for the intimacy of holding her, being held by her. In turn, she genuinely wanted to comfort him and shunned the ultimate lie. He was small and helpless, almost mouselike, beneath her, yet he clung to her so tightly.

She said, 'Sheng Kittegawa will look after you, Conrad. You are not alone now. You must not be afraid.'

'I *am* afraid.'

'The Americans will use the bacterium. They will build others from it. They will turn it against innocent people. You know that is so.'

'I know nothing at all. Only that Upton . . .'

She put her forefinger to his lips. Sweat stood on his brow. On her brow too; a single amber droplet below the hairline, like a Madras jewel. Her eyes were large, solemn, dark, but not mysterious. 'It cannot be used if there is mutation. But use it they will.'

'Mr. Kittegawa?'

Jackie Kyoto pressed her forefinger harder. 'Listen to me, Conrad. Of all the people in the world, you and I alone know what disasters a mutational strain might cause. If the American scientist *has* become infected, then Peking must not be given the bacterium. Sheng Kittegawa is not a warmonger; he is concerned with profit. There is no profit in indiscriminate death. The White Tigers will do as we ask: they will destroy all records of the bacterium.'

'But the Americans have it already.'

'Consequently we must find a counter to it. With Rand's aid, we will disarm it, make it ineffective.'

'But they are lying. I know they are lying. There's no antidote.'

'Truth is hard to find, Conrad. You must go in search of it.'

'Oh, God, no.'

'You know that you must. I ask that you do it for me.'

'Miss Ky . . . Jackie!'

'I cannot love a man who wallows in the sin of omission.'

'Love a . . . ?'

'I am also afraid. Will you hold me, darling.'

'Yes,' he said. 'Yes.'

She untied his robe and opened his pyjamas to bare the front of his body, pale and European, but not flaccid. She had given herself often to less prepossessing men. Slipping to her feet by the bedside, she loosed and let fall the *samang*.

The opulence of her breasts and thighs was beyond his imagining, the hair at the pit of her belly thick padded, like fur. She slid onto the bed and stretched herself along him, hip to hip. Timidly he edged against her, afraid of her womanliness yet eager for her caress. She folded her arms about him and drew him against her, so that they lay, ripe and passive, in an initmate embrace.

The fever in him burned for other satisfactions.

Murmuring, she repeated the poem of the white pony, his favourite. She spoke it tenderly, as if it were her own invention.

'Pure is the white pony, feeding on young shoots in my stackyard. Keep him hobbled, keep him bridled, let him stay through all mornings. So may my lover take his ease.'

'Go on,' Vigson said.

'Pure is the white pony, feeding on the beansprouts in my stackyard. Keep him hobbled, keep him bridled, let him stay through all evenings. So may my lover here have his peace.'

'Please, dearest, finish it.'

'Pure is the white pony who lies in the empty valley with a bundle of fresh hay. He is like a piece of jade. Oh do not be like gold or jade. Do not go far from my heart.'

'Yes,' Vigson sighed. 'I see.'

'You must go. For a little while,' the woman said. 'If only for the joy of returning to me here.'

'Yes.'

'Will you?'

'Yes.'

He placed his hand upon her breast and felt the nipple stiffen massively. His other hand upon the pad of hair between her thighs was moist, her body opening softly without command.

He would do as she wished. Whatever happened in America, he would have the memory of this night to appease him and help him through, a talisman against guilt, fear and hatred.

In the morning, very early, he made love to her while cool teak breezes bathed their naked bodies and dried their sweat. An hour later, strapped by Kittegawa's side, he flew out of Tang Mang Wu in the Bell Kingcobra, flew over the rim of the mountains, out of the valley, out of Thailand, on the first leg of his long journey west.

Below, alone in the bedroom, Miss Kyoto wept for the poor deluded old man. But, soon after breakfast, she began the arduous process of microfilming every research document on file, building up the treasure that would be required to buy her sanctuary and status in Peking.

SUNDAY AFTERNOON THE PAIUTE RANCH

Stein was pleased with his handiwork. In spite of the circumstances, or maybe because of them, he took particular satisfaction in nursing Gordon Rand through the difficult post-operative period. It was one of the luxuries that a surgeon seldom indulged in. Having thirty or forty patients on hand at any given time, out of sheer efficient necessity, aftercare procedures were allotted to nurses and physicians. The mechanics of surgery replaced old-fashioned doctoring. Though he might operate on fifty bodies each week, he had little or no awareness of them as human beings. In this god-forsaken ranch, however, he had precious little to occupy him – except Rand's welfare.

Only the presence of Sarsby's guards indicated that Rand and he were prisoners. No impediment was put on his movements inside the ranch house. He was allowed onto the porch and to walk around the corrals, accompanied by the chemist, Tony. But the guards were there; two teams of Sarsby soldiers, including ranch staff, caretakers and cooks.

The logistics interested him. He enquired of the affable Tony how Sarsby could set up such a stockade and acquire trustworthy personnel at short notice.

'Money,' Tony replied.

'Just money?'

'All the guys you see standing around looking casual are payroll employees. For instance, Earl, the daytime cook, manages catering for Arnold in a motel down in Daytona. He's an ex-convict. He does nothing illegal, pays his taxes and is grateful.'

'The nurse?'

'Medical supervisor in a Sarsby plant south of the border.'

'I see,' said Stein. 'It's corporate enterprise, yah?'

'Exactly right,' said Tony.

'What happens if the state troopers decide to drop by?'

'We have a scout; he radios; we all move down into the cellars.'

'Search would find us.'

'Certainly,' said Tony. 'But it won't come to that. Your *compadres* may not know where we are right now, but if officials did rock the boat, three or four telephone calls would square it.'

Stein nodded. Sarsby's confidence was amazing. He suspected it was based on decades of experience, the tacit assurance that a little bit of bribery and a modicum of weight would go a long way. It worked, he supposed, like the medical establishment; a cabala with its own rules.

If Rand's physical condition gave little cause for alarm, his mental state was puzzling. Since no embargo was put on conversation, and surgeon and patient were frequently left alone in each other's company, they were able to discuss the situation quite freely. Stein, however, was cautious; he believed the bedroom might be bugged.

'So they traded me back again?'

'Yah,' said Stein. 'It was the only way to ensure you got good medical attention.'

'That bloody bacterium,' said Rand, making gestures to indicate that he too thought the walls might have ears. 'I wish to Christ I'd never accepted Jay Rainer's invitation to test it and develop an antidote.'

'Nobody could have known it would mutate,' said Stein.
'I can't understand what the mob hope to gain.'
'They just want to show you off, Gordon.'
'Show off my "recovery", you mean?'
'We are safe here,' said Stein.
'When do I get to get up?'
'Not for a week,' said Stein. 'At least we eat well.'
'But it ain't the Ritz,' Rand said, grinning. 'I'll be glad when this guy turns up and we can do business and get the hell back to civilisation.'
'If the guy turns up,' said Stein.
'What if he doesn't? What happens to us then?'
'I don't know,' Stein said. 'Maybe they bury us in the gotdam desert.'
'You're kidding!'
'Don't excite yourself. It is a joke.'
'Some joke,' said Rand.
'You're too valuable property to ice,' said Stein. 'After all, you are the one with the antidote.'
'Yeah,' Rand said, rolling his eyes. 'Tattooed on what's left of my heart.'
It was Sunday evening before Sarsby visited his prisoner. He brought a guest with him: Senator Halveston. Halveston was nonplussed by the unexpected meeting with Rand and Stein, as if Sarsby had betrayed his secret.
The four men, plus Tony Bulthius, gathered in Rand's bedroom, which had all the appurtenances of an aftercare unit. Stein had already informed Rand that Halveston had been made hostage.
Sarsby made the introductions, like a society host. He seemed proud of the fact that he had a couple of famous men at his beck and call.
Halveston cleared his throat. 'How . . . how do you feel, Dr. Rand?'
'Apart from the pain, not bad.'
'You have much pain?' said Sarsby.
'Some.'
To Stein, Sarsby said, 'I'd appreciate a report from you, sir.'
Stein did not relent his attitude of hostility. 'You are the guy pulled my patient out of Fort Shaffer. You could haf killed him

there and then.'

'Come, come, Mr. Stein,' said Sarsby. 'It was a very elaborate piece of play-acting on both sides. I don't believe that you weren't a party to it.'

'Kidnapping is not play-acting,' said Stein.

Sarsby glanced at Halveston, a question in his eyes. The senator shook his head, as if to answer that he did not know if Stein had been informed of the whole scheme, of the 'contract' between government and syndicate, or if he had been kept in the dark.

Sarsby said, 'Tell us about your patient.'

'The aortic valve I put into place functions well,' said Stein curtly. 'Pain comes from the fractured breastbone, not the heart itself.'

'And stress, how will that affect the valve?' said Sarsby.

'No stress; rest,' said Stein.

'Dr. Rand,' Sarsby said. 'Perhaps you don't know it, but you're a very important man. Important to all of us. That's why you're here. A deal's in progress; an exchange of information. I assume you know of Conrad Vigson.'

'Rand, you can answer,' Halveston instructed the scientist. 'Jay Rainer's only concern is with getting you back in one piece. The Vice-President sanctioned this entire procedure. When Conrad Vigson turns up, you'd better talk with him.'

'I won't talk about the antidote.'

'Yes, you will.' Halveston insisted. 'Don't you understand? Pride or professional ethics have no part in it. Mr. Sarsby here is concerned with survival of his businesses. For Jay Rainer and myself, it's a matter of ensuring that the Chinese – specifically Peking – do not obtain the services of Conrad Visgon. We need you back at work in Stanford; we need that damned antidote. Vigson's bacterium must be disarmed, at all costs.'

'Senator, you make it sound so simple,' said Rand.

Sarsby said, 'If it was, Dr. Rand, do you think we'd have gone to all this inconvenience. How many men in the world are capable of understanding advanced biochemical theory?'

Rand said, 'Couple of hundred.'

'How many comprehend the exact structure of Vigson's bacterium?'

'Yeah, all right,' Rand conceded. 'Now that Professor

Meredith's dead, only two of us.'

'Each representing a different interest,' said Sarsby.

'So we talk to each other,' said Rand, 'and try to find out what the other has up his sleeve.'

'And leave the dealing to us,' said Sarsby.

'Christ, it's the old story told in banner headlines,' said Rand resignedly. 'Vigson and I parley in one language, while you talk another. I don't suppose either Vigson or I will have *any* say in what you *do* with the fucking bacterium or its mutational strain.'

'You'll be consulted,' said Sarsby.

'Only so you and your buddies know what it's worth? I lie here like a cripple, half my chest torn out, and none of you give a fuck. No wonder Vigson skipped. No wonder he accepted the White Tigers' offer of a neat "death by misadventure". If somebody came through with that kind of deal for me, maybe I'd jump at it too.'

'Gordon, don't get so excited,' said Stein.

'I'm not excited.' Rand sank against the pillows.

'You had better leave him,' Stein advised Sarsby.

'Wait,' Rand said. 'You, Senator; I reckon this hood's idea in bringing you here was to let you see the merchandise undamaged and functioning, before he sends you back to Rainer.'

Halveston said, 'I haven't been "released" yet, Dr. Rand.'

'Tell Rainer,' said Rand, 'that he can fold his fucking antidote four ways and stuff it up his ass.'

Sarsby moved fast. He pushed Stein aside. Leaning on the bed, he thrust his face close to Rand's. Anxiety manifest itself in meanness. 'You ever want to see daylight again, *Doctor* Rand, you listen to what I'm telling you.'

'Your ass too,' said Rand.

'Nobody knows the truth,' Sarsby hissed. 'Only you – and Vigson. Vigson'll be here mid-week. Then you'll *talk* to Vigson. You'll tell him what you know. And he'll tell you what he knows. A mutual exchange.'

'Oh, yeah, I'll talk to Vigson,' Rand said, equally softly. 'He may be a raving lunatic, but he *is* a scientist. Put him in that chair and he'll talk. And I'll talk. Not because of your threats, Sarsby – or your warnings, Senator – but because Vigson and I share one all-consuming interest – the bacterium.'

'That's good.' Sarsby drew back a little. 'That's what I wanted to hear.'

'But when we've talked, gentlemen, and dealing begins in the outside room,' Rand said, 'you'd better remember the factor that you haven't taken into account.'

'Meaning?' Sarsby asked.

'Meaning you've no intention – any of you – of letting Vigson leave this place alive. And that'll leave me, just me, won't it?'

'We don't plan to harm Vigson,' said Sarsby.

'Tell him, Senator,' said Rand.

Halveston did not respond. He was smiling his mild patrician smile. It amused him to watch one of the intellects of the new scientific age operating at full power. He wondered how long it had taken Rand to work out the permutations and come up with this manoeuvre. Had it been inductive or intuitive? Considering that Rand hadn't a damn thing to peddle, he put up the best show of huckstering that Halveston had ever seen outside a Senate Committee on Commerce.

Initiative was not the province of the government or commercial dealers. Rand knew they yearned for the big fix, the scientific miracle that would synthesise the whole range of potentialities inherent in Vigson's discovery. Rand also knew that the intimate interaction between technique and application had never been properly understood by greedy, self-seeking agencies who sought only profit or power – Stein's plastic heart valves; Sarsby's morphine-based empire; Upton's personal crusade against Communist mavericks; Marks, betrayed by political chicanery and cannibalism within the world's most complex intelligence system.

What Senator Clark Halveston, who had lost all faith in legislative democracy, saw in the bed before him, at the centre of this deadly vaudeville show, was a vocational scientist who had finally grasped the nettle of truth.

'Go ahead, Senator,' Rand said. 'Enlighten this paragon of capitalism. You're not here as a hostage. You're Jay Rainer's field spotter. You know the score. Tell him what you plan to do to that poor bastard, Vigson.'

'He can't be permitted to return to the Far East,' said Halveston.

'What's the instruction? Bring him in dead or alive? Does it matter which? So long as he creates no more "miracles"?' Rand jibed.

'I know nothing of the government's "arrangements", Dr. Rand,' said Halveston.

'All right.' Rand struggled to sit up. The seering pain in his chest gave his voice a brutal edge. 'Let's talk about my future. If I come out of this mess alive, I'll be minus one heart valve. I'll also know how the Vigson bacterium operates. Stein, when will I be fit to work?'

'Three months, why not?' said Stein.

'I'll go back to my laboratory, develop an antidote to the Vigson bacterium, and its mutant strain. Lead a research team, if that's what Rainer and the Senate decide they want. But after that's done, I'm out.'

'You could stake claim to a high position in academic circles,' Halveston suggested.

'Meredith would have been satisfied with a knighthood,' said Rand. 'But I've learned the score. Before I take the lid off one box of cultures, before I open my mouth and dictate one intelligible syllable, *I want paid.*'

'Paid?' said Sarsby, as if the word was unfamiliar. 'You're a research scientist. You work for the U.S. government.'

'A half a million dollars for openers,' said Rand. 'And a salary of two hundred thousand for the duration of the programme. And a bonus of another half a million, on satisfactory completion. I want my share of the green, gentlemen. I suggest you work out between you who pays me. Maybe you could share costs.'

Sarsby said, 'Did you know this was on the cards, Senator?'

'Don't be ridiculous.'

'Pay me – or I won't co-operate,' said Rand.

Stein said, 'Gordon, take it easy.'

'I'll take it easy all my life, however long that is,' Rand said. 'But for nullifying Vigson's rogue bacterium, I want a substantial fee.'

Sarsby said, 'How can you talk money to us, Rand? We saved your goddamned life, didn't we?'

Rand laughed. It pained the raw wounds.

Halveston put a hand on Sarsby's shoulder. 'Look, this isn't the time or place for haggling. If Rand wants paid, then we'd better pay him. Perhaps he's right.'

Sarsby thought how Frank Varese would handle this extortion demand. But Rand's unexpected outburst had been informative. Rand talked the secret language of the sciences; he could interpret anything Vigson let slip. But he had *something* going already. The antidote? The word reminded Sarsby of the sinister green laudanum bottles that his mother had accumulated during her terminal illness twenty-eight years ago; how his father had prayed on his knees in church for 'a cure'.

Sarsby visualised Rand's antidote as being like 'the cure'; a discernible substance, an entity, something that could be rolled into a pill, cut with a milk sugar powder, or diluted with peppermint cordial. His business was based on medical drugs, on pharmacological preparations. But he had never understood them. Only money. He understood money – what it could do, what it could buy; how to breed it and make it breed. Rand was talking *his* language now.

'Yeah,' Sarsby said, shrugging. 'Yeah, perhaps he's right. We'll put up a piece of the stake, Senator.'

'I don't know if the Vice-President . . .' Halveston began; he didn't complete the sentence. He was staring in fascination at Rand's chest as blood began to creep along the fibres of the bandage. 'He's bleeding.'

'Now you satisfied?' said Stein, fussy and perplexed. 'Get the hell out. I must examine the wound.'

'And settle my price while you're out there,' said Rand.

'Shut up,' Stein told him, as the others left the room.

The bleeding was caused by minute tears round the edges of the stitching. Stein made a thorough examination in silence before he was satisfied that nothing more serious had caused the seepage. He redressed the wound, frowning, while Rand lay with eyes closed and arms by his sides. When it was over, Stein tapped him on the forehead. Rand opened his eyes.

'Nice performance,' the surgeon said, grinning.

'I meant it,' said Gordon Rand.

He didn't trust Stein either.

The chopper was a Fourie-Forrest Springbuck four-seater requisitioned by Lassiter from the Los Angeles Department of Water and Power. Inspection flights were common along the pipelines of the Owens Valley, and WPD craft were occasionally used to fly cartographers, engineers and geological surveyors across the canyons.

The contract pilot brought the bird down in Hammerstone, thirty-two miles south of Liberon, and fuelled there. He picked up Lassiter, Marks and Feldspar who had driven down from the operational base in a rural schoolhouse on the outskirts of Liberon. On lift-off, the chopper headed on a pre-selected bearing of south-south-east, boosted up on the thermals over the ridge of Mount Ladago. Summit slopes were lightly dusted with new snow, a rare seasonal phenomenon, the pilot said, that augured a stormy fall. Few clouds cast shadows on the piebald foothills. The sky was like sheet metal, the sun hazy. The arroyos and deep gulches that scored the vast landscape were filled with powdery purple shade.

They would make one run, cutting a diagonal across the head of the Pronghorn, close – but not too close – to the Paiute Ranch.

Lassiter was tense. He didn't much care for flying of any kind. Feldspar, on the other hand, enjoyed it. It made him feel like a spectator rather than a participant in the up-coming raid. He could not connect a snowbank in Osiris and the contents of the sealed Petri dish with the arid valley below. He had lost the linkage essential for true involvement in any long term assignment. His mind kept returning to the girl, to Dorothy.

Lassiter was radio-tied to Upton's base at Liberon. The FBI chief drawled out comments, figuring approaches. Marks asked the pilot what that straggly road was and where it lead.

'Mine track, into a belt of pine forest, good country to the east;' the pilot answered like a guy proud of his beat.

Feldspar watched vertical rocks slide away below. Glancing right he saw the scribbled old track that Marks had detected. It was paler than the surrounding brush. He saw the forest patch too, clean and green, the glitter of a tiny lake that the pilot identified as Dry Water Creek. The mixed country confused Feldspar. He had no accurate sense of distance. The mountains were too large, the ridges too long, the chains of peaks too congested.

'That's it,' Marks shouted, pointing below right.

The Springbuck drifted out from the face of the ridge, aimed, it seemed, for another vertical wall. But directly below was the valley, the Pronghorn. A discernible dirt road and – the ranch. Steep shadow wedged the prominent arroyo. Feldspar, leaning, put his hand on Marks's shoulder.

Into the radio microphone, Lassiter said, 'Four sedans, two trucks. It's occupied.'

Marks said, 'Be a bitch to push men into a strike position around here.'

'Sure is exposed,' the pilot agreed.

The chopper did not deviate from its course. It did not swing down closer to the valley floor. It looked hotter than hell down there, Feldspar thought, all dried out. He noticed a horse herd on a carpet of slightly more fertile ground.

Marks craned round. 'That track, that mining track?'

Feldspar took the point of the question. He could see the lighted inner wall of the arroyo and the odd configuration on it.

Taking the microphone away from his lips, Lassiter twisted in his seat. 'Yeah. We could bring a small squad in by the back door. In the days when the ranch was operational, that's how Sarsby ferried junk out. The mining camps nine miles down, by Dry Water Creek. Not much left of it, but the road's probably still navigable. It swings round onto the highway again east of the Westgard Pass.'

'Some rough haul,' the pilot said.

The chopper was lifting up once more.

Lassiter returned to radio contact with Upton.

Feldspar watched the ridge soar away beneath them and, with a certain amount of relief, saw the green of the Owens Valley, its villages and townships stretching out below. He had been on raiding missions before, but the logistics were better left to Lassiter and his experts from the local *federales*, gaunt brown-skinned rangers who understood the Sierra Nevada. Feldspar would be in the forward party, the raiding squad. He would claim it as privilege of rank. Marks and Upton weren't likely to argue.

Dropping, swooping, the Springbuck swung over U.S. Highway 6. It was busy with tourist traffic; Angelenos returning to the city after the weekend, vacationers coming out to the big wild. The chopper swept on over Liberon, a low-build wooden town of five thousand residents. Main street and side avenues were cluttered with vehicles, bright and silent in the dusty weathered setting.

Marks said, 'If we put an airlift on standby in Liberon, will it be noticed?'

Lassiter answered, 'We could manage one chopper, like this, maybe larger. How thorough will Sarsby be, though, in checking out the area?'

Marks said, 'Depends what's really on his mind.'

'Yeah,' Lassiter said. 'I don't trust him to play ball with us.'

Marks said, 'Six, eight men in the arroyo. Time it right and they could make it on foot to the ranch faster than we could drop men from here.'

'Much faster,' said Lassiter. 'I don't like leaving it to six men.'

'They can immobilise transport,' Marks suggested. 'Bring in back-up from Liberon over the ridge. Pin them down and we've got them cold.'

'In theory,' Lassiter said.

Feldspar stared down at the traffic – Dusters and Commanches, canoes on the roof, travelling fast and free, soundless between the glutted towns. The chopper was low enough for him to see into the cabins, penetrate the mirror-like surfaces of the windshields, make out the blots that were people. He kept looking for Dorothy – which was crazy. But stimulating. He quit listening to Lassiter and Marks, taking no part in the tactical discussion on how to capture the Paiute Ranch.

Six men bursting out of the arroyo: he would be one of them. He would get her out alive.

Whenever Vigson came, in daylight or by darkness, by air or up that bone-like road, Feldspar promised himself that he would be in at the kill.

SUNDAY NIGHT
SAN FRANCISCO

The bar was on Melmore, a small plush cavern in a row of expensive stores protected by steel grills. The limousine drew up outside. Sarsby gestured Halveston to get out. The monkeys went off with the car. Halveston watched them go, uncertain but relieved.

'One drink,' Sarsby said. 'For the road.'

Halveston shrugged. It was improbable that he would be

recognised in the dimly-lit interior of a 'Frisco bar. Two discreet neon signs said *Sutter's place* and *Air-Conditioning*. Sarsby followed him in.

The booths were crowded, mostly middle-aged men, tired, hot-featured, relaxing after a day with the kids. Sarsby bought martinis at the bar and brought them over to a wooden love-seat close to the doors of the rest rooms. Musak, solo piano in the Shearing mood, was playing in the background. The murmur of many conversations was restful.

'Cheers,' Sarsby said, gulping the martini.

'Absent friends,' said Halveston.

'Yeah, may they not be absent long.'

'You're releasing me, is that right?'

'Right, Senator. Go on home – to Washington.'

'I suppose you know I'll make an immediate report.'

'Tell your colleagues that Rand's doing just fine.'

'Aren't you taking a risk that I'll identify the ranch?'

'Haven't made much effort to hide it, not from your boys,' said Sarsby. 'There's really no need.'

'That's very trusting,' said Halveston.

'Hell no, it's not trust,' said Sarsby. 'It's caution. Your boys wouldn't be stupid enough to set a crack squad on my doorstep, even supposing they do know exactly where I am. Anyhow, you can't tell them to the mile where the ranch is located. It's a big piece of country out there. Marks won't risk scaring off the Chinese. He'll keep his distance.'

'Do the Tigers know where you have Rand?'

'They'd better not,' said Sarsby. 'That *would* be dangerous.'

Halveston said, 'What happens between us now?'

'Nothing, Senator. And I mean *nothing*. You keep your profits and I keep the tapes I had made of some of your conversations with Frank. Just a precaution.'

'Rand's "salary"?' Halveston asked.

'Do you want to be involved?'

'No.'

'Then I'll deal with Rainer, if I have to.'

'Do you want another drink?'

'I have things to do.' Sarsby glanced at his wristwatch and got to his feet. 'Goodbye, Senator. And just remember that you got out of this lightly. If it had been up to Frank, you'd have been dead by now.'

'Perhaps the government will do business with you again sometime,' said Halveston, straight-faced.

'Maybe.'

Halveston said, 'Keep healthy, Mr. Sarsby.'

'And you, Senator.'

He watched the syndicate chieftain leave the bar. He moved lithely through the tables between the booths. Halveston sat where he was for ten minutes, finishing a second drink, keeping a weather eye on the doors. After that he got up, changed five dollars for dimes at the bar, found a payphone and put through a call to Rainer's aide at an emergency number in Washington. He raised the aide almost immediately and assured the young man that he was alive and well. He obtained a number for Upton from the aide and said that he would be back in Washington early the following day. He put down the receiver, lifted it again and dialled the coding that he'd been given for headquarters.

It was Marks who answered.

'Halveston,' the Senator said. 'I've either been dumped or set up. Dumped, I think. But I'm taking no chances. Can you arrange to pick me up with suitable security transport at *Sutter's Bar* on Melmore, in San Francisco?'

'Fifteen minutes,' Marks said.

'I'll be here.'

'What happened?'

'Nothing happened. I got to see Rand.'

'How is he?'

'According to Stein, he's making a normal recovery.'

'Where?'

'Let me get out of here first,' said Halveston.
'Sarsby may have changed his mind about me.'

'All right, Senator,' Marks said. 'Do you want a place on the bleachers for the action?'

'I want a flight to Washington as soon as possible.'

'I'll have it laid on,' said Marks.

Halveston hung up.

Eighteen minutes later two USAF top sergeants, armed and in full regalia, stalked into *Sutter's* and pulled the senator out. They drove him directly to U.S. Air Force Base Forty and, after a short delay, saw him safely onto a Lear jet, reversing his journey to the

West Coast.

When the Lear left the runway, Halveston let out a sigh. He wished to god somebody would bring him a whisky sour. But nobody did. His part in it was over, all over. He felt depressed. Thinking of Sarsby, he was overwhelmed by a peculiar sense of betrayal, temporarily more ravaging than anything he'd experienced in his years as Marks's Judas.

Though the feeling dwindled it did not leave him during the course of the next three days. He went about his duties in a kind of daze.

It was Wednesday night before he got around to opening the safe in the family office in the old brownstone building on Claremount Street and found the two hundred thousand dollars missing. But there was nothing he could do about it, nobody to listen to his complaints or search for the thief.

By Wednesday night, it hardly seemed to matter.

TUESDAY 30 AUGUST
ENSENADA – SAN DIEGO

Jesus, Wing had made it so easy. She could hardly believe it. She suspected a trap. Had they ferried her on down to Mexico to get rid of her? Had the slit-eyed yellow shit found out? Ensenada; wide-open town. He might have hired a fucking butcherboy to slit her throat, ferry her body out to the ocean in a fishing boat, maybe just to drown her, leave her stripped, without identity, on Estero Beach. She was angered by Wing's precision, the detail he'd dreamed up to make the cover story convincing. He'd even packaged two shots of H inside the binding of a thumbed Fodor guide. She didn't know what to do about it. She thought of calling the number Feldspar had given her, begging him to come on down and guard her back. She couldn't understand why she was afraid. She'd never been afraid before. Before, she'd welcomed murderous situations. Time on the Baja, when Wing had used her as a decoy, she'd cut the balls off a greaser with a gutting knife before the Chink thought to crawl out of cover, tell her she'd gotten the wrong fucking Mexican. But she didn't want to die now; not with what was happening to her, with Bobby and all; with the CIA. Jesus, she'd *promised.* She'd been sure, so goddamned sure, that she was home free. Having a future made her nervous.

She got off the trippers' plane and took a cab out to the Pacific Travel Lodge. It was a small, smart motel a mile south of town. It had air-conditioned units and a pool. She was booked into cabin three-four. She went there, carrying the tourist garbage Wing had packed for her, wearing the clean college-girl dress and cheap hat that was his idea of inconspicuous.

In the register she was listed as Miss Margaret Alexander, a single. Next cabin, three-five, was rented out to Robert Alexander.

It means nothing, she told herself, only that the little yellow shit has been *really* thorough. Knows he won't get me easy. Knows what I'll do to him and his fucking bosses, if he doesn't get me first time round. His orders had been explicit: fly to San Francisco, Chinatown. A huge weird bedroom, like Anna May Wong might come through the door. He made her over for half the night before he gave her the shot; then he awakened her early and gave her another session of 'special' loving, the little twisted creep; then he told her he had work for her to do. She could hardly focus straight.

Told her they had Vigson in Mexico. Bring him in for me, Dorothy. Jesus! How raw, how spaced out did he think she was?

But obediently she joined the horde of tourists on the chartered Joytour plane, went on out to the Pacific Travel Lodge and sat in the room on the edge of the soft bed. Then she got up and put her suitcase and the room's tv set in a direct line between her and the door. She closed the drapes with their big guitar pattern, red on sage blue, and opened the bathroom door somewhat, after checking that she could escape through the high back window.

She waited. She had no weapon, except a length of plastic cord she'd ripped out of the bedlight and a broken Pepsi bottle from the six free drinks the management donated. She had wrapped the bottle in a towel and cracked it against the bed leg, picking out three suitable pieces and wrapping them in Kleenex. She put the wrapped pieces under the pillow, held the stump of the bottle on her left hand, plastic cord wrapped around her right wrist with the end across her palm.

It was a quarter after two when she heard the man outside. He knocked, and she told him to come on in. He was nothing, a Mex nonentity. Too dumb even to make a wisecrack about the bottle stump. Keeping her eyes on him, she put down the bottle and told him to leave the keys of the Eldorado and the papers on the floor. She could tell by his brown eyes he hadn't run too many errands of this nature; he thought she'd flipped. She had to tell him to get the hell out and leave her alone.

She picked up the keys and papers, checked them out. Then she began to think perhaps she'd been wrong. Maybe *Wing* had been suckered, *had* trusted her.

The Eldorado had been checked out of San Diego last Sunday, in the Alexander name. It was complete with log, showing a travel mileage that would have taken them down to about La Paz. No passes or auto permits were needed for Ensenada. Even so, the credentials had authority. Even at the Tijuana, with its lax customs and immigration, there was always the chance they would be subjected to a check by officials. Wing had it well organised, down to the last detail; no chances. She knew then she was safe.

Four o'clock on the button, her 'father' arrived. She never did find out who'd brought him. Maybe Kittegawa; somebody. Vigson was helpless, truculent, closemouthed.

He knocked. She told him to come on in. As soon as she saw him, she knew he wouldn't try to get into her pants during the stopover at San Diego that night. He looked haunted – and pooped; kept pressing his thin red lips together as if he was suppressing a yell of torment.

She treated him real nice, as Wing had advised. She put him at his ease, wondering if she should do it along the sixty mile drive to the border and the hell with Feldspar's instructions. She decided against it. Impulse wouldn't get her too far with the CIA. She had to do *exactly* as they asked. She was used to that, working with Wing. Time would come, though. It was all set up and running free. A flawless arrangement, precaution stacked on precaution.

The Tigers valued this little old guy. He was, without doubt, worth killing.

They passed easily and unchecked through Tijuana and across the border into North America. Hoardings and garish neon, hot unsavoury streets, traffic and the stench of gasoline. He hated it now, worse than ever before.

Comparisons were not part of conscious thought. Yet he felt corporeal. Yes, that was the only word to describe his awareness of his body, his sweaty body, robbed of elegance, grace, demeaned by the tall, wide-mouthed whore they had hired for him who, by some calculated joke, was supposed to be the fruit of his loins. Only bored Mexican policemen would be taken in by the deception. They would see only the cheap snap-brimmed straw hat she unearthed for him, the vulgar shirt, the trophies littered in the rear seat of the open sedan. They would smell the beer she'd made him drink, a half can of foul metallic *phizz*, the half pint of bourbon that she'd wafted around, the rancid taco in the paper in his fist. She urged him to sing, like a common drunkard. He baulked at that and lay back against the seat with his eyes closed, the hat resting on the bridge of his nose, beer can crushed in one fist, greasy taco in the other, pretending to be asleep.

She had papers. But she didn't require them.

He closed his eyes, screwing them tight. She nosed the great clumsy car up to the tail of the queue at the border crossing point. He could smell the ocean, unpleasantly mingled with oily fumes. He could hear the blare of radios, the whining strings of guitars tunelessly incorporated into squeals of rubber, creaking of springs, gunned engines. Lights flickered, red, blue, yellow, deathly white. Every muscle in his body was taught, with humiliation, not fear.

Trying the exercises that Jackie had taught him, he dove down into his inner self – visualising the valley of Tang Mang Wu, recalling in every detail the contentment of Sunday luncheons. Miss Jackie Kyoto, his beautiful lover.

That's it, Daddy dear,' the girl said. 'We're through.'

He did not open his eyes.

'Hey, you sleeping?'

'No.'

Speed: acceleration creating cool draughts of night air. What possible truth could he hope to find in this soiled and artificial country. Jackie could not have known how bad it would be for him.

The sacrifice was necessary, however, a final hazard, a last rite of initiation. His return would be triumphal, would make his rebirth complete.

'You're not sick?'

'No.'

'How long you been travelling?'

'I've no idea.'

'Don't want to talk?'

'No.'

He could not sleep. He had not really slept since he had stepped out of his bedroom into the dawn and saw the Kingcobra silhouetted on the pad. He supposed he had dozed a little on airplanes, had snatched an hour in airport lounges, dreaming fitfully of Amelia – and peasants – in a huge cerebral emptiness. He doubted if he would sleep now until he was back again in Tang Mang Wu, in Jackie's arms, in the aromatic breezes that blew from the mountains. He prayed, really prayed, that there would be no undue delay.

'Next stop, San Diego,' the girl said. 'You ever been there?'

He did not even deign to reply.

What did it matter what city they took him to? All cities were the same. Square structures of glass, concrete, steel. Functional modernity. Symbols of institutions that had condemned him to a hypocritical role. He had conducted his own rebellion against Uptonism. And he had been crushed. Reality no longer encompassed him. He found much comfort in that thought. He felt his limbs grow heavy.

Jackie had told him that he must revise his whole manner of thinking to fit himself for the higher status of reality that the new institutions required of the self. Becoming, as he had become, a private man – and what man was more private than one who is dead – was not enough for her. His antagonism was not creative, not healthy for a scientist of his calibre. Already, so Jackie said, he had become another type of person, absolved from the American bureaucratic ideal, moving like a stream towards fulfilment, enrichment of life for all men. It seemed she had found that truth in ancient texts; it married well with what he knew of the students' philosophy, their cheerful, dedicated totalitarianism.

'Los Angeles, you been in L.A.?'

He could not understand the whore's desire for chit-chat. Symptomatic of the empty mind of her generation. Had she no family, no father, no brother, no boyfriend or husband? A girl like that? Perhaps not. She could not make a home as Jackie did, a home for the mind. She needed the tribal conventions of small talk.

Wearily, but no longer irritably, he said, 'No, I have never been in Los Angeles.'

'We fly there tomorrow.'

'So I've been informed.'

How strange! Vigson's brain trembled. Inhibitions faded. He achieved a kind of synthesis, a convenant with Jackie's ideology, temporarily at least. In the girl, he saw the peasant class of America – also victimised. Proof of the polymorphic species, like the ladybird – Jackie Kyoto – and the paid whore. Dominant and recessive. Mutations. Each selected by the environment for a specific purpose, like better-adapted variants.

Yes, yes, this girl too. He could tell.

For the first time, he found himself speculating on what sort of man the American scientist would be, this Gordon Rand. There was perhaps a satisfying irony to be found lying alongside the 'truth'. Rand had become the victim of the very institutions that had driven him out; if Rand, God help the man, had absorbed the poison of change, not in metaphor but in reality.

'No,' Vigson said. 'No, no.'

'Uh?' the girl glanced from the road ahead.

'Nothing,' said Vigson. 'Old men do talk to themselves sometimes.'

'Yeah.'

No, not possible. Not remotely possible. Fusion of the somatic cells of almost unrelated species could not happen outside the controlled environment of a laboratory. The panic was based on inadequate knowledge. Unless the American had been ordered to isolate the bacterium by transformation? R-factor phenomenon? Perhaps Rand had ignored the basic fact that small and primitive organisms proliferate rapidly and are subjected to many artificial selective situations. Had Rand failed to realise that the Vigson bacterium was not without structural integrity?

'Guy I know, he talks to himself all the time. He's not so old, either. And he's not crazy.'

'I'm sure.'

And the so-called 'antidote'? No problem there, only method and patience. Never for a moment had he pretended that the bacterium was impregnable. He could negate its effect on the poppy plant, of whatever variety, simply by inducing genetic change in a related strain – though that would take time. He suspected that the American had attacked the problem by experimentation with chemical rearrangement of the bacterium's DNA and RNA units. Typical of the scientific establishment's approach, ignoring biological risks that could not arise within a natural ecological system. Sooner or later, they would poison everything.

But now? Just what did Mr. Kittegawa expect him to do? He would know within ten minutes whether the American was lying or had a grip on the truth.

Ah yes: the truth. If only they knew what truths he pursued with Jackie in that beautiful valley in Thailand, what fascinating theories evolved, what blossoming experiments were sheltered in the greenhouses. Bacterial genetics was the way to the truth. And to power, he supposed, though that concerned him much less than it used to do.

Hybridizations. Cell fusions. Interrelated mosaics of functional molecules. The composite cell. In contemplating his winter's work in the upland laboratory, he felt restored, made complete.

'This excursion,' he said aloud, 'is inconvenient, that's all.'

'Uh?' the girl glanced at him again. The mile-long open automobile did not waver from its lane. She drove, he noticed, with easy grace, a certain style. She was really quite attractive and not as vacuous as most of her contemporaries.

'Inconvenient, a damned nuisance. This trip.'

'Oh, sure.' The girl smiled. Silently she told herself that all scientists were fucking nuts. 'Look. San Diego. Last stop for both of us.'

But Vigson wasn't listening. He had retreated under the hat brim once more, to think.

The riding lights of American ships sprinkled the harbour of San Diego, an armed city built round amphibious bases, air stations and military reserves; all rather pretty in the velvet darkness, backed by downtown towers and the lights of the traffic on Harbour Drive and Montgomery Freeway.

The Mother Lode Motel was owned by a highly respectable

Chinese family whose paterfamilias, before he retired with a bum stomach, had worked in the Tigers' Singapore office. Coronado was a better place to be than Singapore; the motel owner was conscious of his debt to Mr. Yu-lan. At short notice, he had decanted the residents of the very best suite and given it over to his mentors without question: a four-bedroom unit with kitchen and broad ell-shaped balcony that gave a fine view of the harbour.

Here, at a table on the balcony, Chen Yu-lan and Sheng Kittegawa rolled dice from a wineglass. The first seven would entitle the shooter to accompany Vigson to rendezvous next morning, while the loser stayed in the wings.

On the third roll, Kittegawa shot five and two. He put the wineglass over the dice as if to preserve them as evidence and nodded at his colleague. Sheng Kittegawa was pleased to have won. Yu-lan, though he would die before he would confess it, was relieved to have lost.

From the kitchen bar across the lounge through the sliding glass doors, Mr. Wing looked up from the omelette pan in which he was preparing himself a little snack. He watched the fathers' lips move. Their heads looked smooth and polished, like pebbles. To his surprise, he thought that they looked old, suddenly quite venerable – and vulnerable – as if they needed the heavy embroidered coats of silk and wool that rich sages had once worn to keep soul and body together in the winter of their days. He could not hear their words. He had no need to be party to the conversation.

Outside, Kittegawa said, 'It is settled, Chen. I will go with Conrad to meet Varese and be taken to the place that Sarsby has chosen.'

'When it is over, you will return here?'

'I will return here with Conrad. If we are fortunate enough to have Rand as our guest, too, then he will be in Wing's care – on a separate route.'

'If Rand is still too sick to travel, as Sarsby claims, what then?'

Kittegawa shrugged. 'We will improvise. It is possible that we will not require him for long.'

'If you do not return in a day's time, I will leave alone.'

'By Mexico City,' said Kittegawa. 'You will go to Tang Mang Wu and secure the research material. It belongs to us. You will be required to trade with it, perhaps.'

'And Miss Kyoto?'

'You will trade with her too. It is understood.'

Yu-lan said, 'All will go well, Sheng. We have Wing to look after us.'

Kittegawa turned his head and studied Wing through the glass. 'Speed and cunning,' he said. 'Yes, I will trust to Wing's guile to give us success.'

'Success?' Yu-lan seemed perplexed. 'I am no longer certain what form of success we seek.'

Kittegawa answered, 'All the opium in China, my old friend. Is that not success?'

'It is,' Yu-lan agreed. 'It is.'

At the kitchen bar, Mr. Wing folded the omelette onto a plate. In an hour or less, Dorothy would deliver the cargo. He had ample time to eat supper and check once more with the California Weather Centre before his protégé arrived.

WEDNESDAY 31 AUGUST
LIBERON – PRONGHORN – PAIUTE

A cold salient pitching off the warm sector created freak summer storm tracks, temperate cyclones split into weather edges each of particular harshness.

North of Lee Vining and in the Yosemite, polar airs brought squalls of cold rain, deluge upon deluge, that increased throughout the early hours of Wednesday morning and obscured the dawn in stampedes of blue-black cloud. In San Francisco sinister night fog was stripped away by furious onshore gales that broke at four a.m. Behind the barricade of the San Gabriel, the Mohave desert moved like a yellow ocean. And along the summits of the Pacific Crest pellets of snow drove like buckshot into the hide of last winter's withered drifts and rattled the forests. Trees cracked, boomed, bent. Boughs that had lost resilience snapped and crashed to the sodden floor.

Four packbackers lost their lives in a landslide on a camp site below the Palisade. Trailers at Mammoth Lakes were thrown over. Two foolhardy boys were drowned in a fishing rig on Lake Crowley. Damage and injury were considerable across the mid-Pacific and far into the continent, as cold fronts stirred a vortex through humid layers over the drought lands.

By five a.m. the men in the command post in the Liberon schoolhouse were out of their cots. Funnelled by the mountain ranges that compressed the Owens, big winds straffed the towns and hamlets from Bishop, through Liberon and Hammerstone, Big Pine and Independence, on down the scribble of the aquaduct. The stripping wind, with a fifteen thousand foot ceiling, grounded all but the largest aircraft north and west of L.A. Honed by abrasive dust, daylight was ushered into the valley by a thunderous orchestra of strained timber, tormented piles, and the quick trivial tinkling of shattering glass. The schoolhouse seemed to move bodily with every blast. Desks and tables vibrated demonically, lights blinking and dimming as cables swayed and contacts snapped. Radio wavebands of high frequency and low were scratched by nervous static. Feldspar's voice, and the urgent reports of the scouts this side of the mouth of the Pronghorn, fluctuated plaintively, like ghosts riding the storm.

Though Upton was not superstitious, it was difficult for him to avoid a certain awe at the hostile forces of the environment. It was easy to read into nature a grandiose design intended to thwart the plans of men, a reminder that in macrocosm as well as microcosm lurked forms that were never indifferent.

Eating hamburger cooked in a skillet on a bottle-gas stove, Mike Lassiter leaned against the leeward window in the larger of the schoolhouse's two classrooms. Closed for summer vacation, the schoolhouse was an ideal headquarters. Fortunately the lot was sheltered by a stand of uncut pines that served to divert the full force of the wind. Even so, an angle of the township of Liberon showed Lassiter, through a haze of dust and debris, the strength of the latest enemy.

'Surely they won't bring Vigson into the Paiute today?'

Lassiter looked round at Marks who was pouring coffee into a ceramic mug. In the back, in the smaller classroom, the eight-man back-up team were sprawled on kapok mattresses between the desks eating an *al fresco* breakfast. Assault rifles, shooting vests, radio equipment and a welter of military-looking gear were spread on the raised platform below the blackboard.

Marks said, 'Maybe this is good for the Chinese. I mean, Jesus, at least they can be sure nobody's going to drop grenades on them from a chopper.'

'Have your heard anything from Feldspar?' asked Upton.

'About forty-five minutes ago,' Lassiter answered. 'It seems like your boy's gotten the squad close to the ranch, making use of the lousy visibility. We've lost contact though.'

'That's unfortunate,' said Upton.

He was thinking of the addict, Dorothy Newhoff; of Stein and Rand; of Conrad Vigson too. He was too tense to admit to sympathetic fretfulness that, in a person of less determination, might have deteriorated into guilt. The closer he came to nailing Conrad Vigson once and for all, the more convinced he became that any sacrifice was worth the exchange. He saw the project now not as a loose bundle of secret negotiations, as violence wrought against the system of good government. Like the primary laws of kinetics, the Vigson project *demanded* the invention of unique equations. In processing change in terms of what remained unchanged, he, and others like him, had shaped the philosophy of their enemies.

Vigson was the embodiment of cardinal error. No man of power would stand idly by and permit error to compound error.

Perhaps it was too late. Eliminating Vigson might already be a futile gesture. But there was no other that he could make. It had been destined since the first recruiting, since the initial act of corruption, since the day he had robbed Vigson and the other scientists at Drayton Down of their innocence.

'How long will the storm last?' he asked.

'Who knows?' said Lassiter. 'The weather station at Hammerstone predicts turbulence for the next twenty-four hours. On the other hand I've known it blow itself out in minutes, just kinda roll away.'

'Car travel *is* possible?' Upton said.

'Sure,' said Lassiter. 'Rough, but possible.'

'In that case,' said Upton. 'I imagine the Tigers will not be deterred. We must keep watch as best we can.'

'And depend on Feldspar to make the kill,' said Marks.

Long ribbons of dust undulated across the valley bed as great shovelfuls of wind lifted the loose surface. With no cloud roof over the rump of the Pronghorn, and no threat of rain, Feldspar had glimpses of the mountain wall, ochre and honey-blonde in slanting light from the east. Below and left, clear of the miniature butte at the tail of the arroyo, the horse herd bunched under a canopy of stinging dust hung out from the cliff. Old campaigners, the mustangs huddled, muzzles to flanks, heads dropped, visible for a moment only before being obscured again by blizzards of alkaline sand. Burrowed down against the crumbling rocks, the agents were distracted by the animals. Reluctantly, Feldspar dragged his gaze back to the ranch. He raised binoculars, braced on his elbows. Running, he figured they could make the main building in four minutes, stooped into the wind. They were a long way forward from the intended position, far below the scored defile at the head of the arroyo three or four hundred feet below the crest of the ridge. The IR transport was an hour away, hidden out in a patch of forest in an adjacent valley.

The FBI Special with the radio pack wriggled up by Feldspar's shoulder.

'Can't raise Liberon at all,' he said.

'Keep trying.'

'You know for sure they'll come t'day?'

The agent, a Texan, spoke with a lazy drawl.

Still studying the ranch while he had the chance, Feldspar said, 'I don't know anything for certain.'

Like Upton, he tried to calculate it from the Tigers' point of view. If he were organising a run into the Pronghorn, he would make use of the dust storm. Varese or some other trusted hand would bring the Tigers in. Perhaps Varese would baulk at driving in such a storm. Perhaps there would be argument. But he figured that the Tigers, with Vigson on their hands, would eventually get their way.

If the storm blew out suddenly, though, his squad would be exposed. He would have to back track them to a safer niche higher up the arroyo. That should be no problem. The squad was composed of experienced professionals, used to raiding narcotics dumps. The dust storm didn't throw them at all. They had settled into cover as naturally as mustangs.

They wore lightweight nylon coveralls, hunting vests, trooper boots and pale brown berets. Webbing belts and cross straps kept each man's weapons compact; revolvers, riot guns, two Remington Magnum high-velocity rifles with scopes, smoke and explosive grenades. In preparation for a long watch, canned rations and waterbottles had also been issued.

Timing was vital. Feldspar had to judge precisely when to go in. If it had been a plain grab his task would have been much easier, but he had been instructed not to make the first move. His role was to respond; to prevent harm to Stein and Rand, if possible, but mainly to smother the Tigers' escape plans. He would have to improvise, use guesswork. He was confused now. He did not know whether he was glad or sorry that Dorothy was on the inside.

The storm continued, remorseless yet teasing, diminishing for several minutes then charging up again, coming, it seemed, from no particular direction. Snake trails and twisters veiled the ranch and pasted out the valley track.

Feldspar ate a moist sweet cereal concoction from a can that the Texan opened for him. He washed it down with a mouthful of water. He wished that he could smoke. Three of the agents chewed unlit cigars. He found it difficult to keep himself hyped up. It had all the trimmings of a dud watch. His eyes ached. Grit had infiltrated his clothing so that his groin and armpits itched. Down at the ranch there had been no sign of activity, apart from the caretaker cowboy who crossed from his house to the pickup and painstakingly lashed a tarpaulin over the grill.

From the radio came occasional snatches of Lassiter's voice, but his instructions were scraped by static and Feldspar could not follow the code.

It didn't matter, really. Whatever came out of it, the final strike would be swift and sudden, like two naked wires touched to create an explosion.

At nineteen minutes to noon, a Chevrolet Blazer lurched out of the dust clouds. Travelling slow, it toiled up by the corral and halted hard against the porch.

Belly down, Feldspar froze, binoculars trained on the ranch. Through the lenses the dust seemed solid, like a limewashed wall. Even so he could make out the group that emerged from the Chevvy clearly enough – two Chinese, Frank Varese, Dorothy and a small man in a black topcoat who gave every sign of being impatient to get in out of the raw wind.

By Feldspar's side, the Texan murmured, 'That's them, right?'

'Yes.' Feldspar watched the group go up the steps and into the main block. 'Make ready to move.'

'Now?'

'As soon as I give the word.'

Behind him he heard the soft click of a rifle bolt as the FBI's best marksman prepared to cover his target.

Stein exerted gentle but constant pressure on the plunger of the syringe with his right hand and felt the carotid pulse at the angle of Rand's jaw with his left. Rand had not shaved that morning and bristles made his chin dark. At the open door of the bedroom cell, Bulthius hovered like an impressario awaiting the appearance of a temperamental star. Beyond Bulthius, Stein could see the new arrivals, bunched defensively in the centre of the huge over-dressed living room.

No warning had been given that Vigson was on his way. Neither he nor Rand had anticipated that the meeting would take place that day; the storm seemed too fierce for comfortable travel. The ranch shook under the onslaught of the wind. Dunes of fine dust infiltrated the edges of the window frame and built up in corners. Rand had complained that the thunder of the storm rasped on his nerves. He ate little of the breakfast that was brought to him.

Stein's bedroom was adjacent to Rand's; a bare cubicle with a cot in it. He spent most of his time seated on a chair by his patient, discussing a variety of topics, none of which had relevance to the situation.

Under the circumstances, Rand's recovery had been remarkable. The replacement valve appeared to be functioning efficiently. On the previous evening the surgeon had ordered Bulthius to remove most of the monitoring hardware. Rand was still in pain, of course; discomfort rather than agony. But his surliness, and anger, though hardly recommended therapy in cardiac aftercare, seemed to reduce his stress. Unlike every other case that Stein had handled, Rand did not fret over every twinge in his chest. He gave no indication that he was in the least concerned about his heart. He submitted to Stein's attentions with indifference. Not once had he asked for reassurance that he would survive.

In spite of himself, Stein was more bored than anxious. Apart from the patient, his only relief came in talking with Bulthius, an intelligent conversationalist as eager as the host of a cultural jamboree. From Bulthius – out of earshot of Rand – Stein had learned the details of Sarsby's involvement. With knowledge of Upton's methods, he had pieced together the jigsaw. Now he could more readily appreciate Rand's unshakable distrust.

It was during the customary noon medical check that Varese brought in the White Tigers. Neither Rand nor Stein heard the Chevrolet's approach. Only when Rand raised his head did Stein glance round. The surgeon went on preparing the syringe. Rand's attention was distracted from the discomfort that accompanied the procedure. But soon his face showed that the medication was taking effect, relieving his breathlessness and removing the weight from his chest.

From the living room, Stein heard Vigson say, 'I didn't travel half way around the world to watch a quack work on a charlatan. How soon can I talk to the man?'

Ingratiatingly, Bulthius said, 'As soon as the drug takes full effect. It's fortunate you arrived at precisely this hour.'

'Uh?' said Vigson. 'He looks well enough to me.'

He was lording it over them, a cocky little figure. He unbuttoned his black topcoat – how he could bear to wear such a garment in the heat was beyond Stein's comprehension – and stood still while the younger of the Chinese helped him out of it, folded it and passed it on to one of the three guards that Sarsby had in the room. Sarsby had arrived the previous evening, very late. Stein had been unaware of the incident and had been surprised to meet the boss at the breakfast table. Now they were all assembled, the entire cast – Sarsby, Varese, Bulthius, an elderly and affable Chinese, and a fit-looking young Oriental who had a girl with him. She was obviously no ornament, no hanger-on. Stein studied her covertly through the open door. Blonde, sleepy-looking, tall – an operative, for sure.

But Vigson was the figure at stage centre. White hair crested back, his little hands fluttered imperiously as he allowed curiosity to supercede caution and stepped in front of Bulthius to peer into the bedroom.

'I take it that *is* the scientist I'm supposed to examine?'

'Dr. Gordon Rand,' said Bulthius, 'of the Vereker Laboratory in Stanford.'

The two scientists stared at each other, neither betraying emotion. Rand's chest heaved under the bandages. Standing by the bedside, Stein continued to record the pulse, his back to Vigson, a pointed rejection.

'You, Stein?' Vigson said. 'How did you become involved in this transparent charade?'

'Charade?' Still Stein did not turn. 'Do you want me to cut him open so you can see the valve replacement?'

'I believe you would do it to prove the point.' Vigson twisted his head and peered up now into Bulthius's face. 'Are you responsible for bringing me here?'

'I am,' Sarsby came forward now.

'Why?' Vigson demanded. 'I am not needed here.'

'Only you can tell whether . . .' Sarsby began.

'Drivel! Sheer bloody drivel,' Vigson snapped. 'Do you suppose that man and I are two halves of a treasure map, that by putting us together you will have the key to profit?'

'Conrad,' chided Sheng Kittegawa, softly. 'Conrad. Please!'

Before Stein could prevent it, Rand levered himself up on his elbow and called out, 'Vigson, you stupid shit, they don't understand us any more than we understand them. Never have, right?'

As if he had been snared with a lariat, Vigson jerked his body round again. 'You are *not* part of it?'

Loudly, Rand said, 'Part of what, for Christ's sake? Do you really think I'd *let* the sons of bitches slice up my heart just for the sake of America.'

In silence, Vigson's arrogance diminished. He studied Rand with more respect. He was not so poisoned by the pus of his own psychic injuries that he could ignore Rand's suffering.

'Ashley Meredith,' Rand said, at length. 'You knew him, Vigson, didn't you?'

Vigson nodded.

Nobody in the room moved; they were as motionless as waxworks in tableaux.

Rand said, 'Meredith died because of your experiments.'

With less confidence, Vigson said, 'I have no proof of that.'

'You have me, Vigson,' said Rand. 'Right here. Once, so I've heard, you were a humanitarian with a heart as big as a house. What happened? Don't you care any more about people?'

'You must have been aware of the dangers of tampering with a synthetic bacterium?'

'Meredith respected you too much to realise that you'd let a lethal bacterium out of your laboratory without adequate testing.'

'It *was* tested; *tested and re-tested.*'

'What happened to that notorious conscience of yours, Vigson? Did *it* "die" in the Mexican plane crash?' Rand said. 'Along with eighty innocent passengers?'

'I am more valuable than . . .' Vigson let the sentence hang. Cynical sentiments sounded false.

The storm filled the silence like ocean waves breaking over the roof and walls. The battering vibrations were constant now, backed by the hiss of sand upon the windows and a roaring in the throat of the chimney.

Stiffly hoisting himself from the pillow, Rand said, 'Come in here, Vigson. We mustn't disappoint our sponsors. We were brought here to talk, so let's talk.'

Stein said, 'You haf one hour.'

He moved back from the bed as Conrad Vigson stepped into the room.

Bulthius said, 'Do you want me to . . .?'

'Close the door, Vigson,' Rand commanded. 'And let's you and me converse in a language we both understand.'

Vigson nodded again and, with care, closed the wooden door behind him.

Lassiter said, 'Sweet Jesus, they've reached the goddamned ranch already.'

Marks asked, 'How come your scouts missed them?'

Lassiter said, 'Who the hell knows or cares. Feldspar raised us on the radio. Didn't get much from him. But enough. Vigson's reached the goddamned ranch.'

'Very well,' said Upton. 'Let's get on with it.'

'We're going in? asked Lassiter.

'Of course,' said Upton.

'All the way?'

'All the way, said Marks.

Solicitously, Conrad Vigson asked, 'Are you sure you're strong enough for this meeting, Dr. Rand?'

Rand replied, 'Does it matter?'

Vigson said, 'Why are you so belligerent? Surely, sir, you don't hold me responsible for your misfortune?'

Rand said, 'Misfortune? You really think I got sick by accident?'

'By design then?'

Vigson seated himself on the stout wooden chair. He wore a vested suit of pale grey cloth, a silk tie in the collar of a silk shirt. The styling was too dandified for the little man's outdated manners and the formal rhythms of his speech. He folded his hands in his lap, fixing his attention on Rand with complete concentration. Arrogance had been left outside with chauvinistic entrepreneurs, the mobsters and dealers.

'Was it, sir, by design that you suffered this dreadful incapacity?' He pressed the question.

Rand shifted himself into a more comfortable position. Arms supported the weight of his torso to take pressure off the healing chest wounds. During the past couple of days he had brought himself to an acceptance of death. Each hour brought him closer to it. He was scornful of fear, in himself and in others. But sheer waste made him mad. Now he nursed a steady smouldering anger. He wanted revenge; not on Vigson, on the others. Carefully, he had plotted that revenge, dovetailing it into the complicated plan that Rainer, Marks and the Englishman had originated.

With a valueless future, Rand had no need to protect himself or his career, was absolved from participation in all forms of politics. The truth was carved on his flesh. His carping about a share in the profits had thrown Sarsby off the scent. Even Stein had been taken in by it. He trusted Stein no more than he trusted Rainer, Upton or Marks. If they thought that he would meekly return to Stanford and continue research into the Vigson bacterium, then they had sadly underestimated the effect of their cynical treatment. They had – quite literally – cut out his heart.

Perhaps he should have felt empathy with Vigson, the dead man. But Vigson had been more fortunate than he had. At the cost of his principles, by selling out his soul – for want of a better word – Vigson had escaped. Rand vowed that his revenge on

Vigson would be no less appropriate than that planned for the others. He would bring down Rainer by revelation; he would bide his time, then talk, blab, spread his filthy story all over the newspapers. He would appear with chest bared on every talk-show that would risk having him. He figured he knew how to push that snowball along. Rainer had selected him because he was a man of no personal value, just talented enough to communicate with genius and be convincing.

He would be convincing all right. Now and later. First he would hand them Vigson on a plate. After that, in course of time, he would peddle his story in vivid detail, make the horror public. He was no romantic idealist as Vigson had been. The only tools capable of disengaging the government machine were revelation and public opinion. He would make them regret the day they had extracted his card from the computer and set him up as a sacrifice.

There was no honour in it. He wondered if Vigson had missed that subtle reward, if the White Tiger Company had handed him dignity in its place. In defiling *his* body, as they had defiled Vigson's mind, they had forced him to actualise his identity in real experiences, homeless and cut off from the institutional roles.

A storm seemed appropriate to the meeting, creating a still centre in the middle of parched wasteland. Vigson and he would do battle nakedly, without the full regalia, in a lesser reality of self.

Only flower children, radical innocents that occupied the campuses, would understand his disregard of the major issues that appeared to be involved. In their sweet and simple wisdom, the youngsters had embraced the paradox of total political reality.

'Well?' said Vigson. 'Will you answer me honestly? Did the bacterium mutate, Dr. Rand? Or was it the search for an antidote – what a silly word in the context – that lead to your infection?'

'The bacterium,' said Rand carefully, 'did not mutate.'

'I thought not,' said Vigson.

'But you couldn't be sure?' Rand asked.

Vigson considered, then answered, 'The bacterium was *designed,* Dr. Rand, to perform a specific task. I assume that you, or Ashley Meredith, treated my bacterium as an artifact of low-sensitivity?'

'That's what it is?' said Rand.

'No, it's not synthetic,' said Vigson. 'Many years ago, in Drayton Down, Rafe Poggendorf and I induced genetic changes in several simple bacteria. We did not openly broadcast our findings.'

'Transformation phenomenon?' said Rand. '*You* were into transformation by DNA manipulation as long ago as that?'

'As you know,' said Vigson, 'the DNA of bacteria is – chemically – extremely complex.'

'You forget, I'm not a trained bacterial geneticist; neither was Meredith.'

'Neither am I,' said Vigson. 'I've always believed, however, that bacterial evolution is the richest field of study for those of us concerned with the chemical machinery of plants.'

'So you calculated from the plant the precise chemical environment necessary to the sexual reproduction of a specific bacterium,' said Rand. 'Christ, Vigson, did you *really* do that?'

'Calculated is putting it too basically,' Vigson said. 'I discovered the methodology of adaptation in bacterial genes by a clumsy process of trial and error. Chance bolstered by imagination, you might say. I ignored daunting mathematical numbers, the odds *against* being able to induce – even in an artificial situation – fruitful combinations. As you know, mutations in all species arise at random regardless of evolutionary usefulness.'

'Yeah, but mutations make the wealth of adaptive possibilities in every species,' said Rand.

'Ah, yes,' said Vigson, smugly. 'But the *principle* is so much more fundamental. An image, a kind of icon, for the life process; one I kept firmly in mind throughout the years.'

'Image? What the hell are you talking about?'

'A flower,' said Vigson. 'Or a tree; any variety of tree. The tree is only a means by which the progressive cycle of evolution expresses itself.'

'Chemical circuit, sure,' said Rand, impatiently.

'If only social systems were so perfect, so ordered,' said Vigson.

'Skip the analogies,' said Rand.

'Each tree, each plant, each fragment of living matter is subject to mutational disorder. The vast majority of mutations play no part in the evolution of the individual species and have no enduring effect on intricate genetic coding.'

'Obviously, that is only true of complete systems,' said Rand. 'How did you design a bacterium that would inhibit the morphine bearing properties of the poppy?'

Vigson's lips lifted in a bleak smile. 'Haven't you "discovered" that, Dr. Rand? I was led to believe that you and Meredith solved many so-called problems already; that you were, in fact, in process of testing a so-called antidote to my so-called "poppy-killer".'

Rand said, 'The bacterium is a selected hybrid?'

'Yes,' said Vigson. 'Bred, if you like, to produce a genetic copy of itself only by intervention in another genetically patterned process, the alkaloid formation in certain plant species; Solanaceae – tobacco – and Papaveraceae, the famous poppy that has everybody so heated up. If you had thought to conduct a tracer experiment on the latex of the unripe fruit of the poppy, using carbon dioxide labelled with radiocarbon, the differential rate would have given you a strong clue. Did you conduct such a test?'

'We didn't have time.'

'Time,' said Vigson. 'Yes, that's one commodity I've used astutely. Time – and imagination. Meredith was always lacking in imagination. I assume that you realised quite early in your "official" examination of the stolen culture that my bacterium must in some manner affect alkaloid formation.'

'Sure, we deduced that,' said Rand.

'What else did you deduce, Dr. Rand?' asked Vigson in a syrupy tone.

Rand realised that he had no hope of deceiving Vigson, no hope at all. The matters that Vigson spoke of so lightly were shadowed corners of research. In Vigson were combined a sound knowledge of biochemistry, biophysics and bacterial genetics, and a flair for isolating problems, a rare synthesis that enabled him to approach experimental research with a vision almost unknown in orthodox science. What other achievements had he buried in his sanctuary in South-East Asia? What did he plan to do with them?

Rand said, 'As a plant physiologist, naturally I approached the problem from study of the whole plant and the interrelations between its processes. Yeah, I considered alkaloid malfunction, the failure of bacterially infected poppies to produce morphine-rich opium.'

'That's what you were employed to do, I suppose,' said Vigson.

Rand said, 'Not all the products of metabolism are necessary to plant function; the morphine accumulations, for instance, in the unripened pod of the poppy. Your problem was to breed a bacterium that would impair a highly specialised process without destroying the plant or unsettling the delicate balance of its reproductive ability through any of its stages of growth. I find it hard to believe that you could have achieved this by design.'

'I told you, chance had a part in it,' said Vigson. 'But I was prepared to accept the bounty that random chance gave me; to go on – slowly and uncertainly – from there.'

'The introduction of the bacterium into the poppy plant at any stage of its growth inculcates a fusion between the bacterium and the metabolism of the plant? The plant is not affected, except in that one particular, by the bacterium?'

'No,' said Vigson. 'You're beginning to grasp it, I see.'

'How long have you studied the results of field tests?'

'On and off,' said Vigson, 'ten seasons.'

'Climate and environment, soil type?' Rand asked. 'What effects?'

'Marginal.'

'The bacterium is dependent on the plant – on a specific chemical recurrence in the vegetable cycle – to sustain its reproductive faculty.'

'You *do* understand, Dr. Rand.'

'I'd be lying if I claimed to understand the structure of the bacterium. I figure it correlates to natural auxins in the poppy. Auxins produce highly varied effects. Auxin is reckoned to be active within the individual cell only when united with a protein molecule, a regulator of plant growth and specialised functions in the life cycle.'

'Your conclusion, Dr. Rand?'

'The Vigson bacterium causes an irreversible genetic adaptation in auxin regulation, perhaps by inhibiting cellular fusion.'

Rand closed his eyes. He could see the fundamental chain almost diagramatically in his mind's eye. Beautiful and brilliant in concept. For a few moments now he had no thought of revenge or of the mission he had selected for himself. He longed to know more, to learn from this oddball genius. The techniques and methodology were presently beyond his comprehension.

'Yes,' he went on. 'That must be the key. Auxin to enzyme. Most enzymes activate only one kind of substance in the metabolic process. You have discovered, built maybe, a bacterium that inhibits, through natural auxin reaction, the enzyme that controls the formation of basic organic compounds – the alkaloids – at the time of the fruit's ripening.'

'What *is* an alkaloid, Dr. Rand?'

'One of the end-products of nitrogen metabolism.'

'Do you understand that process?'

'I haven't applied myself to it.'

'You should, you know.'

'Maybe I will, Dr. Vigson.'

Reaching between his knees Vigson drew the wooden chair closer to the bed. Rand let his weight rest on his right hip. His brow almost touched Vigson's now.

Glancing round, Vigson cupped a hand to his mouth and whispered, 'Is this room bugged?'

'I don't think so,' said Rand.

'You can't be too careful.'

'The sound of the storm will drown our voices.'

'Yes,' said Vigson. 'So, Dr. Rand, let us talk about the so-called antidote.'

Rand said, 'Meredith and I hadn't gotten far.'

Vigson's eyes crinkled with amusement. 'I am aware of that fact. Oh, I admit I had doubts. I mean, it wasn't until I really *seriously* thought it through, during the journey, that I realised you *must* be bluffing. All along, of course, I suspected a bluff. Since Upton was involved, any kind of cheatery was possible, indeed likely.'

'I'm not working for Upton, not directly at any rate.'

'But he's here, isn't he?' said Vigson. 'In California. Probably lurking not far away, waiting to pounce?'

Rand's silence served as an affirmative.

Vigson continued, 'We are kindred spirits, Dr. Rand. I sense an affinity with you. You too are embittered and anxious to take revenge. Am I correct in my assessment?'

'It's close enough.'

Vigson said, 'If Upton had been here, perhaps I would have kept my mouth shut. In fact I'm *sure* I would have. But I trust you, Dr. Rand.'

'Thank you,' Rand said.

'Trust is perhaps too forceful a word. I feel sorry for you.'

Rand licked his lips. 'What do you want me to do?' he said. 'Return to South-East Asia with you?'

'Good God, no,' said Vigson. 'That's the last thing I want. Stay here. Stay in America. Deliver, in due course, what the authorities demand.'

'A counter to the bacterium?' said Rand. 'Do you have such a thing?'

'There's no "antidote", of course. Bacterial reactions are not some sort of poison. They are quite natural events – albeit the process *is* triggered by the introduction of an exernal agent – within the poppy plant. No, no. No antidote.'

'A counter bacterium . . .'

'Perhaps,' said Vigson. 'I suspect there are many ways of reversing the effect. It's not a major problem. The solution is perfectly simple. Crude in its application, too crude, I suspect, to occur to researchers immediately. They would prefer to dissect molecules, manipulate chromosomes. The answer comes in a truck, not a tissue sample.'

'Wait,' said Rand. 'Why are you telling me this? Your bosses, the White Tigers, I thought they desperately required a counter to the bacterium?'

'Yes, *they* do,' said Vigson. 'But the White Tigers are only the managers of the affair. I owe them much. They have provided me with security and a wonderfully happy environment. I have no desire to sacrifice that, not at any price. I wish only to return to Tang Mang Wu, to my laboratory.'

'It may not be safe now.'

'Probably not, said Vigson. 'However, I have value in the Far East. I am respected, protected – loved.'

'So you're willing to work for the Red Chinese.'

Vigson smiled modestly. 'I work for them already. Not until I left the nest, as it were, until I was persuaded to return here on this lunatic errand, did I realise the whole truth. I suppose I've been dimly aware of it for years, pushing it to the back of my mind.'

'Don't tell me you want to make a deal for repatriation?'

'Disinterment, exhumation?' said Vigson. 'Never. No, never.

I hate America. For a scientist it's like working in a terminal ward. England is no better. I will return willingly, eagerly, to China.'

'And deliver them a truckload of antidote?'

'In due course of time,' said Vigson. 'But I am . . . what, under the eye, shall we say, of gentlemen from Peking. I think they will take what I offer and welcome it, in lieu of the poppy stuff.'

'What was your scheme originally?'

'To create a Chinese monopoly in opium, as an economic weapon,' said Vigson. 'Understand, Rand, that I am not opposed to this use being made of my discovery. In fact, I designed the programme. I can put it into effect in short order. I can reverse alkaloid inhibition, stimulate the Papaver Somniferum to produce a richer latex, more morphine. Not only that, I now have the means to double the annual crop.'

Rand said, 'What else do you have locked away in that laboratory of yours?'

'Many things,' said Vigson. 'Many marvellous things.'

'All based on bacterial fusions?'

'The most advanced of them, certainly. But that isn't my only field of interest,' Vigson boasted.

'And who'll benefit? The People's Republic of China?'

'Why not? Answer me that, Dr. Rand? Why *shouldn't* the Chinese benefit? Would you have me hand over my researches to the *American* government? To turn against other weaker nations, to transform into economic weapons to benefit an already affluent society?'

Rand said, 'Yeah, it would happen.'

'I'm not foolish enough to believe the American government is composed of evil men. But its systems have become too devouring. The balance of power, like the balance of nature, has been tilted. Do you know what was done with my research here? Do you realise the *extent* of intervention in the ecology of Vietnam? In spite of everything that the scientists said for nine years, the U.S. defoliant programmes continued. Fifteen million gallons of defoliants. Over a million acres of mangrove forest totally destroyed.'

'Yeah, I read . . .'

'You *read*, Dr. Rand. But I *saw*. Film, photographs, material suppressed at highest level,' Vigson said. 'Six hundred thousand people deprived of food supplies. Bad enough. Heinous. Horrible. But only a part of the story. The "inexplicable factors" – have you heard, read, of them? No regrowth. Abnormal births. Human mutants. It may be forty or fifty years before we can assess the damage done, not just to the poor natives of South-East Asia but to mankind's knowledge of himself. And I, Conrad Vigson, I was in part responsible. I had no wish to participate in war. I had no wish to be involved in death and killing. That was the price America demanded for allowing me to live and work, for donating money to my laboratory, for employing technicians, purchasing equipment. That was the price they asked.'

'And the price you paid,' said Rand quietly.

'Oh, Christ in Heaven, yes. *Yes.*'

'You weren't to blame, Conrad.'

'I'm too old, too wise, Rand, to foster an alibi mentality,' said Vigson. 'I am out-dated, old-fashioned. I cannot abrogate moral responsibility. I do not believe in the promises of the counter-culture, the sterile rhetoric. Nor do I believe that all governments are repressive and tyrannical. But I haven't the strength left to struggle against their cunning agents and do the work I must do.'

'It's different in South-East Asia?' said Rand, tauntingly. 'Red China is more moral, is that what you're telling me?'

'When I left my home in Tang Mang Wu I was confused,' said Vigson. 'I did not realise quite *how* confused. I am no longer confused. I know what must be done. What you and I must do together, Dr. Rand, if you will.'

'Go ahead, Conrad. I'm listening?'

'The opium monopoly, the building of a blackmail weapon, is dangerous. That I admit,' said Vigson. 'It's the promise I've used to buy the time I need. And to make myself known, as it were, to agents of Peking. It's an ambitious scheme. But fundamentally administrative, a problem in agriculture. The Chinese are excellent agronomists. They could introduce it, make it work, inside a year.'

'Hold the West to ransom for its pharmacological drug supplies?' said Rand.

'Yes, just as Upton and the others fear might happen,' said Vigson. 'The scheme is thoroughly practical. I have the means, the methods, to bring it about.'

'But?'

'Benefit without power,' said Vigson, 'is my true objective.'

'Meaning?'

'Root crops, flowering grasses, wheat, rice, cereal staples,' Vigson said. 'I have discovered the means to control growth in many crop species.'

'That's not novel.'

'Oh, yes, Rand. It is, it is,' said Vigson. 'The *degree* makes it novel. Bacterial intervention in natural flowering and seeding processes. *Precise* botanical engineering. The reprogramming of the life cycle of entire species. Yes, yes. It's *practical. I can do it.* All the research is complete, many of the methods of application worked out. Some of the testing has been successfully conducted. It's no "ultimate objective", no dream to be overhauled. It's something that can be done *now* – using *my* bacteria.'

'Abundant wheat, let's say, would upturn the world market.'

'Years of glut, years of famine. The politics of grain,' said Vigson. 'Subsidy, dumping; the pouring away of millions of tons of precious nourishment. Buy and sell. Trade, barter, bargain. Gain for gain. While in the Third World, men, women and children starve. I mean *starve*, Rand, not merely suffer the inconvenience of poverty, of having less than the family uptown. I mean *die* of starvation.'

'And you think that handing over your research data to the Chinese Communists will solve this at a stroke?'

'Of course not,' said Vigson. 'But in decades to come, by the end of the century, it won't be oil that concerns the heads of state; it will be food.'

'I think you're exaggerating.'

'Upton doesn't think so.'

'Upton? Listen, I hardly know him.'

'Upton is alive to the dangers. You see, Rand, he knows what I'm capable of doing, what my aim has been, ever since those miserable years in Drayton Down after the war.'

'Dr. Vigson, what do you want from me? I've no line to power.'

'You will have, can have – after this insane escapade is over.'

'If I survive.'

'That,' said Vigson, 'is in the lap of the gods.'

'What do you intend to do?'

'If I tell you how to reverse the effects of the Vigson bacterium on the opium poppy crop, will you, in six months or a year, pass off the discovery as your own?'

'As Meredith was persuaded to do with the Vigson bacterium?'

'Yes. Will you? Please.'

'Where will you be then?'

'In China, I imagine,' said Vigson.

'Christ, you're asking *me* to defuse the opium bomb, to prevent *your* honourable friends in Peking from using *your* bacterium to monopolise the world market. If they knew . . .'

'By that time,' said Vigson, 'I will have given other, better signs of my good faith.'

Rand said, 'I . . . I . . . figured I'd retire. I don't know what my new heart can take. I . . .'

'Dr. Rand, I've no time left,' said Vigson. 'I must trust you. In a few minutes, my mentor will come to enquire what I've discovered. I must denounce you as an impostor.'

'But . . .'

'Vehemently, indignantly denounce you, Dr. Rand,' Vigson pushed on. 'If I don't, then my friends will attempt to take you out of here, perhaps smuggle you back to Tang Mang Wu. Certainly, they won't let you keep your secrets and live.'

'And if you do spill the truth, Conrad?'

'We each have a fifty-fifty chance of survival,' said Vigson. 'It will become a barbarous game, with shooting and killing. My protectors against your protectors; the White Tigers against the American gang. Out there.' He waved at the window. 'Out there, possibly on the very doorstep, Upton will have men lined up. My protectors are fully aware of the risks. They have plans, I believe, to get me out in one piece.'

'I hope they do,' said Rand sincerely.

'You will also be gravely at risk,' said Vigson. 'The very instant that I inform all and sundry that you are nothing but a dupe, an impostor, then the young Chinese man will make an attempt to kill you. Be prepared to barricade the door. Every second gained at that time will be precious.'

'Conrad,' said Rand, 'they led me to believe that you were crazy. They lied about that too.'

'Will you do as I ask and as I say?'

'Yeah.'

'Listen carefully, then. The answer, the counter to the action of the Vigson bacterium lies in the soil. Most poppy crops are grown in soil depleted to some degree or another of nutrients. The band of variation is wide. My bacterium is not so weak that it cannot accommodate itself to natural variations in soil type. But to a massive dosage of . . .'

'*Nitrates,*' Rand exploded, sitting up. 'Treat the soil with *nitrates.*'

'That's it. That's all,' said Vigson. 'Massive quantities of nitrate salts; sodium nitrate or potassium nitrate. Fertilisers of standard commercial composition. But in *huge* infusions worked into the soil of the crop region.'

'The increased activity in the nitrogen cycle kills off your hybrid bacterium?'

'Completely,' said Vigson. 'The plant is restored to full and natural function, without impairment. In fact, the bonus in soil enrichment will benefit most crops.'

Rand shook his head. 'It might have taken me months to work around to that solution.'

'It's the answer,' said Vigson. 'In an area subject to attack by the Vigson bacterium, full alkaloid production can be restored by increased fertilization. There are, Rand, no side effects. The bacterium cannot reproduce; it dies. Crop areas treated in advance will remain immune.'

'You want me to sit on this information, then release it through my government at a strategic opportunity?'

'Yes.'

'Play their goddamned game?'

'For a while, Dr. Rand.'

'Conrad, what if . . .?'

'What if neither of us survive the next few minutes?' said Vigson. 'In that case, we will leave behind an interesting legacy; a puzzle, won't we?'

Rand nodded, grinning. 'Good luck. I hope you make it home.'

'Thank you, Dr. Rand,' said Conrad Vigson, then, raising his voice to a shrill, almost hysterical pitch, shouted, '*Lies. Lies. It's all a pack of lies.*'

He flung open the door and, deliberately protecting Rand with his body, bellowed indignantly into the huge western-style living room. '*We've been deceived. This man has nothing to offer.*'

At that precise moment, a split-second before any of the others could react, Mr. Wing had made his move.

The search for weapons had been thorough. At the airport Varese's henchmen had ensured that Wing and Kittegawa, even the girl, had no knives or guns hidden on their persons. Kittegawa did not protest the injustice. Mr. Wing needed no weapon. Besides, it was Sarsby's right to treat them as hostiles in neutral ground.

Even Kittegawa, however, was shocked by Wing's physical agility. Once Wing had made his decision, the time for talk was over.

Wing had planned his strategy during the twenty-minute wait. Seated in a big black leather chair that commanded the most favourable position, sipping coffee and eating cookies, he assessed the guards carefully. Three of them, each armed with a handgun tucked into his waistband. Varese was heeled with a bulky weapon in a shoulder holster. Sarsby and Bulthius were clean. The pugilistic-looking doctor, Stein, was clean too, but Wing recorded the possibility that the doctor had a blade on his person.

As his first target, Wing chose a rangy young guard with sleepy eyes. He would have preferred to go for the oldest of the three-weapon-carriers, but that man was restless. Wing could not be sure that he would be in a proper position.

A survey of the living room provided an embarrassment of choices when it came to weapons. The longhorns above the fireplace were tempting – foolish: cumbersome things. The coffee table was too heavy to manipulate effectively. Another table to the left of his chair looked light enough to use as a shield or a battering ram.

Dorothy had split herself from him. She was over by the rear door. He thought she had taken that stance to distract the young guard and to assess the kitchen as an escape route. As always, she was very still, very graceful.

He did not tune in to Sarsby and Kittegawa's small talk. He did not even hear the wind howling around the ranch. He breathed from his belly, filling the cells of his body with oxygen, keeping his muscles slack. He had decided that he would go for the young guard's gun. It was visible above the waistband. If the young man did not shift away, he would be the first to die. Rand, naturally, would be the second.

Keys to the Chevrolet Blazer were in Varese's pants pocket.

The Italian-American had been careful to lock the ignition. Of the other automobiles in the vicinity of the ranch-house, only the Toyota offered a possible alternative.

It would be tight, however the sticks fell. He did not know the strength of the forces outside. He had discussed tactics with his father; Sheng was of the opinion that government agents would not be far off. Many imponderables challenged Wing's ingenuity.

Wing had arranged a series of six boltholes based on an assumption that Sarsby would not transport the ailing scientist far from the San Francisco–Los Angeles area. In both cities, 'friends' of the White Tiger Company had organised hideouts and made arrangements to smuggle Vigson out of North America. In Sacramento, Fresno, Bakersfield and the township of Barstow, Tiger employees had laid similar plans. Finally, in a tourist lodge close to Lake Tahoe, Wing had installed four more 'friends'. They could be depended upon to ferry two men in safety across the state line into Nevada where, at a private airstrip in Shelley, a white dealer loyal to his suppliers maintained a small executive jet plane.

The plan had occupied Wing for two days. But now he could be sure that he was never more than a hundred miles or so from an escape hatch. His task was to run that hundred mile stretch and, aided by Dorothy, carry Sheng and Vigson to safety. Wing marked it out in stages – the guard – possession of the handgun – Varese – the Blazer's keys – Rand. He depended on Kittegawa to protect Vigson during the first frantic moments and on Dorothy to clear a route from the living room. He assumed that she would have selected her own weapons; a ceramic lamp, a glass coffee bowl, bottles. She was attracted to bottles. He did not anticipate intervention from Sarsby.

The disposition of opposing elements – that was how Wing thought of it – remained unchanged during the twenty-minute lull. It was as if they were actors in summer stock positioned for the opening curtain: Kittegawa, Sarsby and Bulthius together on the davenport, Stein leaning against the wall close to the bedroom door, Dorothy behind and to the left, covering the kitchen entrance. Varese was seated opposite Wing, unspeaking, scowling, watching him like a hawk.

The wind swallowed up all sounds from the bedroom. Then, at last Vigson's plaintive denouncement filtered through.

'Lies. Lies. It's all a pack of lies.'

Heads jerked. Sarsby began to get to his feet. Varese twisted in his chair as the bedroom door flung open. Harsh light penetrated the cell-like bedroom. Wing could see little of the room's interior. Vigson's body blocked it out.

'We've been deceived. This man has nothing to offer.'

Wing rolled over the arm of the chair. He landed in a cat-like crouch. in the same movement, he drove his fist into the young guard's genitals and plucked the Colt Commander automatic from his belt. As the guard pitched, screaming, to the floor, Wing threw himself left and shot Frank Varese in the centre of the forehead before the big man could reach for his gun. Out of the tail of his eye he was conscious of movement.

Dorothy had gone for the ethnic lamp. Ripping it from its socket she swung it like a baseball bat. The base of the lamp broke into the old guard's face. Smashing his nose, it imploded shards of bone into his air passages and soft palate. Like a Cossack dancer, Wing pivoted in the crouch. He fired two shots into the belly of the third guard just as the man dove for cover by the davenport.

Vigson was still standing in the doorway. The tunnel of blonde light behind him narrowed. Wing projected himself forward. All he had to do now was to kill Rand. At that instant everything began to go wrong.

Dorothy released the lamp at the moment of impact. The man had hoisted the gun out of his belt. She saw his fingers open. She saw the gun carried upward and begin to fall. She was too far from Vigson to reach him before Wing. She had blotted out the living room. It was like fucking with Bobby, a series of seemingly small, languid motions, heightened to explosive climaxes by her own nervous excitement. The automatic struck the floor. She scooped it up.

Vigson was frozen in the doorway.

The doctor had gone from his place against the wall. She'd figured he would be fast. He had less to consider than anybody else, his choice of action limited by a single purpose. The bedroom door began to close.

Against the rectangle of light, she saw a cocoon of bedclothing spread across the floor of the cell. The man, Rand, had struggled free of the sheets. They were draped behind him, trailing to the bed. Tramping over him, the doctor appeared to have no contact with the floor, to be suspended within the room, hanging in mid-air over his patient. But it was the doctor's strength and weight that was slamming the door.

So far, she had blanked out the others – Sarsby, Kittegawa, the soft-bodied, soft-talking New Yorker, Bulthius. But they had been moving too, all three of them, angling away from the davenport. And Wing, incredibly quick, was heading for the closing door.

Abruptly the space between her and Vigson was crowded. She fired twice, saw Bulthius jacknife, and fired again.

The bedroom door slammed shut.

Kittegawa and Wing had both reached Vigson now. Sarsby had swooned out of her view, fading, though; she did not think he had been hit. She squeezed the trigger for a fourth time, saw Kittegawa flail. Wing's moon face angled towards her, eyes slitted, lips pursed, the Colt rising. She toppled sideways as he snapped off the shot. She had lost the advantage of surprise and Vigson was still alive.

Inside the bedroom, Rand and the doctor were secure.

All at once there was an onrush of reality, a dull flash of pain in her hip and shoulder as she landed, the furnace-like roar of the wind, the crisp *pah-pah-pah-pah* of Wing pumping bullets into the woodwork of the door. Wildly she let off two more shots as she came to her knees.

They were moving, like some weird, ungainly beast with six legs – Kittegawa, Wing, Vigson.

She fired again and heard the impertinent *snick* of the empty clip. She hesitated. Though she loathed the yellow bastard, she had respect for him.

A fresh weapon? The dead guard's gun? Wing's feral eyes swept round the room as Vigson's hand closed on the handle and the big outside door swung inwards. She was thirty feet from them. And she did not particularly want to die. In the open, she might prove smarter than the fucking Chink. Vigson faded from her thoughts. She balled the hot anger in her belly into an image of Wing and thrust out of the living room into the kitchen corridor. She found her feet, ran on through the kitchen and out of the side door onto a patch of beaten ground below the end steps of the porch at the gable.

Far out, some forty yards away, she saw the body of a man in denim jeans and cowboy boots gut down in the dust. The wind piled handfuls of grit into the folds of his clothing. A bullet whanged into the board left of her head. She dove for the shelter of the porch steps.

Somebody was yelling through the slats of blown sand. She was aware of blue sky among the storm coils. The voice was faintly ethereal, as if it came from that vanishing sliver of blue.

'Feldspar,' she shouted.

Drawing her knees to her chest, she covered her breasts and throat with folded arms, and lay along the base of the board wall. Dust particles sucked into her mouth, making her gag. Stinging grains made her cry. Lying helpless as a baby, without a visible target, she experienced a moment of absolute terror. There was more gunfire; not random now, not loud.

Dorothy whimpered and shouted again. '*Feldspar. Feldspar. I'm here, Feldspar.*'

The wind carved out the corner of the porch steps in yellow-red dust. Screwed clouds obscured the yards and adobe buildings, flattening them into shapes like cut paper. The howling wind carried her cries away.

She saw them running, running like dummies on a conveyor belt, coming no closer, running silently, energetically – three men with assault rifles at the port.

I'm on your side. Jesus. Christ. Jesus. I'm one of your people.'

She clawed herself up and raised her hands, smiling hideously. 'Ask Harold, you don't believe me.'

Feldspar sprinted out of right field: heroic poses, an overhand lob, bodyswerve, check, the final run. He caught her round the waist and carried her down into the dirt.

She nuzzled her face into his neck as the grenade exploded in front of the ranch in a floury spray of earth and shattered glass. The running men had thrown themselves flat. But now they were up and in motion at last.

Yanking Dorothy to her feet, Feldspar clasped her shaking body.

'Rand? Where's Rand?'

'In . . . in . . . inside.'

'Is he dead?'

'No, listen, I don't . . . think so.'

'And Vigson?'

'With Wing.'

'Christ!'

The Toyota had been Feldspar's target – three shapes in the skin-stripping blizzard. But he had missed the men and the transport. Wing had slung the vehicle into reverse. Hauling the girl behind him, Feldspar plunged around the porch and drew her down by his side.

She was functioning again, becoming rational. The pit spread out like divot-mark, already filling over with sand. The broken corral fence made three interlocking Vees. Shards of glass littered the porch. The Toyota was nowhere in sight.

Catching her by the arm, Feldspar jerked her close. He didn't look gentle or understanding now. She knew that she had disappointed him, had failed the Agency. She burned with shame.

'You're sure Vigson was with him?'

'Sure. I missed them all. Vigson, Kittegawa and Wing.'

'I need wheels.'

'The Chevy; the key's inside the ranch.' She spoke like a child promising obedience, a kiss to compensate for misbehaviour.

'Get it.'

She left him. Running fast, she threw herself through the open door into the living room and, giving no thought to the corpses or the injured, leaped over Varese and kicked him onto his back. Sightless brown eyes stared into hers as she knelt astride him and rifled his pockets. She found the keys and ran out of the ranch again.

Feldspar had disappeared.

The wind tore at her. She let it bowl her along. Grabbing the upright at the angle of the porch, she brought herself to a halt.

Three men in battledress were kneeling in the yard firing into the dust cloud. Yelling instructions, Feldspar leaned on the rail. The Toyota's tail lights winked and vanished.

Dorothy fell back, ran again and jumped from the porch. She swam through the wind to the Chevy, pulled open the door, scrambled into the cab and fired the engine. She slung the lever into Drive, wrenched the wheel and gunned the motor. Tyres bit and the pick-up combo shot forward. At the end of the porch she braked.

Feldspar vaulted the rail. The revolver was stuffed into his coveralls, an assault rifle in his left hand. He looked madder than hell. He dumped himself in the seat and slammed the door.

'Can you drive this thing?'

'Sure.'

'Then go.'

'Where?'

'There's a track of sorts above the arroyo. If Wing finds it, it'll take him clear across the ridge.'

The Blazer was already in motion. Powering forward, it weaved between the snipers. Dorothy flicked on the wipers to clear dust from the shield. Visibility was better up ahead, mountain rim and foothills defined. The Blazer lurched and slowed.

'*Left, left*, for Christ's sake,' Feldspar told her.

A solitary figure with a rifle trotted out of the mouth of the arroyo.

From the open window, Feldspar shouted, 'Get word to Lassiter. Dry Water Creek on the Christobel Road.'

'Wha . . . ?'

Craning from the Chevy, Feldspar bellowed. '*Tell Lassiter. Dry Water Creek.*'

Confidence was coming back to her, exhileration. When she looked close she could see banners of dust whipped up behind the Toyota. The terrain was steep and rough, but the air was cleaner. Below the ranch was shrouded. Above the blue sky widened.

The Toyota seemed to hang like a moth on the face of the escarpment. Both feet pumping, Dorothy felt strong, strong and relaxed, like after a nightcap of fine grade.

'Shit!' said Feldspar. 'Wing knows where he's headed.'

'Maybe not,' Dorothy said. 'He's just lucky.'

'What happened back there?'

'Vigson came out the bedroom after buzz with other guy. Shouted *lies, lies*; and Wing started shooting.'

'What did you do?'

'The best I could.' She sounded anxious. 'I really did.'

'That's okay,' Feldspar assured her.

The Blazer wallowed in powdery dunes that had drifted along a rock edge. The angle steeped, the combo strained for adhesion.

The girl's hands nursed the wheel, not fighting it, letting the machine run, finding the line. They had made ground on the Toyota now. It was no longer veiled by dust clouds. They could see it falter, grind into motion, pull, falter, pull again.

'I got the one called Kittegawa. Arm, I think.'

'That's okay.' Feldspar was hanging on tightly. 'That's terrific, in fact.'

'Wing went for Rand. I had to stop him. That's how I missed out on Vigson.'

'You did right.'

'In the open. I can take Wing in the open.'

'You're doing fine, kid.'

The Toyota revved desperately, listing. For an instant it seemed it would heel over and roll off the cliff, then it dragged over the summit out of sight.

'Shit!' said Feldspar again. 'He found the road.'

'You know where the road goes?'

'Yes.'

'Can we cut him off? Cross country?' Dorothy said. 'We got more machine here than he has.'

'It's a broad valley, with a loop track down the mountain.'

'Can we?'

'Maybe.'

The Chevy's front wheels stretched over rocks. Dorothy slackened power, then laid it on again. The vehicle lifted up, kicked high and skidded onto a flat, pitted plateau.

Rotted staves held back the hillside. Ridges soared on each side. The track followed an even chicane, broad but messed over by debris from rockfalls and sand spills. Sitting up straight in the seat, still loose, she eased the throttle and weaved the combo between the hazards. The valley opened. The track snaked east. They could stare down on turbulent levels of storm, on forest, and the serpentine trail of the mining road's descent to the valley floor.

She didn't ask him again. She assumed that he trusted her now. Slinging the lever into Reverse, she coaxed the Blazer across the bulge of the track and aimed it at the lip in a diagonal towards the treeline.

Wing had taught her how to make madness work. The selfish, alien, shit-dispensing prick had exploited her weakness.

'I don't have to be that way, you rat-fuck. I can choose my own way, can't I? You don't own all the juice in the fucking world.

The shadow of the monolith of covert society cooled her passion, brought rationalisation. She smiled. She had been given a chance to make amends, to do good for the country.

Bobby, sweet baby, you're dropping behind.

'Tell me what you want?' she asked.

Feldspar didn't hesitate. 'Conrad Vigson.'

She touched the agent's arm. 'I'll get him for you, Harold. Hold on.'

She slammed the gear shift unerringly into Drive.

On arrival at the Paiute, Marks and Upton found Feldspar's special squad in command of the situation.

There were four dead – all Sarsby's men – including Frank Varese. Tony Bulthius, an elderly guard and Sarsby himself had suffered injury. Shot in the stomach, Bulthius had lost much blood and only Stein's intervention had pulled him back from the grave. Sarsby had caught two bullets, in the right hip and the left knee. In considerable pain, he was begging for a second shot of morphine as Upton entered the living room.

The Englishman wasted no time. He strode through the wreckage to the bedroom where Rand was propped up in the broken bed, arms folded, an expression of weary arrogance on his face.

'Are you all right, Dr. Rand?'

'As well as can be expected,' said Rand sarcastically. 'When do I get out of this dump?'

'Ambulances are on the way,' said Upton.

'I suppose you want to know what happened?'

'There will be time for that later.'

'Another "secret" report, I suppose?'

Upton said, 'Did you speak with Conrad Vigson?'

'Yeah, we had a long, friendly chat – before he told them I was a faker.'

'What did you learn from him?'

'You mean, did he drop me a hint about the antidote?'

'Yes.'

'He didn't give much away,' said Rand. 'But I did learn that the bacterium is a hybrid that affects the auxin formation in the poppy plant and other species.'

'Do you have a sufficiently intelligible lead to work on, upon which to base a research programme?' Upton had no time to mince words.

'I think so, yeah,' said Rand. 'Did Vigson get away?'

'Oh, we'll catch him, I'm sure.'

'I hope you do, Upton.' Rand played the first move of the new game. 'That guy is dangerous.'

Lassiter appeared in the doorway. 'They headed up for the old mining track. Feldspar's gone in pursuit. I've sent a car back to Liberon to order a roadblock at the Westgard. I'll try to make radio contact with the state police to block all possible exit points.'

'How much of a start do they have?' Marks asked.

'Ten minutes is all,' said Lassiter. 'Your boy, Feldspar, was right behind them.'

Upton glanced at Henry Marks.

'We'll take the jeep,' Marks said.

Feldspar would not have gambled. For all his rebelliousness, he was company trained. He would have figured the odds and counted on organisation to do what courage could not. Nothing would have motivated him to drive the Chevrolet over the edge of the track; to be that simple, that direct. He was scared. For all that, he did nothing and said nothing to check the girl.

He was paralysed by her display of animus. Like a whirlpool it absorbed the energy of his will. He did not think in symbols, only in terms of the result. And that was obvious – if the Blazer reached the bottom level of the track before the Toyota then Dorothy would have achieved victory. She would have Wing's head as a trophy and, to her way of thinking, would have won her spurs as an agent. In other circumstances, the naïveté of such an ambition would have been comical. But Feldspar understood.

The steep terrain was strewn with rocks, crumbling defiles, mining and logging debris. Stumps and timber dumps made hidden obstacles in the brush along the forest margins. Mercilessly, the wind lashed the breast of the mountain. Below the track was a smeared sheet of dust, a thousand feet down.

Ochre spindrift billowed into the valley bowl. Dry Water Creek and its thumbnail lake were hidden by trees. But Feldspar carried a map of the region in his head. For eight miles or more the track zig-zagged, gradually descending to a tarred surface – the Christobel Road – at a deserted mining hamlet. By this route the FBI Specials had come to the ridge. In fact the IR transport was hidden up top, not a half mile from the spot where Dorothy had quit the track.

Across the valley, the Frogmore range was draped with hanks of black cloud, bruised cushions of rain buoyed on the dust storm. Colours were vivid, stark, frightening. Straggle pines and stunted saplings on the forest's edge bowed under the weight of the wind.

The Blazer bucked and plunged wildly. Feldspar hung on grimly, the assault rifle braced securely in back of his knees. He felt as if his bones were being shaken loose, joint by joint, as if his eyes were rolling in his skull like dice in a cup. He clamped his teeth to prevent himself from biting his tongue. He did not share in Dorothy's elation as she steered the combo at breakneck speed down the diagonal towards the trees.

He wondered if Wing had missed them yet, if the Chink was smart enough to deduce what his former bedmate would do. Maybe the Chink was just too damned busy whipping the Land-cruiser down the track to give much consideration to the absence of pursuit. With no choppers in the sky and luck running for him, Wing's chances of clearing the valley were still good. Feldspar cursed himself for screwing up the raid. He should have been faster on the strike. It would serve him right if the Blazer smashed.

Hell, what was he coming to? Death before Dishonour was a schoolkid fantasy. He had no wish to die. The realisation frightened him even more. He squinted at Dorothy. She remained a performer, skilled, graceful and determined. Many virtues were amassed in her: except that she had been drained of moral sense and corrupted by a society that supposedly exhalted independence and still cherished a frontier concept of woman-hood. To them she was a dirty junkie, dependent for sanity on a distillation of chemicals from plants that grew in foreign soils. She needed them to maintain precarious balance, to keep her mind on its gimbal. If she had been gotten young enough, she would have made a perfect agent. But it was far too late for that. Far too late for Bobby Hoffmann to backtrack to his smalltown origins. Too late for Harold Feldspar to kick *his* habit, to be cured of ambition and synthetic loyalties.

The Blazer crashed over the shoulder of the draw. Her reading of the downward route was amazing. Whaleback hills shielded them from the worst of the wind and, more important, hid them from the track. The forest on his right was a green and amber tapestry in the stained window. The slope eased. He could not see the valley now. On rugged ground the Blazer ran a parallel course to the trees, heading towards the edge of nothingness.

She braked. The Blazer nose-dived, reared up, and then surged over the edge. Feldspar's shoulder battered the windshield. He saw the track, straight below. Three, four hundred feet of scrub. Glancing left, he saw the Toyota slither out of a ragged corner in a comber of dust.

Christ: we've missed it. It will be past before we hit the track. There seemed to be no ending to his pursuit of Conrad Vigson.

'Open the door.'

'What?' he shouted.

'Open the fucking door.'

'Dorothy, wha . . . ?'

She tramped on the gas. The Blazer bounded downhill, gathering speed. Speed changed to a kind of plummeting momentum.

'*You want him, don't you*?'

'For Christ's sake, Dorothy. Let him go.'

'*I want him.*'

Even as the Toyota braked in a final bid to avoid the inevitable, Feldspar knew that they were going to hit.

He grabbed her shoulder. She flung him off.

He abandoned the rifle. He opened the passenger door and swung the upper part of his body out on it, weight against weight. Scrub flooded past like a river rushing beneath him. He kicked with his knees and hung, monkeylike, to the door. he released it, dropping flat, taking the shock on his elbows, hands cupped to his jaw.

The impact winded him, but he was not dragged. The edge of the door scythed clear over his head. He rolled automatically, rolled again, not realising the force that had propelled him until he felt his left knee snag and searing pain shoot into his thigh and belly. He grabbed with his left hand, ripping flesh from the palm, curled up like a beetle and fell, sprawling. And stopped. Through the pain, he dug the gun from his coveralls and dragged himself forward to watch.

The Blazer was suspended in mid-air, like some gigantic robot from a Martian jungle leaping on its prey. Still braking, the Toyota was beginning to shimmy out of line, the back end coming hard to the inside of the track. He could not see the men inside. The Blazer's grille guard rammed into the driver's door. The Toyota's body slammed and crumpled, locking. The shapes were lost, melding into a berg of metal that drove on over the far edge of the track.

Dragging the busted leg, Feldspar slithered down the scoop and hobbled over the track. The wreck was not far down. There had been no spectacular plunge, only a short fall that had embedded the Blazer deep into the flattened Landcruiser. He started on down, then smelled the pungent tang of gasoline and changed direction, veering wide.

In the twisted aperture, he could see Dorothy's head. She was sitting upright at the buckled steering, that part of the cabin thrust clear, like a canted turret. Lazily a wheel spun on a snapped axle close below her face. She was staring straight ahead, eyes wide, mouth closed, hair fluttering back from her brow to which clung one huge drop of blood, bright as the ruby of a favoured maharanee.

Shouting her name, Feldspar started forward.

Dorothy's head began to turn then, as metal settled on metal and the stink of gasoline became overpowering, it toppled sideways from her severed neck.

Feldspar fell to his knees and covered his eyes with his hands.

The big groaning berg exploded in a sheet of flame.

Dispassionately Vigson watched the young man pull himself over the edge of the track. Oily plumes of smoke, teased from the burning wreckage, feathered out over the valley. Slightly dazed, Vigson sniffed and found that he could smell nothing. He explored his legs with his thumbs, prodding experimentally. He was scratched and bruised but otherwise undamaged. On Wing's instruction he had thrown himself unhesitatingly from the speeding vehicle. Tussocks of grass had miraculously cushioned his fall.

Mr. Kittegawa had been less fortunate. But Mr. Kittegawa had been very close to death in any case, shirt and dark suit sleek as sealskin with blood pumping from the bullet wound in his chest. As one would have expected, the oriental has been stoical throughout. He had spoken only once, saying, 'Wing, will you escort Conrad home?'

Wing had not answered, only patted the wet sleeve. Features pinched, pupils invisible, Wing looked as if he might weep. But there was no opportunity to indulge in sentimental rituals. The lively vehicle and its murderous descent had demanded his full attention.

Shakily, Vigson seated himself on a rock by the roadside. Frowning, he spread his feet and leaned his forearms on his knees, making a solid shape in the gale.

Strange, it seemed as if Wing had sensed that the Chevrolet would reach that exact point in space at that exact moment in time. It was as if he had contrived not to escape but to keep the rendezvous. Within such men as Wing dwelled an acceptance of the creed of All or Nothing in its most literal terms.

It would be illuminating to discuss the point with Jackie. But there was no hope of that now. He concentrated on shaping his own small model of revenge.

Now he could smell the backdraft from the wreckage. It was greasy, sickly, tainted. Poor Wing's funeral pyre. He inclined his face away. Mr. Kittegawa's body was visible in the grasses below, neck broken, head twisted at an inquisitive angle as if mutely asking him what he intended to do now. He was relieved to have survived the crash without injury. How undignified it would have been, at this stage, to be helpless in their hands.

Patiently, he watched the young man hobble towards him along the track. He held a revolver in his right hand, extending it before him like a talisman.

Broken leg, by the look of it. Bleeding from the left hand too. Lucky to get out of it alive.

'Are you Vigson?'

'I am.'

'You jumped clear?'

'I did.'

'Are you hurt?'

'Not to speak of.'

'What about the others?'

'Wing was at the steering wheel at the moment of impact. I think we can take it that he's dead. The third passenger, Sheng Kittegawa, is lying down there. Dead, too, I'm afraid.'

The young man swayed as the wind gusted violently against him. He came closer, but not too close.

Rain was visible, elegant swan-necked clouds shedding sweet moisture into the parched mountains. Only a Turner could capture such grandeur on canvas, Vigson thought. It must be difficult for Americans to live up to such magnificence, to expand their dreams to match the scale of the country. Perhaps that was why they were so dissatisfied with themselves. He thought of Jackie, her sureness of purpose.

'So you're Conrad Vigson,' the young man said. 'You're not what I expected.'

'Oh?' Vigson said. 'I'm sorry to disappoint you, after all that effort in bringing me back from the grave.'

The young man looked faintly sheepish. His eyes were red, as if he'd been weeping. Perhaps the smoke had caused it or the pain in his leg.

Vigson said, 'Do your employers have any inkling where we are?'

'Yeah.'

'I expect they'll turn up soon in that case.'

'Don't try anything.' He shook the revolver.

'I wouldn't know how,' Vigson said.

The young man *had* been weeping. He did not trust himself to speak. Vigson felt sorry for him, though he had no reason. He assumed that the pursuit would be considered a triumph, that the young man would be given a hero's welcome by his superiors. Again, Vigson thanked his stars that he had not been rendered unconscious. As it was, he would be a burden to them, an embarrassment. Still, it was better than being an embarrassment to himself.

Would they inform Amelia? He could think of his wife now without bitterness, withour fear.

'I've . . . I've got to sit down,' the young man said. 'Over there. I really wouldn't make the mistake of moving, if . . . if I were you. I . . . I'll use the gun, if you force me.'

'I won't move,' Vigson promised.

Would they inform *anyone*? He doubted it.

Chen Yu-lan would find out what had happened. Poor Chen. In some ways, Kittegawa had got the best of the bargain. It would be Chen's job to carry the news back to Tang Mang Wu. But he would probably arrive too late. Peking's ears were larger than the Tigers'. Peking would know all the ins and outs of it before nightfall.

He remembered the opium caravans trailing down from the patches; scrawny mules, occasional lumbering elephants, tended by remnants of the Kuomintang. True Nationalists no more, the KMT ranks were shot through by guerillas and refugees from other, later wars, all governed by hunger for profit, that levelling appetite. In March and May the caravans passed close to Tang Mang Wu. Trusted ones brought cuttings and samples from different zones of growth.

Within the week, a different kind of caravan would set out from his laboratory. How would the traffic be conducted, the cargo spirited away? In two unmarked helicopters, strapped to ten elephants, or a hundred mules? If Jackie had freedom, she would steal it all, not just the important files – everything. She would take herbs, plants, doctored seeds in fibre pots, troughs of earth and moss, glassware, cultures, living cells in nourishing mediums. The greenhouses of Tang Mang Wu would stand empty against the sky. All the students would be gone. He felt no sadness, only a wistful optimism. Jackie would carry his work into a safe country, like seed in her womb. And in America, Rand, the gullible botanist, would set up his watchtower. The game was for the young. He had *won* his little contest. Almost.

Perhaps she would remember him with love. He could ask no more. The beautiful Miss Kyoto, in her greenhouse in Peking.

Though he had no intimate knowledge of such procedures, he assumed that he would be removed to a safe and secret establishment for prolonged interrogation; treated, in effect, like a spy. Who would have charge of him? CIA, FBI, some hybrid group so secret that the Senate could not tamper with it or knot its purse strings? Perhaps they would give him to Upton to ship to England, as Herod had rewarded Salome with the Baptist's head.

He watched the young man lower himself to the dirt. The young man settled with one leg awkwardly bent under his buttock, the other stretched out before him. He reminded Vigson of a beggar at the Buddha's Well in royal Bangkok. The revolver was a sad anomoly. It did not waver in its aim.

Neither man spoke again.

Five minutes later, a jeep cautiously rounded the corner at the foot of the long descent. It braked gradually and halted some fifteen yards away.

Vigson brushed dust from the lapels of his smart gray suit. Finger and thumb fussed with his silk tie. Smoothing the frayed lining, he tucked it inconspicuously into the top of his vest. Listlessly now, the young man watched. Stiffly, Vigson got to his feet and turned to face the new arrivals.

It was going to be all right. The cadences of the ending had the perfection of verses from the *Tao te ching*; a distillation of awareness, the coming of wisdom, of meetings and partings, indisoluble wholeness. He wiped his mouth with his fingertips and took a step towards the Englishman.

'George,' he said. 'Somehow I hoped it would be you.'

'Conrad,' said Upton. 'What a merry dance you've led me.'

'Now it's over, it seems.'

'Yes, Conrad. I'm afraid it's over.'

'It seems,' Vigson said.

He cracked the capsule of hydrogen cyanide between his teeth and inhaled the burning fumes. He visualised the woman's slender fingers sewing the capsule into the lining of his necktie. In the same suffocating image, he imagined Jackie's fingers serenely unspooling the thread of his mortal life.

Upton reached for him and clamped a hand around his throat. But it was too late, far too late.

Across the valley in the Frogmore range a storm broke violently, driving in from the east. Squalls blue as midnight raked the ridge and pealed out the day's first thunderclaps.

In a last act of clemency Upton acknowledged the inevitable and lowered his prisoner to the ground. There, cheek pressed to the toecap of an English shoe, Conrad Vigson died within the minute, hearing no sound from the hills.

The Minotaur Factor

Stuart Stern

The cause:
THE BIRTH PILL

The symptoms:
LETHAL CATATONIA

The result:
CERTAIN DEATH

A young woman goes berserk at a party and mutilates three people with a knife before collapsing into a coma. She dies and acute lethal catatonia is diagnosed as the cause of death, an unstoppable and incurable chemical malfunction of the brain.

Sir George Upton, head of the medical team investigating the epidemic, discovers that it is linked with a brand of birth pill. But what is the link? In desperation the team selects a group of human guinea pigs for a series of experiments as deadly as the disease itself.

THE MINOTAUR FACTOR is a terrifying extrapolation on the theme of the possible long term effects of the birth pill – effects which are still not wholly known.

THE CAESAR CODE

Johannes Mario Simmel

Beneath the peaceful, prosperous surface of today's Europe – a twisting trail of guilt and terror . . .

A young man searching for his father's mysterious assassin . . . the woman who might be the dead man's mistress or murderess or both . . . a harmless old bookseller with a carefully concealed past . . . the madame of a brothel that caters only to the most bizarre erotic appetites . . .

These people form part of the spellbinding mosaic of suspense and intrigue in this magnificent novel. THE CAESAR CODE combines the explosive power of a great thriller with a terrifying investigation into the horrors of the violent past and present.

SHARP PRACTICE

John Farris

Pretty Joe has already signed his name to three plastic bags, each filled with the remains of a woman he'd raped and meticulously butchered. Anne Ramsdell should have been next, but somehow she survived a violent assault and a three storey fall. Battered, shocked and suffering amnesia, she escapes to America – running from a man she can't identify, running from a fear she will never forget.

And all the while, close behind her followed the maniac, cruel, cunning, treacherous, waiting for a second chance . . .

'Masterfully devious plotting, shatteringly effective use of violence, in-depth characterization and scenes of gibbering horror.' *New York Times.*

'An epic among thrillers' *Evening Gazette.*

'Intensely readable . . . I couldn't put it down.' *Daily Telegraph.*